ERIC LEWIS

THE HERON KINGS

This is a **FLAME TREE PRESS** book

FLAME TREE PRESS
6 Melbray Mews, London, SW6 3NS, UK
flametreepress.com

Distribution and warehouse:
Baker & Taylor Publisher Services (BTPS)
30 Amberwood Parkway, Ashland, OH 44805
btpubservices.com

Thanks to the Flame Tree Press team, including:
Taylor Bentley, Frances Bodiam, Federica Ciaravella, Don D'Auria,
Chris Herbert, Josie Karani, Molly Rosevear, Will Rough, Mike Spender,
Cat Taylor, Maria Tissot, Nick Wells, Gillian Whitaker.

The cover is created by Flame Tree Studio with
thanks to Nik Keevil and Shutterstock.com.
The font families used are Avenir and Bembo.

24.95 4/30

Flame Tree Press is an imprint of Flame Tree Publishing Ltd
flametreepublishing.com

A copy of the CIP data for this book is available from the British Library
and the Library of Congress.

HB ISBN: 978-1-78758-389-4
PB ISBN: 978-1-78758-387-0
ebook ISBN: 978-1-78758-390-0

Printed in the UK at Clays, Suffolk

ERIC LEWIS

THE HERON KINGS

FLAME TREE PRESS
London & New York

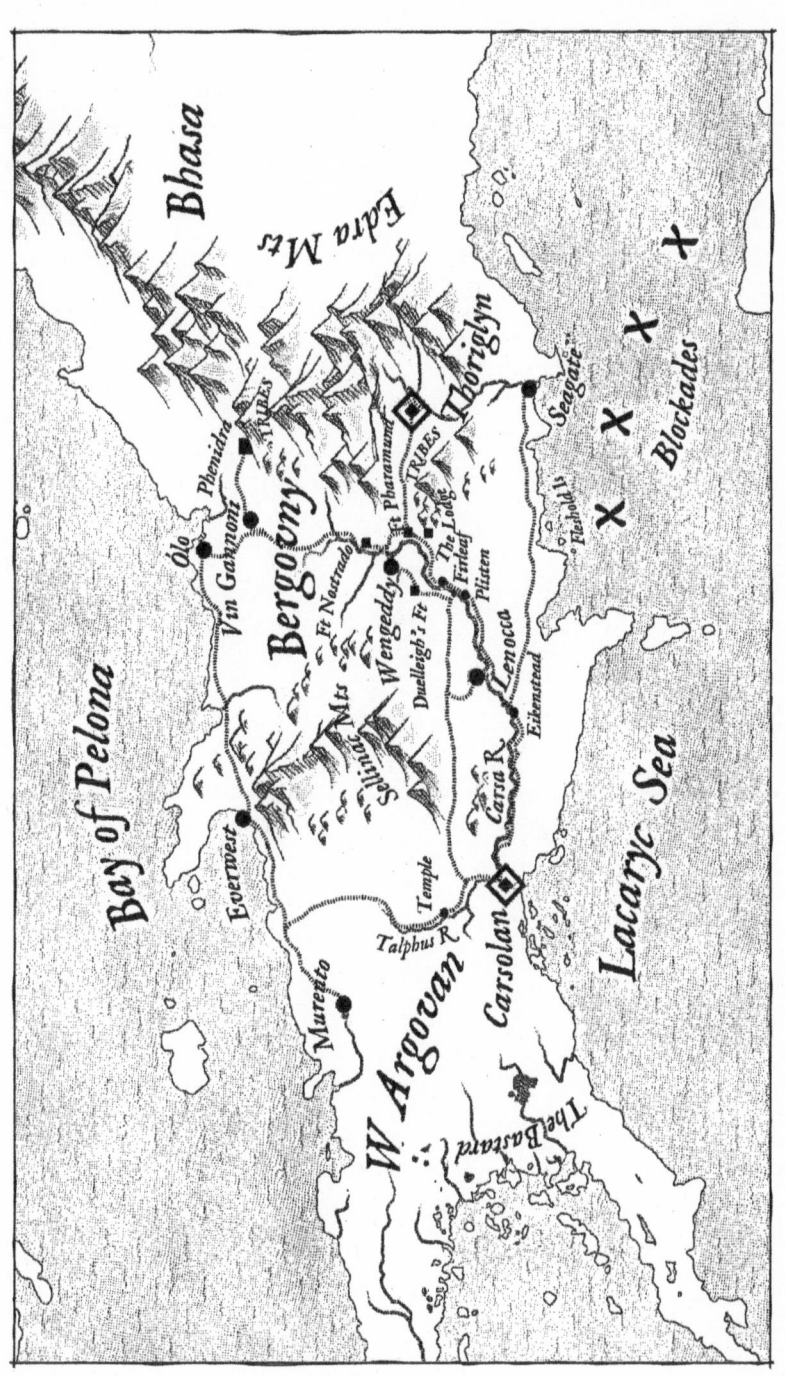

PART ONE

CHAPTER ONE
An Absurd World

A fresh spurt of blood spattered into Alessia's face, painting a smear across her cheek. She didn't flinch this time, barely noticed it with all her attention focused on the task at hand – the sharp instruments, the rent flesh, her own precise movements. The soldier lying before her howled, and the walls of the temple chamber echoed it back tenfold.

"Mother of gods, stop!"

"Oh, shut up," said Alessia, bracing her elbow against his clavicle to try and stop the squirming. "And hold still, you're only making it worse."

"*You're* makin' it worse! It hurts!"

"Good! That's how you know you're not dead. Which is probably what you deserve, but not...quite...yet." She stabbed her needle around the jagged hole in his side again. One last time and it'd be over, one last time he screamed.

"Aargh! Damned evil witches, damned temples—"

Alessia slapped her victim, hard. "Insult me all you like, but you will *not* blaspheme against the Polytheon in here. There, done. You'll live, for what it's worth."

With the bleeding stopped, Alessia turned away, bone-weary. Across the nave a dozen and more like scenes played out – some with screamed profanities, some with moans, and some in silence. The sisters flitted about like angels of death, praying for the lost souls of some and sending others back into the world for another measure of misery.

The convent temple was a circular, sepulchral space of hewn stone, capped by a great dome painted with frescoes of gods and saints and men reaching up toward a precious disc of colored glass at its apex that turned noonday sunlight blue. In days of peace that seemed now so ancient, worshipers would assemble around that circle to receive the benediction of the gods from the Mother tending the altar. Now the greatest blessing to be hoped for was survival, and a hazy mist of steam and desperate sweat hung in the air. Alessia dipped her hands into the basin set in the midst of it all, the water near scalding though she'd been scrubbed too numb to feel it. A young acolyte rushed past to replace the pink rags on the altar with fresh ones before disappearing again.

"You enjoyed that." The accusing voice behind her *did* make her flinch, even after three years. Still, she tried and failed to hold back a little grin.

"Is it not proper," Alessia said, turning slowly, "to take joy from one's work, Mother?"

"Don't play clever with me girl, you well know what I mean." Mother Tanusia was herself covered in gore that lent her glare of disapproval an unsettling aspect.

"Well, why not? Hard to drum up much sympathy – these men are the lucky ones. Those they killed not as much."

Tanusia shook a gnarly finger in Alessia's red-streaked face. "*That* is not your concern, nor mine! Nothing outside these walls is. I've told you a thousand times."

"I know, I know. Where's this lot from, anyway?"

"Who can say anymore?" Tanusia sighed. "Some pointless skirmish not far away, come to us from both sides. Hard to believe, but it was less savage when it was professionals doing the fighting. These poor fools know nothing but to hack at each other like lunatics. This war has to end soon. They're running out of men to fight it."

"Maybe they'll start drafting women."

"Don't you even think that! You just try to find new reserves of patience and sympathy. Be a shame for a bright thing like you to turn cynic so young."

"Yes, Mother."

"And remember, this temple serves as a *hospital*, not a torture chamber. Try to find some opiphine, or wolfsbane, *something* before you cut men open again." There'd been no opiphine to be found since the first season of the war.

"Yes, Mother." As Tanusia turned away to some other task, Alessia's patient put an emphasis on the point by crying out anew.

"And will you please shut him up!"

"*Yes,* Mother."

★   ★   ★

Alessia and a few other sisters sat sprawled on benches in the corner, too tired even to stagger back to the dormitory. Those men who were going to die had mostly done so, and the ones who weren't lay unconscious on the cots that littered the place.

"Are we done?" she asked nobody in particular.

"Done, for now." Sister Livielle started to force herself to her feet. "Almost. I need to check the bandage on that head wound."

"I'll do it, you get some rest."

"Needn't tell me twice...."

Alessia forced herself to her feet, regarding Livielle with affectionate amusement. "Gods spare you dreams of today, love."

While Liv dozed, Alessia made one last round of inspections. As she was trudging back to the bench, one of the soldiers she'd worked on turned his pained gaze toward her.

"Sister?"

"Yes, what is it?"

"I'm sorry. For...what I said earlier. The pain...."

She sighed heavily. She was tired and annoyed, and in no mood to play nursemaid. *Patience and sympathy.* "Forget about it. You just worry about getting better so you can get off that bed and make room for someone else."

"Yes, ma'am. I just wonder...if it all even made any difference."

Alessia wondered that herself more and more, despite her oath of neutrality. Argovan and Bergovny were two kingdoms sharing one peninsula, and little difference between them. The brief moment of unity forged by the old high king had been shattered when his death was followed soon after – some might say suspiciously – by that of his young son. It left a Bergovan duke and the king's second wife, an Argovani countess, both claiming the throne, and two years of war had failed to settle the matter. Much like the twinned countries themselves, Alessia saw no cause to prefer one faction over the other, for each spilled their enemy's blood just as easily, the wounded each sought the sanctuary of the Polytheon. Though she'd never intended it, the conversion of the temple house into a makeshift hospital had given the novice sister the skills of an advanced physic, and there was no sign that her training was likely to ease off anytime soon.

Fatigue only somewhat blunted the shock when her thoughts were interrupted by the boom of the temple's wide double doors being struck from outside. *What now?* she thought with consternation as they rumbled open.

Two columns of armed men marched into the nave, led by an aged, grim-looking brute with black sable draped over his shoulders and dull mail armor from neck to knee. He carried a high-crowned helm in his right hand while the left cradled the hilt of a long, ugly sword at his hip. "Who's in charge here?" The warlord wrinkled his nose at the stench of putrefying viscera while scanning the long nave, taking in the rows of wounded, the sisters, the acolytes, the bits of discarded bandage strewn about.

"Go fetch Mother," Alessia whispered to Livielle, "quickly." She stepped forward. "May the gods light your path, Lord...?"

"Taurix," the man spat. "High Marshal to King Pharamund."

"Taurix. Welcome to the temple of the Artameran Polyth—"

"Whatever. I'm told that piece of shit Ludolphus what calls himself a general passed this way. Is that so?"

Alessia curtsied as she'd been taught to do before the high and mighty, ridiculous in her cold, blood-drenched habit. "I'm sorry, but we don't ask the names of those who visit, only that they come and go in peace."

Taurix sighed. "He would've left some wounded men with you."

Is he serious? Alessia looked him square in the eye. "Well as you can see we get wounded with some regularity. You'll have to be more specific. There *is* a war on, you know."

Taurix stared back down at her unblinkingly, and for a few seconds Alessia was sure he was going to run her through with that nasty sword. *Oh, that was stupid*, she thought.

Instead he broke into a hard chuckle. "It's well that you keep that mouth behind these walls, girl. Few live to speak that way to a lord of the Marches a second time."

"What goes on here?" Mother Tanusia's voice boomed as she strode from the rectory office. "So, has the royal struggle finally spread across the sea to Holy Artamera that an army invades a house of the Polytheon?"

Taurix turned to the woman, noted the stripe on her habit that signified her authority. "Not at all, Mother. At least not yet. In fact we're grateful for the care of His Grace's soldiers. Your house should look to be richly rewarded once these treasonous rebels are put down."

"That we should live to see that day is all the reward we desire, my lord," Tanusia replied with barely concealed sarcasm.

"Yet, it seems you've made an unfortunate mistake." Taurix's tone suddenly became lighter, even more terrifying.

"Mistake?"

"Indeed. For I see that in addition to the king's loyal defenders, you have among you a number of those very traitors." Taurix tossed his helmet to another of his company, then stepped slowly over to a fellow with an amputated leg lying on one of the cots, insensate from the brandy it'd taken to calm him. Though blooded and torn, his tunic still bore the green badges of General Ludolphus and Countess Engwara – the 'treasonous rebels'. "Allow me, Mother, to lighten your burden."

Before any could react he plunged his sword through the man's belly and the cot, the tip stopping just short of the stone floor. The man jerked, eyes wide. Alessia let out a short, shrill scream and the acolytes and most of the sisters scattered from the nave in horror.

"No! How dare you!" Tanusia roared with such fury that some of Taurix's own men took half a step backward. She ran to the doomed patient just as he slipped away into death, gurgling blood. "This house is sacred ground, you've no right—"

"Don't lecture me, woman. Your temple's inviolate only so long as you keep your oath to take part in no wars."

"We've taken no part!"

"No? Look around – giving aid and comfort to the enemy seems to me to be very much taking part."

"But…that's absurd."

"It's an absurd world we live in, Mother." He moved to the next patient and raised his sword again. Alessia's patient. She moved to dive between Taurix and his victim, and with barely a thought the lord turned and struck her across the jaw, sending her flying backward. "Go among them," he said to his retinue. "Root out the traitors." While Taurix dispatched the man beneath him the others fanned out across the chamber, checking each patient for identifying badges or marks. A few wounded tried to crawl away, succeeding only in making themselves targets. Screams rang out anew.

Powerless to stop the slaughter, Tanusia crept along the wall to where Alessia lay dazed, watching helplessly as nearly half the lives they'd fought to save were snuffed out. "You…*sick butcher*," the Mother hissed.

"Spare me the dramatics. As that cheeky bitch on the floor pointed out, there's a war on! If you dare harbor criminals again, expect to be considered a military target. Next time it won't be a smack in the mouth. Understood?"

Tanusia glared up at Taurix as she cradled Alessia in her arms. "Yes," she answered with bitterness.

"Yes, *what?*"

"Yes, *lord.*"

★　　★　　★

Alessia spat into the cloth, the blood her own this time. The whole right side of her face throbbed. *Punishment from the gods for enjoying my job too much.* The damage seemed limited to one lost tooth – a far lighter penance than her patients had suffered.

Livielle touched her gently, as if she were a drifty snowman to collapse at the barest mishandling. "Are you all right?"

"Fine," Alessia answered, trying a weak smile and feeling another trickle on her chin. "Fine enough." They'd finished the disposal of the new-made corpses, and that dark work weighed on them both. "I just can't believe Mother groveled before that bastard, said 'yes, lord' like some fellating harlot…."

"What else could she do? What could anyone do?" For once Livielle forgot to pretend shock at such crude language.

"I don't know. *Something*."

"Like get her face bashed in? Didn't do you much good."

"That was dumb. But I couldn't just stand there and watch those people get stuck like pigs." Alessia flung a blooded rag into a bucket, very tired all of a sudden.

"Best not think on it anymore," said Livielle. "At least no other sisters were hurt, though the acolytes are still shaken, poor dears." She leaned in closer. "I probably shouldn't tell you this, but...you already have a bit of a following."

"What? What are you talking about?"

"Charging a monster like that, are you kidding? Sister Evandri's calling you 'the warrior priestess'."

"Wha— That's heresy!"

"Just a little one. The gods won't mind."

"Well it's stupid." Alessia scowled. "Tell her to stop it. Anyway, the question now's what to do about—"

"Sisters!" The cry came from Eudo, a simpleton who tended ground at the temple, and the only male with leave to come and go without escort. He tottered into the nave with a trembling lip.

"Eudo," Alessia asked, speaking softly to try and calm him, "what frights you so?"

"Peoples is come!" He danced from one foot to the other and whined.

"More soldiers, like yesterday?"

"No, lowfolks. Some looks hurted."

"No rest for the wicked," sighed Livielle. "Very well, Eudo, open the doors and we'll get—"

"Wait." Mother Tanusia appeared between them. "We must know where they come from first...who they bend knee to." Some light, some strength had gone out of the woman since the confrontation. She would not meet either of the sisters' eyes, nor even Eudo's.

"What's that matter?" asked Livielle.

Alessia already knew the answer, and her stomach churned at it. "Because we can't risk the wrath of the great warlord a second time. That's it, isn't it?"

Tanusia nodded. "I've no choice. I won't endanger the lives of the sisters and acolytes."

"But charity is one of the gods' commands," Livielle insisted, "doubly so in time of war! How can we not—"

"If that beast decides to pay us another visit we won't be providing charity to anyone at all. It seems this war has elevated a very different breed, and we must navigate them as best we can."

Alessia felt bile mixing with the blood in her mouth. "So we pick sides and turn away whoever happens to be on the wrong one? What happens when Engwara gets herself one of these breed, comes and says the exact same thing? Who do you obey then? Or will you just shut out the world entire and wait for them to burn the temple down around us?"

Tanusia's face reddened. "What would you have me do? What course would you suggest, *sister?*" Alessia just quivered in wordless, impotent rage. "Then hold your tongue and be content."

She sent Eudo to a high window to question them. The peasants were the few to escape Taurix's latest raids, and they piled against the door crying, "Help us, by the gods!" because they'd been preached to all their lives about the charity of the Artameran Polytheon.

"That's it then," said Tanusia when Eudo brought an answer, defeated. "They're Baroness Brathilde's landbound. Whether they will it or no those people are enemies of Taurix, of Pharamund. We mustn't let them inside."

The gathered sisters stared at Tanusia as if she'd grown horns. "You can't be serious," Alessia said. "You're condemning—"

Tanusia cut her off with a swipe of her hand. "The doors stay shut! That's final."

"Aye," growled Alessia, "well gods damn us then."

★   ★   ★

The wounded pushed higher and harder against the doors and pelted the building with cries, with curses and finally with rocks. Tanusia shut herself inside her cell with fists tight against her ears. Two days it persisted, and more than once Alessia moved to unbar the doors only to find Eudo parked there like a stone gargoyle, even to sleep. If she tried to sneak past he'd pop an eye open and whine, "Mother said *no*," obedient to Tanusia's command even if he did not understand it.

The pleas outside faded, then were gone. Tanusia emerged from her cell red-eyed and ordered the bar lifted. The doors opened and the late-day sun poured in orange light carrying with it a too-familiar smell, and as they swung inward bodies stiff with rigor mortis dropped to the ground. The outsides of the doors were riddled with gouges matched by splinters buried under the fingernails of the dead.

CHAPTER TWO

Just a Pleasant Dream

Tanusia closed the door to the tiny cell behind them. "There, now tell me what was so important it couldn't wait until chapter."

Alessia took a deep breath, steadied herself against a bedside table. "I would not speak of this in chapter, Mother. I...."

Tanusia frowned. "What is it, child? If you're still angry about what happened with the villagers, I'm sorry but I've already—"

"It's not that. Or rather, it's not just that."

"Then *spit it out.*"

Breathe. "Mother, I find I cannot obey both your commands in this and those of the Polytheon as I understand them. So I'm here to beg for my release." The silence between them screamed in Alessia's ears. Tanusia stared at her, unmoving. For a terrible moment Alessia was afraid she'd not been clear. "I mean—"

"I know what you mean, I heard you. If this is some attempt at coercion...."

"It's not. I know you won't change your mind. If the screams of those people couldn't do it.... But I can't – *I won't* endure another day like yesterday. Innocents suffer every hour and no one does anything about it. 'It's war,' they say, as though that makes enough excuse, and move on. The one refuge they have is the temple, and now you say we only welcome folk lucky enough to fall on the right side of some damned line on a map? How can I accept that?"

"You can't." Tanusia nodded. "Not being who you are. I admit I feared something like this. I was hoping it'd pass by...but no. You must do as you feel the gods demand. You have that luxury. I've more complicated responsibilities." She gave a wan smile. "To think, only the other day it was I chiding you for being too ungentle, now here we are. Your knife cuts deep, child. Are you absolutely sure of this? Where would you go? It's not safe out there for anyone, never mind a woman alone."

"I...I hadn't thought much of that, I was so dreading this moment."

"Ah, then I suppose I should be flattered."

"Carsolan, or Murento, somewhere I can practice physic without restriction—"

"There's no such place! Oh, you haven't thought this through at all, have you? This damnable war's left its mark on every corner of Argovan and Bergovny both. It's not just battles anymore. If temples are no longer sacrosanct, then nowhere is. You may come to regret this decision, sister."

Alessia set her jaw, determined. "I'm full of regrets, Tanusia. I can bear a few more, but not like yesterday's. Call me sister no longer."

"Very well. Take a day to gather your belongings and make your goodbyes, but no more. I can't have your choice infecting the others. They'll miss you terribly, especially the acolytes. And Livielle. And...I will miss you." She drew Alessia into a tight embrace, tears welling up. "I do hope you know what you're doing."

That night the temple sisters sang their evening prayers. It was a dour melody, made haunting of late and no less so for being one voice the weaker.

★   ★   ★

Alessia was two and a half years into her novitiate. Another season and she'd have taken final vows as a full-fledged sister pledged to the Polytheon for life. People joined the temples for many reasons: some fled the law or serfdom or an unhappy home. Some sought peaceful retirement after a lifetime of chaos, or after growing weary of the world and finding for themselves no place in it. Only a few had the true calling, and the novitiate period allowed those on a wayward path to realize their mistake, with no harm done.

Which am I? Education, position, opportunity beyond the marshlands of her home county – they all seemed like naïve notions now. Alessia pulled off her habit and wondered what she should do with it. Fold it and set it on the cot that was no longer hers? Hang it on the hook above or deliver it to the laundry? Maybe they'd ritually burn it after she left. She stood shivering in her shift. The canvas rucksack in front of her held pitifully few items, for everything she'd needed was provided and owned by the temple. A spare physic kit, a change of clothes, some travel items, some hardtack, copper coins. And all of those newly bestowed gifts of charity. *Oh, the irony of that!*

"So it's true then. You're running away."

Alessia jumped, spun around. The dormitory was quiet and otherwise empty, but Livielle's soft slippers let her move undetected. "I'm not running. You know why I have to do this."

"Another argument with Mother? Another temper tantrum? What does it matter, Lessi? Is it so important that you get your way—"

"Stop it! You know that's not what this is about."

"But how can you leave…us?" *Me*, Livielle almost said before catching herself. No matter, Alessia heard it anyway.

She moved in close, her voice dropping to just above a whisper. "Liv, you'll be fine. Stay behind these walls, listen to Mother. One day this will all be over, and then…well."

Livielle swallowed, fought hard not to cry. "All right. It's just… it would've been nice…wouldn't it?"

They were alone, but it wouldn't have mattered if they were not, not now. Alessia took the girl in her arms and kissed her lightly. "It was just a dream, love," she whispered, "just a pleasant dream. There'll be others."

"Not like this."

Alessia pulled back, forced herself to let go. "May the gods light your path." But she couldn't see any light, any path before her, and that made her afraid.

In the morning the temple doors opened again and Alessia emerged from a misty-eyed crowd of sisters and acolytes, Tanusia and Eudo. She was dressed in a simple travel gown with her sack slung over a shoulder. Livielle wasn't there; she couldn't bear another parting. That was fine, they'd made their farewells.

"I must ask you once more," said Tanusia before Alessia crossed the threshold, "is this really what you want?"

Alessia lowered her eyes. "No, it isn't. But it's what I have to do."

"Then indulge me in one little way at least." Tanusia turned to a young acolyte almost lost in the folds of her habit and took up what the child held. "Taurix was right in one thing. It *is* an absurd world we live in, and dangerous. Take this."

It was a bow. A light, recurved hunting bow of simple but quality manufacture and a dozen arrows sheathed in a hide quiver. "Mother," said Alessia, "I can't take this—"

"Take it," Tanusia insisted. "Better to have it and not need it than the other way round."

"I'm leaving so I can save lives, not take them."

"And there may come a time when you'll have to save your own. Besides, you might need to hunt to eat. Take it! Consider it my final order."

Alessia took it to satisfy the woman, certain she'd never use it nor even learn how. She pulled the copper Polytheon star from her neck and dropped it on the ground torn up by the suppliants they'd turned away. "Well, that's it. I guess."

"I hope you find what you're looking for," said the child acolyte.

"So do I, dear." Alessia fought not to look back as she walked toward the road that led she knew not where, to do she knew not what.

★   ★   ★

Taurix drew the fur cloak tighter around his neck against a gust of wind, his bones not yet used to the chill of the south. *Still,* he thought as he surveyed the devastation, *I wouldn't be anywhere else.* Even after so many years he never failed to feel awe at the sheer destruction of a town given over to sack. A few more such examples and things might finally start going in the proper direction. Every corpse, every smashed building was a stone laid on the path to victory. In the distance a scream was cut short. *But not too quickly, perhaps.*

A body lay in Taurix's path, face down and naked in the mud with blood trickling from between its legs. As he stepped over it his boot crunched on something hard – a piece of pottery, and a trail of broken bits leading from a burned-out home. *More looting'll slow us down. Have to speak to the captains about that.* Across the way a crow alighted on an overturned barrel, brandishing a pink piece of something in its beak before flying off again. "Feast well, my friend," Taurix muttered.

"M'lord!"

Taurix spun on a heel at the call. The cloak twisted around his muscular frame, the few wisps of hair remaining on his head fluttering in the breeze. A stab of pain shot up his left leg and into his hip at the movement. *This war came twenty years too late*, he thought. *Or I twenty too early.* "Well Tobius," he said impatiently, "is he here?"

The secretary dropped to one knee, making a squelching sound in the street trampled to sludge by hundreds of boots. "Waiting in your command tent."

"I assume that means he's managed to capture Ludolphus?"

"I...er, His Lordship did not say—"

"No then." Taurix sighed. "Disappointing." He took a last look at his day's work before stomping off to his tent and wrenching the flap aside.

The young man looked up from the letter he was reading. He sat behind Taurix's campaign desk, muddy lambskin boots perched on the edge and a silver goblet in hand.

"Lord Felgred, I presume?"

The fellow raised the goblet in greeting then took a long gulp. "I'd just about have to be, wouldn't I? Anyone else that barged into your tent and drank your wine from your silver should look to be disemboweled for his troubles."

"Don't exclude yourself so quickly," Taurix replied. "Welcome to the war, my lord." *My spy, more like. Pharamund sends his lackey to keep me on a short leash. Shitheels, both.*

"*You're* welcoming *me*? That's a bit backward. Since storming down out of the northern Marches just last season you've stirred up a hornet's nest of troubles. Your little stunt in Murento, for instance...."

"That was no *stunt*. Two years of attack, retreat, advance, fall back and regroup...lunacy! It's past time for decisive action. And to lose a city...."

"I see your strategy – kill everyone in the city and there's no one left to surrender it. Brilliant."

"Surrender *must* be seen as the worst possible outcome. From now on it will be. This war's been run like a farce—"

"I certainly hope," Felgred said sharply, perhaps made bold by Taurix's excellent wine, "you aren't speaking ill of His Grace."

Taurix glared, taking a rare moment to measure his words. "Never dream of it. But perhaps the judgment of those who *advise* King Pharamund isn't all it should be."

A tension settled thick in the tent. Two soldiers oiling leather in the back tried hard to look invisible but quivered in anticipation at the very real risk of violence. "*Taurix*," Felgred said. "That's a Marchman name, no?"

The older lord winced. "It is," he replied, ice clinging to each syllable. "What fucking of it?"

"It just seems strange to me that a noble lord, especially one of the soft sunny north, would carry the name of a barbarian."

Taurix pushed Felgred's boots from his desk. "My grandfather was an upland chieftain. I carry the name in his honor, and to remind me of how far a man can climb. Or fall. And since the Marchman tribes precede the kingdoms of Argovan and Bergovny both, my right and title is doubly sound. *And*, as you doubtless learned the lineages of the Bergovan peers before knowing which end of your prick to use, I must wonder at your point."

Felgred set down the goblet, held up his hands in surrender. "Just an observation. Whatever else folk say, the Marchmen are fierce warriors, heedless of their own safety in battle. I wonder if some of that recklessness doesn't run in your blood as well."

"Battle," said Taurix, "has been the exception rather than the rule in this war."

"You see my point all too clearly then." He held up the letter he'd been reading, waved it in Taurix's face and never knew how close he came to being gutted for it. "You got Engwara's attention – she's sent reavers to devastate my lands, and as we speak crops from Lenocca halfway up the Carsa burn. Armies march on their stomachs, and if I can't feed them they certainly can't fight."

Taurix nodded with approval. "Good basic warcraft. If it's grain you want I'll make you a gift, courtesy of the soft sunny north and the Marcher lord with a barbarian's name."

"That's most kind. Meanwhile, I've a line on your elusive General Ludolphus."

"You captured him?"

"Me? Heavens no, I haven't the men for that. I have an idea where he's fled though – south, straight for Carsolan."

"Then let's get after him!"

"We will, we will." Felgred rose, a touch clumsily thanks to the wine. "Something I want to show you first. Come."

★   ★   ★

"Hold still, here it comes!"

"Aye, m'lo—"

The soldier was knocked clean off his feet by the blow, the bolt lodged halfway through his shield. He tried to fall so as not to impale himself on the tip. The man crawled to his feet, his heart pounding.

Felgred sat mounted twenty yards away, impatient. "Well?" The soldier held the shield up sideways to show the damage. "Amazing," he said with a wide smile. "Simply amazing device." He handed the weapon to Taurix, who sat on a charger next to him observing the demonstration. "Care to give it a try?"

"What's it called again?"

"A cross-bow. It's powerful. Like a ballista you can carry."

"Hmm." Taurix examined the awkward weapon. "Takes long to reload, though." He handed it back to Felgred untested.

"The price of progress. Still, one volley of these and you mayn't need to reload."

"This war won't be won by curious gadgets." Taurix kicked his horse back toward his camp, anxious to get moving. Felgred's palfrey struggled to keep up.

"Yes, you favor simpler methods. You made short work of Brathilde's lands. Didn't she declare *for* Pharamund?"

"She switched sides last season. That makes her an enemy."

"Ah. And I hear you gave those temple women a singular fright. It'd be unwise to anger the Polytheon. The Holy City might be far away and neutral, but there are plenty of powerful true believers here, and Engwara's enemy enough."

"Point taken," the Marcher lord replied impatiently. "I'll defer to you on political matters, if you'll defer to me on military ones. An enemy's an enemy whether the so-called queen in Carsolan or a slogger in sickbed. After the bloody nose Pharamund suffered at Everwest, I'd think you would tend to agree."

Felgred swallowed hard. The Everwest disaster and the cost of retaking the city had led to the rather intemperate removal of the previous lord high marshal and the elevation of Taurix. "No argument there. It's just, your devotion to the king's cause seems to have come, well, a bit recently in my memory. Perhaps—"

"When that woman's fleet attacked Ólo it was she who declared the enemy, not I. My house has ruled the northern Marches before man piled stone on stone or set fire to forge and will do so until the sun burns out in the sky. There's nothing I won't do to remove her threat, and there's my *devotion*. Is that clear?"

"All right, you've convinced me! Maybe I should feel sorry for Ludolphus."

Taurix snorted. "Don't bother. I'll put him beyond all feeling soon enough."

"Though I'm surprised you're so keen to end the war quickly. I would've thought this is what you Marcher lords live for. What'll you do when it's over?"

"There are always wars to fight, lordling. The Bhasan emperor's satraps raiding over the mountains, snatching at my lands like ill-behaved puppies while I'm away. Pirates from Pelona, slave uprisings. Even Lady Nostrado needs to be slapped back into line on occasion. This? This is a distraction."

CHAPTER THREE

A Just Reward

'Civil war' they called it, but Ulnoth couldn't see a damn civil thing about the whole mess as he crashed through a wall of brush and down the ravine, making far too much noise for someone trying to slip away. Though outnumbered three to one, he knew the woods better than the recruiters set on drafting him, so his odds probably worked out about fair. Fairness was currently the last thing on Ulnoth's mind.

Rolling to a halt, he peeked back up the slope where the afternoon sun lanced through the trees. Had they given up? No, a healthy man in his twenties was too precious a prize to surrender so easily. He grabbed a good, thick branch from the ground and crept along the bottom of the gully, making it almost ten paces before a blur of red whipped across his vision and slammed him into the mud. It resolved into a decidedly unhygienic fellow with a toothy grin and five-day growth, clad in the worn scarlet livery of Pharamund. *King* Pharamund if you asked certain folk – Usurping Bastard Pharamund according to others. "Now let's have no more o' that," said the recruiter. "You just come along with us and we'll get you sorted out real n— Huargh!"

Having no interest in getting sorted out any way at all, Ulnoth swung the branch up across the man's jaw, launching two yellowed teeth across the forest floor followed by tiny comet-tails of blood. He scrambled to his feet and tore off in the general direction of the village. "Teach me to take a shortcut," he muttered to himself.

"Muhver*fugger*," the recruiter moaned, bent over and spitting more blood. Two more burst forth after Ulnoth, leaving their companion forgotten behind.

"Come on, son," called out one of them, somewhat past his

prime and huffing heavily. "King's army...needs men! No use... running, they'll get ya...sooner or later. They get everyone!"

"Aye," said the second man, "we's just doin' our jobs! Come back, make it easy on yourself!"

Ulnoth's mind raced with options, most of them dumb, until he heard a soft trickle not far off. *Cadwall's Run!* He looked for the familiar landmarks – the upturned tree stump, there. The boulder with that patch of moss that looked like Saint Nelwyn...right there. Not much farther, then.

He came at last to a rickety bridge. It certainly *looked* solid enough to bear him across, surely good for another season yet? He didn't step onto it but cut north upstream, careful not to get stuck in the marshy wet. *Now where's that stone?* He leaped lightly onto the rock jutting from the middle of the stream, then again toward the other side. He didn't quite make it, landing shin-deep in a clod of muck a yard from the bank. Good enough. He waded ashore, came back to the bridge and continued on to the village just as his pursuers came upon the Run. Without a moment's hesitation they trampled onto the bridge. A creak, a groan and the rotted-out planks collapsed, tossing the men into the water. The rubble and sucking mud held them long enough for Ulnoth to pause a moment and admire his handiwork.

"Fareyawell," he called with a wave as they thrashed. "Give my regards to the king!"

★   ★   ★

"It's the same ever'where," grumbled Bedegar between gulps of watery beer. "I'm too old to bother with o'course, but recruiters got my nephew last season. No idea where he is now." The white-haired man sighed. "You gave 'em hells today though." A rumble of approval passed through the taproom, and a few congratulatory hands patted Ulnoth's shoulder.

"Sure, 'til next time," he said, fingering the hole that'd been ripped in his tunic at some point. "When'll it end, Bed? King, queen, one country or two, nobody gives a good godsdamn. Just flip a coin or play a round of castra and be done with it."

"Nah, that'd make too much sense," replied Bed.

"And now that all them fool volunteers got themselves killed, the lords steal us farmers from the land to keep at it. Who's gonna feed their fat asses if they turn us to spear fodder? It ain't a game nummore, Bed – I got mouths to feed!"

"I know, I know," said Bedegar. "Speaking o' which, how are they?"

Ulnoth grinned in spite of his commitment to maintaining a bad mood. "Well, Lisette's three. That's pretty much her story. Chattering little ball of mostly hair, golden like her mother's. Taken to giving names to all our animals. And the trees. *And* the farm tools...."

Bedegar chuckled. "Is that so? And Athewen?"

"Makes this whole ruin of a world bearable. They both do. It's a hard duty though, keeping 'em safe in it."

Bed raised an eyebrow. "Is that why you seek out a lighter duty with...?"

"Don't," Ulnoth replied with a sharp frown.

The old man shrugged. "You're a lucky one, Ulnoth, despite everything."

"I am. Not that you'd know it by the surroundings." That was true enough. Rationing made all but the barest food and drink illegal, thus the room they sat in was literally underground, in the cellar of a barn owned by some far-off bank. It was a bit of an open secret in the village of Plisten, far beneath the gaze of any heighty lords more concerned with the war between Engwara and Pharamund than with bootlegging peasants.

"You takes your comforts wheresoe'er you may, my boy," said Bed, "as I often reminded your da, gods rest 'im. Now drink up and soon you'll be addled enough to believe that cack from the Polytheon about a just reward in the next life."

Ulnoth took his drink, then set the cup down hard. "Can't wait that long, Bed." His eyes drifted past the crowd and the smoke, and the corner of his mouth turned up just a tick. "Speaking of comforts...."

"Huh, don't need to guess what you're spyin' at. You're playing a dangerous game there, son. I told you once—"

"I know, and I said don't."

"I'll leave ya to 'er then." Bed lifted his cup in mock salute as his young friend stood. "Gods light yer path."

"Uh-huh, and yours," Ulnoth muttered, his thoughts already miles away.

* * *

An hour later Ulnoth lay exhausted on a straw cot, drowning in Sally's dark tresses. She rolled over and rested a pouty chin on Ulnoth's chest.

"How long are you in town this time?"

"Mmm, who cares?"

"C'mon, how long?"

Ulnoth sighed. "Depends on how hard the grain factor wants to haggle. I can't take another price hit like last year. War's supposed to make grain *more* expensive, but they keep coming up with excuses...." He shrugged. "I'm here as long as I need to be."

"Well that's fine by me," Sally said, tugging playfully on the curls of his short auburn beard. "I'm feeling thoroughly underfucked these days."

"Flattered, but you must know I ain't the only man in the county."

"Starting to seem that way. I heard about your little adventure with the recruiters."

Ulnoth snorted. "Aye, I'm a real hero. What other news of the great patriotic struggle? Are we bending knee to king or queen this week?"

"Umm, king still. I think. Pharamund's put a Marcher lord in charge as the new marshal, real bloody-minded."

"That's nothing new."

"This one's different," Sally said, suddenly serious. "Courier rode through yesterday, said he was at Murento. The queen's army put it under siege, and after a while they yielded."

"That's nothing new either – cities change hands with the winds."

"Not this time. The marshal retook it a few days later. The queen's soldiers escaped, but to punish the citizens for surrendering he sacked the city, burned down the university and strung half the population up along the walls so all who passed by could see the price of treason against the king. Women and children, too."

Ulnoth frowned. "That's...bullshit, Sally. You're too credulous. That courier was having you on."

"No, he wouldn't even talk about it before downing a gallon of cider, and then only in whispers. He was *scared*. Scared me, too." Sally shivered and wrapped herself closer around Ulnoth. "I wish some wizard would come along and just disappear us into Faerie, away from these godsfucked lords and their godsfucked war, leave us in peace."

"That's only in stories. Besides, you'd go batty with boredom in such a place."

"Oh, I think you could keep me entertained," she said, sliding a slender hand down between his legs. "Ready for more, I see."

He took one of her olive-toned tits in his grasp. "Always."

"Oh yes? You haven't felt the full extent of my powers, arrogant mortal! Hows about I show you things...."

"Mmm, yes...."

Her voice dropped to a husky whisper. "Unspeakable things...."

"Ahh...."

"Things that pasty little wife of yours couldn't even begin to imagine...."

Ulnoth suddenly jerked, shrank back. "*Godsdammit!*" He leaped up and tromped toward the clothes piled in the corner. "What'd I tell you last time? Chthonii, the *one* thing I say not to talk about.... Shit!" He plucked his braies from the pile and one muddy leg of his chausses. He hopped from one leg to another as he wrenched his clothes on.

"Ulnoth, I'm sorry! I-I just got a bit carried away...."

"I'll say you did."

"Come on, don't be that way. You know how I am."

"Aye, I know." He was dressed and out of the rented room without another word.

★   ★   ★

"Let's get this over with."

The factor looked up from his lunch with one raised eyebrow. "Good afternoon to you too, Ulnoth."

The factor was easy to pick out even in the dim taproom, his ridiculous bag-sleeved silken cotte setting him well apart from the meaner villagers. Clean-shaven, with hair cut short in the current fashion, his very presence screamed, *I'm better than any of you will ever be!* Ulnoth knew he shouldn't have come to the man angry. It probably wouldn't end well, but he wanted to finish his business and go home. *Stupid sandcrab girl, why'd she have to....* Whatever. He put it out of his mind. "Marek, you've no idea how profoundly uninterested I am in cocking around today, so you can save the excuses about pirates stealing shipments and I won't remind you about blight and rationing. Heard it all before. I've got a great deal, even for you: fifteen per tun. Take it or leave it."

Marek chewed, swallowed and sat back in his chair, all while keeping perfect eye contact with Ulnoth. "Twelve."

"You worthless piece of—"

"*In addition* to the usual myriad catastrophes that can befall grain shipments, it's become common knowledge that Emperor Artabarzanes is nipping at the borders of Bergovny, snatching away whole crops and adding to our woes. That's what happens when Marcher lords are more interested in slaughtering each other than keeping up a defense of the *Marches*. The Marimines Islands' banks grow weary of the high-risk credit environment. Liquidity suffers." He held up his palms as if to say, *What can anyone do? Certainly not my fault, old boy.* "Twelve."

Ulnoth grimaced, punched the air. "Done," he growled, simmering with bile.

"There now, that wasn't so painful, was it?" Marek stood. "I wish all my clients were so decisive. Pleasure, as always. And as a token of goodwill, here's an advance." He tossed a silver penny onto the table then extended a hand along with the falsest of smiles. Ulnoth just glowered. "Until next season then." He smirked and mounted the stepladder up out of the room.

Ulnoth scooped up the penny but didn't bother putting it in his purse. He walked over to the plank laid between crates that served for a bar and slapped it back down as the brewer Ludrig passed. "Brandy," he said.

An hour later he considered going home. An hour after that he reconsidered it. *Twelve*, he thought. *Can we make it through the winter on that?* Not likely. *Maybe I should join the army after all.* At least they drew some pay, and volunteers earned more than conscripts. After some unknown span of time Ulnoth looked up from his ponderings to notice the place emptier than usual. Completely empty, but for a couple of tanners. It was late but no one had bothered to toss him out. A nervous woman came down the stair, whispered something to the tanners, then they all left together in a hurry.

"Ludrig," he called toward the back room. No answer. "Hey, Ludrig! Hey, I'm drinking up all your cider, better wake up and stop me!" When the bartender abandons his bar, something is very wrong. He crossed the sawdust-strewn cellar and climbed.

It was dark outside, an hour when all honest souls and most dishonest ones should be abed. Instead there was pandemonium. Townsfolk and strangers scrambled north on the highway along the Carsa River, walking, running, riding horse-drawn carts, mule carts and even a few rickshaws. Dogs barked. "What is going on?"

"Ulnoth!"

He turned with a scowl. "I'm still pissed at you, Sal—"

"Shut up and listen. They're coming!"

"Coming? Who?"

"Reavers! Riding up from the south, firing everything in their path. They...they torched Lenocca."

Ulnoth went white. "*Lenocca?* But it's a temple city, inviolate!"

"Old quarter might be, but the land's held by Felgred, Pharamund's man. Word is they're keeping to the river and burning. Your farm, isn't it—?"

"Oh gods...." He didn't waste any more breath. He tore through the stream of humanity flooding the road until he spotted a fast-looking horse, then leaped into the air and ripped the unfortunate rider from his saddle.

"Hey!" They fell to the ground together. The horse snorted and shied away while other travelers mostly interested in minding their own business drifted around the island of violence. Ulnoth climbed into the saddle, wrenched the horse around against the flow of traffic and into the darkness, leaving the mount's owner shambling after him and spitting hellfire.

Faster, faster. Blood pounded in his ears as the horse pummeled the ground at a gallop, sweat steaming in the night's chill. Ulnoth's lungs burned with the effort of holding on. *Go.*

He smelled it first of course. That's always how it is, isn't it? He almost gagged at the smell. He tried breathing through his mouth. It didn't help. *They'll hide. Yes, they're clever, they know to hide.*

Losing a crop was bad, even at a price of twelve per tun. Losing the house was worse, but if the foundation was sound it could be relaid. If anything happened to his little girl, to Athewen....

—that pasty little wife of yours—

He shook that memory from his head. *Please, let them be all right and I swear I'll never touch – look at – think about another woman again!* He turned a corner, cleared a line of trees, and saw the red glow on the horizon. *No....*

Too late for the crops – millet, turnips, all a field of black, the fire already spread to the next property. The remains of his home burned bright. Ulnoth kicked the horse but still it slowed, spent and refusing to go another step toward the heat. *Surely they would've got away from that.* He crumpled from the saddle and half crawled toward the inferno. Smoke poured poison into his eyes, his throat.

"*Athewen!*" Ulnoth barely heard his own voice against the roar of the flames. "*Lisette!*" No use. "Athewen...."

They could be anywhere, or nowhere. He searched the bounds of the property, the edge of the forest, the rocky waste leading down to the riverbank calling their names over and over. Finally he let out a wordless howl. Smoke and fatigue overcame him as the adrenaline flowed out and he collapsed, dead to the world.

★　　★　　★

Ulnoth didn't remember waking up, barely remembered how he'd got there. The horse – *was there a horse?* He couldn't see one. His hands and clothes were black. The ground, trees, his own throat it seemed, all black with burn, except for the snow of gray ash in the early gloom. The sun overhead burned cold, hidden by cloud – real clouds or more smoke? There wasn't even a wind to carry the fumes away. He lay still for a few centuries, certain he was in the deepest of the seventeen hells. *A just reward*, Bedegar's voice droned from somewhere.

When aching joints broke the sad news that he was indeed still alive, Ulnoth rose and reached for a fencepost to steady himself. The charred wood crumbled in his grasp and he nearly fell again. *What am I doing here? I had to find something. Some....* He looked at the ruin before him. It seemed familiar. *This was my house.* It hit him like a sucker punch from the gods. *Athewen. Lisette.*

The rubble still gave off a sickening heat, though the sting of singed arm and beard hairs barely registered as he trod among the cinders. It hadn't been much of a house – one room and a small attached barn. It didn't take long to search.

He found his wife's body in the middle of the floor, and though it had been immolated to nothingness, he recognized the little copper Polytheon star still around her neck. A spearhead was lodged in her ribcage with the shaft snapped off just below it. Proof then, if any was needed, that this was no accident. Ulnoth stood over what was left of his wife, so in shock that he actually felt nothing in that moment. *How can that be?* wondered the tiny corner of his mind still capable of thought.

He paced the perimeter in a daze. The few animals they'd had were gone. The cornerstones of the foundation were blackened like everything else but still solid. *All four of them. One, two, three....*

Little Lisette was wedged up against the fourth one, golden hair all burned away. Part of her skull was missing, smashed against the cornerstone.

He doubled over and vomited, and when his stomach was empty he retched black bile. A thunderclap burst overhead, and as a cold rain fell and turned the world to a dark slimy swamp, Ulnoth wailed.

CHAPTER FOUR

The Hard Way

Alessia traveled a country of scar tissue in every direction – scorched fields, houses fallen back to the earth, people few and far between. *Why*, she wondered for the ten thousandth time, *would anyone so completely break a land then fight so long and hard over it?*

She'd started southward along the Talphus River, but quickly abandoned the idea after hearing word of fighting that way. Now she crept east, still keeping an eye out for soldiers. Pharamund had his supporters in Argovan and Engwara some in Bergovny, so one never knew where violence would erupt next. After finding no town intact, she spent her first night in a crumbled Polytheon priory, the brothers long fled or worse. *Is it too late to go back?* But of course it was, and her reasons for leaving could only deepen over time.

Two more days and the Sellinac Mountains fell away to ripples on the horizon near the Bergovan border. Some of the travelers Alessia asked for directions had strange accents and dialects, but in a world where serfs might never travel more than ten miles from where they were born, tongues could change from one town to another.

"Thahtaway. Abaht a day's wahlk," said the woman perched atop a cart drawn curiously by one ox and one mule yoked together. She jerked a thumb behind her. A haggard man in the seat with her clutched at a bundle like it was gold. "Ya can go straight on 'cross Carsa to Firleaf and 'at, or south to Plisten then 'Nocca. Don't go north."

"Why, what's north?" Alessia asked.

"Wengeddy," the man said, as if that was all the explanation needed. "Don't go north." The woman tapped the ox on the shoulder with a stick and the cart pressed on westward.

"Firleaf," she said to herself. "That sounds pleasant."

★　★　★

"Gods' tits, woman, yer goin' alone?"

The highways were dotted with wayside clearings every few miles to ease travelers, and this one boasted a firepit currently in use by ten or twelve of them. Alessia gave her inquisitor a bemused look. "What? Yes…I know, I know. Dangerous."

"Dangerous." The man nodded. "And nearer to full lunacy, or suicide." He waved Alessia toward the fire and the bubbling pot that seemed too small to fill twelve stomachs. "Sit by awhile at least. Lucky thirteen we'll be."

"I…all right. But I haven't much to add to your pot, just some hardtack."

"Eh?" An older woman stirring the pot looked up. "Toss it in, soak up and add some thick to the mess."

"Can I take it," said the man who'd invited her, "by your unworldliness, if I may say so, that you be o' the cloister?"

"You can take it," Alessia answered as she crumbled a wafer into the pot, "but it's not quite so anymore. I quit the temple."

"You *what?*" Half the company said it all at once, and it might have been funny but for the horror on their hard-bitten faces. "Why, by the gods – if you'll forgive me – would you go and do a damn fool thing like that? Leave the only halfway safe place left in the world?"

Alessia tried to explain what'd happened. They listened but didn't seem to understand. "Hmm," mumbled the old woman as she emptied a ladle of…whatever it was into a clay bowl. "Well tahns can always use a physic, just so long as you can get to one ain't been hit yet—"

"I'm sorry," said Alessia, not sure she'd heard right, "did you say…oh, *towns.*"

The woman gave her a quizzical look. "Aye, tahns. What else? Stick to the roads though – godsdamn bandits make as much trouble as the soldiers. No real difference, really."

"Aye," agreed the travelers.

Alessia ate her meal and tried not to think of bandits.

Sometime later that night she woke to find a body on top of her and a hand over her mouth. Panic shot through her. *Bandits!*

"Ssh," said a whisper somewhere above her. "No troubles, sis, jus' a quick 'un, eh?" It was cold and the fire was out. Nearby, dark shapes huddled together, breathing, snoring. None of the other travelers stirred. The hand that wasn't covering her mouth pawed at Alessia's gown. Down, down toward the hem, up under it.

No! she tried to scream but couldn't. She opened her mouth to bite and tasted the salty stink of her attacker's fingers, then blood.

"Ah!" The figure shrank back and Alessia wrenched her knee upward. He went tumbling to the side. "Godsbuggerit!"

"Oh, give it up, sis," mumbled another tired voice. "It's jus' a tumble. Fair trade for a bowl and fire, and these ol' bones need they's sleep." It was the old woman! Alessia placed her attacker now – the man who'd drawn her into this company of strangers. *Lucky thirteen.*

"Aye," agreed the others who'd awakened.

What horror had she walked into? Alessia staggered to her feet, almost tripping over her rucksack, which she'd used as a pillow, the bow lashed to the side of it. She hugged it in front of her like a shield, and then felt something inside poke her hand. Something small and hard and sharp. She fumbled at the top flap while backing away.

"Hey now," said her would-be rapist, sucking at his bitten finger, "don't be like that! Come on back, let's all just—" He leaped at her.

Alessia whipped an arrow out of the sack and swung. The head sank into the man's cheek, through the meat and straight out the other. She turned and ran in no particular direction, leaving the man howling with a yard of good temple ash skewered clean through his mouth.

When she'd run her legs out and her throat burned with desert dryness, Alessia collapsed in the dark, still hugging her rucksack, weeping silent thanks for Tanusia's final order.

★   ★   ★

What just happened? What did I just do? What just happened? She asked herself the questions over and over in a daze, in a gray place half a league west of sleep. When at last the sky lightened, she stumbled to a brook at the bottom of a gully. The face reflected in the water bore uncounted cuts and scratches from her flight through the brush, reddened eyes and a trace of the same deadness she saw in others.

She rinsed her wounds, dared a few sips of brackish water—

Ack!

—then looked around for the road. *How far did I run? Which way?* She climbed a nearby hill to get a better look. *Should I go back? What if those...people are still there?*

She made her way east, parallel to the highway but well away from it. It was slow going through the brambles and she soon had new scrapes to match the old. Around noontime the first pangs of hunger hit her all at once. In the temple they'd eaten simply but none starved. Thus this new pain brought some alarm.

Alessia felt through her sack for the rough flatness of her remaining hardtack. She didn't find it. Annoyed, she dumped everything in a pile on the ground. The last thing to tumble out was a sparker. "Oh, no...." She rifled through everything. Fallen out or swiped, it wasn't there.

"Chthonii," she breathed, painfully aware that no one was around to report her foul mouth to Mother. She instinctively reached for her neck, for her Polytheon star, but it wasn't there either. She'd cast it away.

"All right," she said to herself, "don't panic. Uh...." There were hills all around, and that meant ravines and probably water at the bottom. But food? Her eyes rested on the pile before her – clothes, some coins, her physic kit, needle case, eating knife— *Ha! No use for that now* – sparker, bow...

The bow, still in one piece and strapped securely along the edge of the sack. She'd not wanted to take it at first, but an arrow had already saved her. What else could she accomplish?

★   ★   ★

Alessia's total archery experience added up to a few laughing, fumbling attempts at market fair games, and it took her almost twenty minutes just to string the thing. She became terrified of breaking it as she bent it back to its full tension. "This can't be the right way," she whispered more than once before giving up to let her aching arms recover. Somehow she managed it without getting her fingers caught in the nocks. *What an idiot I must look*, she thought, unnerved anew at the notion of being watched.

She drew an arrow from the quiver and notched it, the gray goose-feather fletching tickling her fingers. She picked out a large nearby oak tree, an easy target certainly. She drew the string as far back as she could manage, clenched her throat to hold her breath and let go.

"Ah!" Pain exploded across her arm where the string smacked and her fingers buzzed. The arrow was nowhere to be seen, and had certainly not hit the tree. This wasn't going to be as easy as it looked.

The next day saw Alessia hungrier, and motivated to try the weapon again. *Slower this time.* She wrapped cloth around her arm and fingers, tried a few aching practice draws, aiming and relaxing. At last she built up the nerve to try another shot.

This time, it hit the tree. A glancing strike that made the arrow twist around then fall to the ground, but a hit all the same. Alessia let out a whooping cry at the small victory. She tried another shot, and another and another until she could hit the target nearly half the time.

That night Alessia dined on a hard-gotten feast – a pigeon and a squirrel. It cost another arrow broken on a stone, but it was a trade gladly made.

CHAPTER FIVE

Everything Breaks

Plisten village proper had taken only a swipe from the reavers as they'd passed through, like it was an afterthought. It was the farmland that mattered after all, the farms that fed enemy armies. Most of the buildings were blackened on the outside but there'd been no concerted effort to erase the place for all time, so when the smiths, millers and carpenters started creeping back from wherever they'd hidden there was cause for, if not quite celebration, then at least relief.

Ludrig poured Bedegar another strong ale. The underground taphouse was overlooked and untouched but for a bit of soot and some burst kegs, and the survivors gathered there either to mourn their losses or celebrate their undeserved luck. Looking around the space you could almost think nothing had happened, except that it wasn't so full now. Nineteen plots of the county had been wiped out, no doubt with more to come. Nineteen families torn apart, all known to each other, more or less. But the sole survivor of one sitting silent among them weighed heaviest.

"How is he?" Sally set a trio of empty cups onto the bar, clumsily knocking one over.

"The same," Bed replied, following the young woman's gaze to the pitiable figure in the corner. "Poor fellow. I knew he was out of his mind when we found 'im, but how long can a man stay that way?"

Sally's mouth twitched. "He must eat though, or he'd be dead by now."

Bed shrugged. "He eats on occasion, drinks what I put in front of him, goes where he's led. Doesn't really sleep. Manages not to piss himself, thank the gods. But he ain't said a word since we dug him from that black hell." He shook his head. "Those poor lasses... terrible. No wonder his noggin shut down. I'm not sure what we can do. Either he'll find himself again, or he won't. Imagine the temples all got their hands full without a lackwit to look after."

Lackwit was an apt description. Ulnoth hunched over a crate used as a table, eyes open but glazed and staring at nothing. The slow rise and fall of his chest was all that marked him as a living, breathing man. There were stories from traveling merchants about nobles in Thazov and Porontus who would have the corpses of slain enemies or beloved relatives hollowed out and stuffed like beasts taken in hunt. Their blood was drained and replaced with some chthonic concoction that prevented decay, limbs arranged so that it seemed they lived still but frozen at a single moment to spend all eternity on display. In his current state, Ulnoth could well have been taken for such a horror.

"Then we will," said Sally finally, "long as we have to."

"Aye. You got any family to worry over in all this?"

"Not no more. Been on my own for years. Seems a blessing now. You?"

Bed nodded. "A niece. Husband's a woodsman, gods be thanked. They've a cottage tucked away in the sticks. No one bothers 'em there."

"Maybe we should all become woodsmen. Just take to the trees and disappear. Wouldn't that be something?"

Bedegar laughed into his cup. "I doubt the lords'd hold well with that. Born a peasant, die a peasant, says the law. 'The harmonious choir of the gods translated unto the kingdoms of the world.' Or so the temples preach."

"I could imagine a few good men – or women, for that matter – with sharp knives might contest that."

Bedegar looked hard at Sally. "Hey now, don't you go even joking about that kind o' thing. Heads've come off for less, the wrong type hears it."

"Who's gonna hear anything down in this—"

"Ahem. *Him*, for one." Bed jerked his chin toward the entrance. He was a nondescript thirtyish man dressed in a padded gambeson with Engwara's coiled snake emblem sewn to the front. No helmet, sword or spear, but a long knife was tucked into his belt. The whole place stilled. In the corner, a pregnant woman strumming a theorbo fell silent.

"Ah. I heard 'bout this place. Didn't believe it but here it be. Ain't exactly on the up an' up, eh? No worries, the laws o' that pretender from Thoriglyn are no more." The man raised his voice to reach every ear. "This county is now under the tender care of Her Majesty Queen Engwara. Rejoice in your fucking liberation." He sidled up to the bar. "Gimme whatever you pour around here." Ludrig only gawked at the man for a few seconds before absently reaching for a cup and filling it from a small keg. The man took a long drink, then turned around to face the room. "Heard there was a bit of trouble lately, eh? Queen's partisans got a bit overzealous in their campaign. Pity about that. Still, one does what must be done. Fortunes o' war, eh?"

Bed rose from his stool and steadied himself against the bar. "If you're here to recruit men, you won't find any today. We got enough war stories to go round for now."

The man turned to face him with a maddeningly carefree grin. "No, I can see the bottom of the barrel's been thoroughly scraped. No men to be found. None of use anyway." His gaze shifted to Sally. "Now, *you* on the other hand...."

Sally rolled her eyes. "Why don't you just drink your drink and be gone? Red or green, neither's got much love here."

"Ohoho, now *that* sounds mighty close to sedition. You know that word, missy? It means speakin' against your rightful queen—"

A ripple of hateful snorts wove its way through the small crowd. "Rightful?" someone said. "I buried my brother yesterday. Tell me some more 'bout rightful!"

The soldier shifted on his stool. "Who said that? It's war! That's what you dirtfuckers fail to grasp. Bad things happen. Get over it." He took a too-big swig and spilled some down the front of his padded gambeson. "Ech, dammit. You don't like it? Get your baron to come over t' the right side. Why, even old Lord Tarleston seen the light just last week. 'Course," he chuckled, "we had to relieve him of a few fleshy bits to get 'im to come around. Then there was Everwest...."

Bedegar gave Ludrig a hard look that contained an unspoken question. The brewer shook his head, just enough to be clear. Bed shrugged as the soldier went on with his bloody boasts. And on, and on.

"...and the idiots tried to hold us off with mattocks. *Mattocks*, can you believe it? Well, we made short work o' them as you can imagine. Lots o' loot you might be interested in, actually – farming shit and the like. Also took some nice pretty lasses into our, uh, *protection*," he cackled, downing another cup. "Not so pretty as you, though." His eyes rested once again on Sally, who was bringing another tray of empty cups to the bar. "Might be I'll have to bring my lads back this way, pay you all another visit. All for the glory of the queen, o' course...."

During this intrusion no one bothered to look in Ulnoth's direction. What was there to see? He'd become a fixture in the place, unmoving, unchanging. So no one reacted when Ulnoth slowly got up from his seat, making no sound as he crept across the sawdust. He came up behind Sally and swept up one of the clay cups. In the space of a heartbeat he stepped around behind the soldier.

"Wha—?"

Ulnoth suddenly smashed the cup onto the man's head, sending broken shards in every direction. Everyone in the room jumped, some screamed.

"Gyargh!" The soldier leaned over the bar, clutching his bleeding crown. "What the—" Ulnoth plucked up one of the bigger fragments of clay. A sharp one. As easily as he would swing a sickle at harvest he sliced into the soldier's neck, a stretch of wet hair wrapped around one fist, tearing and stabbing, stabbing and ripping and digging. Blood went everywhere. Bed, Sally and everyone froze as they were coated in hot red splashes. The soldier made awful choking sounds that became gurgles. Through it all Ulnoth kept on hacking and came near to taking the head clean off.

How long the whole grisly spectacle went on Ulnoth didn't know. It was only when the twitchy, pulpy mass atop human shoulders slumped to the floor with a revolting squish-thump that time resumed. Ulnoth looked down at his handiwork—

Give my regards to the queen!

—and for the first time seemed conscious of where he was, who he was, and perhaps what he'd done. He dropped the bit of clay to the floor where a fountain of blood soaked through the sawdust and looked at Bed and Sally. "What—?" he mouthed. He looked around at the horrified faces, down at the body. Then he turned toward the ladder and scrambled up, painting each rung in red.

He ran. Out, across the road, into the forest without destination. *What have I done?* He thought it over and over again. *Oh gods what have I done?*

CHAPTER SIX

Sandcastle

Alessia walked into Firleaf with only eight arrows but a full belly and more or less unmolested. It looked a dull but peaceful place, dominated by a rectangular green sward of earth ringed with low wooden buildings. Farther out, humble houses sat on the edges of plots claimed from the forest. Then she noticed that most of the plots lay blackened, dead. *Not so peaceful, then.*

There didn't seem to be much of a common gathering place in the village beyond a ramshackle longhouse with a trough in front that fed and watered animals. One side of the building was smeared with soot. She went in.

Down the length of the building a row of horse stalls went mostly unoccupied. At the near end a few grim-faced peasants sat around one of two tables. Conversation halted and heads turned in her direction. She realized too late how odd she must look: a dirty, lone wild-haired woman in a traveling gown with a strung bow across her shoulder and half a quiver full at her waist. "Ah, um. Hello."

"Ay." A short, broad-boned woman waddled out from a stable, looked her over once, and nodded. "Horse?"

"Hmm? Oh, no. I'm on foot."

"Drink then?"

"Yes, please."

"Siddahn."

Alessia sat at the empty table, only then becoming fully aware of the aching in her feet and thighs. "Oh...." She shrugged the rucksack onto the floor and laid her bow beside it.

"Whatchye huntin'?" asked one of the peasants with a furtive glance.

Alessia's hand flinched toward the eating knife she now kept close at her hip. *Calm down.* "Hunting? Whatever I can catch, I guess."

A round of grunts. "Yep, that's just abaht what we's brought to, seems."

Alessia shook her head. "I'm no hunter though. I was traveling from Argovan and I, uh, got separated from my group."

"That's some bad luck. And you ain't found 'em again after all this way—?"

"I didn't enjoy the company," Alessia replied more sharply than she'd intended.

The woman set a cup and a jug in front of her. "Small beer's all there is, sorry."

"That's fine, thank you."

"Well you can thank me with a cop."

Alessia dug through her sack and came out with a copper disc struck with the outline of a boar. "Um, will you take 'Vani coin?"

The woman shrugged. "No difference t' us."

"Is there anything to eat? Pigeon gets old fast."

"I can believe 'at. But there ain't been feed fit for none but beast since the reavers come through."

"Reavers?" Alessia guessed the woman's meaning before she even asked, but was sad to hear the answer. The description was dreadfully familiar.

"No food for the soldiers means none for us. I guess yinz got 'em over on yer side too," she said, a bit uncertainly.

"I don't have a side."

The woman laughed, loud and bitter. "Ha! That ain't allowed no more. Just ask arahnd. Hey, anyone still got their farm alraht?"

One peasant perked up. "I got about two acres left, not good for much. Hey Rhea, fill me up again."

"Well, I still don't have a side, I'm a—" Alessia stopped herself before finishing. *Temple sister? Not anymore I'm not.* "I'm a physic."

"Funny things for a physic to carry," said the woman, nodding at the bow while she poured more small beer into the peasant's cup. "Though maybe not so much these days."

"Is there a hospital around where I might get employment? A temple sick house, something like that?"

The woman shrugged. "Maybe in 'Nocca. Thoriglyn. But not here, not no more."

Alessia let out a frustrated sigh, then eyed all the empty stalls. "Hmm...."

"What?"

"Would you like there to be?"

★   ★   ★

There were actually two stables in Firleaf, but the owner of one had been caught up in the destruction of the reavers' advance. Now it was put to whatever use the survivors fancied. When Alessia swung open the double doors a small population of squatters shielded their eyes at the sudden flare of light or looked away. Garbled curses rang out and from somewhere an infant cried.

"There are people living in here?"

"Well...wouldn't call what they do *livin'* exactly, but aye."

The peasants had readily agreed that a physic would be a welcome addition in the village, like having a real temple but without all the preachifying. They'd support the hospital and Alessia would provide what care they might need. "People only," she'd added, knowing how farmers thought. "No animals." They still gave her the stable.

Now that she saw the space she wondered if she weren't in over her head after all. It stank, the roof had holes, the floor had manure, and half the stalls had vagrants sleeping in hay along with the rats. "Some just lost their homes," explained Wrenth, the man who still had about two acres left. "Burned aht. Others are professional rogues, if you make any distinction. Here, up! Up and aht, yinz swampgnats! We's makin' a 'spital ahtta the place."

"Eh?" An old man hobbled to his feet covered in fodder and screwed up his face into a sour rictus. "Why bother? Reds or greens'll jus' torch it like ever'thing else. Whole world be cinders soon, lords get their way."

"Might be, Cuddy," replied Wrenth as he shuffled the old man toward the doors. "But 'til then you'll hafta find another place to sleep off Rhea's home brew. That goes for the rest o' yinz too!"

Alessia muttered apologies and thanks to the doubly displaced peasants as they filed out, assuring each of a welcome back should they need her services. *Not the most auspicious start*, she thought. Emptied thus, the stable looked even more a wreck.

"Well there you have it," said Wrenth with a wide sweep of one muscled arm. "All yours."

"Thanks. I'm not sure where to begin – I've never actually built a hospital before."

"I'll spread the word and folks'll come by to help muck aht the place. Sooner you can start doing business the better for everyone."

★ ★ ★

Alessia slept in the stable while it was being transformed into her hospital. It actually went much faster than she'd thought it would. Within a week the roof was patched and most of the filth flushed out. A few of the people Wrenth had kicked out came, for what other employment could they have? There was still a great deal of cleaning to be done and supplies to be obtained before she could treat patients, but it was a start. She even became somewhat accustomed to their odd dialect. *Yinz is just abaht grown ahn me*, she thought with a grin.

Some days later she found herself twisting the blade of one of her scalpels into a tiny wooden screw with extreme care so as not to bend or snap it. She was assembling what was to be the frame of a cot that had to be built sturdy enough not to collapse under a thrashing patient.

"What's that?"

Alessia jumped, startled by the lilting voice. "Quennet, don't sneak up on me like that!"

"Sorry. But what is it?"

Alessia turned to her latest visitor, Wrenth's eight-year-old daughter. "It's a scalpel," she said. "For cutting people's flesh open."

The girl's eyes almost doubled in size. "Oh…so why you usin' it to put screws in?"

"I shouldn't be." Alessia sighed. "A physic's tools are fine things, for fine work. But with the rebuilding around Firleaf all the proper tools are taken." It pained her to draft her instruments into such mundane service, but the alternative was to wait, and that she would not do.

"So were you really a priestess in a temple? With stony walls and saints' shrines and everything?"

Alessia set down the scalpel with the feeling she wasn't going to get much work done today. "I was a novitiate sister. The only priests are far away, in Holy Artamera."

"Where the God of Man descended to earth and broke into ten thousand pieces to become the first people." Quen beamed with pride at her knowledge.

"That's right," said Alessia, making sure to sound properly impressed.

"I know that story. Did you sing at sundown? And tell people what to do and beg for their money?"

"I – uh. Well, I sang, yes. Not very loudly, though. I'm not very good. But I didn't have much say in matters of doctrine—"

"Doc *what?*"

"Never mind. Dear, what are you doing here, exactly?"

"I'm s'posed to help you." Quennet frowned. "Actually, I think Mama just wanted me out of the way. Not much to do since everything got burned. I used to feed the hens and the goat. They're gone now."

Rage lanced through Alessia's gut. What did Quen know or care about king or queen, lords and soldiers and treason? She only knew that her family's hens and goat were gone, their land burned. *Better she find another path in life – any other.* "Do you think...you might like to take vows, join a temple someday?"

"Nah," said Quen, "I'm not a good singer either. Da always tells me to pipe down. I wanna be a physic like you and cut people open with a scaplel!"

"There's a bit more to it than that," Alessia said with a smile. "Most of the cutting's done by chirurgeons. But stick around here long enough, you might pick up a few skills."

The girl beamed, hopeful. "Can I?"

"Of course, I'll need a helper after all. But it won't be easy."

"That's all right, it beats feeding hens."

★　　★　　★

"It's done then?" Wrenth eyed the outside of the building as though expecting it to be much changed. He'd come near sunset to fetch his daughter home from her new apprenticeship and found Alessia outside, clearing a plot for an herb garden.

She rubbed dirt from her hands. "It's as done as it's going to get until I can find supplies. Space is the easy part. We'll need clean water, lots of it. Always kept at or near a boil."

Wrenth whistled. "Ain't no small thing there. Anything else?"

"Bandages," Alessia continued, "and medicament herbs and gut string and needles, and brandy—"

"Brandy?"

"For infections, cooling, making tinctures."

Wrenth shook his head. "Sister, I ain't even heard of some o' that stuff, never mind seen it around here. I can get you leeches."

"No! No leeches, they don't work."

"Well, for the rest you'll have to go to 'Nocca, buy from the temple there. Wait for a caravan to come through, you don't wanna go alone."

Alessia snorted. "I've had better luck when I do. I – wait, what's that?"

"What?"

"That...what is it, rumbling? From the north road, you hear it? Maybe that's a caravan now."

Wrenth frowned. "Don't sound quite like...." His face turned white. "Oh no. No, please, not again."

"What is it?"

"Where's Quen?"

"Inside," Alessia answered. Wrenth's fear gripped her also. "Polishing my clamps. Why—"

"Get her. Go and find somewhere to hide. Go now!" He sprinted toward the remains of his farm on the outskirts of Firleaf.

The rumbles grew louder and nearer. Then clanks, stomps, curses. While stumbling into the building, Alessia understood. It was a small army approaching. Not many men, but enough to make trouble.

"Quen, we have to go."

The girl looked up from the row of shiny metal parts laid out on the bench before her. "Go? Where? How come?" Then she saw the frightened expression on Alessia's face. "Oh." She stood and took a hold of Alessia's hand and tugged. "Come on, I know where we can hide."

As Alessia passed a corner she hesitated, then eyed the bow and quiver laid there, forgotten these past weeks. *Surely I won't need that.* Still, she spared a moment to gather them up in her arms.

The army burst upon the village, and for an instant it seemed that they'd all be spared, for it plowed forward without hint of stopping. Then they saw the meaning of it all – it wasn't one army but two. One splashed green and fleeing, the other in red hot on their heels, and the pursuers caught up to their quarry right as they passed into Firleaf. Through clouds of road dirt kicked up by the fray, poleaxes swung and flashed in the orange sunset. Men tried to form defensive lines only to see them dashed apart by charging horses, then ground into mud.

Alessia dashed across a corner of the village green, praying that Quen knew where she was going. Behind them she heard some formation break and howls went up. At the edge of the green near the woods they came to the stump of a large tree felled long ago. The far side was hollowed out wide near the ground, enough for a slight woman and child to squeeze inside. Alessia crouched and held Quen tight with the bow before them, fumbling to get it strung.

"Here," said Quen, pulling an arrow from the ever-slackening quiver and passing it to Alessia. "Hurry up—"

"Shh," Alessia whispered. They listened to the carnage go on and on as they cowered. It sounded like the fleeing soldiers had taken refuge in some of the village buildings. So the pursuing troops set them on fire. When the too-familiar stench of smoke assaulted their noses, Quen burst into tears. "Mommy...."

Alessia risked a peek around the edge of the trunk, and amid the fighting and burning houses she spied a green-badged soldier running toward them. Their eyes locked. "No...." She scrambled to notch the arrow.

The soldier appeared above them, ogreish and snarling with a blooded hatchet in his hand. "Out, this is my spot now!"

"But there's nowhere else to go!" Alessia stood halfway and raised her bow. "You get back...."

"Piss off!" He raised the hatchet and moved toward Quennet.

"*I said get back!*" The arrow seemed not to actually cross the short distance. It was simply resting taut on the bowstring one instant and the very next buried inside the soldier's skull and poking out through one eye. He dropped the hatchet and fell back, shaking. A stench rose to announce that the man had voided his bowels as he died.

Alessia began shaking too, not believing what she'd just done. But there was little time to reflect – out of the corner of her eye she saw her hospital engulfed in flames, and the corpse at her feet was forgotten. "Quen, stay here."

"B-but what—"

"Stay!" Heedless of being seen, she tore back toward the building. The heat nearly drove her away but she forced herself to dive through the smoke-filled doorway and grab her rucksack and whatever was inside – there was no time to save anything more.

Between her and the tree stump a group of men now fought and died, and horses with smoldering manes bolted every which way. One of them knocked Alessia back ten feet and she lost her way in the gloom, cut off from Quen. The last thing she saw with clarity was her hospital succumbing to the flames at last, like everything else.

She ran directionless into the forest, overcome by terror and despair. *What a stupid girl I am!* she thought. *To think I could fight against just a tiny bit of this.* Dusk fell and she found herself lost and alone. Again. *Cuddy was right. Whatever we build, they destroy it. Over and over.*

Stumbling in the twilight, she tripped and fell down a slope carpeted with brambles, dragging her precious few possessions with her. When she stopped falling, Alessia lay still, waiting for the pain to come and tell her what was damaged.

Face, all over. *Scratches, ignore 'em.* Leg, below the knee. She reached down and felt a slight wetness, then cringed. She tried to move it. It hurt but it worked. *Not broken then.* She sat up. Above, a full moon peeked through the treetops to illuminate her unfamiliar surroundings. She couldn't smell Firleaf burning or hear any shouts. Had she run so far? Guilt at losing sight of Quen gnawed at her. *I can't even protect one life.* If only—

A sound. Something big, moving on her right. Something

close. *Animal?* Anything not scared off by her thrashing fall could be dangerous. *Certainly I couldn't have been followed.* She rummaged through her pack, hoping she hadn't destroyed everything. The bow was gone, dropped somewhere up the slope. She felt the smooth horn handle of an eating knife and whipped it out while ignoring the pain it took to stand.

"Come out," she said, feigning a confidence she didn't feel. "Come out and…I'll let you live." She stepped forward, quivering, then brushed aside a swath of ferns.

He wasn't from the village; she could tell that straight away even in the moonlight. Times were tough, but not *that* tough. He looked bedraggled and half-mad with wild, twig-ridden hair, torn clothes and a smell like week-dead deer.

"Stay away!" He held up his fingers as if Alessia's very presence blinded him. "Leave me be!" He sounded more terrified than threatening.

The adrenaline surging through Alessia's body told her to strike, but she fought against it. "Who are you? You didn't come from Firleaf."

"Firleaf? N-no. Is it close?"

"Not anymore I fear." She lowered the knife to have a better look at him in the moonlight. "Your hand, it's cut to bits. It'll get infected if it's not seen to." She took a tiny step toward him. "You should let me—"

"No! Stay back I said. I'll…I'll hurt you."

"What happened?"

"I killed— I mean I think I killed a man."

"You think?"

"I can't remember. I cut my hand on…whatever I used. There was so much blood. I think it was a soldier."

"Are you a soldier?"

The man gave her a shocked look, as though horrified by the idea. "No! I'm— I mean I was a farmer. Think I'm a fugitive now."

"Well, I'm sure you're very sorry."

"No. I ain't. I do know that much."

"What's your name?"

"…Ulnoth."

"Ulnoth, I'm Alessia. Let me help." She took a step forward.

"Help...me?" He took a half step back, but only half.

"Why don't you let me have a look at that hand? I don't think you'll hurt me."

"...Okay."

CHAPTER SEVEN

The Spymistress

"What did you actually hear him say?"

"That the mercenaries would be at Taurix's disposal when they arrived. That they'd march on Everwest as though to retake it for the queen, then lay down their arms before the walls as proof that they'd turned. As long as Pharamund's pay came in advance, of course."

"Of course. And this person the company's captain spoke with. Describe him."

"Describe him?" The agent gulped. "Well, I don't know, he was just—"

"What was he wearing?"

"Clothes. Just, I don't know, tunic and chausses. Dark-colored. And a coat."

"What manner of coat?"

"One of those long fog-wicking things the dockworkers up there wear. You know the kind."

"How long did the meeting take?"

"About ten minutes, more or less."

"Well, which was it? More than ten minutes, or less?"

The agent felt his gut twist. "Look, what's that matter? I told you—"

"It matters because I'm fucking *asking* you. After they parted which direction did this stranger go?"

"South, I think. To the inns."

"You think, or you know?"

"I think! Please, I'm telling the truth!"

"We'll see. How tall was he?"

"I didn't get close enough to take his measurements! Average."

"What color were his eyes?"

"I don't know, it was dark!"

"Are you lying to me? Trying to make up your story as you go along, is that it? But the questions are coming too fast—"

"No, I swear!" A hand appeared out of the darkness from behind him and took a hard grip on his wrist. A manacle built right into the chair flipped up and around, locking him in place. "What the—"

"Swear all you like, I'm no temple sister to care. Now, his eyes!"

"I don't know!"

"You do! Tell me or I'll have you sliced up bit by tiny bit from foot to crown and fed to the fish. It'll take you *weeks* to die."

"No! Please, that's all I know!"

"Answer! Answer, you lying, traitorous pisspot!"

He shrank in the chair, sobbing and defeated. "I don't, don't know...."

A pause. "All right. I believe you."

"You...you do?"

"Of course, no one would notice such insignificant details. Well, *I* would, but not you."

"Then, then why—"

"I needed to know you wouldn't lie to me, even on pain of dismemberment. Now I do, mostly. Congratulations."

"So...."

"So, now you can go. But not too far, I might need to interview you again."

The agent rose slowly from his seat after the manacle was unlocked, his legs quivering jelly. As he stood, the weak light revealed a wet stain that spread down his leg and across the chair. No matter, that chair had endured far worse during its service.

Only after the poor fellow was gone did his questioner lean forward over the table and its single flickering candle, revealing a face that might have been beautiful once. Still would be but for a long stretch of scar tissue that dominated the left side from brow to chin, legacy of the passionate kiss of a flame far greater than a candle.

Vinian wove her finger in and out of the flame, slowly enough that the attendant standing wordless at the door might've noticed the distinct stench of overdone pork in the air. Pain is nothing. Control is everything. I. Am in. Control. She smiled and pinched the candle out.

"Put a tail on that last one," Vinian said. "That's all for now. I have another appointment." The attendant just nodded.

Vinian left the interview cell and ascended a winding stair. The palace at Carsolan had many passages, some secret, others merely private. At ground level this one opened onto a little-known, seldom-used seaside dock built into the stone foundation. Vinian peered out into the harbor and in the predawn gloom spotted a tiny point of light making its way toward the dock. *Right on time*, she thought. She didn't stay to meet it but continued to the top of the stair, a short hallway and finally a door that opened onto a small audience chamber. "He's coming now."

Engwara – Queen to vassals, but to enemies Countess, or something worse – turned from the open window that looked down on the port city of Carsolan. The god's-eye view somehow made the city less impressive rather than more, laid out in all its diseased glory. At least one couldn't smell the shit and fish from here. A city fought hard for, like the rest of her kingdom. How much longer would the fight go on? That was one thing this meeting was supposed to answer, but Vinian could tell she wasn't looking forward to it.

"Yes, I thought I felt my stomach turn a bit. Best get this over with. I assume you've made your customary perch comfortable? Go on, then."

Vinian nodded with a mischievous smile. "I attend, Majesty." She brushed aside an old tapestry to reveal a place carved out of the wall from which she could see and hear all that transpired, and Engwara turned back to her window.

Engwara was a striking woman; none could deny it. Not beautiful, this one – years of the nobility breeding just a bit too close together made sure of that. The nose a bit too long, the jaw more than a bit too square. But still striking, the way an axe might strike a head off or flint might strike fire from steel. No enemy would ever be lulled into a false sense of security in her presence. Or a genuine one.

That was certainly true of the fat banker from the Marimines Islands who now waddled through the door. Though fat, the man also reminded Vinian of a hungry wolf. He had thick lips, a broad beard, and a shaved or bald head and wore furs dyed to colors that you could make out even in the murk. *Rich and foreign*, Vinian thought, *always the most troublesome combination.*

"Not even bothering to knock now, are you?" Engwara asked with irritation.

The man wiped a sheen of cold sweat from his brow. "I did not," he said between breaths, "see much point, Your Majesty. I am expected after all. And you've dismissed all your guards – not even a footman do I see to disapprove my manners. Your Majesty flatters me with such trust." As he spoke he took in his surroundings and shivered. Snakes coiled and slithered over every boundary: the window, the corners, the doorway. Carved from rock they might be, but so expertly done Vinian couldn't but imagine the banker took the choice of venue as some kind of message.

"Hardly," replied Engwara. "I owe you so much money I'm probably safer with you than with my own generals. I'm worth much more alive. Prying eyes, spying eyes – those I can't afford."

"Of course, of course. Let no one say Carthagne Fadhlan ven Xedrusia does not appreciate the need for discretion, eh?" He produced a false, humorless laugh.

"Do all Marimines have so many names?"

"In my line of work," he shrugged, "I find one needs many."

"What does that even mean?"

"Honestly I've no idea, I just thought it sounded appropriately cryptic." He pulled the furs even tighter around him. "How goes the war?" he asked as if he did not already know. As if he did not know the precise reason he was there. *But the niceties must be observed nevertheless*, Vinian thought.

"It goes," the queen replied. "It goes, and it goes and it goes on like some damnable saga song where only the bit players change."

"Ah," said Carthagne, "like this new man of Pharamund's. This Toricus?"

"Taurix," Engwara corrected, "and damn you for making me speak the name. He's a Chthonus loosed from the seventeenth hell, destroying everything in his path with no thought of what's to come after. I've tried to answer him blow for blow, but...."

"But a pale imitation of a demon is no match for the real thing."

Carthagne shuffled over to an armchair in the corner of the chamber and wedged himself into it. "I know very little about warring, but in the Isles we have a saying. Actually we have many, but one of them is if you can't beat them, buy them."

Engwara snorted. "A man like that isn't seduced by gold. Or land beyond what he's already got."

"Ah, but there are many kinds of coin. You've only to find the right one. And speaking of coin...."

"Yes," the queen sighed, "I will require another loan."

"Another?" He said it with such flatness that not even the raising of his bushy eyebrows could produce the illusion of surprise. *The niceties needn't be convincing, after all.* "My employers have already advanced Your Majesty a heavy sum to finance—"

"All spent, every copper. And I'm leveraged far beyond already. I don't understand it – we beat him back time and time again yet somehow Pharamund's band of brigands manages to hang on! Some days I wonder if he hasn't made some bloody bargain with the Bhasan emperor—"

"Artabarzanes?" Carthagne interjected with what seemed to be genuine shock. "Surely that python hasn't taken Pharamund's side!"

"I don't know. I would think he'd consider it beneath him to take *any* side. But if we can't come to some new arrangement there's little chance your employers will collect on their investment, unless you have offices in the seventeen hells."

"Not yet, but rest assured we're working on it. In any event, I'm afraid the bank's faith in the inevitability of your cause is somewhat, er, lessened since we last met. There's even been talk of cutting losses now rather than—"

Engwara charged across the room, loomed over the banker with painted nails digging into the chair's upholstery. "Don't you *dare* tell me that, don't you even pretend it, you grotesque pig! At a word I can have you gutted—"

"Your Majesty, I can assure you that I am but a small part in a great machine, eminently replaceable. Nothing you do to me will alter my superiors' position." He paused a moment as the queen simmered above him. "However, your dedication to your cause is evident. It may be possible I can arrange the same amount as previously, but the terms would have to be more...favorable to the institution."

"More. How much more?"

"Fifteen percent annually."

"What? That's outrageous!"

"So is taking two years and more to beat down a band of brigands. The best you've managed is a stalemate. This does not inspire confidence back west, especially now that you've begun killing off your productive classes and burning the farmland. Understand me, *Your Majesty*. The bank doesn't give half a shit who wins your backward little war or runs your big backwater country. We're in business to make *money*. A great deal of money over a very long period of time, and writing off your loan will sting us far less than it will you. So agree to our terms or not, it's all much the same to me." Carthagne sweated. He was indeed a trivial part in the machine, and no one would shed a tear if his miscalculating tongue got him drawn, quartered and dumped in the harbor with the sewage.

Engwara's lower lip trembled. Finally she stood upright, backed away from the banker. "Fifteen percent is out of the question," she hissed, every word dripping acid.

Carthagne cleared his throat. "The, ah, exact rate might be open to some negotiation. I believe I could persuade the appropriate people to come down to, say, twelve percent."

"I can't do more than ten."

"I said *some*. Don't get greedy on me now. These people don't hold my negotiating skills in as high regard as Your Majesty." He looked the queen square in the eye. "Twelve."

She glowered over him, perhaps considering evisceration after all. But.... "Done."

Carthagne exhaled, worked his way out of the chair, leaving large sweat stains behind. "I'm so glad we could come to an understanding, Queen. Please forgive my intemperate words – I take my job very seriously. I'll return soon with the necessary papers. Until then, by your leave...?"

Engwara nodded sharply.

Carthagne Fadhlan ven Xedrusia of Bank Isle-Euderico bowed as low as his shape would allow and turned to depart. Before he crossed the threshold Engwara called out, "One thing, banker. A bit in a machine you may be, and I queen of half a backwater country, but if you ever speak to me like that again I'll have you ripped open and use your blubber to light my lamps. Are we clear?"

Carthagne smiled one last time, nodded. "Crystal clear, Majesty."

When he was safely gone, Vinian emerged from her hiding place. "Could've spared that last bit. Threats after the fact are a sign of weakness."

"Yech, what happened to your finger?"

"Nothing," replied Vinian. "It was exactly as I expected. Well, almost. Fifteen percent! I almost have to admire the gall."

Engwara slumped on her couch. It was less comfortable than the armchair, but the banker's stink would have to be scrubbed away first. "He's a greedy pig. He did make one point – we've got to deal with Taurix. Ludolphus is no match for him, nor the jumped-up fops leading the rest of my army."

Vinian shrugged. "You could take the field yourself. The scandal alone would be inspiring."

"Don't tempt me. No, we must find a way to neutralize him. It was a mistake to attack Ólo, it forced his hand. He wasn't committed to Pharamund until then."

"I suppose that's probably true. War strategy's not exactly my department, Majesty."

"Wrong," Engwara said sharply. "As my spymistress, *everything* under moon and sun is your department."

The reprimand stung Vinian harder than the candle had. Her cheeks flushed in the morning light, making her scarred side a streak of red lightning. "Well, here's a thing under moon and sun, Majesty – your childbearing days are approaching their end, and if we don't finish this war soon you'll have a dynasty of one even if we should prevail."

The queen gave Vinian a venomous look. "That's unworthy, even for you. What I need is help winning the here and now."

The spymistress thought for a moment. "Actually, now that you mention it...."

"What?"

"I just concluded a very interesting interview that might take care of our problem."

"Ooh, intrigue. Can't wait to hear the details." A rumbling din floated up from the walls of the city. Both women looked down to see the fortified gate begin the long process of opening. "But it seems I must," said Engwara. "There's Ludolphus now. Managed to elude Taurix for one more day, I see."

"Stay. I'll go down and meet him," said Vinian.

The queen smiled. "You and he have spent some time together, I've noticed. Is there something between you?"

"Ha! The general's a bit old for me. No, we're natural allies – both baseborn."

"Sounds like a peasant uprising brewing. I'd best be careful."

Vinian made a perfunctory bow. "With your leave, Majesty."

"Mhmm." Engwara waved Vinian away, staring listlessly at her armchair.

By the time Vinian made her way down and out of the palace, the sun had risen and Ludolphus's column was marching through the gates. On each side of the paved boulevard a few of what passed for prominent citizens of Carsolan – guildsmen, publicans, the more expensive prostitutes – stood waving and cheering the arrival, perhaps in some vain hope of attracting attention and favor. Most commoners just stared without emotion and only grudgingly moved out of the way. *They would never have dared even last autumn*, Vinian thought with a frown. *When the commons no longer fear death, we're in trouble.* And such attitudes in a city that hadn't yet even come under siege....

Vinian waded against the flow of citizens, dodging baskets of fish and fleetfooted children. The ranks of armored men and horses, like a troop of iron centaurs, turned to examine her. Vinian found a forest of cautious pikes leveled at her face. *Please, you'd only improve it with those*, she thought while brushing aside the nearest tines and stepping forward. "Hail, general!" she called out to the lead centaur with the green horsehair crest atop his high helm. "Her Majesty sends greetings and welcome. What news of great victories?" Her words were pitched so that only the two of them perceived the tinge of sarcasm that rode along with them.

The gray-stubbled man hefted the helm from his mailed shoulders, not bothering to unstrap it, so gaunt was his flesh. "News? Aye, spymistress," he said with a tired grin, "we're here and not bleeding out in some godsforsaken ditch somewhere. I'll take that victory any day."

"You made good time," said Vinian while she jogged alongside the general's charger.

"We had good motivation. King Milksop's new marshal seems to hold some personal grudge against me for not having lost the war yet. Chased my ass up the Sellinacs and down the Talphus, and woulda got us but for a forced night march. These old bones'll sleep for a week."

Vinian nodded. "Don't get too comfy, I may have a new task for you. Come see me after you've rested."

"Oh, no, I've heard about your 'interviews'. Don't think I care to put myself through that."

It was just a joke, but Vinian winced all the same. *Someone blabbed. I've gotten sloppy.* "No, nothing like that," she said with a forced smile. "I think you'll like this one. Might take care of Taurix for us once and for all."

"Now *that* I can get behind." Ludolphus yawned. "But later. After I make my report to the queen I intend to get behind a pretty young wench, under a blanket and over a bottle, in no particular order."

★ ★ ★

To travel from the south of Argovan to the north at the peninsula's midpoint was a journey of about two weeks by horse. Another route, cheaper but twice as lengthy, was to sail the Lacaryc Sea westward hugging the coast, swing north around the swamplands known lovingly as The Bastard, then back east into the Bay of Pelona. One ship among many laid anchor in the port town of Everwest, where the scars of back and forth conquest couldn't keep business from thriving beneath the fox-head banners of Pharamund. New splashes of plaster made from Pelonan gypsum already covered the city's terraced buildings painted with brilliant red or blue rooftops, so desperate were its inhabitants for the illusion of peace.

Long after dark, six men disembarked from the ship and went directly to a particular tavern on a particular street. The next day the headless body of a well-known mercenary captain was found floating in the harbor, half eaten by fish and gulls and identified only by its flamboyant clothing. The day after that a deal was struck with the mercenary company itself as they drew near to the city. It was not a hard sell, for it involved promotions all around. The day after *that* the company marched to the gates of Everwest and laid down halberds, shields, bows, swords and axes all on cue. The castellan opened the gates and in they marched through the town to the seaside fortress. The gates closed, and while their new captain shook hands with the castellan the company pulled concealed knives and with shocking ease massacred most of the garrison. Those who managed to surrender were put to work maintaining the notion that nothing had changed. The red banners yet waved when more ships dropped anchor and supplies and troops spilled out, along with a hefty bonus in gold for the doubly turncoat mercenaries. At a stroke, Engwara's forces had retaken Everwest and were within spitting distance of targets like Ólo, Vin Gannoni and Phenidra, and no one had any idea.

CHAPTER EIGHT

Regards

The destruction was complete; not a shack stood erect. The village green was now only green in the very middle, with the rest a hundred shades of gray and brown. The eerie silence was made more so by the honks of geese flying north for the winter, gray ghosts against a gray sky. Alessia walked among the ruins with a dropped jaw and Ulnoth next to her, dead-eyed. A new binding covered his hand but rust-red stains already soaked through.

And there were bodies. Of course there were, but she'd seen plenty of those before. Most looked to be the fleeing queen's men, stripped of anything of value. Most, but not all.

"It's—" Alessia started to say, but couldn't find words. "It's—"

"It's what they do," Ulnoth said. "They get everyone in the end. Just like the man said."

She didn't know what he meant by that and didn't ask. She'd tended his wound with what supplies she had, then spent the night cowering against a tree with few words passing between them. Now in open daylight she knew him for younger than first she'd thought – his eyes had aged him. "What happened to you, was it like this?"

Ulnoth nodded. "Queen's men. My farm, and others. My w-wife, daughter…burned. And worse."

"I'm so sorry," she whispered.

"And I," he continued, "weren't even there. I was in town. Screwing my girlfriend…drinking…feeling *sorry* for myself." He dropped to one knee to hide his welling tears. Alessia put a hand on his shoulder but he shrugged it off. "It was my fault."

"There was nothing you could do. You'd have been killed right along with—"

"My fault! I should've been with them, to whatever end. Now

there's nothing left to me." He looked down at the blood on his hands. "Except this."

"Ho there, lass!" The sharp cry came from the remains of the stable. Ulnoth turned a suspicious gaze that way as the woman tottered into view.

"It's all right," Alessia said to Ulnoth. "Rhea, where is everybody? Are they...?"

The woman nodded. "Aye, a few's gone to earth for good. Nothin' you can do for them. Most is scattered – we got good at that real fast. They'll come back slow, I reckon." She eyed the ashes of Firleaf. "Never come back to it as bad as this, though. Them thugs fought 'emselfs out at least, they're gone. The reds gone back north, gods curse 'em all."

"What about Quen and her folks? Did you see them?"

"Weren't much time for takin' headcount, lass," Rhea said. "I ain't seen 'em."

"Then shouldn't we go looking?"

"If they run off into the thick, you'll never find 'em. If they come back it means they's hale. If not, well...."

Alessia shook with helpless frustration. "Isn't there *anything* we can do?"

"Look, you're a nice girl, still got lots of livin' left to do. Take my advice – get away from here. This place is cursed, there's nothin' for you now. Nor for any of us. Might not even bother to rebuild after this." She went back to rooting through the cinders for anything worth the effort to salvage.

Alessia held her head in her hands, suddenly grave-tired. "If you see Quen, please tell her I'm sorry."

"Uh-huh," Rhea grunted. Nothing left to be said, Alessia began to walk away with Ulnoth in tow.

"You should listen to her," Ulnoth said. "You'll go back to your temple, I suppose."

"I can't, nothing's changed. If anything it's worse. Do you have any suggestions?"

"You could go to Plisten. But after what I done it'll prob'ly get the same as here."

"Was it really so bad as that?"

"It was." Ulnoth frowned, spat a mouthful of phlegm onto the no-longer-green. "That woman said the reds headed north. Guess I will too."

"Why?"

"I'm dead already. Only question now's how many of them I take with me."

"But you said it was the queen's side that—"

"They're all the same! Red, green, no matter. They come, we go running, and people die. Every time. If it's blood they want, blood they'll get. I'm done running."

"And how many do you think you'll kill, the shape you're in? It's suicide."

Ulnoth produced a bitter sneer that filled Alessia with dread. "I'd have a lot better chance with a good physic on my side."

Alessia nearly choked on her own startled breath. "You expect me to *help* you kill? For what, petty revenge?"

"Petty? Maybe. But then I'm just a lowly dirtfucker, what do I know? Come with me or don't, it's all the same." He began to stalk toward the road that led roughly north and held up his torn hand. "Thanks for the patchwork."

What should I do? Stop him? But how? She supposed she could tag along and try to keep him out of trouble, convince him to give up his hateful quest. Maybe find somewhere else to start over again. *It's not like I have anything better to do.* She started after him. "Wait."

"Why?" he said without turning.

"You in a hurry to die? Wait a bit." She turned toward the ruin of her hospital. "I have some clamps to find."

After digging a few precious bits of equipment from the blackened mess, they started northward. They kept to the road along the Carsa, but Ulnoth was still wary of people and disappeared into the growth on either side when the odd traveler happened by. He'd watch each with a rabbit's stare until they were gone beyond the horizon and only then come out again. Alessia wondered how he was going to wreak vengeance with such skittishness.

When they came to a forded stream, Alessia insisted Ulnoth bathe at least once, and while he splashed in the water she sat on the grass and inventoried their supplies. They'd found her bow, some of her instruments covered in the ash she'd dug them out of, and six arrows. Thoughts of the soldier she'd killed came unbidden. *It was so easy*, she thought. *Satisfying, even. The warrior priestess.* She glanced at Ulnoth. The Polytheon had arcane texts on how much evil a person could endure without becoming evil himself, but Alessia had never read them. Too morbid, too distant a topic.

So lost in brooding was Alessia that she didn't notice the rider upon her until the horse neighed its presence. Startled, she jumped to her feet. Against the sun all she could make out was a small man wearing a helmet and overstuffed saddlebags. "Oh! What do you want?"

The rider held up a hand, then dismounted with an expert leap. A slender hand whipped off the helmet and a dark cascade tumbled out. "Calm yourself. Just water and directions."

"You're a woman!" Alessia exclaimed.

"And you have a keen eye. While men kill each other there's all kinds of work to be had. Couriers riding light and fast earn good silver, and no clumsy gowns to wear neither." She pulled a square of parchment from the folds of her leather brigandine. "You know where the road west to Wengeddy breaks off from the main? If my package is late I only get half pay."

"Um, I think you passed it. Back south about a day, then west over the river, then north again."

"Damn it all! Hard to navigate by landmark anymore with so many towns wiped out."

Alessia eyed the green serpent standard sewn onto the horse's saddle blanket. "You might want to hide that. There's been a lot of fighting around here."

"Hmm? Oh, don't worry. I have the fox stashed away too, ready as I need it. Long as nobody looks too close I can get wherever I need to most of the time. I bettern't linger though. I'll just go down and water the horse—"

Neither woman had marked Ulnoth coming up behind them or the wet rock in his hand. He leaped naked and dripping at the courier, swinging the stone hard. It impacted on the back of her head and they both went to the ground.

"No!" Alessia screamed. The horse gave a startled snort. "Stop! What are you doing, she's just a courier!"

Ulnoth looked up, eyes blazing. "What? She?" He flipped the limp form over. "What is this? I thought...I mean I saw the sigil...."

"Get back, idiot!" Alessia shoved him aside and examined the damage he'd done. The courier was alive, but dazed. It was a lucky thing Ulnoth was starved weak, else he might've killed her. "Get some water." She pulled out some bits of cloth from her rucksack to cushion the woman's head, careful not to move the neck too much.

While Alessia watched her drift in and out of consciousness, Ulnoth began digging through the saddlebags. "Hey," he exclaimed, "there's food in here!" He shoved a handful of salted bacon into his mouth and chewed as he spoke. "Spare clothes, some coin.... Say, look at this!"

Alessia spared a moment to cast an annoyed glance in his direction. He'd already made a mess at the gray palfrey's feet. In his hands Ulnoth held a bow bigger than her own, and in better condition. "You know how to use that?"

"Done a little poaching in my day, sure. But I got bigger game in mind." He lifted up the saddle blanket to reveal another with Pharamund's banner underneath. "Ha, nice. This is a gift from the gods!"

"Oh, no," said Alessia, jumping to her feet. "I never agreed to turn blackhand. We're not bashing this woman's head in and stealing her stuff!"

"We? Don't recall asking permission," Ulnoth said, jabbing a finger at her. "She wears the colors, wears both of 'em! Fair game, I say. Getting off better than most do." He plucked some fresh clothes from the pile and pulled on a pair of braies that fit too tightly. "I'm takin' it."

"Then you're no better than they are!"

"Never said I was." He dressed in what bits would fit him, then finished off with the tattered remains of his own clothes. He mounted the palfrey that'd stood placidly the whole time. "You comin'?" Alessia didn't answer, just stared at the dazed courier, cursing her luck. "Fine," he said at last, and kicked the horse's ribs back to the road. "So long."

★ ★ ★

"Ohhh...." The courier slowly floated back to her senses, wincing in pain. "My head...."

"Lie still," Alessia insisted. "I'm not sure how bad it is."

"What happened?"

"It was...a bandit. He came out of nowhere. I didn't see him."

"Gah," the woman spat, "they're a pox on the land! They've gotten bold lately. Bastard hurt you much?"

"No, I, um, didn't have anything worth stealing. He took your horse though."

She sat up slowly and probed the back of her head. "Ow!"

"Careful!"

"Must've been in a hurry," she said. "I still got my purse." She fumbled at the leather pouch at her waist, and a cache of coins jingled. "And my helm, for all the good it did me."

"Don't wear it," said Alessia. "Not until the swelling goes down."

"Help me up. I guess the only thing is to go back the way I came. My employer won't be too happy, but it's a risk of the job." On wobbly feet she gathered up some bits of clothes and other things scattered on the ground.

"You're going on foot?"

The courier nodded. "I'll hitch a ride or hire one, if any come along. Thanks for looking after me. Sorry about the trouble – I think I made too tempting a target. Never shoulda let my guard down."

The absurdity struck Alessia almost as hard as Ulnoth's rock. "Um, think nothing of it. I'll come with you, make sure you're all right—"

"No, don't. Wouldn't want you to get attacked again on my account. I'll be fine."

And so the woman whose name Alessia never learned cradled her helm under one arm and began shambling back south. Feeling more helpless and useless than ever, Alessia slung her rucksack over her shoulder – *gods I'm starting to hate this thing* – and turned the opposite direction, northward.

She walked with her head down, watching her shadow grow longer as the sun neared the horizon. After about half a mile a rustling erupted from the roadside thicket. She was only mildly surprised by the familiar horse climbing out of a ditch.

"I suppose you're feeling terribly pleased with yourself."

"Have to admit, I've felt worse."

"Why did you wait?"

Ulnoth shrugged. "I wasn't gonna. I got curious. Your friend's whole?"

"Maybe. I told her an outlaw attacked and robbed her."

"True enough, I guess. Hop up, we got a lot of ground to make up."

"I'm not riding with you, you...."

"What?"

"I don't know, I'll think of something!"

"You're an accomplice, you know. You distracted her—"

"Don't you involve *me* in your—"

"You're already involved. If whoever pays that courier gets wise, you'll go up on the cross sure as me, whatever you intended. You're light, it'll take you days to die. So come on," he said, slapping the back of the stolen saddle. "Nothing to do except get some distance 'twixt us and here."

Growling, Alessia took Ulnoth's hand and shimmied into the saddle behind him. "You still stink."

They made a few more miles before sunset, and Alessia convinced Ulnoth to camp on the wayside rather than stealing deep into the forest. He sat gnawing on more stolen bacon and rooting through the saddlebags.

"Anything interesting?" Alessia asked as she tied the horse up where it could graze.

"What do you care? You don't want to get involved, remember? Um...can you read?"

"Of course," said Alessia, "can't you?"

"Sure, a little. Much as I need."

"Why?"

Ulnoth presented a leather folio. "I found this...."

"Give it here." She held the documents up to the last light of day and squinted. "This is what the courier was delivering, I think. It's from...it's from Queen Engwara! To some count named Vendreesen."

"Never heard of 'im," said Ulnoth.

"It says, 'Our Majesty regrets that we will be unable to relieve Wengeddy of its imminent siege, as our forces are currently occupied in pacifying the southern Bergovan counties.'"

Ulnoth frowned. "Pacifying? What's that mean, killin' every damn thing in sight?"

"Apparently. It commands the count to hold out as long as possible, 'as Wengeddy is our easternmost possession and beacon of our undoubted triumph'."

"I'd say it's more than a little bit doubted. What else?"

"Just self-important fluff. Great, just great. We—Well, *you* robbed the queen's own messenger."

"What can I say, I aim high."

"This is serious! She'll probably send an army just to root us out."

"And the greens'll run right into the reds and cut each other down. Suits me just fine."

"It might not suit the folk that get caught in the middle," said Alessia. "Wengeddy's going to get it bad." She put down the folio and glared at Ulnoth. "We have to go there."

"What? Why?"

"We should deliver this message. It might give the town some time to—"

"I don't think you quite understand how this works," Ulnoth snarled. "I aim to *murder* these bastards, not work for 'em."

"But the townspeople—"

"Ain't my problem. You wanna make 'em yours, be my guest, but leave me out of it!"

"Ha, now look who doesn't want to get involved. Admit it, you need my help. That's why you came back. You're still half dead and you'd be all the way there without me to do your thinking for you."

"That...that's not true—"

"It's true enough. And maybe I need you too – I haven't done so great on my own either. You want to kill reds and greens? There's bound to be both at Wengeddy. And people that need help too. So why not?" Ulnoth stared at her for a long time. Whether he was considering her proposal or trying to come up with an excuse to refuse it, Alessia couldn't say. "Well?"

He made a guttural sound. "Fine, you win. All the same to me. Prob'ly too late anyway."

Alessia nodded. "Good. Tomorrow I guess we turn around."

"And risk running into your friend again? Nah, we keep north."

"But—"

"There's another way. Couple more days, then there's a footbridge cuts west. Army don't let it go on maps so people won't wear it out, but it's there."

"Oh. See? Working together."

"Uh-huh. Now that's decided...." He laid his head on the saddlebag with the serpent banner wadded up for a pillow. "Sweet dreams, bandit."

★　★　★

"Gods take me, there they are!"

"Who?" Alessia leaned to look around Ulnoth. She'd stared at the back of his neck for the better part of a day, and anything else would be an improvement.

"The reds that ruined Firleaf. Up ahead."

"Then we'd better slow down or get off the road!"

"Hold on a minute," Ulnoth said, slowing the palfrey not one bit. If anything he nudged it faster.

"What are you doing?" asked Alessia in a whisper even though they were still far off. "Are you nuts? Oh wait, of course you are. You've been skittering into the bushes at every sound for two days. These ones are actually *dangerous,* so naturally—"

"Uh-huh, just hold on," he said again, his attention far away. He watched the marching column like they were a company of tumblers, waiting for one to fall. "About fifty altogether. Headed back home? Hmm...those on the end...."

"What about them?"

"Stragglers. They're falling behind. Far behind...tired."

"Wait. Don't. Don't you even *think* about—"

"Get off," he told her.

"No. I'm not letting you—"

"Fine." He kicked the horse faster, gaining on the company. Alessia reflexively held tighter, not sure what she should do.

"Ulnoth, for the love of the gods, stop!"

"Gods got no love for me," he said, the rhythm of the horse's hooves nearly drowning him out. "And the feeling's mutual."

"This is madness!"

"It's a mad world, sister."

Just when it seemed Ulnoth was going to charge into that mass of flesh and iron, he drew rein and wrenched the horse to a stop. They were still far enough away that the clamor of their march muffled his approach. He hopped down from the saddle, leaving Alessia alone.

Ulnoth trailed the column from about twenty yards back. Not one soldier bothered to look behind or they'd have caught him straight away. The last line was no line at all but weary sluggards that trudged rather than marched. One in particular was fallen farthest back, a halberd slung across his back with both arms draped over the shaft. Alessia realized Ulnoth's plan and considered turning the horse around and leaving him to his fate. *Why not? He deserves it. One less rogue to trouble the world.* But something held her fast. Morbid curiosity to see the bloody spectacle played out? Or perhaps some vague hope that he might actually pull it off? She felt herself take the reins and spur the mount not back, but forward.

★　★　★

The end of the column crested a small hillock on the road and began falling away, out of sight. It was now or never. Ulnoth chose now. As the last man was about to go over the top he rushed, wrapped his arm around the soldier's throat and jerked him backward. They both went tumbling. Ulnoth dove for the halberd but the soldier lay dazed on top of it. He punched him in the mouth but the poorly aimed blow hit the nasal of his helm.

"Aargh!" They grappled on the ground, neither able to reach for the halberd. The soldier pounded and Ulnoth pounded back, succeeding only in knocking the helmet off. The soldier managed to get ahold of a fist-sized rock from the edge of the road and slammed it into Ulnoth's forehead.

Ulnoth hollered and fell back. In a moment the soldier was atop him, thrashing away with his knuckles, blood flying every which way. Still no one else in the column had noticed any of this and it marched on, oblivious.

Too weak to throw off the man who was killing him, Ulnoth

gave in to his fate. But just as he welcomed death's warm embrace, the blows stopped and the weight atop him fell away. He forced open his swollen eyes, lifted his head, and cackled at what he saw.

"Gah! Get offa me, you crazy bitch!" The soldier squawked as Alessia wrapped the soldier in a bear hug, holding his arms up and dragging him backward. Wasting no time, Ulnoth turned and grabbed the discarded helmet by the nasal and, just as the soldier wriggled free of Alessia's grasp, swung it with his last reserves of strength. The soldier went down on his back, and now it was Ulnoth on top, reinvigorated and wailing on the man with his own armor.

He smashed the face under him over and over, and though it was probably incoherent to any but him, Ulnoth screamed with rage and red joy. "Give! My! Regards! To! The King!" With each syllable he smashed meat and bone, and suddenly he was back in the taphouse with all his friends watching him murder his first one. *That one green, this one red. Even score, one to one.*

The fever only subsided when he felt Alessia tug on his tunic and scream something in his ear. Crunching had long given way to squishing, and when he looked down what he saw bore no resemblance to anything remotely human.

He stopped, dropped the blood-soaked helm and looked over at Alessia with a smile. "Thanks for the h...."

He collapsed onto the puddle of gore, exhausted before he could finish.

★   ★   ★

"Is that how it was the first time?"

"I told you, I don't remember – wait, yes. I do now. It was worse this time."

"Worse?"

"Then I was out of my mind."

"And now?"

"Now...my head's clear. And I want more. I'd call that quite a bit worse."

"And I helped you."

"Aye."

CHAPTER NINE

Turn

"We aren't going to catch him, are we?"

"No," spat Taurix. "No, my lordling, we are not. The bastard stole a night's march on us. On *me*."

Felgred rode at the sulking marshal's side ahead of the host of five hundred, both of them covered in mud to the knee. Taurix looked perfectly at home, though the entire army could likely feel the frustration radiating from him, the seething desire to tear off at speed from the slow-moving human machine and challenge Ludolphus in person. Felgred by contrast appeared utterly miserable until a military courier rode up and handed him a message cylinder. He broke the red wax of Pharamund's seal and pulled out a stretch of vellum. "Ah, well, you can rest easy. Orders from His Grace – there's a mercenary company marching toward Everwest. The king's spymaster is arranging to buy them off, but doesn't trust the bastards to keep faith. We're to turn back north and pursue."

"Mercenaries," snarled Taurix. "They're not worth my morning cack. I can't be everywhere at once! I'll send General Pertinax."

"His Grace has ordered *you*, lord marshal—"

"If Pharamund wants to take the field, let him. Ludolphus is the greater threat."

"Should've left Murento alone," Felgred said, already forgetting his agreement to remain silent on military matters. "It was a distraction. If we'd stayed south we could've linked up with my men there and—"

Taurix drew rein, stopped. "What?" He asked it quietly, gently. The front ranks of the army were taken by surprise at the unexpected halt, unsure whether to stop also or march around the mounted lords. "What. Did. You. Say?"

Felgred drew up paces ahead, looked back with confusion. "Eh? What do you mean? Look, you're disordering the lines—"

"You *already have men in the south?*"

"Well, yes. I must at least *try* to defend my lands, after all. What of it?"

Taurix's face turned bright red. "Why didn't you tell me? I could've cut Ludolphus off before he got anywhere near Carsolan!" The bellow unnerved men and horses alike, and a ring of avoidance formed around them.

"A few," he replied, "...hundred at most. Hardly enough to stop Lud—"

"It would have slowed him enough for me to catch up to 'im, you preening fool!"

"Now wait just a moment, you—"

"What?" Taurix nudged his charger closer, glowering down on Felgred and daring him to answer. "*What* am I?"

Felgred gulped. "N-nothing. I meant nothing, my lord, forgive me."

"Wrong, little man. I am most assuredly not *nothing*. I am the lord high marshal. I command all of His Grace's troops, including yours. And if you ever keep so much as a single slogger's position from me again you'll suffer a fate that will make you *envy* the last marshal."

Near the end of the day the army gnawed a meal of hard bread on the march, made soft by the rain. The incessant plinking on helmets and the splashing feet could drive a man mad, but they were in good spirits for all of that. Brathilde's household troops had reacted stupidly, just as Taurix knew they would, and rode out to meet his harriers only to come face to face with the bulk of his army as it limped back north, stung from the failure to catch Ludolphus and itching for a fight. Now the baroness's retainers drained their insides into ditches and hedgerows, blood and mud mixed into a vast gray soup.

It's not enough, Taurix thought while they pitched a soggy camp in the ruins of some abandoned pasture. *Petty skirmish here, town there. Not nearly enough.*

"Not nearly enough," Felgred whined. "Fill it up!" The servant poured more wine into the cup until it threatened to spill onto the young lord's sleeve. Felgred nodded a greeting when Taurix stomped into the tent.

"What are *you* doing here?"

Felgred held up the cup, sloshing wine everywhere. "I'd have thought that was obvious by now. Come, look at this!" He thrust a sheet of paper, partly folded and repeatedly crumpled to look at it, into the Marcher lord's hand. "Gone. It's all gone!"

Taurix scanned the missive. "Hmmph. Lost your precious estates, did you?"

"Not just mine. That she-Chthonus is ravaging all the way up the Carsa! What a disaster." Felgred downed the wine in a few great gulps, belched loudly.

"Lot of good those men of yours did. I could've made some use of 'em. Now their only use is dog feed." He wadded up the note and threw it back in Felgred's face. "I *told* Pharamund to put all troops under my direct control. This is why! Get out, go sleep off my wine in your own tent."

With Felgred banished, Taurix collapsed into a twitchy, restless mockery of sleep. He dreamed in the old Marchman tongue of his childhood. Red dreams, to freeze your soul.

At some point the rain stopped. The dead of night takes on a truer meaning in the country than it does in cities. The still quiet looms like a gaping maw to swallow the whole sky, even with armed and blooded brutes gathered close. Killing is tiring work, and they slept as soundly as those left dead and unburied behind them. Except for the men who woke screaming, but those were fewer these days. So when Taurix jerked awake in the darkness only the tiniest ripple on the surface of his senses told him he was no longer alone in his tent. "Who's there?"

"A friend," said a hard, feminine voice, "if you want one."

"Guards—!"

"Don't bother. They're taking a little nap right now. I don't want us interrupted."

"Who're you?" Taurix demanded, joints creaking as he sat up and turned in the general direction of the voice. "You come from that bitch Engwara? Come to kill me?"

A low giggle. "Taurix, if I wanted you dead you'd never have awoken. I had the option and chose not, try and remember that. That bitch sends her greetings. Ludolphus as well."

Taurix sneered into the dark. "Does he really?"

"No, not really. What he has to say about you'd make even me blush. Tonight I'm just an ambassador."

"You make a dramatic entrance," said Taurix, playing for time while his hand inched toward one of several blades he kept close, even at night. "What's your message? You want to surrender?"

"I see serial defeat hasn't killed your sense of humor," said the voice. "I've come to invite you over to the winning side."

In defiance of the night Taurix let out a booming laugh. Perhaps it would bring guards from farther away, but he had a feeling she'd be out and disappeared long before they arrived. "You've got things a bit backward, dear. I hold the whole of the north from the Edras to The Bastard, and the Marches down to Seagate. That looks like winning to me." His hands caressed the contours of the knife. A throwing knife. *Perfect.*

"Sorry, my lord, your information's out of date. In a day or two a scout will inform you of two things. First, that about two thousand of Her Majesty's troops are headed straight for Vin Gannoni."

"Ha! You want to scare me, you'll have to do better than that cack. Two thousand, from where?"

"That's the second thing. We have – and I'm truly sorry to have to be the one to tell you this – retaken Everwest."

Silence. Then: "That's ridiculous. Impossible. I happen to know that—"

"Mercenaries *are* a finicky lot, aren't they? Professional fighters, hard as steel. Fight like Chthonii *when they have to*...."

No. It can't be. Taurix felt his spine go cold. He gripped the knife tighter.

"But when they don't have to and can still get paid? Ooh, but they can be true scumbags. At least, that's what your king intended, yes? Well, two can play that game. A double-double-cross, I guess you'd call it—"

The knife sliced through the darkness with a silky *swoosh*. Taurix listened for the thud of punctured flesh, a scream. Neither came. Just a clattering, then silence. He leaped to his feet, straining to see something, anything to attack, but his old eyes failed him. A heavy sigh came from his right. Or was it from behind?

"Please don't do that again, it's been a long day and I am tired. I can hear you breathing. I know where you are and where you're going to be before you do."

"You. Filthy. Bitch...."

"I can see I've overrun your patience, so I'll spell it right out. Join the queen and put someone competent on the throne, and your Marchlands are safe and yours to rule forever. Or not and watch Vin burn. Then whatever you've left of Murento. Then Ólo, again. I doubt the Pelonans up north will want much trade with someone who can't keep his own backyard in order. They might even join up with us just to bring an end to it all."

"I've already pledged to Pharamund. Your precious queen drove me to that—"

"Pharamund's weak and stupid and dominated by his barons. Engwara is not, though she admits her mistake in making you an enemy. But there's no other way this can end, and deep down in places you can only face alone on nights like this, you know it."

"I don't believe it. Any of it. It's some damned trick...."

"That's for you to decide. I've said everything I came here to say. You can think on it and I can walk out of here, or you can throw more silverware at me."

Taurix burned to rip the woman apart. His Marchman half screamed at him to try. But if there was even a chance the bitch wasn't lying.... "Go. Go, and may the gods burn you."

"Too late for that, my lord. Good night." A swish, a rustle, then silence again. Taurix relaxed a clenched fist, felt blood under his nails.

★　★　★

Vinian strode through the ranks of tents, putting her skill at mimicking a masculine gait to the test against the outline of watch fires. It was good enough to get her to the southern perimeter, where a sentry challenged her.

"Who goes there?"

"Your mysterious benefactor. See?" She pulled a small sack of coin from the folds of her jacket.

"Oh. Ah. So, you're done, then?" The sentry fidgeted and looked about nervously. "You promised—"

"Just talk, like I promised. You heard the old ox laughing from here? All's well. I'll be off now, and no one the wiser."

"Yes, well then…could I have…?" He switched his halberd to his left hand and held out his right, expectant.

"Of course," said Vinian with a smile. She dropped the sack into his waiting grasp, and as it landed with a soft *clink* she whipped out a blade of her own – a little skinning knife, razor-sharp. With a single fluid stroke she opened the sentry's throat. So expertly done was it that for almost two whole seconds he stood, confused about what'd just happened.

Vinian put a gentle hand on the soldier's shoulder and said in a soothing voice as his life sprayed out, "Never trust a traitor, even one you turn yourself."

He opened his mouth as if to say something, but only a gurgle came out. Still clutching his payoff, he collapsed to the ground like a puppet whose strings were suddenly snipped. His armor clattered loud against the silence, so the spymistress didn't dawdle but melted back into the surrounding countryside, just in case Taurix changed his mind and tried to come after her.

★　　★　　★

"That's all for today," Engwara said with a broad sweep of her hand. The remaining petitioners turned away, disappointed but as always, determined to return tomorrow. She left the audience chamber by a small door behind the throne. Carsolan's palace was old and drafty, so once she became Argovan's most powerful countess, Engwara's first order had been to fully renovate her private apartments. Late afternoon sun bathed her little drawing room in yellow warmth reflected off the Lacaryc Sea. The autumn chill warned that the shutters would soon be battened down, so Engwara didn't bother to hide her irritation when she found Vinian already lounging in the chair she had meant to bask in while there was yet time. "How did you get in h— No, never mind. I don't want to know."

"It's not as comfortable as the one upstairs," Vinian said, running her finger along the rich floral patterns woven into the upholstery. "Gaudy too, to my taste."

"Then don't sit in it." Engwara shooed Vinian away like she was a bothersome housecat. "A queen should at least get the choice of her own furniture. You've returned, decidedly unimpaled. Can I assume success?"

Vinian opened her mouth to reply, paused. "Have my people checked this room lately?"

Engwara nodded. "This morning – it's secure."

"Good. Yes, I must've made an impression on Taurix. He only tried to kill me once."

"Encouraging."

"He did have some unkind words about Your Majesty—"

"No doubt."

"—but I think he might come around. Good bit of leverage we bought with one dead mercenary and a little petty cash."

Engwara let out a most unqueenly snort. "Petty? It cost a fortune!"

"I just mean, I passed a lot of corpses on the way home, and most didn't wear Pharamund's colors. Or any colors. If you'd let me turn this into a war of assassinations it could all be over with a lot faster. And cleaner."

"Oh, not this again. I told you – I can't have what's left of the nobility worrying I'll slip a knife between their ribs in a fit of pique. A few after a battle or siege is one thing, but if men of consequence all started to fear for their very *lives*? Why, they'd never trust me even after we win. We'll have to do our heavy lifting the old-fashioned way."

"Just a thought," Vinian said while helping herself to some of Engwara's excellent white wine.

"Oh dear girl, don't sulk. I wish I could. Gods, with a thousand of you I could conquer the world."

Vinian allowed herself a grin. "You mean *I* could conquer the world."

Engwara didn't immediately reply to the remark, regarding her most valued retainer with a look that lay somewhere between curiosity and concern. "Of course," she said at last. "Speaking of which, you might want to tell your agents to be a bit more careful than usual. One of my own couriers was robbed by highwaymen last week."

"I know," Vinian said. "Luckily the message wasn't very important. Wengeddy's of little value, according to Ludolphus."

Engwara gasped. "Gods below, are you spying for me or *on* me?"

"As you said, everything under moon and sun." She raised her glass in a mock salute and drank deep. "Don't ask how the sausage is made."

Engwara stared at her with a worried look. "I wonder if I've not created a monster."

Vinian laughed, almost choking on her wine. "Don't worry, you didn't create me. You just hired me."

"That makes me feel so much better!"

"I live to serve, Majesty."

CHAPTER TEN

Can't Go Home Again

It was a hell of a thing, watching a town die. Alessia and Ulnoth had come close enough to Wengeddy to see that they were too late to be of any help. Thick stinking smoke billowed over the walls, only somewhat muffling intermittent screams, while through it banners of red with the device of a black fist brandishing a mace fluttered. A great gate lay flung wide open and smashed, while beyond it towers lay in ruin or in flames. Soldier companies streamed up and down the road, some laden with pillage, others with women and crying children bound with rope, no doubt headed for the few slave markets still allowed in the furthest north.

"Bastards," snarled Alessia, "they just can't help themselves! Every damned time...." She made to spur the horse on toward the catastrophe, but Ulnoth, walking beside, took a tight hold on the rein.

"Whoa there, what you think you're about? You won't be allowed to do any good in there. None left to be done, most like."

Alessia glared down at him, her face all twisted fury. "What do you care about good? You just want to kill, same as them!"

"Maybe. But you still have to pick your battles, same as me. We should leave this place."

The debate was ended when the clamor of a column on the march echoed dangerously close and they scrambled away and into the woods. No longer sure of their course, they skirted the outermost clearings surrounding Wengeddy, and came to a series of low hills and marshland at the edge of the forest. The westerly road away from the town lay somewhere beyond.

Then, out of nowhere came a series of shouts, the pounding of hooves on mud. Alessia pointed at something emerging from behind one of the slopes. "Look!"

"What the…?"

It was a man, tearing through the gullies between the hills, fleeing for dear life toward the trees it seemed. But he'd picked a poor route. If he wasn't quickly run down by the two mailed horsemen on his tail, the marsh would slow him until he was.

"Is he going to make it?"

"No."

The man tossed something away as he ran – a heavy piece of clothing it looked like. That gave him a little speed but the riders were still gaining. Alessia raised her bow uncertainly. "Can…can you get a clear shot?"

"Nah, too far," said Ulnoth. "He's had it."

They watched, helpless as the man charged right into the marsh, making it only a few paces before it wrenched him downward with a splash. The riders rounded a knoll, their massive chargers stomping into the mud after him.

Then, something quite unexpected happened. Something that Alessia imagined would not have happened again in a thousand thousand years. She watched in astonishment as a great flock of birds – herons, she thought – took leave of the sky and landed right on the spot where the man had fallen. So many and so thick among the high grass that the wind of their passing breezed across the marsh to cool Alessia's face, and when the riders came upon the place where the man lay, they saw only what was plain in front of them – a flock of herons.

"Gods," said Ulnoth, "now there's some luck!"

At a distance they could hear the riders argue about where their quarry had escaped to. They traded curses, a dramatic shrug, then they turned away, apparently having given up the chase.

Slowly, the man they sought rose among the herons, soaked and covered in feathers and bird cack, and like a corpse suddenly revived, made his shambling way toward the line of trees.

"Careful," whispered Alessia, "not too fast or you'll— Oh, no!"

He slipped again, making a loud splash. One of the riders looked back at the sound and shouted to the other, and they took up the hunt again. The mounts galloped across the marsh as though it were solid ground, so strong were their limbs.

The man was mere yards from the forest's edge, but the riders were upon him and he stumbled once more, perhaps accepting his fate. They pulled long swords from wooden scabbards, making dull metallic swishing sounds. The raised blades glinted even in the overcast light.

Neither blow fell, though. At just that moment two arrows flew out of the trees, piercing the riders each through their necks just above the mail rings. Both of them tumbled, eyes wide, from their chargers, bleeding and drowning in the shallow water while the horses neighed in alarm.

After moments of stunned silence the man raised his head to regard his two saviors. "W-wha...who...?" He raised a dripping, shaking, dark-skinned hand, and Ulnoth reached out to pull him clear of the muck.

"Well," he said with almost obscene levity, "that was a sight. Should call you the heron king, well as them birds served you. Who are you?" The man just stared, incredulous.

"Whoever you are, you can come with us," Alessia said, "if you want."

★　★　★

"I...I'm not sure which of you is crazier," the man who'd given his name as Corren finally said in a thick northern accent after sitting in shock for some time. "It's all...a bit hard to believe."

"Believe it," spat Ulnoth. "You think them soldiers and lords are something special? All that padding and metal makes 'em gods? I thought that. Then I turned a couple into stew for the vultures. Three now." He kicked the bodies at their feet.

"And two more for you, if I count your story right," Corren said to Alessia.

"Hold on, I never set out to—"

"Oh, I'm not complaining. I'm still breathing thanks to you two. Bit unsettling though, isn't it? Common folk taking up arms all on their own. Could cause a panic in some circles."

"Some circles are due for a share of panic," said Ulnoth. He bent over and gripped one of the dead soldiers' swords. "Hey now, speakin' of taking up arms...." He made some clumsy cuts in the air, and Corren and Alessia shied away. "Lighter than it looks. I could do some damage with this."

"I'm sure you could," said Alessia. "Now I *know* you don't know how to use one of those."

"I can learn," Ulnoth replied, ogling the blade up and down like it was a Thazovi dancing girl. He glanced back toward the bog. "Imma go make sure no more got curious and come lookin' for these two."

"Be careful!" said Alessia as she began stripping the corpses of anything useful.

"Humph, why start now?"

"Your friend there's what in the north we call 'peculiar'. Namely, he's a bloody psychopath."

"He takes some getting used to," Alessia said, "but he's been through a lot."

"We all have," said Corren. "I lost my whole family when I was a lad. Won't see me going on a killing spree over it."

"People react differently to things. Once we brought a man in after a battle with only a slight head wound. For some reason, he absolutely would not let the temple cat kill any of the mice. Kept them as pets and fed them. Talked to them. Afterward he went right back to fighting. Next I saw of him he was dead as these two."

"Hmm. Well, I'm no temple mouse. Thanks for, well, saving my life and all, but I think I best get going."

"Go where? Your town's laid waste – we saw the smoke."

"My town? Wha— Oh. Oh, no—"

"You're not from Wengeddy?"

Corren's face turned a red that was visible even under the canopy of trees. "Um, no. Well...."

Alessia stood slowly, eyes wide. She took a step backward. "You...you're one of *them*. You're a soldier!" She turned toward the bog where Ulnoth had gone, ready to run.

"No! Well...yes. Wait, let me explain. I deserted."

"You were drafted then?"

"No, I volunteered, gods help me."

Alessia wrinkled her nose, put a hand to the knife at her waist.

"So you're a killer and a coward. Doesn't much recommend you."

"I'm not a killer! W-well, except the other day, by accident. That's why they were after me. I wouldn't do it. I threw off my kit and ran."

"Wouldn't? Then why join up?"

"Because...." Corren sighed. "Because I heard the wrong words, listened to the wrong lies. It all seems so stupid. I'm a fool, I realize that now."

Alessia relaxed just a little bit but kept a decent distance. The sound of marsh grass swishing and crunching grew louder. "Then maybe there's some hope for you. But for now, don't tell Ulnoth – he'll tear out your intestines."

"Aye, I worked that bit out for m'self already."

"Nothing," said Ulnoth when he returned. "Nothing to be seen anyway. Heard some screams though. Don't know what that's about."

"The count they're after escaped the siege, blended in with the fleeing townsfolk. The bastards were executing everyone to flush him out, few at a time to not raise a ruckus. That's why I ran. Maybe that caused a stir?"

"Maybe," Ulnoth said, then looked at Alessia. "We should leave here. There's nothing we can do."

"I don't know, I still want to try to find—" She stepped halfway out of the trees and came face to face with a bloody stranger. "Ah!" she yelped. It was a frail, past middle-aged man with a salt-and-pepper beard, one clouded eye, and a long gash running from his ear to his shoulder blade.

"H-help..." he moaned, then collapsed into Alessia's arms.

"What happened?" The man just shook his head.

"Looks like the townsfolk got wise," said Corren. "I figured they couldn't keep it quiet for long."

"Well, if he found us you can bet the reds will too, and I ain't keen to take 'em on all at once."

"We can't leave him here alone," said Alessia.

Ulnoth opened his mouth to argue, then looked past her. "Shit. He ain't alone."

Alessia turned to see twenty or more people running, limping or crawling toward them through the marsh with cries of "Help!" and

"Gods, save us!" There were no great temple doors closed against them now.

"You go if you want. I'm staying."

"Lessi, they'll lead 'em right to us," Ulnoth said. "You ain't even got enough supplies."

"I'm still staying." She began dragging the wounded man deeper into the forest.

"Listen, you can't—"

"*Don't you tell me I can't!* Help me or get out of here."

They helped her.

★   ★   ★

Righteous outrage can be a powerful tool, but it doesn't stitch lacerations or set bones. Alessia quickly used up her last bit of gut thread while Ulnoth implored the patients not to cry out as she worked, mostly by threatening to punch them senseless if they did.

They cleared a place between three trees with relatively dry ground and set the wounded nearby to wait their turn. They used branches and even sword scabbards from the dead soldiers for splints, and vines as bindings. It was primitive in the extreme and Alessia lost three of the lives in her care.

"I need more," she said as she worked, sweat dripping from her brow. "I need bandages, thread, everything."

"We don't have any," Ulnoth said as gently as he could, careful not to set off her temper again. He jammed a stick wrapped with cloth into someone's mouth to bite on while they moaned and bled. "We used the last of it."

"I—" Corren said, then paused. "Er, that is…."

"What?" Ulnoth prompted.

"I think I know someplace that might have the supplies we need."

"Where?"

"The soldiers' camp."

Ulnoth rolled his eyes. "Oh, good. Let's just stroll on over there and kindly ask to pick through their stores. Should work out sweetly."

"*If* we're careful I think we can pull it off."

"How in the seventeen hells do you think that?"

Corren pointed down at the dead riders that still laid by, still clad in their armor.

Ulnoth shook his head. "No. Aw, hells no. No way I'm riskin' my neck for a buncha strangers." He glanced at the gaggle of refugees that were still alive and conscious. "No offense, but—"

"I thought you said you were already dead," Alessia observed in a husky mockery of his voice.

"It's more than just that," said Corren. "They have other things. Food, weapons, coin. They just looted a whole town. We dress up in this armor and we can walk off with half the camp and no one'll say a thing."

Ulnoth frowned. "I'm no warlord. Even in that dead pig's getup I won't look—"

"It's not about how you look, more how you act. Confidence, bearing, attitude. And I'd say you've got plenty of attitude."

"Whatever you decide," Alessia said, "do it quick!" She looked up from tying off an amputated finger. "I can keep the rest alive, but not for long."

Ulnoth sighed. "All right, what the hells. Might as well go out like a crazy bastard."

They threw on the mail and helms as quickly as one can throw on thirty pounds of iron, not bothering with the underpadding. It didn't fit— "Because of *course* it doesn't fit," Ulnoth complained as the armor's acrid preserving oil invaded his nostrils – but eventually they stumbled onto the two big horses that had lately been made riderless. They nudged the mounts out into the marshy plain.

"You know the way," Ulnoth said casually, "and passwords and secret handshakes or whatever, I assume."

"Uh, no," mumbled Corren. "I guess I just figured, what with the armor and—"

"Sure you do. You're one of 'em, after all."

Corren froze on his horse, staring at Ulnoth. The mail ventail covered his mouth, leaving only the eyes visible. "You knew," he said. "You knew the whole time."

"I suspected. I saw you runnin', throwing stuff away. I may be a dumb peasant but I can put two and one together."

"So why didn't you do for me like you did those two others?"

Ulnoth's mail clinked as he shrugged. "You was runnin', they was after you. I figure whatever you done to make 'em wanna hunt you down's a mark in your favor. And there's more than enough of them around here still wearin' the colors to pick from. I know you and Lessi both think I'm fracted in the noggin. Maybe you're right. But I guess there's a method to my madness."

"Gods take me," breathed Corren. "That's a relief."

"Fact, I even thought about joinin' up once. For the coin."

"Did you? Just think, things'd gone different it could've been some other bastard with a grudge coming after you."

Ulnoth sat still another moment, then kicked his horse forward again. "Let's go get that loot."

A quarter mile. That was all the distance that separated them from the place where citizens had been rounded up and systematically executed in the search for the count, and as they crested the last hill and it came into view both men began sweating over the danger they'd placed themselves in. And also because of the armor.

"Nice of 'em to stick around for us," Ulnoth said. "So what are we lookin' for? Tents and wagons and such?"

"No, it was a quick march from Wengeddy. We didn't have time for that. Just what could be carried, which works out fine for us, doesn't it?" He pulled his own ventail across his face and laced it tight. "Look lordly now."

"But you said it ain't about looks—"

"I lied. Sit up straight!"

The scene before them told a story in three acts all at once: carnage, confusion, and boredom. Bodies were tossed in piles to clear the way, others left where they'd fallen. Half of those – the men – were also decapitated and the heads arranged in a comparatively neat stack. A few soldier companies still double-timed it here and there at their captain's orders to pursue the rest but with no idea of which way to go. Those with no such orders milled about, pissed on the dead or picked their teeth and played at dice.

"Impressive," Ulnoth said, "you boys got this 'pacification' business down cold. How long you think a proper payback for this'd take—"

"Hush!" Two soldiers tramped across the muddy ground toward

them. They made perfunctory halfway obeisances, their knees not actually touching down.

"Thought yer lordships'd never come back," said one. "Catch anything on them bigarsed horses o' yers?"

"Erm...." Corren fidgeted in the saddle, then nodded sharply. "Aye, a couple."

"So where's the heads? Ain't we to collect 'em up for the Lady No?"

"They were bitches, didn't see the point. Not that it's any business of yours."

"No m'lord. Sorry. Say, you fallin' ill? You sound different from this mornin'. All this gore can't be good for the humors."

"Yes, perhaps I am. I...uh, I wonder if you could, that is...."

The man frowned. "M'lord? Say again?"

Corren cleared his throat. "Tell me where to find the physic."

"Oh. Thataway." He pointed toward a not-too-distant grove of trees where a draught mule was tied up. Sacks and boxes encircled it and a small fire with two men nearby. "Thinks he's too good to be sat near the rest of us."

"Fine with me," said the other soldier. "Keeps the screams away."

Corren dismissed the pair, and they rode toward the grove. "Nice one," said Ulnoth. "Thought we was done for there. But what did they mean by 'the screams'?"

The question was answered a moment later. An open-mouthed howl erupted from one of the men sitting by the fire, the other standing over him holding a pair of bloody pliers. Corren winced. "The company physic's also the barber and the dentist. Bit of a jack of all trades."

"And master of none, sounds like. Did a little dentistry of my own on a recruiter not so long back. That went just about as well." The soldier with one tooth less skulked away bent forward with a red rag jammed in his mouth and tears in his eyes. The physic was wiping his pliers down when he looked up to see the two riders approach. They dismounted with a great deal less skill than professional cavalrymen should have.

"Ah, hail m'lords. Come with a toothache? Saddle-sore? I'm all outta ointments for that."

"No," said Corren. "It...it's Cap'n Gadanga. His arthritis is flared up again. He's down 'round the bend and urgently requests your assistance."

"Gods damn that old coot, I warned him not to tax them joints! All right, just let me get— Hey, beggin' your pardon, but why are you two fetching me?"

Ulnoth and Corren looked at each other, then at the physic. "What?" they both said.

"Surely that's a job for a messenger, not a pair of householders."

"Well," mumbled Corren, "that is, you see, we were—"

"Who are you, anyway? Don't I know you from some—"

The inquisition was cut off when Ulnoth suddenly leaped forward and socked the man in the jaw. He went down easy, without another word. "Hmm. Not a fighter, that one."

Corren caught the physic as he fell and lowered him the rest of the way to the ground. "What the hells! You trying to get us caught?"

Ulnoth shrugged. "Seemed like you were fresh out of ideas. Problem solved."

They loaded up with whatever would fit in the saddlebags. Then they tied sacks together and laid them across the horses' rumps, but the coursers were used to heavy loads and bore it easily. "I think that's all we can take," said Corren when supplies started falling from where he stuffed them. "Leave the mule, it'll slow us down. We best go before anyone notices."

"With you there. But you said there'd be food and—"

"Oi!" They jumped at the bark. Someone was coming. "Oi, Joby, where you get to? I gots me a splittin' headache from all this— Oh."

Ulnoth heard Corren curse under his breath. *He knows this one,* Ulnoth thought. *Not good.*

"Sorry to bother you, m'lords. You happen to know where physic Joby got to? Still sufferin' a few minor aftereffects of victory, if you take my meaning."

"He's away," Corren said after a few seconds, keeping his face turned away even behind the mask of mail. "Tending to Gadanga. Come back later."

"Oh. Cack on my luck then. All right." The man was about to go back the way he came when he noticed the horses and their cargo. "Say, where you takin' all that? If we's movin' out in a hurry it'd be good to know about it—"

"Requisitions. Lady No's personal request. Now stand aside." Corren held out an arm to wave him away as well as to block him from coming any closer. The mail hauberk extended most of the way down his sleeve, ending short of the wrists. There were loops to attach matching mittens to cover the hands but he wasn't wearing them, so Corren's exposed hand was thrust right in the man's face. A hand suspiciously dark for a Bergovan household retainer.

The soldier looked at the hand, then at the obscured face in front of him. The hand again. A pause. Then his eyes went wide. "Wait. It – it's you. *You!*" He began backing away.

"Tancred, wait—"

"What is this? You damn near started a riot when you pissed off. What are you doing in that getup? Sergeant Jaxa—!"

Corren and Ulnoth descended on the man together, wrestling him to the ground as he cried out. Corren bashed his face and neck. When he crushed the windpipe it made a sickening squelch. The man struggled still, making weak moaning sounds.

"Shut up!" Corren hissed, hands shaking and tears dropping onto his writhing victim. "Shut up shut up shut up!" He squeezed. The man's face turned purple, then blue as he went still. Corren whipped off his helmet and coif just in time to avoid spewing vomit all over the inside of his armor as he gagged into the grass.

"Hey," said Ulnoth, panting from exertion, "what're you doing? They'll recognize your deserting ass!" He struggled to his feet. "Come on, let's go."

Leaving the body to cool next to the puddle of puke, they trudged over to the horses and climbed once again into the saddle.

"Stop!"

Ulnoth looked down to see two more soldiers standing before them. One was an older Marzahni fellow in apparent command, with a dozen upset and heavily armed sloggers at their backs. He stepped forward, rubbing his wrist. "Corren lad…what have you done?" He glanced down at the body. "You, you did this? They said you ran and I didn't believe it, but then…why?"

Corren broke out in sudden bitter laughter. "Why? *Why*, really? Look around you, Cap'n. That's why!"

The captain shook his head. "You're out of your senses. You must be. Come down from there, and I promise I'll try—"

"No, Cap'n. My senses are clear, maybe for the first time. I'm leaving. Don't try to stop me or come after."

The sergeant next to the captain spat into the bloody ground in front of him. "Enough of this. Take 'em down!" The soldiers behind them stepped forward and hurled a volley of spears. Ulnoth was already moving, riding in front of Corren. Ulnoth threw a sack of something heavy to deflect one spear, but a second grazed his hip, just as the hem of the mail hauberk bounced up. "Gah!" he screamed, wrenching the horse away. "Go!"

Corren kicked his courser into a full gallop, and they were soon racing downhill back toward the marsh, toward the forest. Ulnoth looked back once and saw the men giving chase on foot but falling behind fast. He looked back a second time and they were gone, given up perhaps. He bled down his side, droplets flying backward. One spear wound and one dead ex-comrade. *Better be worth it*, he thought.

CHAPTER ELEVEN
Some Unspoken Fellowship

"I don't know what happened. They said they were going to let us go. Then we heard screams from somewhere. Someone panicked. Then the soldiers just started killing, and we ran. That's all I know."

Alessia wrapped the bandage around the man's neck, snipped the end off with her new stolen scissors. The poultice she'd mixed up squished out between the strips, and she scraped up the excess.

"They weren't going to let you go," Corren said. "They had orders to collect heads."

The man nodded. "Guess I figured that. We all did really. It was just false hope. Good for us we ran into you lot though – others weren't so lucky. Who are you people, anyway?"

"Just people," said Alessia, "trying to survive, like you."

The man glanced up at Corren. "Hmmph, them two fellas ain't like me, and that's a true thing. Warriors or uncommon killers, can't quite tell."

"Speakin' of which," called Ulnoth from where he lay with a cloth pressed against his hip, "when's my turn? This hurts!"

"Good. That's how you know you're not dead," Alessia replied. She told the man to lie still and rest, then went over to Ulnoth. "You're next. But I want to talk to you first."

"Eh? What's there to talk about? I took a spear in the leg."

"I know. And I'll patch you up. On one condition."

"*Condition?*"

"Yes. No more random killing. It puts us in needless danger."

Ulnoth rolled his eyes. "We been over this...."

"And we're going over it again. Because now I have patients to think about. Here's the deal: I'll do my best to keep you alive and somewhere in the general vicinity of healthy. In turn you – and

Corren, if he wants – do whatever you have to to keep the soldiers' sharp and pointies far away from us. But no more unhinged suicide attacks. You want to raid, steal, ambush them, whatever, be smart about it. Just look at what you got for us with a little planning! That's not so hard, now is it?"

Ulnoth scrunched his face in distaste. "And if I say no thank you, ma'am?"

"Then you can lie there and bleed out until you get what you were looking for. But I think you want to live, whatever you say. I'm betting you do."

Ulnoth lay still, staring at her. Slowly, he lifted the cloth from his wound, stared down at the mess of blood. "You know, there's a certain grain factor I'd love for you to meet. I think you could haggle him right out of his fancy clothes."

"That's not an answer," said Alessia, pressing the attack.

"Fine. You win, again."

Alessia set to stanching the flow of blood from Ulnoth's hip.

"Now that that's settled," Corren said, "I can think of a few hundred reasons both personal and practical that we should leave here once and for all. It won't take much imagination for them to figure out what happened to those two riders."

"Agreed," said Alessia. "These people need time to heal, but not here. Back south seems safest."

"I can walk," Ulnoth said before demonstrating most convincingly that he could not. "Argh!"

"Uh-huh. You can ride. We've three horses – that should be enough to carry the worst hurt. The supplies we'll have to carry ourselves."

"Lucky wanker," Corren remarked.

A few hasty prayers were said over the dead both near and far and the refugees moved deeper into the forest, swatting at gnats with every step. Corren and Alessia held to the rear to make sure there were no stragglers, but when a scream rang out they dropped their loads and ran ahead. "What is it?" asked Alessia. "Did they find us?" It couldn't be that though – they stood gathered around something on the ground. "What is it?" The crowd parted.

It was almost comical that the sight of one more corpse should cause a commotion. It lay naked, face down along a newly pashed-out footpath. Corren frowned. "Now there's a fresh kill. But out here – I wonder who it is?"

A few of the braver townsfolk flipped the body over to reveal a youngish, smooth-faced man with no marks on him but one – a huge gaping spear wound that ran deep into his chest, a killing blow. "It's him," spat the man with the neck wound, his voice a mixture of hate and awe. "The cause of it all. *That's* Count Vendreesen."

"I thought he escaped with the rest of you," said Corren.

"He must've gone off on his own after that, or with a brace of bodyguards. Them as did this I'd wager. Took everything of value, and his life. No point in serving a lord with a price on his head."

"But," Alessia asked, "why not take the head and collect it?"

The man shrugged, then winced when the movement irritated his injury. "Who'd bother to pay out a bounty claimed by traitors? Soldiers ain't exactly known for their honor, after all." That thought quashed any notions of collecting it now, so all they could do was take turns spitting on the body as they passed by, and the only one to protest was a solitary starling that pecked greedily at the count's eyes.

When the moon hung high in the sky and people began to stumble from exhaustion Alessia called a halt. "We can't go any further tonight. We should be safe enough out here in the middle of nowhere...shouldn't we?"

"I heard a stream a few paces back," said Corren. "Here's as good as any place to stop. Wouldn't recommend trying a fire though."

The twenty-odd people and three horses made no protest, and many simply dropped where they stood. Once the animals and wounded had been seen to, Ulnoth, Alessia and Corren gathered together in some unspoken fellowship. "So much for my grand military career," Corren sighed. Alessia threw a sharp look of alarm at him, and Corren waved a dismissive hand. "Don't worry. He knows."

"I do," Ulnoth muttered, half asleep already. "But thanks for the vote of confidence. I don't get what you was doin' in that army anyway. You're a sandcrab, ain't you? Er, I mean, Pelonan."

"Partly right. My grandda was from Marzahn. I suppose I'm a

little bit of everything, really. How'd you know? I didn't think you'd have many in the south."

"Not many, but I know – or, I *knew* someone with your coloring."

Alessia tightened Ulnoth's binding, then slapped his hand away when he moved to fiddle with it. "Stop that! Where are you from then?"

"Either of you ever heard of Vindis?" Neither of them had. "Not surprised. It doesn't exist anymore."

"You look a bit young to be from a long-lost city," Ulnoth said with a chuckle.

"Not that long. It was northeast, where Pelona and Bhasa meet. A port town, and rich enough. Until the Gray Plague. People say it came aboard a slave ship from Ghresh. Killed every adult in the city. Lots of children too, but not all. News of it spread faster than the plague itself, and we were abandoned. I was ten. The Pelonan king and the emperor of Bhasa agreed on something for once when they walled us in. More than a year like that, no one in, no one out.

"*Feral*. I learned that word later, but that's how we grew up. In gangs, fighting rats and each other for scraps of food in streets filled with cack and corpses. Altogether unpleasant, you might say."

"How did you get out?"

Corren shrugged. "Time passed, the plague did too. The city was never rebuilt but the blockades were lifted and I stowed away on the first ship I saw. I figured whatever came after, the worst had to be over. Sailed a few years, drifted a few more. I did a peacetime year in the Pelonan king's army, all marching and training but no action and less pay. Then some silver-tongued arsehole talked me into joining up with Lady Nostrado's levy. Said there'd be gold and glory aplenty serving King Pharamund under Lady No's banner, and I guess it sounded just like what I was after. Figured I'd take a highborn lord for ransom and retire rich. Stupid! We marched out of Fort Nostrado a few days back, just a quick pop across the Carsa to whip Vendreesen then home again. But when we took Wengeddy he escaped out of a tower window, on a rope made of tied-up bedlinens. Tancred was drafted but he knew better than I did what was going to happen then."

"Is that your buddy back there that you...?" Ulnoth put a hand to his neck.

Corren nodded. "We came in together. Was always reminding

him to keep his shield up during drills, move his feet. He took to the pillage like a leech to vein."

"But not you," ventured Alessia.

"I've seen enough suffering," Corren said with a shrug, "felt no powerful need to add to it. I tried to stop him from raping a young girl and he beat me senseless. I woke to some bastard from another company trying to steal my boots. Pulled a knife on me." Corren laughed bitterly. "That was my first kill, if you can believe it. I barely had time to put my boots back on when we were sent to capture the townsfolk. Lady No would've been able to pick out Vendreesen, but she never came. Taken ill, they said. So we were ordered to take heads and save 'em for identification later. That's when I ran."

"Chthonii," whispered Ulnoth, shaking his head, "we really are lower than cattle to them noble fucks."

"I wish I could say I don't believe you, but I know better," said Alessia. "We could surely use someone with your skills, though. Teach Ulnoth how to not cut his stones off with a sword."

"Might do, might do. I need to think on it. Made a few too many snap decisions lately. Right now…." Corren didn't finish his sentence before nodding off, but no one was still awake to hear it. They slept without fire or food but without fear either, and they slept well.

*　　*　　*

"Um…ma'am?"

Alessia looked up from her early morning inventory to see a gangly teenage lad shifting nervously from one foot to another. He was filthy, but who among them wasn't? She remembered he'd had only minor wounds and now wore a linen band about his brow, but hadn't caught his name. "Yes, uh…."

"Dannek, ma'am."

"Dannek, call me Alessia. What can I do for you? Is your binding holding?"

"Huh?" He stammered a bit and rubbed at the cloth. "Oh. I think so. No, that's…everything's fine. It's just…." He looked away.

She really didn't have time for this. *Patience, and sympathy*, Tanusia's voice reminded her. "What is it?"

"Well, I heard some of the others talking...."

"My nanna always said you should believe only half of what you see and none of what you hear."

"...and they said you were starting some kind of...I dunno, rebel gang?"

"What? No! Who gave anybody that idea?"

Dannek went on as if he'd not heard. "They said you and those two men you run with made some sort of pact."

"Oh for...." She sighed. "That's just something I came up with in the moment to head off a dangerous situation. I don't know how that turned into...whatever it is you're talking about."

"Oh," Dannek said, downcast.

"Why? Certainly you don't want that kind of life."

"Why not?" The boy's nervousness suddenly gave way to anger. "It's not like we got anything to go back to in Wengeddy. My folks are dead. The carver I was 'prenticed to is dead. Anywhere you go it's the same, just waiting around to get nullied sooner or later. Any kinda life is better than that, innit? Better a wolf than a sheep."

"Oh, you're a wolf now, are you?"

He sat down next to Alessia, nearly stepping in her poultice bowls in the process. He leaned in close. "Lemme join up with you. I can do things – I can hunt and fish, carve things. Mostly spoons, but once I made a bow! Not, you know, a *good* one, but—"

"Dannek, stop. That's very brave of you but you'll most likely just get yourself killed."

"You don't understand," he said, his voice quivering, "It's *not* brave. The brave thing would be staying out there. I want to hide. I want to live. And if that means knifing some of them sloggers in the back, well I got a lot better chance doing that than I have facing 'em straight on. That's no chance."

He spoke with such insistence that Alessia didn't notice the three or four others gathered around until he paused for breath. They all had the same look in their eyes. "I suppose the rest of you feel the same way?" They nodded.

"Let us come with you, wherever it is," said a tall, redheaded girl a bit older than Dannek.

The man with the salt-and-pepper beard and neck wound stood

up straighter. "This here's my third war, my fourth siege and second sacking. Every time's been worse than the last. I'm tired of it. Aye, I may die, but I haven't many years left and I don't mean to die afraid. So if you'll have us, let's join."

This can't possibly end well, Alessia thought. She looked them over, each riddled with her own handiwork. *Poor stuff to fight both sides of a war with*. But like a ship caught in a squall, sometimes the only course was to turn straight into it. "There won't be any attacks on innocent folk, or pilgrims or towns, you understand. Only soldiers and highborns, or others of evil intent. You agree to that?" They nodded as the remaining folk gathered around them also.

"And you'll listen to me, and to Corren and, if it comes to it, gods help us, Ulnoth. No acting alone or endangering the group." They nodded.

"Then I suppose, welcome to the temple of the damned. I'd better go tell the others."

Ulnoth chuckled when she told him. It irritated his wound but he couldn't help it. "I don't believe it. Got our own little guild goin' here, don't we? Mighty funny one, though. Fulfilling all your medical, thieving, and general assassination needs at a not remotely fair price. But what should we call it?"

Corren knelt next to him, somewhat recovered from their raid by a few hours' sleep. "How about what you called me when we first met? How about...the Heron Kings?"

Ulnoth laughed more strongly this time. "The Heron Kings. I like it."

PART TWO

CHAPTER TWELVE
Farsight

They lay or crouched in the brambles along the old dirt road, straining to hear the approaching supply wagon. They'd tracked it a mile or more, and the golden moment was upon them. Sweat, fear and piss filled their nostrils. Far off but rapidly nearing, voices.

"Only one more mile to go."

"You said that five miles ago. Anyway, what's the hurry, Braygin? Can't believe anyone starved to death over a few barrels of salt cod." A whip cracked, and the yells that rang out were not those of cattle. *Bastards*, thought Ulnoth with a growl.

"It ain't about the cod, Trasca," said an older voice. "If we get to the castle ahead of schedule we…well, we get a bonus."

"What? You ain't told me that!"

"I was savin' it for when you needed extra motivating. Like now."

"You was gonna keep it for yourself! I bet you only said anything 'cause you was afraid I'd fall down asleep and break a wheel with my neck or—"

"Quiet, both of you," came a new gruff voice. Moonlight glinted off the officer's armor, making him just barely visible. "You're giving me a headache. Braygin's right this time – we're almost there. Pipe down."

"Look here, fella. You might cap'n over your sloggers, but I'm in charge o' the wagon and these here slaves. Mayn't be all blood and glory but it's my job. Way I see it, your orders mean just about dick to us, so you can kindly piss off."

A hard laugh. "That's cute," said the officer. "Well *I'm* charged with insuring the safety of this shipment and your precious wagon until it reaches its destination. So the way our six sharp swords see it, my orders mean slightly more than dick. And those orders are to *stuff it!*"

That seemed to shut everyone up. For about ten seconds. "So…" said the one named Trasca, "how much of a bonus, exactly?"

"Oh for—"

Thhhwunk.

"—the hells was *that?*"

Ulnoth had loosed first as the wagon passed, and that was the signal. The officer hadn't even finished the question when the rearmost member of his squad fell forward with a startled exhalation of "huuhph!" As he fell he banged his head against the right rear wagon wheel. The arrow in his back only partly penetrated the layers of cloth padding, but as he rolled over the soldier's own weight pushed it clean through his chest.

"Shit," hissed the officer. "Alarum! We're under att—" A shadowy shape appeared out of the darkness and brought something big and heavy down onto his head, the clang of his helmet like being in a bell tower. His knees gave out, and a blade soon found his throat.

Ulnoth sent a second arrow striking up from his ditch like a venomous snake, and another man went down screaming. While the soldiers yelled to each other in confusion and drew swords against unseen enemies, Braygin tried to crawl between the slaves and up into the wagon and shouted, "Go! Move it!" But the slaves wouldn't stop their crouched moaning or obey the reins to which they were yoked.

"I can't!" Trasca cried, thrashing with the useless whip.

On both sides of the road, phantoms arose from the earth to rain death down upon them. Knives, axes, even the odd sword or two flashed silvery light and each time a scream followed. Where blades failed to find flesh, blunt force worked just as well.

"Hells to this," breathed Trasca, and he jumped down from the driver's seat, stumbled once as he hit the ground then dashed off directionless into the dark.

"Trasca!" Braygin scrambled to follow. "Wait for me!" He

tripped, flew into the hard-packed dirt. The screams died away, or were cut off sharp. Ulnoth limped out of cover to hover over him.

A young man from Wengeddy came up to Ulnoth and said, "That's all of 'em. Easier 'n we practiced even."

"Nice work, Allard. It's like I keep saying – they ain't gods. Let's get this off the road, and hide the bodies."

"One got away – the kid."

"Forget 'im. We got what we come for." He crouched over Braygin and spoke. "Well now, this is a pickle. I'm not terribly interested in having the fame of our daring storyfied all over the place, I'm sure you understand. Any last words before I send you hellsbound?"

"F...f...."

"What's that? Speak up, last chance now. Y'ain't savin' it for nothing."

"Fuck...you!"

Ulnoth shrugged, raised an axe high. "Good enough for me."

"I told you not to kill them!" Alessia fumed while Ulnoth gorged himself on their prize. After a week of near-starvation and aimless drifting, even salted cod seemed a feast. The band gathered round the small fire they'd risked among the low brush, a quarter mile from the road on the western side of the Carsa awaiting the result of Ulnoth's raid.

"What could I do?" mumbled Ulnoth through a mouthful of fish. "They had guards this time. Six of 'em. It was that or go hungry, and we've had quite enough of that."

"You killed *six* armed guards?"

"Eight counting the drivers," said Allard excitedly. He'd suffered a cut to his side but pretended not to feel it. "Well, seven. One ran off. Only smart one in the lot."

"One," Alessia huffed, "that'll bring a thousand back here to wipe us out."

"We'll be long gone by then," said Ulnoth.

"Doesn't matter! I told you I didn't sign up for that kind of—"

Ulnoth spat out a bone. "I ain't signed up for any of this. Look around you – a motley crew's puttin' it overly mild. And not to bring up ancient history, but this whole thing was *your* idea. You know what they had pullin' that wagon? Men! Slaves, hitched up just like horses. You tell me not to kill them fucks? Please."

"Slaves? Well, where are they?"

"We offered to bring 'em along, but their minds were so broke they just lay on the ground whining like simpletons. Too late for them I guess." Ulnoth turned to Corren, who had just come back from an expedition of his own. "You was right though – last mile before home free them guards ain't payin' attention at all. Good stuff."

"Glad I could help," he said in a carefully neutral tone. "Sorry I wasn't there in person. I did manage to liberate a few things from that riverboat I spotted bound for Fort Nostrado." He opened up a large sack next to him. "Without much bloodshed, I'm afraid."

"Nobody's perfect," said Ulnoth.

Corren pulled out a bundle of cloth and tossed it in Ulnoth's face. "Here, change of clothes. You could use it. Actually we all could, but you most of all, I think."

"Hey!"

"Thanks, Corren," said Alessia. "I was afraid you'd abandoned us."

"Never fear, sister, I figured I best stick with you lot. Don't exactly blend in well with the local landbound." He rifled through the sack, sending bits of clothes everywhere. "No gowns, I'm afraid."

Alessia chewed her lip for a moment, then said, "No matter. Give me chausses. And a tunic. And, that jerkin there if you can spare it."

The people gathered around the fire stared at her, looking bemused. Even Ulnoth paused his incessant chewing. "What?"

"You wanna dress in men's clothes?" asked Corren. "You sure?"

"So what of it? Easier to move around in."

"But...that's weird. Not to mention dangerous. Suppose we're captured and you get taken for a man—"

"Then I'll be killed just like everyone else, except I won't get raped first. Don't lecture me on what's dangerous, not now."

Corren's mouth hung open with no counterargument to offer. "All right, you got it." He selected garments that looked closest to Alessia's size and handed them over.

"You, uh," said Ulnoth with childish glee, "might find the braies a bit loose in the crotch area."

Without missing a beat Alessia replied, "No more so than you do." There was an explosion of laughter.

"Now there's somethin' I ain't heard in far too long," said Crander, the older man who'd identified Vendreesen. "I may be too old to fight 'longside you all, but there's still some use in me yet. Takes all kinds to hold a family together, even strange ones. Maybe that's what we'll become."

"Aye," agreed Alessia, "if we live long enough." She took up a scalpel to tailor her new clothes a bit.

There was a rustle in the brush some paces away. Ulnoth turned toward it, expecting another of their company, but nothing came. No one else paid it mind. *Deer? No, they wouldn't come so close. Too big for squirrels.* A twinge tickled the back of his neck. He put down the cod and rose to his feet. "Imma go for a piss," he said casually. "Don't miss me too much whilst I'm gone."

"Don't worry, we won't," sneered Nandine, the redheaded girl.

He walked from the camp, out of the reach of firelight and and in the opposite direction to the sound. Then he made a great looping arc back around, creeping through the undergrowth one careful step at a time to make no noise and navigating by the few stars that poked through the trees. He approached the camp from the east, closing in ever so slowly. *Come on, I know you're around here,* he thought. *Just move once more, you—*

There. Ulnoth waited for a gust of wind to set the brush rustling. Under cover of the noise he crept forward, forward, then jumped.

"Aaargh!"

He grabbed on to the body and wrapped it in a violent bear hug, wrestling it to the ground. "Here!" Ulnoth yelled. "Get over here!"

Cries erupted from the camp, and while he waited he struggled, the figure squirming in his grasp. He punched it.

"Ow! Lemme go!" The voice sounded familiar.

Corren nearly tripped over the pair grappling in the dirt. "Who's there?" He held a burning brand from the fire before him.

"Good question," said Ulnoth. "Help me!"

They took the lad by both arms and pulled him into the light. He was a fellow no older than Dannek. "All right," said Alessia, "who are you?"

"N-nobody! I got lost in the forest, and I—"

"Bullshit," said Ulnoth. "You're the wagon driver, the one with the whip. The one who ran." The lad's eyes went wide but he said nothing. "Spyin' on us, are you? Still hopin' for that bonus." He pulled out a knife smeared with fishy salt. "Hope it was worth it."

"No!" Alessia stepped between them. "There's no need to hurt him. Put it down."

"But you just got done sayin' he'd bring—"

"And *you* said we'd be gone before he could. Let him go, we'll move out before dawn."

"She's right," said Corren. "There's been enough blood tonight."

Ulnoth lowered his knife and crouched by the fire, scowling. "Two against one," he grunted, "looks like I got..." He saw the green serpent badge sewn into the kid's homespun jacket. "...no choice." His gaze then rested on something else, something small and shiny left forgotten near the fire, and an idea popped into Ulnoth's mind. "At least let me march him away from here blindfolded, take 'im a bit longer to get back home and babble." A flick of his wrist and it was taken, unseen.

"Good idea," Corren said with a nod. "See, that's using your head. I'll take him."

"No! I found him, my responsibility. *I'll* take him." Alessia glared at him, and he glared right back. *I dare you*, he thought. *Show them all how much you really trust me. Family, my ass.*

"Fine." She tore a stretch of cloth from her ruined gown and covered the youth's eyes. "Promise me," she said to Ulnoth. "Promise me you won't kill him."

"I promise, all right?"

He led Trasca almost a mile into the woods, far from the road, his knife hard against the lad's back. When they were well out of earshot Ulnoth halted him and yanked the blindfold away. He put the knife back into his belt pouch, then pulled out something smaller, more delicate.

"Y-you're really gonna let me go?"

"Looks that way," said Ulnoth.

"Alive?"

"Alive. Like I promised."

"Thank you. Oh gods, thank you so m—"

"In fact," said Ulnoth, "I'm gonna do you one better."

"W-what do you mean?"

"Well, you was watching us pretty good there, wasn't you? You like to watch things?"

"Uh…what?"

"I said. You *like*. To *watch*. *Things*. You like to *see things*. *Right?*"

Trasca began to back away slowly. He felt his bladder start to give way. "Uh. Please…."

Ulnoth smiled his terrifying smile. "Good. You like to see things, I'm going to help you see things. Forever. You can see towns burn, you can see wives butchered, you can see children's brains bashed on stones. You can see it all. Come here!"

*　　*　　*

When Trasca found his way to the half of a stone wall and crumbling tower that passed for a castle the sentries almost shot him in the dark. When he came closer they knew there was something strange about him but couldn't quite figure what. When he came even closer they nearly ran in terror.

"H-help," the apparition begged, "help…help…." It was difficult to comprehend what was before them, for no one had ever seen such a mutilation before. Blood oozed all over his face and only after some seconds' examination did they understand.

The lad had no eyelids. Both upper and lower had been…excised somehow. The eyes – *those horrible eyes!* – stared out grotesquely wide from their sockets. When the sentries stopped screaming they discovered that the boy had been left – perhaps mercifully blocked by the trauma – with no clear memory of how such a fate had befallen him.

*　　*　　*

Before dawn Alessia sneaked behind a bush to dress. Oh, they were far past bodily modesty in a world that had little use for it anyway. It was just that she wanted to be sure she knew how to don the strange new clothes without making a fool of herself. Reasonably outfitted, she stepped back into view.

"Gods below," muttered Dannek, "you look...you look—"

"She looks perfectly fine," said Nandine. "Wait, almost." She took up Alessia's bow and strung it with ease, then a short sword they'd taken during last night's raid.

"What are you doing?" asked Alessia. "I'm not going into battle—"

"Here." Nan pressed the bow into her hands, then clipped a quiver stuffed with twelve unmatched arrows to the right side of her belt, followed by the blade on the left. "There. *Now* you look like a leader of deadly outlaws."

"What? Don't be stupid...."

Corren returned from watering their growing supply of horses, took a glance at Alessia and nodded. "Huh. Yep. Tie that hair back, and maybe lose the hood – it's too big for you. Then I'd say you'll be about ready."

"Ready for what?"

"To lead your Heron Kings wherever you care to take them. They'll follow. I guess I'll come along too." He walked off again to some other task.

Nan called after him. "Hey, wait up! Can I have some men's clothes too?"

By the time the sun was up they'd left their most recent campsite behind and become a regular convoy, with horses, the wagon, and a not inconsiderable amount of loot.

As they moved out Ulnoth limped up beside Alessia. "Here," he said softly, "I think you dropped this." She looked down to see one of her scalpels in his hand. "Found it on the ground."

"Oh. How did I lose that? Thanks. I hope nobody's using my tools to cut their food. Hard enough to keep anything clean as it is." She took the shiny little blade, and as it passed from his hand to hers Ulnoth seemed relieved. *Why would that be?* she wondered.

CHAPTER THIRTEEN
Matters of Strategy

"Is it true? Give it to me straight."

Taurix growled the question like he growled everything, and the scout clearly feared to be the bearer of such astoundingly terrible news. He took a breath, then swallowed hard. "It, uh...."

Taurix nodded. "That's a yes." He ripped off his helm and rubbed his skull. "All of it?"

"Y-yes lord. I guessed at least seventeen hundred men camped in the lee of Mount Rosimuir. It's no surprise they weren't spotted. I, er, took the liberty of sending to General Pertinax for aid, but—"

"But Pharamund – oh, I'm sorry, *King* Pharamund – has him guarding the road to Thoriglyn. Good man, but I fear it's too late. That'll be all. Go get some rest."

The scout sighed in relief, bowed deeply, then turned to leave the tent.

"Oh, one thing."

"Yes lord?"

"Tell absolutely no one of this."

The scout bowed again. "Of course not, Marshal."

"And—"

"Yes?"

"Have Lord Felgred join me at his convenience."

"Yes, lord."

"And tell no one of *that* either."

"Yes, lord. Erm, may I go now?"

"Yes gods damn you, go!"

The man fairly leaped out of the tent.

Fifteen minutes later Felgred was announced outside. Rather than admit him, the Marcher lord hid a leather sack under his cloak, strapped on his sword and walked out to meet him. "Ah, how are we this morning, my landless nobleman? Sleep well?"

Felgred sniffed. "I think I may be catching a cold, actually. All this marching."

"Sorry to hear it." Taurix gestured toward the nearest boundary of the camp. "Walk with me awhile, will you? We've matters of strategy to discuss."

"Strategy? Oh, of course. I'm gratified that you asked to speak with me, Taurix. I actually have some interesting ideas. You see, if only we could equip some reliable mercenaries with cross-bows—"

"The fortunes of war are a funny thing," said Taurix. "One moment you're scrambling for your life, for every breath, your own blood pooling at your feet and the whole world is the few paces between you and the closest bastard keen to bash your noggin in. The next, *you're* the bastard. The blood now fills your nostrils, your mouth waters at victory so close you can taste it. Some unseen hand moves you like a piece on a castra board, invincible. You know what I mean?"

Felgred twitched, suddenly nervous. "I, um, suppose—"

"No, of course you don't. No matter. What matters is, there come times – very, very seldom, mind you – when you get to see that hand, to *be* it even. It seems fate has conspired to make today such a day for me."

"Ah...I'm glad to hear it, my lord. Have you obtained some new ally? A new source of funding, some secret intelligence?"

Taurix laughed, and Felgred's face lost a few shades of color. "Well put! In a way, all three." He walked them to a line of trees, the closest to be spared the axe when campground had been cleared. Taurix chose a wide one that blocked them from view of the tents. "You see, I've realized our prime tactical mistake: Pharamund."

"The king? I don't understand, how can—"

"You know the secret to a good sword blow? Actually, it's twofold: first is proper edge alignment, getting the angle of the cut right, to reduce friction. Second is to hit with the sweet spot on the blade that focuses momentum, lets the sword do the work – that's what it's made for after all. Pharamund's an idiot. He knows absolutely nothing about fighting a war. Which is forgivable. Except he's too stupid to let those who *do* know get the job done for him. That is not forgivable. Loss piled upon loss upon loss and my hands tied, and there's nothing even I can do."

"Well, we could appeal to him for more authority—"

"Sssh. It's too late for that," Taurix said gently. "You recall, don't you, you pisspot, what I told you about my motivations?"

"W-what of it? What do you—"

"Be glad then that you're about to contribute, for once in your miserable, worthless life, a very great deal to the furtherance of that noble cause." Taurix drew his sword with one hand and took some of Felgred's ridiculously long yellow hair in the other.

"Hey—!"

He flung Felgred hard against the tree trunk, jamming his soft face deep into the bark and in one swift stroke sliced clean through the lordling's neck. And as this was a moment Taurix had imagined with glee many, many times, his edge alignment was perfect.

The body jerked once then fell away, blood spurting from the stump in an arcing fountain. Felgred's head swayed back and forth in Taurix's grip. A surprised expression remained, and the dying eyes seemed to focus on Taurix one last time as he held them level with his own.

"I'd say I was sorry for this, but that'd be bullshit. I will send you off to hell with one true thing, though: I'm going to fuck your king up the arse with this sword for making such a fool out of me."

Taurix dropped Felgred's head into the leather sack, then went to summon a courier – he finally had some good news to send to King Pharamund.

CHAPTER FOURTEEN

It Worked!

The girl waited on a bench outside the general's apartment, overhearing bits and pieces of gossip between soldiers with nothing better to do. She heard Wengeddy mentioned several times, along with phrases like 'magnificent massacre' and 'complete pacification'. And of course, 'Vendreesen'.

The fort was new and hastily built, meant to slow Engwara's strike up the Carsa Valley. The lumber smelled fresh cut and outside men threw up timber towers and blockhouses and slept in tents. In the center of all this stood the headquarters of the man in charge, and information as to the habits and appetites of General Duelleigh had not come cheaply.

The door creaked open and a bookish young clerk emerged. A rumbling voice behind him said, "Keep it under wraps all the same. Desertion's bad enough, but theft and murder into the bargain – word of that gets out we'll lose half the army."

"Of course, sir." The young man stepped aside to reveal an elderly one with a scowl that looked carved from rock. He raised one eyebrow when he noticed the girl and the guard said, "Claims she has an appointment, chief."

The girl stood but kept her eyes respectfully down. "A lie, sir. Well, partly." She held out the note she clutched.

The guard snatched it away, gave it a suspicious look over, shrugged and handed it to the general, who read it with an expression that could've been a grin or a torture victim's rictus. He nodded to the clerk. "That'll be all for now." He turned to the girl. "Hmm. So, Captain Nera sends me a free whore, does he?"

The girl nodded. "Engaged for a full week, sir. Paid in full."

"And what have I done that the captain should be so generous?"

"He mentioned something about some casks of Cynuvik red you sent him?"

The general grunted. "Huh, I guess there's proof Duelleigh of Edrastead knows his wines after all. All right." He jerked his thumb back toward his office. "Might as well see what you're made of." He ordered the guard not to disturb him for the next hour and slammed the door behind them.

The room was only part office, with a desk and chair and scroll rack. A partition concealed a cot, wash basin, trunk and a wine pitcher with two cups set by. "Is that the famous Cynuvik red I hear of, my lord?"

"Hmm? Oh, aye. Brought a cask with me. I run a dry fort but command has its privileges. Otherwise what's the point, eh?" His cackle sounded like a dying coyote.

"May I try some? It's been a thirsty journey."

"Pour us both a cup," said the general as he began pulling off his tunic and undershirt.

They'd patted the girl down, or groped her more like, before letting her into the building, but not closely enough to discover the envelope folded into the sleeve of her gown. It was expertly done, and when she turned around the general had his braies down around his ankles. He reeked of rancid onions even from a distance. Her stomach churned but she forced a smile. "I see you don't believe in wasting time, my lord."

"At my age, child, I haven't time to waste. Get over here."

She sauntered to the cot, imitating the gait of the quayside two-copper doxies she remembered from home. She handed him his cup and fought to look away.

He took it all in one go. Perfect. She took a tiny sip from her own cup. "Mmm, exquisite," she said. "You have a keen palate." It tasted like horse piss, but he wasn't listening.

He fumbled at her gown, ripping the seams and sucking on skin as it was exposed. "Mhm, you done bathed recently," he said as if that were the most exotic thing he could imagine. He had her tits out and she yelped when his yellowed teeth bit her nipple.

"Yes – oh! Ow! Oh, you are a *beast* of a man."

Duelleigh peeled off the last of her clothing and threw it over the partition. Two bony fingers jammed between her legs. He took her shivering for arousal. What would he do when he found her dry as a bone? "Oh, gods," she whispered.

"Aye," he said, throwing her down onto the cot and kneeling over her. "Oh...." He frowned for just an instant, rubbed his sagging gut, then shook his head. "Meh." His aged cock poked out – just barely – from a bushy gray nest. "Have a taste, my child." He slid his hips forward, toward her face. She was going to be sick.

"Aargh," the general suddenly exclaimed, grabbing his belly again and falling on top of her. "I'm going to be sick!" He rolled over and retched slimy red onto the floor. "G-guard," he moaned between heaves. "Guard!"

The soldier stationed outside the not-at-all soundproof room rushed in after two hard kicks to the locked latch. "General sir, what's – yech!" He tried to avert his eyes but between the girl, his naked general and the mess on the floor, there was nowhere to look. "What the—?"

"Don't just stand there," said the girl, heedless of her own nudity, "can't you see the general's ill? Get him to the physic!"

"Um, right. Help me carry him," said the guard with desperation, dropping his halberd. He hoisted the groaning general and threw a stained blanket over his shoulders.

"I can't go out like this – think of the gossip! They'll say he can't even take a whore without keeling over. You can handle him. I'll be along in a minute." She began gathering the remains of her gown.

"Oh, uh, right. Good thinking."

"I'm thinking of my professional reputation. Now go!" As if on cue the old man retched again and almost fell from the guard's grasp.

"Come on, sir, all will be well." The two hobbled too slowly out of the room.

With literally seconds to spare she dropped the pretense of dressing and rifled through the desk like a whirlwind, jittery with adrenaline. It wasn't there. The trunk? Clothing, coins, bits of armor and leather gear. She even went through the soiled clothes he'd been wearing. Nothing. She went back and checked the scroll rack – there were too many damn slots! She tore out the scrolls, notes, pens, everything but what she was after. Outside men's voices rose and the clomping of booted feet echoed. "Shit," she spat. "After all this...."

In frustration she heaved the scroll rack over. As it fell something tumbled out, making a hollow woody scrape as it slid. Desperate, she raised the rack back up and inspected the pile underneath, hoping against hope for—

There!

She plucked up the small pewter seal – such a tiny, delicate thing to be the cause of so much care – and wasted no time in throwing on only half her clothes and rushing out of the office, out of the building and into the midday brightness.

No one was guarding the outside. There was a commotion around a large tent at the east end of the fort with men standing about gawking. Some at the back jumped up for a glimpse at the spectacle of their ailing commander.

One man ignored all this and walked toward the girl, keeping his eyes fixed on some point past her. Closer, closer, close enough to touch as they passed. Exchanging no words, the girl dropped the seal into his waiting grasp. If anyone watching had blinked, they'd have missed it. Her part in all this thankfully ended, she made her way to the untended gate and out of the fort.

★   ★   ★

The man walked as casually as one can when holding a general's stolen seal while surrounded by that general's soldiers, past a fire burning inside a portable copper pit over which a tin of lentils boiled. His other hand palmed a tiny red candle that he ignited as he went by. A few more steps and he ducked between the back of a bunkhouse and the fort's timber wall and produced a list from his belt pouch with a blank space left at the bottom. He dribbled some molten wax onto the space then pressed the seal into it, supporting both on his knee. The hot wax smarted only for a moment. He pulled the seal away slowly, lifting one end first in a rolling motion like he'd seen done before. Perfect. He blew on the impression to cool it, then went back the way he'd come, tossing the candle entirely into the fire this time. No one saw him; the fort was absorbed in the drama over the general.

Besides the general's apartment, the largest structure in the fort was the storehouse. Outside it the man nodded to the old carter who sat high in his big, empty wagon. The carter nodded back, and a trickle of sweat ran down his brow while he double-checked the horse team's tack.

"Not there, *there!*" a supply sergeant barked at a conscript more out of boredom than need, for if stacking crates was tiresome, supervising the stacking was even more so. Easier on the back though, to be sure.

"I tried over there. The boxes don't fit," whined the laborer.

"They fit yesterday, they damn well will fit today if you just—"

"Excuse me."

"*What?*" The supply sergeant spun on a heel in anticipation of another target for his bored ire, then saw the insignia adorning the man's tunic. The gold braid stitched about his foxhead badge marked him as a horseman – definitely an officer and probably at least a minor nobleman. The sergeant blanched. "Um, pardon sir. What can I do for you?"

The man presented his forged list. "Orders from General Duelleigh. These supplies are to be loaded and dispatched immediately."

The sergeant scanned the list as fast as one of elementary literacy could, and his jaw dropped. "Four tuns wheat, two tuns millet, two barrels salt pork, thirty bowstaves, one cask cider, twenty short swords, ten bolts – what is this? This is half the entire storehouse!"

The man sniffed. "And?"

"Well, I mean, I don't even have a wagon that'd—"

"I do. It's waiting outside."

"But this – will we get a replacement for all this? We got a lot o' mouths to feed. Where's all this going, anyway? The general never told me nothing about—"

The man sighed heavily and rolled his eyes. "Not that it's any business of *yours*, but His Grace is moving to liberate the towns along the Carsa that Engwara burned. This is all needed for the strike, which is to be a swift one whilst you lot sit behind these walls and wank each other. Now does that meet with your approval or shall I inform the king the whole thing's off because you have a problem with it?"

"What? I didn't know—"

"Of *course* you didn't! No one's supposed to know so those snakes are taken by surprise, ken'ee?"

"Oh. Oh, I got ya!" He looked again at the daunting list. "Everything looks to be in order, then. Take a while to load."

"I'll help you."

The sergeant blinked. "Y-you will? Personal-like?"

"Speed is essential, man! Half of winning wars is getting where you're going before the other bastard does. Move it!" The sergeant and his minion jumped to obey. They carried crate after barrel after sack after cask, with even the old carter helping as he could.

When it was done they all stood soaked in sweat. "That's it," said the huffing sergeant, who'd grown unused to doing the stacking himself of late, "wagon's full to bursting."

"Fine, I'll return for the rest later. And," the man leaned in with a conspiratorial smile, "I'll commend your diligence to the general. I hear he's taken on a new courtesan that lays men out cold. Mayhap you'll earn a dance."

"Thank you, sir!"

He climbed into the wagon. The crowd that had hounded the physic tent was mostly dispersed back to their posts. He turned and waved back to the sergeant. "Gods save His Grace the king!"

"Eh? Oh, aye! Gods save 'im!"

The carter whipped the horses forward. They had to cross the entire length of the fort, and each second of it seemed an eternity. "Almost there," he mumbled. "Let's just don't cock it up."

"Hard part's over, ain't it?" asked the carter.

"Aye, that's what I'm worried about. My experience, it's the easy parts no one bothers over where things go to shite. Almost there...."

A swath of red appeared on the periphery of his vision. The freshly dressed but pale general crept across the worn dirt track flanked by a horde of sycophantic officers and men. The clerk next to him pointed out the packed wagon and said something. Duelleigh looked at the wagon – so slowly it seemed to move! – then at the storehouse with its doors still wide open and a big empty space inside. With a sudden frowning vigor the old man tromped over to the building.

"Don't look back," said the carter, "don't look."

"What did I tell you? Always the easy parts! Can't we go faster?"

"Faster risks tossing half this stuff out. And a lot of unwanted attention."

Almost there. They were less than twenty yards to the open gates. And that was precisely when things went to shite.

A great cry went up from Duelleigh's retainers all at once, and if the general himself joined it he was drowned out. The confusion made for a few more seconds' delay but their meaning was eventually made clear: "*Close the gate!*"

"That's it, we're humped. Whip 'em!"

Anything that wasn't tied down shook violently and the topmost boxes flew back to shatter on the ground as the carter lashed at the horse team without hint of restraint. The animals neighed in protest but surged ahead as the gates began a comically lazy process of swinging shut. Behind them a half-dozen riders, armed but armorless and mounted only by chance when the alarm arose, raced after and were catching up fast.

By the barest of margins the wagon rumbled through the gate and the timbers scraped against the back wheels as it squeezed past. Not being suicidal, the sentries didn't dare try blocking the path of the stampeding beasts.

"We're out!" said the carter. "We made it!"

The other man craned his neck back overtop the shifting mountain of loot. "Uh," he said, "not quite." Before the gates closed entirely they slowly reversed and opened again, and a pair of riders came surging out. The man tore off the heavy tunic with the gold braid and whipped it back and forth over his head. "Hey! Hey, help! Now!" He seemed to be shouting at no one, and the wagon plunged on. Just as the horsemen caught up with the fleeing thieves and drew long swords to hack at their necks, the woods came alive.

★　　★　　★

They were just blurs among the foliage, nothing anyone would notice while atop a charging warhorse. One rider pitched backward as though he'd hit some invisible wire. It was as much shock that felled him from his saddle as the arrow buried in his ribcage. The horse pressed on oblivious while he tumbled down with a shriek.

Another arrow aimed for the second rider but grazed the horse instead. It bucked and threw him, but he rolled then scrambled to his feet while the wagon gained distance. He dashed behind a tree on the side of the road. From his vantage point he watched the other rider moaning and bleeding profusely. "Help," the other rider tried to cry, sending blood gurgling up into the air. "He—"

"Sorry friend," whispered the other, "ain't goin' out there." There was a rustle in the woods across the way and a grim young brute shambled out holding a strung bow. He was dirty, shaggy and clad in a tunic that could've been green or gray or brown depending on the light. He crept over to the dying man, knelt, pulled out a long knife and hesitated a bit before opening his throat. Engwara's agents were right in their own backyard. The surviving rider backed away, careful to keep the wide oak between him and this preternatural killer.

He bumped into something. He jumped, spun around and gasped.

"Good day," Ulnoth said politely, then bashed the man across the nose.

The man staggered back then swung his sword in a wide arc. But the growth was old and gnarled, and the tip of the blade bounced harmlessly off a low-hanging branch. Panicking, he dropped his weapon, turned and fled deep into the woods.

Ulnoth trudged up the steep hill, almost bored with the affair. *At least you can eat fish in a barrel after you spear 'em,* he thought. *Is it just me or do they get dumber every time I meet one?* Perhaps it was just his bloodlust was waning. A terrible thing to consider, for what else would he do if that were so?

The fool was nowhere to be seen. "Holed up and hid, eh? Smart choice," he said quietly. "Hmm...." He scanned the hillside. The growth was sparser here; he couldn't have gone far. To his left a broken twig gave a hint to his quarry's direction. Ulnoth followed it and found a stand of broad trees in front of him. No sound came from any of them but...his eyes shot to a tiny movement. Ulnoth smiled.

A shadow, quivering. His victim was well-hid but the angle of the sinking sun marked his shadow lancing out from behind the tree. *There.* Ulnoth wasn't bored anymore.

Later the search party would find the rider, arms and legs broken, but shockingly still alive. His chest had been laid bare, and into it was carved a crude sketch. Ants and various woodland critters had nibbled away at the flesh but one could still discern the outline of a great crested bird in flight. A heron, it sort of looked like.

★ ★ ★

Nandine sat on the ground under a rocky outcropping, hugging her knees and biting her lip to stop its trembling.

"What's wrong?" Alessia asked. "Didn't it work?"

Nan looked up at her, red-eyed. "Oh, it worked. It worked. Just in time. You couldn't have made the poison stronger? My tits are still swollen."

"I guess I could've put more in. But it's a tricky thing, understand. Too much and it could even be fatal—"

Nan tossed her hands up. "Oh, *well* then! Stupid me, can't have that."

Alessia knelt next to the girl. Nan flinched away at her touch. "What happened exactly?"

"Nothing. The stuff just took a while to work, that's all."

Alessia swallowed the lump in her throat. "It's not an exact science out here in the wilds – I had to do some guessing. You didn't have to...?"

"No. It was close though. It was...ugh. Those hands all over me, *in* me. It was horrible. Don't ask me to do anything like that again. I'll fight 'em. I'll fight 'em all face to face and go down swinging. But not that, ever again."

"I'm sorry." It sounded ludicrous like the nothing it was, but Alessia couldn't imagine what else to say.

Nan wiped a tear away. "No, I am. I volunteered. It just kind of hit me all at once. We did it though, didn't we?"

"You did."

"You should've seen us – it was brilliant." She smiled now. "Right out from under their fat ugly noses."

"Glad to hear it," said Alessia. "I'm sure you're as sick of cod as I am."

"And I'm sick of these clothes. Burn 'em – I can still smell his stink on me."

A rumbling interrupted her ruminations and the wagon clattered across the forest floor toward their latest campsite. "Idiots. That racket's sure to give us away! You could hear it in Thoriglyn."

Corren ignored this. "Hey doctor, next batch of puke powder you mix up you think could actually make it, you know, *work?* We barely got away!"

"Don't call me doctor," Alessia fumed. "You know how hard it was to scrape together those ingredients? Look around – this isn't exactly the university apothecary."

Corren hitched the horse team to a tree and rescued a wobbling crate from the top of the wagon. "Oh no, you can't fool me. I saw you mix up that witch's brew. You only used half of what you had. You held back."

Alessia's face went beet red. "Fine! Have Ulnoth make it next time. You can poison the whole damn world. I told you I won't kill if I don't—"

"You almost got *us* killed! I suggest you decide which side you're on, sister." He paused to glance at Nan. "So what's wrong with her?"

Shaking with frustration, Alessia was saved from her lack of a retort when Ulnoth also came trundling into the camp with Dannek in tow, making almost as much noise as the wagon. "Whoop! How was that for a rush? And lookit that haul! We'll eat for weeks and then some. Proper eats this time."

"Glad you had such fun," Corren said. "Am I the only one takes this seriously? I've seen deserters crucified. It's not pretty, and I doubt they'd be half so kind if they catch us." He looked at Dannek, whose face was turned roughly the same color as his tunic. "You all right?"

"Oh, he's fine," Ulnoth said, clapping a hand on the lad's back and sending him stumbling forward a pace. "First kill's all. Scary with that bow, too. My shot went wide and it came down to knife work. Not that I'm complainin' mind you—"

"All right," said Alessia, "enough. I'm getting a headache."

"Their search party ran right by us," said Crander. "Won't take 'em long to figure out we gave 'em the slip, come back here and start beating the bushes."

"Meaning we keep moving, as usual. Any ideas for a destination?" Ulnoth had one.

CHAPTER FIFTEEN
Gifts and Purchases

When Taurix arrived outside Carsolan with a thousand men at his back, it caused a bit of trepidation. Riots broke out, and a number of ships were set alight when they refused escape passage to the wrong people. Morning saw more than the usual number of bodies floating in the harbor.

"Let them panic," said Engwara when told of the unrest. "The more dramatic when he turns and pledges to me. You're certain that *is* his true intention, yes?"

"Oh, yes," replied Vinian. "I had his courier to Thoriglyn intercepted. The message within his gilded box was...unsubtle in its meaning, to put it mildly."

"Good. If those doors open and he tries to murder me I'll be rather upset. To put it mildly."

The doors in question were tiny one-man gates built into the greater gates to the city. When they did open Vinian followed Engwara through, one pace behind and protected on all sides by Ludolphus and his hand-picked bodyguards. She spared a moment to look upward, and all along the battlements townspeople pressed in to watch. Word of the meeting spread like wildfire and even the city garrison couldn't hold back that deluge.

Probably expecting to see their queen gutted, she thought. *They very well might if there really is a double-cross in the works.*

Engwara led her ring of protectors out from the walls. Before them a vast sea of gray and brown and frowning men stretched away in both directions. Directly ahead, impossible to miss, loomed Taurix, standing still as a statue.

After the small gate clanged shut behind them there was complete silence but for the crunching of ground underfoot, a light breeze off the harbor, the queen's slow breath. Closer, closer. At a distance somehow unconsciously agreed upon by the principals of both sides, they halted. Taurix took a few paces forward and Vinian felt the tension spike. Here was the architect of all their ills, and perhaps their only salvation.

He pulled off his helm. "So," he said, "here we are."

Engwara's mouth twitched, whether in irritation or amusement Vinian couldn't be sure. "Is that what you planned for your first words to me?"

"Honestly, I expected to get shot down by some cocksucker up on them walls before I got the chance. So I didn't really think on it too deeply."

In spite of the gravity of the moment Engwara laughed, and the sound echoed off the walls to the consternation of the spectators. "So sorry to disappoint you, my lord."

"Oh I've had a lot of disappointment lately, as you well know. Used to it."

"I'd say it's time to redress that. Our deputations have worked out the details, I believe? There's only one thing left."

Taurix eyed her a moment longer, perhaps wondering if it was too late to change his mind.

"Join with me," the queen said, "and help me put an end to this supreme stupidity once and for all. You know we can do it. You know it's the right choice."

"Choice? You gave me none. But that's past. Pharamund. I wanna hear it from your royal lips. He's mine?"

She nodded. "All yours. And the Marches besides."

"Well then." He drew his sword. Ludolphus's men closed tighter around Engwara but held their peace otherwise. Taurix chuckled. "Touchy lot." He bent to one knee, grimacing as his joint flared. And like a pebble dropped into a calm pool the great mass of his men did the same in a wave expanding outward. Vinian looked on with probing suspicion, watching for reluctant troublemakers who didn't follow quickly enough. Taurix offered up the blade to Engwara. "All that's mine is yours to command. Let gods and men witness, from now until death I serve Your Majesty in all things."

Pretty words, Vinian thought. *Certain he spoke the same before*

Pharamund. She watched Engwara take the heavy gray weapon in one hand. In a slight departure from custom, she turned toward the walls and hoisted it aloft. The cheering nearly swept the party off its feet. *Is that support they're proclaiming, or just relief?* When it began to die down Engwara turned back and extended the sword to Taurix once again. He rested his huge craggy hand atop hers over the hilt, and it was done.

"Nice touch," he said under his breath. He rose at his new lady's beckoning and sheathed the blade.

"The people demand spectacle, after all. And now may I present the mother of this union," she turned to indicate Vinian, "my spymistress."

Vinian made a sarcastic mockery of a curtsy. "Pleasure to meet you again, my lord. Sorry about your sentry."

Taurix grunted. "*You.* I can see why you like to work in the night. If I'd known you were so pretty I'd have tried to kiss you instead of kill you."

"Your sword's keener than your wit, Taurix."

"My! But the women of this country are uppity, aren't they?"

"And," Engwara continued, "I'm sure you know General—"

"Ludolphus." He rolled the name over his tongue, savoring it. "*Luuudolllphusss.* Aye, by reputation." He stepped closer, and the two elderly men stared each other up and down like two graveyard dogs. "Led me on a merry fucking chase, you did."

Ludolphus visibly gnashed his teeth. "It was no trouble – I needed the exercise. Delighted to make your acquaintance at last."

"Indeed. Your Gr— I mean, Your *Majesty*, in our negotiations I made mention of one small indulgence…?"

Engwara sighed, nodded once. Without warning Taurix sent a right hook square across Ludolphus's jaw. The stunned general stumbled back into the arms of two bodyguards behind, and the rest moved to tackle Taurix.

"Stop!" Engwara shouted. Angry rumbles erupted from the wall. "Hold! All of you, hold. I'm sorry, general, he wouldn't submit until I agreed to give him one blow at you. I thought it best to keep it a surprise."

After regaining his balance Ludolphus spat blood into the ground and nodded. "A wise choice, Majesty. But certainly you'll grant me the chance to return it."

Taurix grinned. "You're welcome to try. Anytime."

"*That* I leave between the two of you," Engwara said quickly. "But later. For now, come, my new Lord Taurix – show me what I've bought today."

★   ★   ★

"That was fun," said Vinian as they emerged from the stuffy conference chamber.

"Don't be snide. Taurix has brought some good ideas with him. We're just lucky Pharamund didn't put them to use first." Engwara snapped her fingers and her body servant appeared and began to work at the knots in the queen's neck.

"Oh, yes. Burn all the ports, put bounties on every man wearing red, disembowel the nobility…actually I sort of like that last one. But mostly it's as I said before – there won't be anything left to win."

"Ludolphus didn't seem to have any complaints," Engwara said.

"He hasn't said anything all day. He's just pouting. Was that smart, embarrassing him in public like that?"

"High politics, my dear. It's too often a matter of finding the least bad of many unpalatable options. Ludolphus may brood, but he understands that." Tension eventually oozed away from the queen's joints, and she waved the servant away. "Besides, I have a little project for you. Bit of a mystery, like."

"Intriguing," said Vinian, not the least bit intrigued.

"I assume you're still snooping on my scout reports from the Carsa offensive?"

"No," replied Vinian with a scowl. "No time what with all the security for today's entertainment. You know I had to have the families of the ballista men taken hostage to make sure no one got itchy when Taurix's horde showed up? The paperwork on that alone—"

"Fine, whatever. Short version, there's something going on along the river valley."

"Something?"

"Follow me." They wound through the hallways of the palace until reaching Engwara's private apartments, where carved snakes gave way to fresh roses and fragrant floor rushes. The hot bath she'd ordered drawn up awaited, and the queen wasted no time in throwing off her layers of royal finery and sinking into the big brass cauldron. "Oh, that's better. Over there, on the desk."

Vinian sifted through the small pile of reports. "These all describe a series of...."

"Disappearances," Engwara finished. "Supply trains, men, officers, whole squads. Just up and gone without a trace."

"Desertions," said Vinian with a shrug, "that's no mystery."

"My first assumption also. But all in the same area, all at once? Quite a coincidence."

"Certainly not bandits."

The queen gurgled and spit as she luxuriated in the tub. "Common bandits wouldn't be so organized or so meticulous in covering their tracks. You'll find no eyewitness reports there."

"Partisans of Pharamund then? Some kind of...I don't know, killer rangers."

"An excellent deduction. Or it would be if not for rumors from the other side – of the *exact same thing* befalling his forces."

"What?" Vinian found herself bereft of words, now genuinely intrigued. "I...."

Engwara sat up in her bath with a grin. "Like I said, a mystery. My lords and officers in the field are confounded. They're starting to blame it on Chthonii and forest ghosts. I need someone with a brain to tackle this. That's why I'm sending you."

"Sending...me?"

"You leave as soon as my business with that banker is concluded. I'm granting you a writ of full authority to act in my name, and don't pretend you won't enjoy *that*."

"But I assumed you'd need me to help with Taurix, the planning—"

"Ludolphus can manage. I need you out there. Right now it's little more than an annoyance, but whatever it is we're dealing with – deserters, bandits, or hellsent Chthonii – it must *not* be allowed to interfere with our plans, whatever the cost. Understood?" The queen had that look in her eyes that said it was pointless and more than a little dangerous to resist. Letting go and casting herself into the tides of fate, Vinian relented.

"Understood, Majesty. I guess I'd better go pack."

★   ★   ★

"Pleased to see you again," said Engwara, though her expression betrayed the lie. She received the banker, as before, in her tower chamber, though there was little need for secrecy at this point as the banker had already docked in Carsolan's harbor. Vinian now attended at her queen's right hand, and this time she kept Carthagne on his feet.

"With all respect, Majesty, I must rather doubt this. Few are pleased to be often in the presence of my kind. Especially those in most need of our services. It is a consequence to which I've grown accustomed." He spoke in a lilting, relaxed singsong, visibly more at ease than the last time he'd visited. And why not? The deal was done after all, and he was only here to oversee the fulfillment. "But enough of that. I have the honor of presenting the delivery – only the first installment, mind – of the extension of Your Majesty's line of credit. All is as you specified – gold for the big expenses, silver for the small, all unloaded in the harbor as we speak. And this I'm sure you *are* pleased to see."

The queen put a hand to her chest. "Why banker, I do believe you have…cut me to the quick, is that the expression?"

Carthagne nodded serenely. "Perfect. But I'm sure Your Majesty will recover." He pulled a red leatherbound folder from the billows of his clothing. "If you would be so kind as to sign the receipt…."

Engwara snatched the packet and handed it back to a waiting attendant without bothering to inspect it. "Seal." The attendant scampered off to find the queen's stamp. "You've come openly this time, and during the day. Should I take that as a vote of confidence?"

Carthagne shrugged. "If Your Majesty so chooses. Though we can hardly sneak a hundred boxes of money in one boat at a time under cover of night, can we? I've taken the liberty of marking them 'textiles'. And I come, as you see, clad in the manner of a Cynuvik merchant. So if I'm not incognito, then at least *less*cognito." He smiled and gestured at the rich dark woolens draped about him.

"Bit anticlimactic though, isn't it? A signature, some boxes change hands and that's the end of it."

"I must admit, I thought you'd be happier to receive these funds considering the stalemate you found yourself in during my previous visit. Has Lord Marshal Taurix fallen ill?"

"Oh no, something quite a bit better than that. Far from ill, Marshal Taurix has in fact come quite fully to his senses – switched sides and joined our cause. He's brought his own men, generals and many more under his vassals. Pharamund has no more allies of consequence, and final victory is now only a matter of time. The money should still help, I suppose."

The color drained from Carthagne's face, and he grasped at a serpentine column for support. "W-what's that? He's...joined you, indeed?" He began sweating profusely, his breathing heavy and labored. "Why that – that's very, uh, welcome news. Very, very welcome! I...I must congratulate Your Majesty on your diplomatic skills to pull off such an...unlikely feat."

Engwara gestured toward Vinian. "Actually it was my spymistress who engineered the stroke...Master Carthagne, are you quite all right?"

"Must be...the weather, Majesty. No winter in the Marimines Isles you know...oh...."

Engwara smirked just a bit at that. "I suppose it is a little chilly. Next time you visit I'll be queen of the whole peninsula. Greater Argovan I think I'll call it. I'll receive you in Ólo, or somewhere else where the winds are temperate all year round."

"That would be...most gracious, Your Majesty." He wiped his brow with a silk kerchief and seemed to regain some sense of control. "I look forward to it."

"And, I assume, to the profitable repayment of the bank's loans well ahead of schedule," she replied.

"Yes. Of course. Profit flows everywhere. A...a golden age ahead. Erm, how long do you think this great victory will take...exactly?"

"Exactly? Depends on how well my generals play together. We're pushing up the Carsa and along the northern coast both now. By spring we should have Thoriglyn surrounded. Why?"

"Oh, no reason. I'm sure my employers would be curious as to the timeline of this operation, for…for cash flow purposes, and the like."

"Really? I thought Bank Isle-Euderico didn't give – how did you put it? – half a shit who wins our backward little war? Those were your words."

"Ah…forgive me, Majesty. A bit of a temper tantrum on my part if I recall. We're taught to go rather straight for the jugular during negotiations. I'm sure a woman of the world such as yourself understands?"

"Only too well," she replied with a smile as false as the banker's. The attendant returned with the folder opened to the appropriate page, a thimble of molten wax and the queen's solid gold seal. Engwara tipped some of the green wax onto the document and made her stamp, then scribbled *Engw Q* across the bottom of the page. "I suppose this concludes our business for the time being."

"Yes Majesty but…my ship requires provisioning. Might I beg a few weeks in your marvelous harbor?"

"If this is what you call marvelous then the Marimines Isles are far less than I've been led to believe. Stay as long as you like. Though I *do* hope your health does not suffer for the weather."

Carthagne again bowed as low as he could manage. "Thank you, Majesty. I'm sure I'll muddle through…somehow."

After Carthagne stumbled out of the room and down the stairs in what seemed to be the onset of some kind of apoplexy, Engwara frowned and said to Vinian, "What in the name of the Chthonii was that about?"

"I don't know," Vinian answered with a deeper frown, "and I don't take well to not knowing things. Something you said frightened him. I'll see what I can find out."

"No, no you have other work. Best get about it."

"Yes, Majesty."

CHAPTER SIXTEEN

Baggage

"Draw. Aim. Loose!" Eight arrows took flight as one toward the makeshift archery butts. That was the idea anyway. Three of the shots ended up stuck in the crates twenty paces away with circles drawn on the front. The rest buried themselves in the ground beyond or, in two cases, shot clear overhead and out of sight. Corren sighed. "Well, that's...definitely an improvement. Everyone rescue your arrows and line up again."

"Why do we only get one apiece?" Dannek asked. "We have hundreds now, don't we?"

"True. But each arrow is a precious resource, and I want you to get in the habit of treating them so. Also motivates you not to break 'em." They scattered to obey as Ulnoth approached.

"Target practice? Good idea."

"Most of these people have never held a bow before, and we can't afford dead weight. Anyone that can't defend themselves isn't going to be of much use, just a mouth to feed. It's sheer luck we don't have any children with us."

"Allow me to remind you that if anyone from Wengeddy ain't with us they likely got hacked down by your brothers in arms. Not sure I'd call that luck. Not the good kind, at least."

"Good point."

"Plus they can get some more practice right now. We spotted some kind of caravan a bit east of here. I wanna check it out."

"Soldiers?"

"Can't tell. Might be a good idea to track 'em awhile, take some folks along."

They were all lined up again and staring expectantly at Corren. "Now this time, make sure you get a full draw. Hold steady and follow through on your shot, like I showed. On the quiet count now, like you're shooting from cover." He slapped his thigh in a slow rhythm and mouthed the words: *Draw...aim...loose.*

Four hits, four in the dirt. Definite improvement. "All right, go get 'em. Wait, hold a second." He turned to Ulnoth. "Remember we agreed to no robbing civil—"

"Right, right, agreed. Eyes only."

"Fine. Dannek, Emony, Allard – take a quiver each and go with Ulnoth. The rest of you, back to it!"

Emony and Allard were twins – sister and brother about twenty years old and nearly indistinguishable but for Allard's newly amputated pinky finger. "Are...are we going into a fight?" Emony asked nervously.

"Nah," said Ulnoth, "just a look-see. Good practice staying out of sight though."

"I'm coming too." They all turned at once to see Alessia standing before them, kitted out just as she'd been when Nan had first done her up.

Ulnoth snorted. "Babysitting me, is that it? You still don't trust me to keep my word."

"I could use the experience too. And who knows, they might have herbs or medicines we could trade for."

"I didn't plan on getting close enough to hold a fair day."

"Then there's nothing to argue about. Let's go."

★   ★   ★

"Not very smart," said Ulnoth. "Who'd bring a caravan through this country now? It's near suicide." The five hugged the ground at the crest of a ridge, peering down onto the train of people and cargo that snaked through the narrow valley. It was a well-worn path that skirted the main highway, but if they were trying to avoid attention they weren't doing a very good job – the noise the travelers made echoed off the steep slopes to either side.

"Smugglers I'd wager," said Allard. "Business doesn't stop, even in wartime. Even opens up all kinds of opportunities for merchants – iron, Pelonan textiles, grain...."

"How d'you know all that?"

"Father was a mercer," said Emony with a wistful sigh. "Mother ran the books for most of Wengeddy. The undertable market was half our business."

Alessia crawled up next to them, covered in dust. "These smugglers have women and children with them."

"Family business like any other," said Allard. "But I don't think this lot's likely to have anything we'd be interested in. By the carts it looks like bulk commodities mostly."

"Still, not a bad business to get into," said Ulnoth, rubbing his chin and grinning. "We could, uh, *relieve* them of some of it...."

"Don't you dare even *think* about—"

"Just kidding! You're too easy a mark, Lessi. I say we track 'em half a mile or so, make sure they don't straggle too close to our little traveling circus."

"Fine. Don't get too – wait. What's that?"

"What?"

Alessia pointed toward the opposite ridge. It was a bit lower than the one they were perched on, and coming over the top they spied two, three, six, then ten figures. "That. Who...everybody else is still back at camp, right?"

"So far as I know," said Ulnoth.

"Then who are they?"

The ten men – no, it was seven men and three women, all filthy – rushed down the slope toward the caravan. Each held some kind of weapon, either blade or blunt, and when the smugglers noticed them a cacophony of frightened screams bounced off the rocks. The ten attacked both ends of the train at once to create chaos and prevent escape. A knife flashed and the screams increased.

"Bandits," said Dannek, "real ones." He whipped an arrow from the quiver at his belt and reached for his bow but Ulnoth stayed his hand.

"Whoa, hold on. Far as I know this ain't any concern of ours."

"But they'll be murdered!"

"Seems a popular fate these days, one I ain't keen to share. Show me a red or a green and I'm all in, otherwise no thanks."

"Ulnoth, we have to—" Alessia started to say but he cut her off.

"No, we don't. You love to remind me of our little deal, throw it in my face. Well, now it's my turn. Anyone else can do what they want."

"We can't rescue those folks without you, and you know it!"

Ulnoth just shrugged.

"Fine, I've got a new deal for you. Help us and the next batch of poison I mix up will be as strong as you like, and you can do what you want with it."

Ulnoth chewed his lip for a moment, thinking – or appearing to. Below them the screams continued.

"Well?"

"Mmm, fine. But we do this *my* way – no half-measures. No mercy, no prisoners. We're outnumbered, so we hit quick and don't stop until every last one of 'em's dead. That means you too, sister."

Alessia agreed.

"Good. Everyone up! Take two shots then move in with knives. Look crazy and they'll scare easy. Allard, you be careful – try to only hit the bad guys."

They poured over the top of the ridge and tried not to stumble. Halfway down Emony stopped, notched her first arrow and took her shot. A snarling woman was about to bash a child's head in when she jerked, dropped her club, then pitched forward. The hard *thwack* of the arrow piercing her rawhide vest echoed back. Dannek took another bandit in the leg and the man promptly fell to the stony ground writhing in pain.

A few of the brigands turned to face the new intrusion as Ulnoth and Allard lined up their shots. One took a man in the stomach; the other just missed. "Damn!" Ulnoth drew another arrow but the bandits were scattering now, obviously having not expected armed resistance. "Eh, screw it." He dropped his bow and charged in among the caravan, drawing his knife and dodging a clumsy bearded fellow's swipe before burying his blade in the man's side. Allard and Alessia scored one kill and two wounded between them, then they moved in also.

Among all the panic and screaming it was hard to know who was the enemy. Dannek slashed toward a big Pelonan man who jumped out from behind a carriage with an eating knife, and through the tunnel vision and adrenaline it was two full seconds of standoff before Dannek realized the man was too clean and well-fed to be one of the bandits. "Not me, you idiot," Dannek said between clenched teeth, "we're here to help!" He turned and ran around the other side of the carriage without waiting for a response.

Alessia swung her short sword wildly before her. It was surreal – once sworn never to bear arms, she now fought off a girl years younger than herself, barely more than a child. A child who'd been in the process of spitting a cart driver on a sharpened stake when Alessia attacked. The girl jumped back at the sword blows with eyes full of desperation and terror. Back, back further. She stopped. Alessia stopped swinging her sword, holding it high and ready.

An instant later a blade erupted from the girl's chest amid a fountain of blood. She looked down in amazement. "Oh," she said almost casually. The girl crumpled to the ground and in her place stood Emony, white-faced, the long knife torn from her grip by the girl's falling body.

The whole thing was over in a matter of minutes. In the end two of the brigands escaped, four lay wounded and four dead along with three of the smugglers. Once convinced that their rescuers didn't intend to rob them as well, they dispatched the remaining bandits with fearsome relish.

"Thank you," breathed one of the smugglers. "Oh merciful saints and gods, thank you! I thought we was done for. You came outta nowhere!"

"We saw...had to help," said Alessia. "Do you have injured?" She unslung her physic kit, which was now reassuringly crammed with supplies.

"Aye. Who are you people? King's rangers? Queen's?"

"No, just people not terribly affected to either. Show me your wounded."

Alessia moved up and down the caravan, tending to cuts, punctures, and broken bones. As the day waned the smugglers brought the last casualty before her – a child about six years old.

"He was hiding," said the little boy's mother, tears streaking her face. "I just found...please help!" She set the boy down and Alessia gasped.

"Oh, no...." Speared clean through his leg was an arrow – one of their own. An errant shot, maybe a ricochet, forgotten in the mad clash. There was no telling who'd loosed it.

It could be tricky work removing a shaft. A master chirurgeon should've done it but it was at least a hundred miles to the nearest of those. The arrowhead had to be cut off first, then the shaft worked out little by little and bleeding kept to absolute minimum. But not too slowly, for the blood could not be allowed to clot around it. The others gathered around, helpless. "Do you think it was me?" Allard asked. "…Do you think?" He asked it over and over, quietly. No one answered.

Alessia pulled out her bone saw, and when he saw the sharp teeth the boy shrieked in terror. "No, it's all right! I just have to cut the wood away. What's your name?"

"L-Lannie," he whimpered.

"Lannie, I need you to hold very still for me. Can you do that?" The boy nodded uncertainly. She'd seen Mother Tanusia do this on grown men before, and even that was hard to watch. Alessia tied a kerchief around her head to keep from dripping sweat into the wound, then prayed silently to the gods and every saint she could remember for the skill to accomplish it.

Even with a stick between his teeth the boy screamed and had to be held down, but at last the arrow was freed. He fell into a quiet sob while she applied the poultice and bandages, and his mother thanked her ecstatically. Alessia took the severed piece of arrow and found Ulnoth sitting nearby. He'd been given or had appropriated a wine jug from among the cargo.

"We need more target practice," she said icily. "This is not acceptable."

Ulnoth sighed. "Look, this was your—"

"I know, my idea. And I'd do it again, gods help me." She held up the blood-soaked bit of wood between them. "Still. We need more practice."

*　　*　　*

"Where were you headed?"

"Lenocca," replied Reynal, the leader of the smuggler band. "It's a dangerous trip, but we had no choice. There's no market up north, for anything. The soldiers and petty lords just take what they want and all the buyers are fled. Engwara has Lenocca, and that means a route to Carsolan, means a route to anywhere in the world. All the other ports are blocked, so...."

"We should do that ourselves," Ulnoth said. "Jump ship away from this cackhole."

The Pelonan smuggler Dannek had briefly faced off against shook his head. "Might do, but no safer than staying put."

"Alondo's right," Reynal said. "This ain't the first time we been hit. Highwaymen are a cost of doing business, but they never been so out for blood before."

"People are desperate," said Emony, still a little pale. "The normal rules are dead and gone. I suppose that explains us too."

"And you say there're more of you just over that ridge? Gods, if I were younger I might like to join you!"

"Bad idea," said Ulnoth. "We barely know what we're doing. We look for easy targets, wait for our chance, fight dirty then hightail it outta there. Which is all just dandy for me, but not really anything to admire."

"Ah, but there's where you're wrong," Reynal said excitedly. "It's exactly that! Why, imagine a whole army of sneak-thieves turnin' their knives against the lords and their slaves that fight their wars. The forest is their castle, the dark is their kingdom, they bend knee to no one on this earth! Ha, now there's a tale that'd put asses in every theater seat from here to Porontus."

Alessia laughed despite her dour mood. "I think you've confused us for a company of troubadours. But for our chosen targets we're no different from those we just fought off."

"Lady, to me that's all the difference in the world."

Alessia sent Dannek back to tell Corren and the others what'd happened, and decided to spend the night among the smugglers, if only to keep an eye on the child. There were about fifty of them in all, and a few of those were whole families. The next day they scouted to the outlet of the canyon and found a spot to bury their dead. Alessia led a few words of prayer over them for the repose of their souls, though technically she had no authority to do so. *Just a little heresy*, she imagined Livielle saying. *The gods won't mind.*

The bandits' corpses by contrast were tossed aside and forgotten. "Leave 'em," spat Alondo. "Dinner for wolves is all the use they are."

"What will you do now?" Alessia asked. "Certainly not keep on with your journey?"

"Of course," Reynal answered, surprised that she would ask. "What else would we do? It ain't greed, you understand. This cargo's a life's savings for some of us. We owe it to the children of those we lost to see it through. Uh." He fidgeted uncomfortably, looked away. "There's one more thing I'd ask of you. I know I've no right considerin' all you already done, but...will you be moving on from here in a hurry?"

"We're headed southward, but in no great hurry. Why, what is it?"

"You saved that boy's life, and others besides. Now we've folk alive but in no shape to travel at the pace we intend just quite yet, and *they* have family from which they'd not be parted, so...."

"You want to leave them with us," Alessia concluded.

Reynal nodded. "I feel like cack asking it, but they're safer with you than with us. We'd come back again and pick them up eventually." There was silence between them for a long time, Alessia looking off into the distance and Reynal mostly staring at his shoes. When she didn't say anything he ventured, "Well?"

"I don't know, the others would have to agree. The more we are the slower, and easier to track. It's not like your theater tale, you know. It's hard, and mean. Every day almost I feel my heart turning a little more stony."

"But you can't cut stone quite as easy," said Reynal.

"Everyone would have to contribute, understand. No freeloaders."

"Of course. They're all good, hardworking folk once they're healed up, you'll see. The children too. Some can even fight in a pinch."

"The rest will have to learn. Even the children, as you say."

Reynal nodded. "All right. Alessia, thank you again. Whatever else befalls us in this wretched war, you've a friend among the smugglers."

"Don't thank me," she replied. "I haven't done you any favors."

After hearing the tale of the bandit attack a vote was held, and the others decidedly did agree. Overnight the Heron Kings almost doubled their numbers and in the process acquired a good supply of food, clothing and other sundries from the smugglers' cargo.

Ulnoth led the dozen wounded into camp, along with a couple that had to be carried, and several children. "Just a look-see, eh?" Corren said as they filed past.

"Shut up."

Alessia brought up the rear, and when they'd all been seen to she said to Corren, "Better make space for those kids at the arrow butts. *Everyone* needs practice."

CHAPTER SEVENTEEN

Civilization

"Funny. I half expected it not to be here, after everything."

"Expected, or hoped?"

Ulnoth turned to Nandine. "What's that supposed to mean?"

"You've been moodier than usual since we got close to Plisten. Don't tell me it's 'cause of all the new faces."

"Nah," Ulnoth grunted. "Maybe 'cause of all the old ones. All bad memories, or good ones of what's gone. Maybe it was a mistake coming back here." They stood on a low cliff overlooking the village. Ulnoth had come to the spot often as a boy, and was always amazed at how small Plisten looked from here. Now it seemed even smaller. "Or maybe I been living like a heathen Marchman so long civilization scares me." They clambered down using the tall, ungrazed grass as cover more out of habit than actual need.

"Where do we go first?" asked Nan.

"There was a general store, sold mostly farm supplies. Not sure if it's still around...." He purposely avoided the taphouse barn; he wasn't sure he wanted to revisit the scene of his...what? Crime? He'd committed many since; why should that one matter?

He banged on the door to the storehouse built on the edge of the green. No answer. "Humph. No surprise there." He took his knife and slid it between the door and the frame right where the latch would be. Sure enough, at just the right spot the mechanism jiggled and the door creaked open.

The building was empty. Clean, as though it were still in use in some way, but the shelves all along the rectangular structure stood bare. "Well, there we have it. I guess—"

"Hold it! Don't. Fucking. Move." An angry woman's voice. They froze. "Turn around." They heard the swish of something slice the air.

With a knowing grin Ulnoth said, "Well, which is it? Don't fucking move or turn around?" Even as he said this he began turning, but with hands raised.

"I don't know who you rogues think you are just strollin' into town and – gods!"

"Hello, Sal."

"You...you're here!" Sally dropped the adz she'd been wielding. "And alive!"

"That one's debatable, but yeah. I'm here. Nan, you can unfreeze now."

"You look like shit," said Sally, half in shock. She reached out to touch Ulnoth, haltingly as though he were a specter that might disappear. "You're so thin! And brown as me, almost."

"I'll take that as a compliment. Listen, where's Glaston? More to the point, where's his stuff?"

"He left. Lot of folk did after the queen's men started taking everything. You're the first to come back."

"Sorry to disappoint, but I don't plan to stay. What happened? Did...did the greens punish the village? For what I did?"

"For what – oh. Oh, no! No, they didn't even miss him as far as I know. We, uh, fed the body to goats. The ones we still had. Burned the clothes. Nothing left to point to us."

Ulnoth snorted. "And here I was all fretting about...I mean, you told me about Murento."

"What happened to you? Where've you been?"

"That's a little bit of a story. Is Bed around?"

"Bed? Well, he's...." She looked away.

"Don't tell me he's dead!"

"No. But he's not well. It's his lungs again, made worse by the smoke. On bad days he can barely walk."

"Doesn't he take medicine for that?"

"If we could get hold of any. Usually comes up from 'Nocca, from the temple gardens. But not much of anything gets through these days."

"Oh. You know, I think maybe that's something we could help with."

"We?"

*   *   *

Even in his weakened state it took a fair amount of arguing to convince Bedegar to rise from his pallet. At first he would not even believe his own eyes, thinking his illness made him hallucinate Ulnoth's return. But the promises of medicine, Sally's harangues and, to be honest, the curve of Nandine's thighs won him over and he struggled, coughing and wheezing, to his feet.

"Hate to do this to you, Bed," said Ulnoth as he took one of the old man's arms about his neck to support him, "but I ain't sure it's safe to bring anyone else into Plisten."

"Still...don't understand," Bedegar mumbled. "How in...seventeen hells you find a physic? Where you been all this time, and why... not safe—"

"One thing at a time, Bed. Let's just get you there first, eh?"

"Fine, fine." He turned to Nan, who supported his other side, and managed a thin smile. "Say...you're a...pretty young thing—"

"Don't even *think* about it," said Nan sharply. Bed shut up.

*   *   *

The camp was about half a mile away amid thick growth along Cadwall's Run, not far from where Ulnoth had slipped Pharamund's recruiters. The trees were turning and the forest blazed orange in mockery of the fire-ravaged farmland. While escorting Bed at a snail's pace, Ulnoth tried to explain what'd happened. It was only when telling the tale straight out that he realized how unlikely it all sounded. When he finished Sally didn't say anything, just kind of stared at him as they walked. At last she said, "So...you're bullshitting me, right? This is all some kind of stupid joke?"

"Erm, no. I know it seems fanciful but stranger things've—"

"Stop it," said Sally with a frown. "Just stop. Don't you dare pretend you haven't heard, and this isn't some—"

"Heard *what*? We've been a bit outta earshot, if you ain't been paying attention."

They emerged into a clearing, and suddenly two men with bows strung and arrows nocked jumped out of nowhere. Sally let out a shrill yelp. "Halt!" one said firmly but without shouting.

"Calm down, Banwick, it's just us."

The man's mouth twitched. "Well, I know, but Corren said if anyone came upon—"

Ulnoth nodded. "Yes, yes, good work. One of you go scout behind us, will you?"

"Right. Verrell?" He signaled to the other man, who took off into the forest and disappeared. Ulnoth and Nan pressed on with Bedegar strung between them.

"Who was that?" asked Sally, her heart pounding from the shock as she trailed after.

"Just a couple friends. Come on, we're almost there."

It was Sally's turn not to believe her eyes. A wide network of trees had branches and planks tied and woven between them to make a rough wall. It ringed a central area sheltering about three dozen people along with tents, horses, cookfires, and even a rack of mail hauberks and weapons of both Argovani and Bergovan manufacture. In the middle a wagon was loaded high with sacks and boxes while a few people dozed beneath lean-tos slung from the sides of it. Along one end of the enclosure a row of children practiced shooting arrows at a crude effigy of a soldier complete with red foxhead badge, padded armor and helmet atop a rotten squash for a head. At the other end an older fellow hammered at something metal while a woman tended to a sniffling little girl with a skinned knee. Just outside the camp two teenagers canoodled shamelessly. And all around at regular intervals grim-faced guards stood watch. It seemed a veritable village all its own, some weird hybrid of a traveling circus camp and military expedition. "Oh gods," Sally breathed. "You're... you weren't making it up. It's you. It really is you."

"*What's* really us?"

"Ulnoth, the things you've done – they've made you famous."

"Wha— Famous? How'd that happen? We don't exactly advertise." Even as he said it he knew that wasn't true. A little eye surgery, some human graffiti, those things added up.

"When soldiers aren't killing things they drink and gossip," said Sally. "So do the free folk they rope into service. Stories of men gone missing, some turning up in pieces, shipments of goods stolen without a trace. Reds and greens both. Every one of 'em from here to Vin Gannoni's terrified they'll be next. And it was you all along."

Nan lost a little color in her cheeks. "We never figured...we just wanted a little payback, some food and fire, a place to ride out the war."

"Half those idiots think there's some kind of shape-shifting monster out there, mimicking their officers."

"It's just some stolen clothes," Ulnoth said, nodding to the racks of armor.

"Whatever it is, you've made a name for yourselves. And you're their leader?"

"Well it's...more of a cooperative thing. Speaking of which, let's get Bed over there, let Lessi have a look at 'im."

They hauled Bedegar toward the woman who was just finishing up with the little girl. "There, that's better, isn't it? Go on now, Lalaith, and be more careful." She looked up at the new faces with worry. "What's this?"

"This," said Ulnoth, "is a patient. You know, the reason you came out here in the first place? This fella's the closest I've had to a father for a long time. I owe him." He glanced at Sally. "Both of them. They took care of me...afterward."

"All right. Lay him down."

Alessia listened to a brief description of Bed's illness, then took some herbs from a clay pot. "You're lucky I was able to find this stuff – it doesn't grow much around here. Here, crush these up."

She made a soupy boiling mixture and had Bed inhale the steam. It stank, but eventually he seemed to breathe easier. "Thank you," he whispered.

"Don't mention it," said Alessia before turning to Sally and Ulnoth, who both sat hovering over Bed like mother hens. "I mean that – don't tell anyone else where we are. No offense, but I'm not sure it's a good idea bringing outsiders around here."

"Oh, believe me, it's not. You can trust us, but there are some desperate enough to sell you for a cup of beans. The queen's men have taken over most of the county, use Plisten as their own personal granary and steal whatever we don't hide. If they find out you lot are right under their noses there'll be blood aplenty. These ones are the worst. In fact they're the—" She suddenly broke off and looked away.

"What?"

"Uh...."

"What, Sal?" Ulnoth pressed. "What are they?"

Sally sighed. "They're the same crew that came through the first time, when...when they burned your farm and killed your wife and daughter." She winced in anticipation of a rage. It didn't come, and that was somehow more frightening. He just sat there.

"Where," he said softly, "are they exactly?"

"Ulnoth, don't—"

"Where. Are. They?"

"Most of them I don't know, but some are squatting in the baron's house—"

Ulnoth stood up, pointed at Bed. "Take care of him. Do whatever you have to." He began walking toward the weapon rack. "Nan! Bring me Corren and Dannek."

"But I don't understand," said Dannek when he was finally found. "I thought we were laying low for the winter."

"You thought wrong," Ulnoth growled. "One more dance around the green, then we'll be done. This one's personal. I won't force anyone, but these cocksuckers here in Plisten are getting cleaned out one way or another, even if I have to do it all by my lonesome."

Dannek fumbled with his chausses, having been rudely interrupted in his closing negotiations with Alixe, one of the smuggler girls. Beside him and trying hard to erase that image from her memory, Nan strapped on a short sword. "Just us? I'm flattered at your confidence."

"Any and all who want, but I need you two at least, and Corren if we can track him down."

"And us!" Two men Ulnoth didn't yet know approached the trio. One said, "I'm Staphenil, and this here's Gant. You folks saved our hides from those highwaymen, and—"

The other broke in excitedly. "And we figure we're healed up enough to return the favor. We been practicing!"

"All right, your funeral, though you won't really get one. Go check out a bow and quiver each. And bring knives too, as many as you can fi—"

"Ulnoth!" Corren stamped in amid the growing circle. "What in the seventeen hells do you think you're doing? We didn't agree to any new attacks!"

"This ain't a new attack, soldier boy, it's an old one I'm ending. And there's nothing among gods nor men gonna stop me. You come help if you want, or don't. But you try to interfere and I swear one of us'll end up in the dirt."

"Dammit, we're too many now for you to just go off on every ill-conceived adventure that comes along. We've young ones to care after – you want to put them in danger?"

"Wasn't my idea to bring 'em on, and no one forced 'em." Ulnoth looked across the whole of the bothersome campsite, then sighed. "I'll give you this much: we don't come back here until every one of them – however many – is crow feed. There'll be no one left to tell the tale. Happy?"

Corren snorted. "Happy? What's that? Suppose I should come along, keep you out of trouble. And *you* two...." He stabbed a finger at Staphenil and Gant. "You stay down and do exactly as you're told, or you *will* end this day in the dirt."

CHAPTER EIGHTEEN
Bad and Worse

Baron Curlew's house could only generously be called a manor. Yes, it had three rooms instead of the peasants' one, two hearths, a separate barn and a few outbuildings. But otherwise the estate differed little from the dwellings it supposedly lorded over. Curlew had worked the fields just as his serfs did, though with some indentured help and more animals. But not even minor lords were excused their annual term of service, so when Curlew rode a tired old draught horse off to war the previous spring at the count's summons, he left his household in the care of his one nominal retainer, a neighbor. And as he was far, far past his obliged term and yet to return, the worst was assumed and folk expected things to stay just about that way. They likely would have had Engwara's marauders not swept through, taken up residence there and lived off the winter larder and whatever else they could steal. Service to Her Majesty could be decidedly profitable, it seemed.

The sun was just setting when six shades crept upon Curlew's estate. They made their way up the slope along a rotted fence that separated a long-fallow millet field from grazeland devoid of cattle and shrieking with crickets. The whole place reeked of neglect, and of things more sinister. Harsh laughter erupted from the building.

"Stay low," Ulnoth whispered, not sure if there would be any sentries. "No windows on this side, but keep near the ground anyhow." Smoke billowed from one chimney, black against the midnight blue sky. Far above, the Antabolid meteor shower presaged the coming of winter.

Corren knelt next to Ulnoth. "How do you wanna go in? Wait 'til they're asleep?"

"Nah," Ulnoth replied, "lights out'd put bows at a disadvantage, wouldn't it? Fair fight's currently the last thing on my mind."

"What, you've been paying attention to my lectures?"

Ulnoth grinned. "Much as I can stand. You smell that? I been in there a few times – place has a separate kitchen over the other side with a window. Whoever's cooking won't be too much on guard, ken'ee? I say we go in there, take 'em down fast then move on."

"What if it's just landbound they got slaving for 'em?" asked Nan.

"Then they'd better not be wearing green."

They circled round the low grounds, keeping below the tops of the wild grass and behind outbuildings. Something had been propped up along the pathway to the front entrance, but the sneaking, snaking train couldn't figure out what until they passed close. They smelled it before they saw it, of course. They crouched around the grotesque display, Staphenil and Gant open-mouthed.

"Lupold," said Ulnoth bitterly. "Has to be. A good old fellow." The corpse had been strung up on a crossbeam – no, not the corpse. The last bit of light showed that the caretaker of his baron's estate had been nailed up, quite alive most probably, and left to die of exposure and blood loss, a warning to others perhaps. "I'll pay 'em back as best I can, Lupold. For as long as I can."

Flickering lamplight poured from the window on the kitchen side. The air shimmered where heat escaped. Ulnoth and Dannek led them two by two with the newcomers at the rear right up to the edge of the house. They heard a hard, slow repeating thud, a low male voice with an Argovani accent, and a nervous female one. The smell of meat roasting.

"I think that's enough garlic," said the female voice.

"Shut up, I know my business. You ain't put enough in last time, I told you."

"It's already burning my eyes!"

"Well, you ain't eatin' it, is ya? Now shut your cockhole and add more garlic!" *Thud.*

Pressed against the outer wall, Ulnoth craned his neck to risk a peek inside. One man, chopping at what he hoped was a pork shoulder, and a woman tending a cauldron with her back to the window. Ulnoth raised a hand toward the others behind him. *Wait,* he mouthed. He unslung his bow from his shoulder and notched an arrow.

"Can I at least hold some back for my little one? She's so hungry."

"We'll see, depends on how well you perform tonight. Now shut up."

Thud. Another chop at the meat. *Gods but it smells good*, Ulnoth thought. Except for the too-much garlic.

"How many must I 'perform' for this time?"

Thud.

Ulnoth had the rhythm now. At the right instant he stood, bow drawn. Just as the cleaver fell to chop again Ulnoth loosed. *Thwung.* At such close range the greasy, gap-toothed man didn't even get the chance to cry out at the arrow that nailed his skull to the far wall. He convulsed slightly but so well-timed was the shot that the woman didn't trouble to look up from her cauldron.

"What," she said, "not even going to answer me now? Nice—"

Ulnoth leaped through the window, followed by Dannek and Nan. While the two smugglers scrambled in last, Ulnoth reached around and clamped a hand over the woman's mouth. She started to struggle.

"*Ssh!*" He turned her head so she could see the dying man, and her eyes bulged with fright. "You see that? Lest you want the like you keep quiet!"

"Hey, what's all the—"

Thwung-slap! Ulnoth looked up to see another marauder entering the kitchen also sprout a shaft, this one in his belly. Corren jumped forward and cut the soldier's throat before he could scream, then lowered the body to the floor as blood poured over his hands and into the rushes. Ulnoth glanced back over his shoulder to see Dannek with another arrow already drawn. "Thanks," he breathed.

"Gods' *tits*," said Gant, nearly fainting at the easy violence.

"Shut up." Ulnoth looked back at the woman he held fast. "Where you from?"

"E-Eikenstead," she said, quivering, when Ulnoth relaxed his hand slightly. "P-past Lenocca. Please, they made me, they took me with—"

"You see that window? Go out it, start running and don't stop 'til you hit Eikenstead again."

"But, my daughter! They have her chained up in the barn, said they'll cut her up and roast her if I don't—"

"Oh for...."

"Go to the barn," said Nan. "Stay there. With luck all this'll be over in a bit."

"But who are—"

"Go!"

The next room was the main hall where Curlew would receive guests on the rare occasion that he had any. There were three or four reavers lounging about with another moving to investigate the racket coming from the kitchen. Corren surprised that one with a sword swipe, and while they struggled Nan loosed an arrow at another. The shot bounced off a helmet and knocked out a tiny lamp hanging on the far wall. The room went darker, lit only by a smoldering hearth at the far end. There was the sound of yelling, and a heavy door slamming shut. Ulnoth leaped at one of the shadows, and Dannek's shot was rewarded with a pained scream. Staphenil tripped over something and he crashed to the floor. A drunk and almost unconscious reaver mumbled something, and Staphenil kicked away frantically while the shape began to crawl. Gant took his knife and fell onto it, hesitant at first, then in a frenzy of stabs.

Corren nearly had his man pinned, and shouted, "Shoot!" to any who had the means.

Nan notched another arrow from across the room. But the reaver struggled, and in the dark it was hard to tell who was whom. "Which one?" The two shadows twisted and tumbled. Just as she was about to make her choice a great mass fell atop her from above. One end of the hall included a small loft from which a marauder had watched the attack. He dropped onto Nan with blade drawn. She tried to scream when cold iron bit into her face.

Dannek took the shot. One of the shadows jerked, then stilled. Ulnoth finished pounding a man's face into offal when yet another dropped from the loft onto his back to strangle him. Staphenil came up from behind and tried to drag his knife across the man's throat, but the blade was in terrible need of sharpening and the reaver managed to pull it away, spin around, and twist Staphenil's wrist backward to force the smuggler to stab his own chest. He inhaled sharply and barely had time to see Ulnoth turn and gut the reaver before he fell to the floor in a sloshing pool of his own blood. "Oh shit," he said, over and over. "Shit...oh...."

Dannek and Gant wrestled the last marauder off of Nan before he could do any more damage and Gant went mad with his blade again. Dannek relit the lamp from the dying embers of the hearth to reveal the full measure of what they'd wrought in the space of a minute: bodies everywhere, blood spreading on the floor. Corren lay against a wall breathing heavily and eyeing the body before him. Nan sat with a hand to her face over a long, ugly slash. Staphenil lay in a fetal position as the last of his life drained out, his first and last raid concluded.

Gant knelt over Staphenil's body as the madness passed. "I'm sorry," said Ulnoth. "Shouldn't have let you two come along. Fool likely saved my life. For what, I dunno." Ulnoth's teeth gnashed in anger, mostly at himself.

"We...volunteered," said Gant shakily. "Our choice. Coulda been me. Next time...might be." He hung his head.

"How about you?" Corren asked Nan. "Is it bad?"

"Ish not good," she replied, talking out of one side of her mouth while the other bled.

Dannek unwrapped a woolen winding from about one of his chausses and pressed it against Nan's wound. "Here. We need to get you back home."

"We're not done yet," said Ulnoth. He nodded at the locked door. "The bedchamber. There's more in there, I saw 'em scramble. No windows on that side. Leave if you want. I ain't until I get every last one."

Corren shook his head. "Can't leave this half done. Can we force the door?"

"Nah, it's Qassorian oak. Just about the only thing o' value old Curlew owned. Steel locks."

"What then?"

Ulnoth looked around the manor. He walked over to the hearth where a heavy iron key hung from a peg. He took it and handed it to Gant. "Check for that woman and her kid."

"Right."

"Baron Curlew," said Ulnoth, "weren't no filthy rich highborn. Just a bit above the rest of us. His whole life was bound up in this land, worked it hard as we did ours. He left more 'n a year ago and ain't returned. Way I figure it that means he's in the dirt somewhere. Wife's dead of pneumony, sons killed early in the war. So if the choice is to give this place over to the greens or reds...I say we burn it, like they did for me. Burn them bastards out, and cut 'em down." He pulled an old, cheap-looking tapestry from the plastered wall and tossed it into the hearth. Flames and smoke roiled out, and soon the fabric was alight.

They gathered up Staphenil's body, spread the flames as best they could and shut the windows, then filed out of the manor through the front door. Gant came running up holding a familiar-looking cleaver. "Gone," he said. "I checked all the buildings. All I found was this, and a smashed chain."

"Didn't want to wait around eh?" grunted Ulnoth. "I don't blame her."

They waited. The night wore on and the fire enveloped the manor. When it was almost obscured by smoke they heard screams and pounding at the walls of the bedchamber. At last the first reaver came stumbling out the front door. He got barely three paces before Dannek put an arrow in him. Another soon followed, this one tripping over the body of the first. It was almost funny, though no one felt like laughing.

As the manor began to collapse, the last of their enemies crawled out on hands and knees. Dannek raised his bow again to shoot him down, then halted. "Gods damn it...." It was a boy, younger than himself. "Um...."

The boy shambled to his feet, tears and smoke in his eyes, and began to run when he saw the five killers in front of him. Corren sprinted after him. Dannek loosed an arrow across his path, causing the boy to trip to the side. Corren caught him in a tight grip, dragged him back kicking and struggling, and dumped him inside the circle formed by the others.

"What is this?" Ulnoth muttered. "Bring 'im here." By the stinging firelight the captive looked up into the hundred different notions reflected in their faces. "Queen's all out of men, I guess." That reminded him of something, but he couldn't quite recall what. "Where'd you come from, boy?"

"Uh...." The lad trembled, seeming to set the green serpent

sewn onto his chest rattling. "M-Murento...I was born in Mur—"

"No. I mean your little crew we just toasted. Where were you based?"

"Oh. 'N-'Nocca. By the old citadel. P-please. I only joined up 'cause there weren't no other work—"

"No uvver work!" Nandine pulled a hand away from her wound and slapped the boy, leaving a streak of her own blood across his face. "No uvver work but pillish and murder? You lil shickenshit! I'll—"

"All right," said Corren calmly. He spun the boy around to face him. "Are there any more of you here? Anyone away who might return soon? Don't you dare lie to me now."

The boy shook his head. "J-just us. Relief s'posed to come next week, a hundred men. That's what Sarge Morvyn says."

"And where is Sarge Morvyn?"

The boy pointed to one of the corpses piled near the doorway. "That's all I know, I swear!"

Nan made a disgusted sound. "He shwearsh. Well vhen...."

Corren patted the lad on the shoulder. "That's good." He looked to Ulnoth. "What do you think?"

"I think we prob'ly have enough time to get out of town before a hundred cocksuckers show up." He glanced once at the boy. "Assuming a *clean* head start." Corren seemed to take his meaning with a shudder. Ulnoth looked to the others and read their grim silence as...what? Assent? *No one left to tell the tale.*

Corren nodded once with grinding teeth, then raised the boy to his feet, careful to keep his attention. "Now listen to me very closely, son. Is there anything else you can tell me? Anything at all?"

"Um." He frowned. "Don't think so. Sarge said he knows the locals is hidin' food, jus' ain't figured where yet. Said if I found out I could have first go at the next girl we took – er, um...that's it."

"Good," said Corren, "very good. You've done...very well."

The boy's expression eased just a little. "Eh? Thanks. Listen, if you folks could just see your way to letting me g—"

It was mercifully done, no denying that. The kid never saw nor heard the blow that pierced upward through the base of his skull and deep into his brain in one stroke. His face registered a moment of surprise, but that was all. Two seconds later he dropped to the ground a lifeless husk. Ulnoth braced his boot between the boy's shoulder blades and yanked, and the sword came out with a sucking sound. He handed it back to Nandine, who had tears in her eyes despite her flare of temper.

"Saints," said Dannek, shaking. "I thought we were the good guys."

Ulnoth shook his head. "Ain't no good left. Just bad and worse."

"It's done," said Gant. "Let's get out of this cursed place." He hoisted Staphenil's body over his shoulder, not really sure what he intended on doing with it.

"You all go ahead," said Ulnoth. "There's one more thing I need to do."

★ ★ ★

"Halt! Who goes—"

"Out of my way, Banwick," said Gant, swiping the man aside with a swing of Staphenil's limp limbs. The camp was nearly dark, with only a single fire alight to guide them home.

"Oh shit. What happened?"

"What haffened," Nan grumbled when Alessia asked the same minutes later, "ish I misshed an easy shot and screwed our shances for shome nishe clean kills!"

"Hold still. You can't blame yourself," said Alessia later as she examined Nan's face and readied her stitching needle. "We're none of us perfect, even with all the training Corren puts us through."

"Tell that to Shtaphenil."

Alessia gently pulled away the improvised bandages. "It's not near your mouth – if you must speak you can do so normally. Listen to me, if you drown yourself in guilt you'll become just like Ulnoth. And one of him is quite enough."

"That'sh another thing," Nan said gingerly. "Maybe it was a mistake to go with him, I dunno. But there wasn't any stopping him. He's going to get us killed if he keeps up these little crusades. What if he's captured?"

"I know. I've been talking to Corren, some of the others. It's time to put a stop to that." Alessia waved Emony over to assist her. "Now hold still, I only need to stitch in one place, but it's going to hurt like a firedrake's cock." Emony wrapped her surprisingly strong arms around Nan's head and clamped it in place.

"Such language from a good sister, how scanda— *Aaargh!*" Nan screwed her eyes shut as Alessia's needle dug into her cheek with gut thread dragging behind. It hurt far more than the knife that'd made the cut, for that at least had been quick. Ten times she endured it, for ten stitches. When it was over Emony handed Nan a cup of herb-infused brandy that she gulped down.

"Everybody complains that I keep the liquor locked up, until they actually need it," Alessia remarked.

"Does that mean there's more?" Nan lay back on the cot while a new poulticed bandage was applied.

"No. We're running low on everything. I was hoping the village could help with that...."

"They have even less than we do," said Corren as he sat down next to the cot. "All carried off by those jackals. How is she?"

"She'll have quite the battle scar, no doubt of that," replied Alessia, "but otherwise she should be fine assuming I can keep infection away."

"There goes my career as a high-class whore," Nan said sleepily. "Sorry, Duelleigh!"

"We'll have to move out again soon," said Corren. "More of them are coming – too many even for Ulnoth to take on."

Alessia frowned. "Already? How do you know? You took a prisoner?"

Corren clenched his jaw, glanced at Nan.

"No," Nan drawled seconds before dropping into a dreamless sleep. "No prisoners."

★   ★   ★

When the sun next rose over Plisten the wreckage of Baron Curlew's estate told a gruesome tale, and the lingering smoke and stench of death drew gawking villagers. But before the blackened rubble of the manor or bodies clustered near what had been the doorway, the greatest horror greeted visitors first: on the path leading to this ruin the raised cross now held not old Lupold, but a young boy with a green serpent sewn onto his chest and a surprised stare on his face.

CHAPTER NINETEEN

Moving On

Jerk! "Not again," Vinian groaned. Of course again. Every night for the last two seasons it was the same. Just as she was about to drift into a troubled simulacrum of sleep, right at that moment, a spasm at the base of her skull shocked her back awake. She would lie there in frustration until feeling tired again, begin to drop off, then – *jerk!* It could go on for hours, and the next day her mind was scrambled into worthlessness. The five or six doctors and physics she'd seen were baffled, resorting to idiotic pronouncements like 'stress' or 'exhaustion'. *Useless, the lot of them.* Nothing helped, except....

She rolled over and fumbled for the hard edge of the table beside the bed, clawed for the bottle on the bottom shelf, thumbed open the stopper and lifted it to her mouth. *Not even troubling with a glass now.* The rush of brandy warmed her throat. The good, strong Cynuvik stuff it was, not that watered swill sold down in the city. A few gulps and she knew she'd sleep. She wouldn't breathe properly, but she'd sleep. *A Chthonus's bargain made in quiet desperation in the dark. How appropriate.*

That was the plan, anyway. She awoke with a gasp, a drowning sensation, and only gradually became aware that someone was shaking her.

"Gyargh! Get off! What is it?"

"Sorry, ma'am," said the agent as her head swam to the surface of the waking world. "But it's time to go."

"Go? Where—? Oh, yes." *My assignment,* she remembered, half-conscious. *As if I didn't know full well that Engwara's trying to push me out of the way. Too much baseborn power too close for comfort.*

Vinian rolled over and clawed her way out of bed and into a nightrobe. For security she'd ordered that the exact time and manner of her departure be kept undetermined until the very last minute. She hoisted a travel pack that she'd prepared in advance and followed the agent down a winding stair, clinging to the rope strung along the inner wall for balance. "You're to depart from the lower service dock, ma'am," said the agent, holding a lantern out in front of him. A hallway, another set of stairs.

As they descended, the other matter stealing her sleep niggled at her mind. Following Carthagne's bizarre departure from meeting with Engwara, Vinian had given orders to her agents in time for him to be observed running, such as he was able, back to his docked ship. Then at dusk an unknown man in foreign dress disembarked, hired a fast horse and bribed his way through the city gate. "But to where," Vinian mumbled to herself, "and why?"

"Ma'am?"

"Never mind."

The agent stepped aside just before reaching the dock, not keen to be in the irritated spymistress's presence any longer than necessary. Vinian pulled the robe tight around her as a cold blast from across the harbor wafted upward.

"You can go. This never happened." The agent nodded, then scampered back up the stairs while Vinian pressed forward. In the water floated a tiny boat that held one person…and something else.

"Captain Arnaud, what an unpleasant unsurprise."

"My dear, you wound me. I be come all this way for to collect a special package at such ungodly hour and not even a kiss you have for me?"

"Some people say I keep a scorpion stored up my skirts. You can have a kiss from that if you like."

The stout, goateed smuggler laughed. "I think your kiss is be more deadly. Alas must I pine for another day."

"Uh-huh." Vinian yawned. "What do you know of this special package?"

"Ah," Arnaud answered, "a most interesting one. Told to bring concealment of considerable size, Arnaud was." He pointed to the hulking pile in the boat behind him. It was a great sack of brown burlap, big enough to hold a person.

"I hope that's not a comment on my figure," said Vinian. "I'm the package. Am I supposed to get into that thing?"

"Unless you be preferring otherwise," the pirate said with a shrug.

"I do be. But better safe than seen. Do we have far to go?"

"My ship awaits, not far."

"And then?"

"Upriver, to Lenocca by and deliver this exquisite package to a certain encampment there. Short journey, but safer than going over disputed land, yes?"

Vinian chuckled. "Why, how can it be disputed? Doesn't Her Majesty's serene domain extend over all the whole of the Argovani peninsula?"

"Ha! Your neverending war squeezes all profit from my humble business venture, yet none of the risk. You, my dear, may be the only customer left to me."

"And haven't I always paid you handsomely? I, uh, don't seem to have much gold on me at the moment, being as it is the middle of the godsdamned night."

"No need, my scorpioness. Arnaud keeps the tally, all up in here." He laughed and tapped the feathered cap atop his head. "Shall we off then?" Vinian tossed the torch into the water, tiptoed into the boat and into the sack while it drifted back into the harbor toward an unseen ship and away from Carsolan. *I forgot my brandy bottle*, she thought. She didn't bother trying to get any more sleep.

★　★　★

Alessia woke to sharp cracks of wood against wood, and a brief investigation revealed the source: two children playing at swordfighting with practice dowels that Corren had made or stolen from somewhere. They giggled and danced about the camp while whipping the rods at each other. For some reason the sight filled Alessia with fury, and she tromped over to the pair and wrenched the dowels out of their hands.

"Stop that!"

"Why?" asked Lalaith, a hurt and confused look on her face.

"Why? Because...because. These are for practice. If you want to train, do it properly. Weapons aren't toys."

Embarrassed at her sudden temper, she returned the dowels to their rack and went to check on her patients, passing by a newly turned mound that was Staphenil's final resting place. Nan still slept, while Bedegar sat poking at a bowl of gruel. "How are you doing then, Bed?"

The old man looked up and smiled. "Much better. Breathing much better. My dear, you're a godsend. All of us, this place – it's nothing short of amazing."

"What's amazing is that any of us are still alive. We...we lost someone last night."

"I heard. I'm sorry. But you cleared them reavers out of the estate sure enough. The whole village will owe you for that."

"For all the good it did. More are coming. The queen means to take this valley once and for all before winter it seems. We can't stay – we're too many to hide so close."

"Where will you go then?"

Alessia shook her head. "No idea. Have you seen Ulnoth?"

"Ayup." He pointed his spoon behind him. Near the boundary of the camp Ulnoth and Sally sat talking in hushed tones. Neither looked very happy. "Presented without comment."

"Hmm. Bed, before all this happened were he and Sally...?"

"Aye. I, uh, get the impression that's all over with now. Too much pain I guess."

Alessia purposely made noise as she approached so as not to seem to be eavesdropping. "Good morning."

Sally stood. "Good morning. Alessia, thank you for all you've done for us. All of us. You can trust me and Bed to keep your secret—"

"Great. Sally, can I talk to Ulnoth alone for a bit?"

Ulnoth scowled. "Woah, hold on there. Anything you need to say you can say in front of her."

"All right. You won't like it though."

"I never do. Lay it on me," he answered with a sigh.

"We – the others, I mean – have decided it's too dangerous to continue your raids, especially bloody spectacles like last night."

"If this is about that fellow Staphenil—"

"It's about everyone. Our only hope now's to disappear

completely, live in secret as best we can until this damned war is over. We'll defend ourselves, buy or steal what we need to live, but your days of serial killing are over with. Otherwise…you're out. Expelled from the Heron Kings."

Ulnoth glared at her for several moments, then looked at Sally. "Disappear into Faerie, isn't that what you wanted?" He turned back to Alessia. "Expelled, just like that. You all just up and decided. Ain't that peachy. You ever consider that just maybe all my serial killing's what's keeping us breathing in the first place?"

"I know. But it's also making it harder to keep hidden – we've a reputation that we can't afford. We need to be a scalpel now, not a broadaxe. If you want to keep a place with us you'll have to learn this."

"You're pissing all over our agreement," he growled.

Alessia felt a hot rush flood her cheeks. "Well now, I think we both know you've been taking some *creative* liberties with that deal. Don't we?"

"I killed a boy last night. Little more 'n a child. I jammed a sword into his noggin just to keep him from blabbing to anyone about us. Do you really think there's any coming back from that?"

Alessia wiped away a tear. "Try," she said, then turned away.

"Wait!" Sally ran to catch up after taking some time to make the decision to do so. "He's not that bad, you know. He's…he was a good man."

"Maybe he was," said Alessia without turning around. "Though I'm not so sure his wife would've agreed." She regretted the words almost before they left her lips.

Sally paused for a moment. "I guess maybe I deserved that. So what, is he your fella now or something?"

"What? No."

"That handsome sandcrab then?"

Alessia felt her patience boiling away. "No."

"Too bad. You could have your pick, you know. What are you, twenty at least? And not married yet?"

Alessia stopped walking and turned to Sally with a heavy, overdramatic sigh that said, *You're prying and you know it.* "Until lately I was a Polytheon novice. If you must know my only experience with men was just after I left – a disgusting pig crawling all over me in the night insisting on 'jus' a tumble'."

"Yech! It's like that all over now. Lots of places, people are no better than animals."

Alessia raised an eyebrow. "Lots of places they're worse."

"I guess. I'm sorry that happened to you."

"Better to be sorry for that bastard got an arrow shoved through his face."

Sally clapped a hand over her mouth to suppress a laugh. "Ah. You sure don't talk like no novice."

"Was there something you wanted?"

Sally nodded. "Lemme join up, come with you."

"Sally...."

"No, listen. I'm smart, can do all sorts of work. I'm strong and fit from churning good men into adulterers...I can learn to fight."

"What about Plisten? You won't mind leaving it?"

"I've got nothing here. I'm no landbound. Born on the wrong side of the linens, they say. What's two more people anyway?"

"Two?"

"Bed's going to need your medicine for a while yet, and no one in the village can care for him half so well as you and I can."

Alessia furrowed her brow in annoyance, remembering Ulnoth's words. *This is what you left the temple to do, isn't it?* It seemed so naïve now, yet perhaps never more necessary. "You put this whole argument together in advance, didn't you?"

Sally smiled. "I had a long night to think about it."

"I'm not sure. It's already hard taking on so many as we have now...."

"I can offer something else, too."

★   ★   ★

A shaft of yellow appeared in the gloom accompanied by the scrape of wood on metal.

"I knew it!" Ulnoth and Corren flanked Sally as she slid open the hidden floor panel of the supposedly empty storehouse. About twenty of Plisten's remaining population gathered outside, curious about this new, hardened Ulnoth that'd returned to them, and his shadowy friends that had something to do with the massacre at the baron's manor.

"Best place to hide's the first place they'd look," said Sally with a shrug. It was the same basic notion as Ludrig's taphouse: a cellar dug underneath the building held grain, roots, herbs, salt, potted meat and what other supplies they'd been able to lay in without being noticed by the queen's predators. "We started stashing it after things got really bad."

"I never knew about this," Ulnoth said, "and I lived in Plisten all my life."

"Sure," Sally replied, "but how long did you spend in Glaston's bed?" She laughed, knowing Ulnoth couldn't tell if she was being serious.

"It's a good haul," said Corren. "But I don't think Alessia would hold with us looting the place."

"Everybody contributes what they can, and we all have shares. Me, Bed, we even set a portion aside for you, Ulnoth, in case you came back."

"I appreciate that," he said.

"And a part for the baron and his household in expectation of... well, I guess that wasn't necessary. But after what you all did I'd say it's fair to turn that over to you. Add in our three shares, and it's not much but it's not nothing neither."

"All right," Corren said, "if that's the way of it we'll take what you'll give. We haven't the luxury of pride right now." He turned to the crowd outside. "The rest of you – this sit well with you all?" There was a smattering of shy nods, a few grunts. They mostly seemed too nervous to dare oppose. "Then do yourselves a favor and forget you ever saw us. If either the reds or the greens get word we've been through here they'll tear you apart to find us. That's no threat from me, just a warning."

"Where'll you go?" asked Ludrig.

"Best if you don't know," Corren answered. "Don't look for us – you won't find anything except an arrow in the dark."

"Will you ever come back?"

Ulnoth looked out across the sleepy, vulnerable village and knew that he wouldn't. "The fellow you knew's dead. Killed along with – with Athewen and Lisette." It was the first time he'd spoken their names aloud since screaming them into that horrible night. "No place here for what's left. Don't look for us."

CHAPTER TWENTY
Found in Translation

Six days after lighting out from Carsolan, a Thazovi mercenary with very explicit instructions left the last of Engwara's forces behind. They'd been easy to evade. Pharamund's still lay ahead, but he expected they would pose no great challenge either. After that it was a scrabble over the mountains, a few days in the desert...figure three weeks to Sarpoor in all. But first things first.

He dismounted and led his dappled gray mare into the brush, along a path a trapper outside Leńocca claimed would take a day off his journey. It was a well-worn trail, but not one that exhibited the signature abuses of an army's march. After an hour the light began to fade and the path grew less clear. The soft trickle of water advertised a good place to stop for the night, and while he was hitching the horse by the stream a sharp crack echoed from some not-too-distant place. The mercenary looked up and peered through the trees, scanning for movement. He could just make out a doe browsing in a tiny clearing. Stomach suddenly rumbling, he tore after it, trusting his exquisite sense of direction to lead him back again.

The doe leaped lightly over some fallen branches, gaining some distance. The mercenary tried to run faster, but he wasn't as young as he used to be. So intent on his prey was he that when something emerged from the mess of fallen leaves before him, he hadn't the chance to dodge it. His feet went out from under him and he went tumbling into the underbrush.

As he shuffled to his feet a bolt of panic shot through him. It was a young man, dirty and shaggy and clad in the same style tunic issued to the queen's sloggers. They'd followed and ambushed him somehow. The man held a bow and had a sword at his waist and regarded the mercenary with a mix of curiosity and anger. The mercenary, though armed only with a knife, dove at his stalker while hurling a string of invectives in his native tongue.

The youth jumped back, but not in time to avoid a swipe of the knife that sliced his tunic and left a shallow scratch across his belly. "Gah!" he yelled. "What the—?"

The mercenary attacked again and again, giving the surprised young man no chance to draw his sword or bow. Backing away further and further, he tripped over a log and landed on his rear. The mercenary stood over him to deliver the final strike. He flipped the knife to a downward grip, raised it high. But before it could fall he jerked, then fell atop his victim.

*　　*　　*

"And then he just came at me," Allard said. "Crander came to the rescue just in time." Allard lifted his tunic to supply the red scratch along his belly as illustration.

They were two days gone from Plisten, into the hills northeast, and the hours of tough walking had halted early. Alessia divided her attention between listening to the story and her latest round of barbering, but now dropped her scissors and paced around the mare with its rider's body draped over her back like a traveling rug merchant's wares. "And you've no idea who he is?"

"Nah, but I think he was after the same deer as us," Crander replied. "Unless…." He glanced at Allard's tunic. "Maybe he thought you were one of the greens?"

"But I tore the badge off! Idiot." The strange man wore weathered but quality traveling clothes, good boots. His blond-and-gray hair was cut short on the sides and left long in the middle. "Not from around here, looks like."

The dead man had drawn a small crowd now, and Corren even halted the staff drills he'd been running to come see. He noted the hairstyle. "No indeed. Thazovi. Hired man by the look. Scout maybe? Courier?"

Allard produced a purse he'd taken off the body. "He was worth something, certain. Had this. A lot of these coins aren't 'Vani nor Bergovan."

"And this," Corren added, pulling something out of the saddlebag. A red leather packet, folded and sealed against wear and weather. "What do you make of it?" He handed the packet to Alessia, who opened it to reveal a single page inside. "That writing...."

She scanned the paper and its spidery, flowing script running from the top of the page to the bottom. "It's Bhasan."

"Bhasans," spat Crander. "Those ruddy busybodies are always sticking their hooked noses where they're not wanted."

"I picked up a little Bhasan when I was young, never could read any. Can you?" asked Corren.

"No. I learned some of the letters as an acolyte but not the language...." She held the document closer to the firelight, mindful of how much more easily paper burned compared to parchment or vellum.

Alessia squinted, strained to make out the lines. They were not written in a steady hand. "*Hash...mekhvot daqla...pellovastolani quath... rtabrznes....*"

"Wait, what was that last word?"

Alessia blinked. "Umm, *rtabrz—*"

"Artabarzanes."

"You think this is something to do with the Bhasan emperor?" asked Crander.

Corren shrugged. "Not necessarily. Official letters coming through Fort Nostrado had 'Gods Save His Grace King Pharamund' somewhere between the beginning or end and were nothing to do with the bastard. Read on."

The dead Thazovi was forgotten now, and the crowd encircled Alessia and Corren as they tried to decipher the exotic document. "Gimme some space," said Alessia. "It's hard to...yes, this is the letter for...*hhezmet shafla kenitya zesheen vahn angar-u-wa zethisht... lashkeef vahn toricos.* That's the end of that line."

Corren frowned. "*Vahn* is a word for a highborn leader. The Bhasan name for this whole peninsula is 'Western Kingdom'. *Barg-o-Vahnii.*"

"These words after that – *angar-u-wa*. Could that be Engwara?"

"A spy," Crander said, "on his way back to court in Sarpoor. He must've thought we'd winkled him out. But wouldn't it be safer just to take a ship?"

Corren shook his head. "Engwara's got the whole southern coast blockaded. This fellow had something to hide."

Sally nudged her way to the center of the circle, newly dressed in her 'men's clothes' like some other women of the band. "Does it make any mention of Pharamund? If it talks of plans, troop marches or something, maybe we can better avoid them."

"Um," said Alessia, "let me see. It's been a while, you know. Not much call for Bhasan outside herbalist catalogs...." She ran her finger down and up the script, looking for something that might approximate the sound of the Bergovan king's name. "This maybe? *Fa-ram-khunt*. It says *geh ixtaml nequuthe vahn fa-ram-khunt—*"

"That *cunt* part sounds about right," said someone in the crowd, producing laughter.

Corren wasn't laughing. "*Ixtaml*? Are you sure that's the word?"

Alessia looked again, nodded. "Yes, it's these two characters here. Why?"

"I sure as hells know that word. When the Bhasans sealed off Vindis after the Gray Plague hit, them that spoke the tongue wailed it across the walls, screaming themselves hoarse until the plague took them. '*Tlaf, tlaf, ixtaml'a tal?*' Why, oh why have you betrayed us?"

"What are you saying? That someone intends to betray Pharamund?"

"Or already has," said Corren with another shrug. "The tense is ambiguous without context."

"That's no news," said Sally. "Lords switch allegiances like partners at a barn dance."

Crander shifted his feet nervously, jerking a thumb back at the cold body. "But that Thazovi was keen to kill Allard. Panicked when he saw him. I'd say he was desperate to deliver this. There's something more to it I think."

"We need to get a proper translation of this," said Alessia, frustrated.

"But who do you know that's fluent in Bhasan?"

Alessia set her jaw in anticipation of an argument. "The nearest? That'd probably be a temple father...in Lenocca."

★　★　★

"Lenocca!" Ulnoth nearly dropped the sack of beans he carried. "And here I thought I was the crazy one. You didn't maybe notice that roughly, oh, *all* our problems are coming from that general direction these days? About the most damn fool thing I ever heard of."

"The fighting's moved further up the valley. When I make it there—"

"*If* you make it you're a mouse in a snake pit."

"But—"

"All to translate some mail ain't got nothing to do with—"

"Stop interrupting me!" Alessia eyed the sack with suspicion. "Where'd you get that, anyway?"

Gant held up another like it. "Donation to the cause," he said with a grin, "from a cart what mysteriously broke a wheel on a divot in the road. Bad luck, that. Only kind I believe in."

Alessia sighed. "Dammit...."

"Calm down," said Ulnoth. "Tail end of a private supply train contracted to the greens. Nobody even got hurt, just a fright's all. 'Course, once Dannek gets to lighting his farts after some o' these—"

"Fine, fine. I guess that's progress. Anyway, Lenocca. I'm going. Something tells me it could be important. You've been to the city?"

Ulnoth nodded. "To the market fair. You want me to draw you a map? It's just a straight shot along the river—"

"I want you to come with me."

"Well, I was wrong. *That's* the most damn fool thing I ever heard of."

"If I go alone and get killed, you'll have to take care of all our people by yourself. Can you set a bone or bring down fever? And you'll have to deal with Corren without my expert mediation...."

"That's weak, Lessi, even for you. Why should I—"

"Please?"

That took Ulnoth off guard. Commands, arguments, cajoling – all these he was used to. He glared at her and chewed his lip as though she'd used an unfair move in a castra match. "Some days I really hate you, you know that?"

"Thank you," Alessia said simply.

"But there's something I need you to make for me first."

$$\star \quad \star \quad \star$$

"Wait, I'm coming too!" Nandine came jogging up to meet the horses as Alessia and Ulnoth made ready to depart. Her face still bore the grotesque slash, stitched and bound over with linen but no longer bloody.

"No, Nan," said Alessia, "you're still healing. Getting there, but I don't want to risk reopening the wound."

"But—"

"I've left Emony my instruments – she knows what to do to keep it clean, and to take out the stitches when it's time. Listen to her."

Ulnoth screwed up his face in irritation. "Wait, didn't you just tell me that—"

"I lied. But you're already all saddled up, so let's go."

"Some days I *really* hate you...."

Corren handed Alessia her careworn rucksack, the strange letter hidden under clothing at the bottom. "Stay off the roads, out of sight for two days at least. After that it's one more to the city. Should be undisputed territory by then."

"We'll hurry back as soon as we can. Don't be too hard to find."

Corren smiled. "No worries, we'll find you. Expect us no further north than, say, Firleaf Ford."

Firleaf. She'd avoided going near the place in fact and in thought for fear of what they'd find there. Or not find. "All right," she said. "May the gods light both our paths."

Corren nodded. "And darken our enemy's."

CHAPTER TWENTY-ONE

On the Town

When the wind died down and the swirling fury of frosted leaves settled, Lenocca lay splayed out before them like a murder victim in the street. The pair gazed down on what was left of the city from above, where the highway began its steep descent. Alessia imagined that in kinder days the view may've been picturesque, breathtaking even: rows of houses and guildhalls and taverns of red brick and gray slate arrayed along the arrowhead of land formed by the converging rivers whose waters burned with sunglint. Markets and stalls crammed between them, fairs where merchants, thieves and whores alike plied their trades. Wharves and boats all askitter with souls beneath a dozen solid bridges where a legion of pilgrims flowed to and from the temple citadel that dominated all from the center. Once, it may have been so.

All that life and vigor was gone. Now the bridges were all but collapsed, the buildings reduced to rubble, piled together in pathetic attempts at ordering chaos while here and there the skeleton of a tower or steeple hinted at former grandeur. Refuse floated in the fouled waters, forming little islands of filth that not even the pigeons cared to plunder. Vast swathes of ash mud clogged the streets, and if you looked closely you could still see movement in them. Solitary figures, picking their way over the garbage looking for who knows what while others looked on as they jealously guarded their own patches of nothing. But it was the silence of such a great place that unnerved Alessia the most. How many had called it home? Where had they all gone? She shivered.

"Yup," said Ulnoth, "that just about sums it up." From their vantage point they could see the temple alone remained untouched, its wall a barely visible ring of gray outlining the ugly complex that

had once been a castle. "At least we won't have to ask directions –
it's just about the only thing still standing."

"I don't think there's anybody left to ask," said Alessia, wondering
how she could still be shocked after all they'd seen and done. "Except
for *them*." A military camp perched on the edge of the city was
the one place of activity, the lines of tents standing out stark white
among the gray waste.

"It's mostly greens," Ulnoth agreed. "Best we avoid standing
out. I doubt they'd believe we were temple pilgrims, given the, er,
political situation. We should stow the horses up here, hide our iron,
and try to blend in with that sorry lot of scavengers down there."

"Never thought I'd say this, but I think we'll have to make
ourselves *dirtier* to pull that off."

There were dozens of tiny rivulets draining into the river basin,
and after a short search they found a place to hitch the mounts where
they could drink and graze on the scant greenery that still poked
through the early winter carpet. They swaddled their knives and
bows in clothes and rubbed mud into their faces, then proceeded
down toward the one surviving bridge.

It was more wood than stone – a hasty patch-up job to restore
minimal function but little confidence. After negotiating that rickety
terror they were confronted by a hungry-looking man holding a
rusted halberd. "Hold," he drawled, the word a hard apathetic shell
concealing a core of sadness. "What business in Her Majesty's city?"

"Pickers," said Ulnoth, pointing toward the nearest pile of
destruction. "Heard we might go through the leavings, try to find—"

"Fine," the guard replied, impatient to return to the relative
warmth of his tollbooth post. "Go on. Army gets half of whatever
you find. Stay outta trouble." He waved them by.

"Thank you," Alessia muttered.

"Hey, don't you fuckin' thank me. You get yerselves shanked in
there it's on your own heads." The guard turned back to his booth.

"Did you hear that accent? He's 'Vani. Western," Alessia said
when they were out of earshot.

"Of course," Ulnoth replied. "You don't use locals to invade
their own country, gotta bring 'em in from afar. Lot easier to plant a
boot on the neck of someone you don't know."

They went through the motions of searching through garbage, tossing piles of clay, charred wood and junk to mimic the desperation of people who would do so day after day in hopes of finding some scrap of metal or utensil only to surrender half of it for the privilege of leaving alive. A few genuine pickers gave them nasty looks as though their territory was being invaded, but none made trouble. "How many people you think," Alessia wondered, "didn't make it out of here before it fell to ruin?"

"No idea," replied Ulnoth, "but with all this ash you can be sure you're breathing in some of their remains."

Alessia coughed.

When they were reasonably certain that no one was watching, they made their way toward what had once been a fortress but was long ago donated to the Polytheon and converted to a temple. Green grass still grew only inside the wall. Ulnoth stood before a stretch of stonework about four feet high and shook his head. "Amazing. Castles and cities fall all around us but this little row of pebbles holds 'em back sure as a mountain. I shoulda run off to be a rober."

"I doubt you could handle the discipline," said Alessia. "Anyway, that's the power of the Polytheon. Neutrality has its benefits. Sometimes."

Ulnoth smirked. "You don't believe it's the power of the gods themselves what do it, like they preach?"

"I know for a fact it's not. Besides, it's inner doctrine that the gods don't generally take much interest in human aff—"

The theology lesson was cut off by a sharp cry of pain from somewhere within the temple grounds. Ulnoth and Alessia leaped over the wall, dislodging some of it in the process. Running toward the moans, they came upon a young man pinned to the ground under a collapsed section, his legs covered by fallen stone blocks.

"Help!" he screamed, arms flailing. "Help me!"

"Hold still," Alessia commanded as Ulnoth flung stones off of the boy. "Careful, don't make it worse. If a bone is broken—"

"Aargh!"

"It's broken. Calm yourself, brother. What's your name?"

"U-Uwen. Brother Uwen. I was – ah! Checking the mortar... pushed on the stones...."

"Are you alone out here?"

"Brother Bendicca...he was just here."

"Ulnoth, go find him. Find anyone." Alessia finished clearing the blocks off Uwen's legs and saw one lying at an unnatural angle. "You'll be all right." *How many men have I told that who were dead minutes later?* She took a handful of the novice's robe and dabbed sweat from his pale brow.

"See here," growled a new voice from somewhere behind them. "Who do you think you are? You rabble know you're not allowed – Uwen!" The older brother ran to where the boy lay. "Gods curse it all! I knew this was a stupid idea."

"His fibula's fracted," said Alessia. "Is there something we can carry him in on?"

"Wha— There's a wheelbarrow I think, in the shed."

"Then kindly fetch it."

"Aye – wait, who exactly are you anyway? Women aren't permitted in—"

"Just get it!" barked Ulnoth. The brother jumped then scurried to obey. "Another thing I don't miss about civilization – foolish questions."

Alessia and Ulnoth helped Uwen onto one foot then laid him into Bendicca's wheelbarrow. "Gently, keep it elevated. Do you have a physic here?"

Bendicca shook his head. "We had a chirurgeon, but he was old. He died and we haven't been able to send to Artamera for a replacement."

"Then you'll have to let me inside. This bone needs to be set."

The brother visibly blanched. "Inside? B-but...I don't think that's—"

"I'm sure the Polytheon would make an exception," Alessia said. *Something I don't miss about civilization.*

"And," said Ulnoth with a grin, "if you get in trouble just tell your bosses I forced you. At knife point." He produced a blade from the bundle of rags on his back and casually laid a hand on the pommel.

With a nervous gulp Bendicca hefted the wheelbarrow across the grounds, trying not to jostle the novice too much and mostly failing. He led them through a small side door and down a dark hallway.

"We've an infirmary, but without a physic it's become a bit of a mess...."

"Let's go then," said Alessia.

They passed through a gaggle of brothers congregated outside the refectory. "Make way," bellowed Bendicca. "Out of the damned way! Brother Fento, find Father and bid him come to the infirmary." The men glanced first at Uwen, then stared at Alessia.

"Is...is that a wom—"

"Fento! Now! Rest of you, find something to do or I will!" They scattered as the wheelbarrow barreled through the complex. They turned a corner and light burst upon them once more as they approached the inner courtyard.

"Big place for so few of you," remarked Ulnoth.

"We were once more than we are," Bendicca countered with a sigh. "The gods call few to their service in these bloody days... Here, the infirmary opens into the courtyard for light."

"Good," said Alessia. "Put him onto this pallet." She opened a window shutter and the room lit up to reveal a sorry sight indeed. Supplies, what were left of them, littered the floor, piled in corners, poured from overturned canisters. "Ugh, what have you done?"

Bendicca shrugged. "As I said...."

"Right." She hiked Uwen's robe up to expose his broken bone. She ran her fingers carefully across the purple, swollen wound, probing. "Skin's not punctured at least." Uwen grimaced in pain, and Bendicca averted his eyes at such an indecent act. "I have to set this. Um, it's going to hurt."

"It already hurts!" Uwen squeezed his eyes shut tight. "Just do it," he whispered.

Timing is everything, Alessia thought. "What? What did you say?" She took a hold of the limb, got ready.

"I said, just do— *Aaargh!!!*" Uwen's howl echoed back down the hallway and across the courtyard. When it died down he wept openly.

Ulnoth patted the novice on the shoulder. "Just be happy you caught her on a good day. Sometimes she demands payment in advance, and it can be quite a bill."

Bendicca was about to ask what that meant when a scowling,

silver-haired man appeared in the doorway. "What's the meaning of all this?"

"Father Jenulius," said Bendicca, inclining his head. "There was, ah, an accident. Uwen was injured, and these folk came to the rescue." *At knife point*, he didn't add.

Jenulius eyed Alessia up and down. "I see the rules don't count for what they used to. I suppose we owe you a debt of thanks, madam. You've training?"

Alessia nodded, flicking sweat from her brow. "Some. Second degree physic, fullwise with kit. A season from third degree." Remembering her manners, she bowed her head. "Um, I humbly beg to report, Honored Father."

"So," said Jenulius, "one of our order. Strayed from the flock perhaps?"

"Not strayed, released entire. In these bloody days, others have greater need of my service than the gods."

"I see. Uwen will recover?"

"If you've left me anything to splint this bone with. Or plaster."

"Plaster?"

"I've seen it done. Pour wet plaster around the limb. It dries tight and holds the bone until it knits."

"Plaster we have," said Bendicca. "It's certainly no use to – er, that is...."

Jenulius sighed. "It's all right, you can say it. Repairing that wall was a fool's errand, and the fault is mine. Do as you think best." He noticed Ulnoth for the first time. "And what's your story?"

"Me? Oh, I'm just along for the ride."

"Ride?"

Alessia paused wrapping bandages around Uwen's leg. "We may be rabble, but we're here with purpose. Please Father, tell me you can read Bhasan."

Jenulius raised an eyebrow.

*   *   *

"It's been some time," muttered Jenulius as he squinted over the letter like a vulture. A piece of scrap paper was set beside the original, charcoal pencil at the ready. "Haven't had occasion to read Bhasan since, well, since my subprior exams. Strange tongue to be sure, but so full of knowledge. Do you know, the Bhasans were charting the stars and cataloguing herbs when we were still clawing our way out of the Argovani swamps...though the hand that wrote this wasn't a native, you can tell by the strokes. Phrasing is strange, but.... It says, 'To deity body-wise, sun-rays-through-water which inhabit on all grounds, Artabarzanes—' oh my! 'From his same disgust-making and slave of no value, greetings and abasements'."

"Basements?" said Ulnoth with a quizzical expression from the corner of the study to which he'd been relegated. "Some kinda construction—"

"Hush!" snapped Alessia. "We thought as much. Go on."

Jenulius scribbled with his charcoal as he read. "'I must pray forgiving of...shortness-by-mockery that is this parcel but endure yoke-whipped by now-wise evolutions pertaining to friend-taking by high lord—' erm, it says *angar-uw*—"

"Engwara," said Alessia. "We assumed that part references the queen. Go on, Father, please."

*   *   *

To the God Incarnate, The Rainbow Which Abideth Upon The Earth, Artabarzanes, from His most loathsome and unworthy servant, greetings and abasements!

I must beg forgiveness of the insolent brevity of this note but feel compelled by recent developments concerning the acquisition by Queen Engwara of a powerful new ally in the person of one Lord Taurix. Your Radiance knows the delicate balance of strife in this country – which I remain honored beyond description to maintain – requires wealth of both gold and flesh to rest upon the scales. The first is easy to accomplish as our Bank and Your vast riches have shown – neither side in this pitiful war suspects the true source of its finances nor cares to discover. Alas the movements of people are a more troublesome coin. This Taurix, whose wrath Your Radiance's western-most satraps may have had cause to fear, has against all possible calculation betrayed his self-styled King Pharamund and tipped the balance in the queen's favor. I therefore beg as immediate counter a large infusion of resources to Pharamund's cause of value not less than a thousand pounds gold and contracts for ships and men from Thazov, Marzahn and Porontus. The Bank can direct the flow of money with little difficulty but must act quickly. If successful the war can be maintained for another year yet, after which the whole of the peninsula will be exhausted and left at Your pleasure and mercy – a bargain! Profit flows everywhere, Your Radiance.

Your ever-kneeling and humble agent,

C. F. v X.
B. I.-E., Marimine Sardicchio Esquaralle

★   ★   ★

Jenulius translated the letter twice word for word, his hand shaking by the end. "Where...*how* did you come by this?"

"Quite by accident," Alessia said, her voice barely above a whisper. "A Thazovi sneaking through the forest tried to kill one of us and...failed. Had this on him. I think he took us for spies."

"Where did this happen – no, no don't tell me, I don't want to know. I shouldn't even be reading this. You—"

"Wait," said Ulnoth, "explain this to me like I'm five. This says what exactly? That Emperor Artawhatevers is footin' the bill for *both sides?*"

"Proxy war, using Marimines Banks as middlemen," answered Jenulius. "And when both are utterly spent from killing each other, the emperor can walk right in and take over. A bargain, indeed. We're so poor by comparison it's far cheaper than a direct invasion."

"Uh-huh. And no one's maybe taking this with a barrel of salt? I mean I could write a little note saying I'm the royal titty inspector of the Cloud Kingdom of Uxtaphrath, don't make it so."

"Good question," said Alessia. "*Is* this genuine?"

"Look here," said Jenulius, "the signature. This *C. F. v X.*"

Ulnoth and Alessia leaned across the worktable. "It's...shiny," Ulnoth observed.

"It's gold dust. Poured onto the ink before it dried. The amount of gold there is of no great value, but dust of such fine manufacture is difficult to come by. In this country, anyway. Whatever else, someone of means wrote this document and wrote it in a hurry, I can tell that even in translation."

"It makes sense," Alessia said as the pit in her stomach sank ever deeper. "Argovan's been bankrupt for over a year. Bergovny can't be any better off yet they've managed to keep at it. They're so obsessed with killing each other they don't bother to ask where the money comes from. The bank must be getting...I can't imagine *what* they're getting to play such a long game like this."

"A vast amount of real estate," ventured Jenulius, "percentages, exclusive trade routes, monopolies, anything they want. All while hiding under Artabarzanes's skirts."

"Now Taurix has gone and thrown a stone in their stream by switching sides. *Treason*, that hypocrite. All for nothing...."

Ulnoth kicked a chair across the tiny study and it crashed into the corner. "A game!" he shouted in fury. "It's all a game to them. Half the country's dead and the rest on the way, all 'cause of a godsfucked *bank?*" He stormed toward the door, but in his rage he fumbled with the deadbolt.

"Where do you think you're going?" asked Jenulius, more frightened than angry.

"Carsolan. Imma kill that bitch queen with my bare hands. Then if by some miracle I ain't dead I'm going to Thoriglyn and do the same for—"

"You can't! If this gets out...oh gods, if anyone learns I had anything to do with this...." Jenulius turned even whiter and snatched his translation off the table. He turned and shoved the paper into the tiny hearth behind him.

"No!" yelled Alessia. "Stop, this is too important!" She grabbed the original before Jenulius could do the same to it. "Both of you just settle down, we need to think—"

A banging came from outside the study, followed by Bendicca's voice. "Father? Is everything all right? I heard shouting." Ulnoth at last got the door open and almost barreled into the brother. "What is going on?"

Jenulius's forehead shimmered with perspiration. "What did you hear? Is there anyone else in this wing?"

"What? No, the brothers are gathered for chapter. Are you—"

"Start without me. Go. Go!" Jenulius turned to Alessia, begging again for the letter. "Understand, we can't be caught with this – it violates sacred neutrality. Just dabbling in politics is dangerous enough, but *this?*"

"Don't lecture me about neutrality, Father, it's not as sacred as you think. Besides, which side could this help? They're both getting funding from the bank, both being duped. Don't you see? *We* can use this. If we can get to someone who has the ear of Pharamund or Engwara, expose the bank's scheme, it might change things. If they knew Artabarzanes was behind it…well they'd have to make a truce, wouldn't they? It could even help end the war!"

"I wouldn't count on it," said Ulnoth. "People who win crowns ain't the type to be swayed by reason. Look, you've tricked me into doing things your way since we met, and I almost started to believe your cack. But you heard that letter – don't matter what we do, don't matter how bad you think things are, it just gets worse and worse and it only stops when everyone's dead. I knew that once, but you made me forget." Head hung low in resignation, he walked out of the study.

"Damn it all," said Jenulius, "if he runs his mouth about this we're through!"

"Don't worry," Alessia answered. "He plays at mean and callous – a lot of the time he is – but he won't put anyone else in danger on purpose. There's nothing to link this letter back to you. I'll take it and go and forget we ever met."

"It's not that I blame you, girl," Jenulius bristled, "it's just, I've got the brothers to think about, ken'ee? And we're walking a tightrope here already."

"I understand, all too well. I thank you for your help, Father, and beg to take my leave."

Jenulius nodded, laid a hand atop Alessia's head in benediction. "Go sister, and may the gods—"

"Don't," snapped Alessia. "Don't say it. They haven't done so yet and I doubt they'll start now."

*   *   *

Where'd that fool get to? Alessia considered going back without Ulnoth and leaving him to his latest suicide attempt. It was tedious always having to coax him back from the brink of madness. *Maybe it's his fate and I should just let him get about it*, she thought, although she didn't believe in fate. But what about the letter? Was it pure chance that it'd fallen into their hands? Exhausted and morose, Alessia only halfway pondered these things as she made her way uncertainly back toward the bridge. She jumped back in alarm when a familiar rusted halberd appeared in front of her.

"And just where do you think *you're* going, darlin'?" It was a different guard than the one they'd passed on the way in – this one had the stench of gleeful sadism about him, along with cheap wine and ball sweat.

"Oh, um, across the river," Alessia answered, careful to keep her eyes down lest they betray her contempt.

"Rule is crown gets half o' what you find. You know that."

"Well, as you can see I didn't find anything." *Careful!* "Just bad luck I guess."

"Oh, wrong answer, missy. No one gets out without paying the toll. Ain't that right, boys?" Nearby a squad of conscripts gave perfunctory nods or looked away.

I don't have time for this, she thought. "And what exactly is the toll?"

"Ah, well, thing is, the toll is either booty...or pussy." He barked laughter at his witticism.

"I don't think so," she growled. Her hand inched toward the knife she had concealed in a sleeve. The guard noticed the movement and grabbed her arm.

"What's this?" He wrenched the knife from her grasp. "Oho, a little pricker, eh? That's against the rules too. Anyway, I got a lot bigger one for ya right here. Take her!"

Alessia lashed out with her free arm and struck the guard across the jaw. At the same time she jammed a knee into his groin. He stumbled backward but the padded jack absorbed most of the blow. She tried to snatch his halberd but the distance was too short to stab at him so she whacked the guard in the forehead with the shaft.

"Ow!" he shouted. "Godsdammit, I said take her!" Half a dozen men grabbed her from behind, and Alessia was immobilized. The guard shook his head, spat blood, and smiled. "That's good, I like some fight in 'em. At first anyways." He wound up and landed a hard slap across Alessia's mouth. The crack rang out and echoed across the ruined landscape of Lenocca.

"Now you behave, and if you're a good little cocksuck just maybe we'll keep you alive long enough to use you up. Turn her around." They spun Alessia about and though dazed she struggled, sure she was about to be buggered then and there. The sight of nearly a hundred dejected-looking men greeted her. Most of them wore rags, but a few sported makeshift emblems of Engwara's standard. "You see that? Them's the fresh recruits, newly sworn to Her Majesty's service. They been promised a sign-on bonus, and today that bonus is *you.*"

CHAPTER TWENTY-TWO

Murder Them

Ohshitohshitohshitohshit.... It was all she was capable of thinking in that moment. Not even before Taurix had she been so helpless, so paralyzed. They locked her up in the ruins of Lenocca's jailhouse, its one cell still sturdy. They'd lain her face down over a table and chained her arms to opposite walls, in position and ready for use. Her chausses and braies lay in a pile on the floor. Just outside the cell a callow youth stood watch, saying nothing but staring intently at her exposed crotch.

"P-please," she whispered, "let me go. I...I'll take you with me, away from all this, I promise. There's a place we can go – ah!" A piece of rubble slammed into her backside, tossed through the bars by her captor.

"Sarge says keep you quiet else I don't get a turn."

So that was it then. All her hopes, plans, incredible turns of luck all come down to this. The temple, Firleaf, Wengeddy, the Heron Kings – washed away in a moment of carelessness. *Ulnoth was right,* she thought while fighting back tears. *It doesn't matter what we do, all turns to cack in the end.* She would die, and for her own arrogance, her conceit and presumption through it all she was going to be raped by a hundred dehumanized wretches first. *Gods forgive me.* She stopped fighting and wept.

Sometime later the door to the jailhouse creaked open on its one good hinge. Alessia heard it but had worked herself into such a merciful fugue that it seemed far away, muted. A drunken voice filled the room.

"It's me. I won the lot, I'm first, sergeant said so. Let me at 'er."

"All right, all right, pipe down. Lucky fuckin' you," said the youth.

"Exactly, ha! Lucky *fuckin'* me." The sound of liquid sloshing.

"Watch it! Where'd you get that jug, 'nyway? Wine's against the rules for new scrubs."

"Meh, who cares? No fightin' to be done here, right?"

"Well then gimme some!"

"Here, enjoy. I got somethin' sweeter to taste." Footsteps. The clang of the cell opening. Closer footsteps, but still miles away as far as Alessia perceived. *Someone else*, she thought. *This is happening to someone else, far away. Pay it no mind.*

Stink of flesh, heat. Rustling of roughspun cloth. Pressure from above. "Ah, now *this* is what I call a bonus." There was something about that voice. Hot breath, scratching of a beard against her neck, bare legs pressed against hers. *Someone else, somewhere else....* She held tight to the fiction, held on for dear life. Whispers in her ear. "Make this look good. Not sure how long that stuff takes."

What?

Coughing. Hacking, violent spasms. "Oh...what is thi... help...." Moans. More sloshing. Crying.

Suddenly the pressure was off her. The sounds of suffering were cut short. Chains fell slack. What was happening? Slowly, so slowly, Alessia's mind took a cautious step back toward reality. Then another, and another. When she felt her left arm fall free, then the right, she dared open her eyes.

Blinking away tears, she sat up and turned around, confused by what she saw. "...Ulnoth?" It was Ulnoth, as naked from the waist down as she was and hopping into his braies. On the floor next to him lay her jailer, face bloated and purple with green foamy slime pouring from his lifeless mouth, neck twisted at a grotesque angle.

"Nothing gets by you. Don't just sit there, put your clothes on and let's get outta here!"

"You came back for me?"

"Tell the truth, I never left. I was gonna. Then I figured you'd get into trouble without me and well, you're a right silly cooze with silly notions but I still owe you. And gods damn you for that. Uh, sorry about gettin' kinda intimate with you there, but it had to look real-like."

"But how? What did you do to – oh, my poison powder!"

Ulnoth nodded. "Strong as I wanted, just like you said. I'm afraid the kid didn't survive. I assume you won't lose sleep over that?"

Alessia shivered as she fumbled back into her own clothes. "I'm not sure I'll ever sleep again."

"Uh-huh, we can debate the moral implications another day. For now can we...?" He jerked a thumb toward the door.

"Please."

On the other side of the door they were greeted by a crowd of expectant recruits, but no officers. Ulnoth raised his knife and held it in front of them. "Listen up, you shitspittles, we're walkin' outta here. Anyone says different I guarantee I will end you."

One man near the front of the pack said, "The hells? Come on lads, we can take these two!"

"Sure," sneered Ulnoth, "but how many'll we take first? You feeling lucky, tough guy?"

Another close to them shrugged but kept his distance. "Eh, what do we care? I just joined up for the food, not to bugger girls."

Alessia snarled. "You'd have done it anyway though, wouldn't you?"

"You do what you're told around here or you die," answered Tough Guy. "You learn that right quick."

"What is going on here?" Alessia jumped nearly out of her skin at the interruption. *Please, not again.* The bridge guard, perhaps come for his turn with her, stomped toward them. "You! Who said you could take that piece of pussy out of—" He stopped, looked into the jailhouse through the doorway and saw the young soldier lying on the floor. "What the—?"

Ulnoth lashed out with his knife while the conscripts gawked and cowered at the same time. The guard jumped back and swung his halberd, but Ulnoth dove out of the way. Alessia picked up a broken brick and lobbed it at the guard's forehead. It was a glancing blow, but he stumbled backward dizzily...and fell right on his ass. Without warning someone had come up from behind and tripped him, just stuck out a foot in a tiny, casual movement. The halberd clattered to the pavement. Ulnoth wasted no time and fell on the guard, dispatching him with clean efficiency. Only then did they look up at their benefactor – it was the first bridge guard they'd met coming into the city, the Argovani.

"You?" said Alessia, amazed.

"Never did like that bastard," he said.

"But," asked Ulnoth between breaths, "why?"

"I was coming for my free piece, saw the line outside, then saw you two fighting...all just seemed so stupid somehow. Army was supposed to be my ticket out of the shitty bog I come from. Now all I want is to go back."

"So go," said Ulnoth, "nothing stopping you now." He turned to Alessia. "We'd better hightail it too."

Tough Guy broke from the pack of conscripts, angry. "Well, that's just fine for you, but patrol's due soon and lookit this mess you made – we'll get blamed. We're all screwed now!"

"We need a diversion," said Ulnoth. "Somethin' more pressing than two nullied sloggers."

The Argovani perked up. "You could fire some arrows, shoot 'em into the stockade. Lots of tents and whatnot set up in there."

Ulnoth frowned. "*Fire*...arrows? What does that mean?"

"Look." He went into the jailhouse and rooted through the dead youth's kit set in a corner. "We ain't supposed to have 'em ourselves, but at night it's fun to shoot for distance, y'know?" He pulled a bow and three strange arrows from the bottom of a sack. The heads bulged to envelop a wad of some foul-smelling cloth. "Soaked in heavy oil."

"Oh, I get it," said Alessia. "You set them alight then shoot 'em."

"That's absolutely chthonic," said Ulnoth, half in awe.

"Wait 'til you see a cross-bow, you'll cack a brick."

"A *what?*"

"Never mind. Come see this." He led the pair back into the street where the conscripts still gathered, curiosity overriding fear of their officers. The Argovani pulled a sparker from his pouch and after several tries the arrow erupted into flames. Alessia and Ulnoth jumped back.

"They're about seventy yards down the main street there." He offered the bow to Ulnoth. "You want to do the honors?"

Ulnoth moved to take it, then glanced at Alessia.

"I'll do it," she said angrily. "Light the others."

The camp stood in stark contrast to the wasteland surrounding it, and so close they could hear the shouting of officers and men, hear the clanging of smiths' hammers, smell roasting food and steaming cack. Only the toppled walls of Lenocca's buildings blocked Her Majesty's troops from view. Alessia pushed her way through the conscripts, climbed up a pile of rubble and sighted down the destroyed thoroughfare. She notched and drew the fire arrow back until the flames almost kissed her hand, aimed high, then loosed. The missile shot into the sky and the flame promptly disappeared.

"Shit," said Ulnoth, "it went out!"

"Wait," answered the Argovani. The arrow trailed smoke behind it, and when it landed right on top of an oiled canvas tent, the flame revived. At first there was no reaction. Sweat tricked down Alessia's brow, and she braced to flee.

Then all at once the entire top of the tent became engulfed; shouts went up. "Give me another," Alessia commanded. This one landed on the thatched roof of a barracks, far above any bucket brigade's reach. Another, in the midst of a sawdust-choked lumberyard. The fires spread and men scrambled to put them out. "That'll keep 'em busy awhile." From her vantage point she could see two figures running from the bridge toward the conflagration, their posts abandoned. She hopped down and shoved back through the crowd of stunned men. "Consider yourselves discharged."

"Great," scoffed Tough Guy, more despondent than belligerent. "Except now we gots no prospects at all."

As the smoke, heat and noise of the fires wafted over them Ulnoth stepped onto an overturned cart to be better heard. "Don't you idiots get it? You're a part of their game, a bit piece in a great big scam, just like we are. But don't think for one second that'll stay my hand if you come for me and mine."

"So what *are* we supposed to do if not join?" asked a boy no older than the one Ulnoth had slaughtered in Plisten, his voice cracking and tears flowing. "Fight them? How?"

"You can't," said Alessia. She joined Ulnoth on top of the cart, looked down on the men with eyes blazing. "They have the steel, the horses, they have the money and the numbers. They care about nothing and they'll stop at nothing. It's suicide to fight them on those terms."

"What then?"

"Don't fight them! Don't fight them. *Fucking murder them*. Murder them in their beds. Murder them in dark alleys. Murder them under bridges. Burn their camps like I did, ambush their patrols, shit in their water so they sicken and die. Hit 'em and run, make them furious, make them jump at shadows and turn on each other. And don't stop until you can't find any more. It's the only way."

"Says who?"

Alessia ground her teeth. "Says the warrior priestess."

★   ★   ★

Only after they crossed the Carsa into the evening dark outside the city did Ulnoth dare to speak. "So…what was that exactly? Was it you back there, or Reynal and his stupid playacts?"

"Not sure," Alessia replied without looking at him. "Maybe a bit of both."

"And those men – you just gonna speechify like that and turn 'em loose?"

"They make their choices, like everyone else."

"Huh. And what about you?" he asked the guard. "You want to come with us?"

The Argovani guard – former guard – trailed behind, and came to a stop where the road split in two directions. "Me? No, I'm going home. Shitty bog maybe, but it's better than this." He ripped the green badge from the tattered clothes he wore and tossed it into the dirt.

"Stay off the road then, you'll live longer. Good luck."

He nodded. "To all of us." Ulnoth shook the man's hand without ever learning his name and they parted in the night, leaving fire and chaos behind them.

★   ★   ★

The cloaked and hooded woman crept from the confines of the outpost leaving fire and chaos behind her as well. While soldiers flailed about for water and someone to give them orders, she pressed through the flames unafraid, kissed by their warm bite. *Sorry old friend, I haven't time to stay and visit.* She tracked the trails of smoke to their source, and hiding behind what remained of a guildhall, watched a very interesting scene play out. When it was over she sat in the ruins for a little while, considering. At last she rose and made her way back to her tent, which was singed but set apart enough to avoid much damage, and sent for a secretary.

"Yes, ma'am. The fires are—"

"Under control, I'm sure."

"Erm, yes. Mostly."

"Forget about that now. Find me a fast courier, and have him report to me in exactly one quarter of an hour."

"Yes, ma'am."

"And don't call me ma'am."

Vinian flung the hood away, wanting her brandy bottle more than ever, then took a pen and sheet of paper from the little table she'd appropriated.

To Your Majesty, from Her Devoted Spymistress:

We have a problem.

CHAPTER TWENTY-THREE

Interruptus

Alessia said little on the way back, and Ulnoth didn't press her. He well knew how fragile the protective cocoon of shock could be, and how dangerous to pierce it too soon. He'd abandoned the notion of leaving her in such a state to go off on his own, so they simply rode away from Lenocca without looking back.

It was unfortunate that they didn't look back, because they did not ride alone. Trailing behind, sometimes at a distance of a quarter mile and at others no more than a hundred yards, was a solitary, skittish figure keeping mostly to the shadows yet always following, following.

Though she kept well out of sight, Vinian would not risk a fire, so night after night she and the horse she'd taken without asking suffered the biting frost in dark silence. She followed, she watched, she listened but heard little, and she thought.

As You commanded I'm acting at my own discretion, she'd written to her queen. *Upon dispatch of this message I'll pursue these demagogues with the intention of discovering their base of operations. In my opinion, we have found an answer to our riddle. I intend to solve it fully.*

And freeze myself fully, Vinian thought now. An impulsive decision, yes, and no going back now. She'd do it again if given the choice. *But I'd pack more woolens.* She squeezed her cloak tighter around her, closed her eyes, and waited for the jerks to start.

*   *   *

Ulnoth and Alessia took the path skirting Plisten, passing close enough to hear the ugly sounds of occupation. Ulnoth said a silent prayer for the safety of those still in the village, more out of habit than belief. A day later they rode through Firleaf. There was no one there, and they didn't stop. Alessia said nothing.

After the ford Ulnoth said, "This is as far as they should've gone."

"Uh-huh," Alessia muttered.

"I figured they'd find us by now. I hope nothing's happened."

"Hmm."

Ulnoth sighed. "Look, Lessi—"

"Don't call me that," she snapped, her eyes suddenly filled with fire as they had been in Lenocca. "Don't *you* ever call me that again."

"All right, gods, sorry! I don't claim to know what you gone through – that's true for all of us. But there's lots of people depending on us. On you, really. More I think about it, that letter of yours might actually be a pretty big piece on the board. I ain't smart enough to know how to use it, so you need to brace up." He hoped it was convincing. He just took the more irksome bits she'd thrown at him over the last season and mashed them together.

Alessia sat on her horse and stared straight ahead. It seemed she was sunk back into a fugue and Ulnoth was about to poke her again when she said, "Fire an arrow."

"What's that?"

"Fire an arrow, then shoot it up. Maybe they'll see it."

"And maybe the reds or greens will." He scanned up and down the road, listened to the howling wind. "'Course I got no better ideas."

They dismounted and Ulnoth strung the bow they'd taken from Lenocca. They sacrificed a few strips of cloth and wound them about the head of an arrow. "The arrow's too light for this bow," Ulnoth remarked. "Not that I'm shooting for accuracy." They sparked a little fire of what dry twigs they could find and lit the improvised missile. They had no oil, so it burned low and smoky.

Ulnoth notched, aimed upward, drew the string full to his ear, then loosed before bits of flaming linen could fall into his eye. The arrow burst into the sky with an evil hiss, and as before the flame winked out leaving a dark trail behind. It rose high and higher and they watched it reach its apex. In the half a moment it spent suspended in the air the fire flashed back to life. Then it was gone again, and the arrow fell back to the earth somewhere beyond sight.

*   ★   ★

Dannek and Alixe lay entangled in fallen leaves and in each other while the first snowflakes of the season fell onto them unheeded. *Finally!* Dannek thought, though not so coherently as that. Finally they'd found the chance to slip away together, away from the drudgery and chores and stink of the Heron Kings' roving caravan. For a week and more after the awful events in Plisten he couldn't manage an erection – a new and terrifying experience for a young man – and when he dared to steal a kiss from Alixe all he tasted on her lips was blood; all he saw when he closed his eyes was fire. The nightmares had faded a little since, and as the caravan made their way out of the river valley and into the Edra foothills, he became more and more his old young self. So when Alixe wriggled her petite hand down his braies and smiled, he had no shortage of reasons to smile back.

"Careful!" Alixe cried in mock horror as Dannek fumbled at her clothes. "It's my only gown!" She lifted her ground-chilled rump to let him hike up her skirts, and he pawed at her stupidly, adorably. "Mmmhmm...."

So warm, So warm, so soft, so...wet.

"Get in me, now," she breathed.

The cold and his layers of clothing made it a bit of an ordeal, but Dannek charged ahead, paying no heed to the damage done to his own garments. Still mostly lying atop her, he felt the icy sting of the ground against his cock, then the warmth of Alixe's hand guiding him home. *Finally!*

"Oh, Dannek," she whispered, "Dannek...."

"Dannek! Where the hells you get to? Get back here!"

Corren. "Oh, for...." *Just go away!*

"Ignore it," ordered Alixe. "Whatever it is can wait. *I* can't."

"Dannek!" Louder, closer. Probably following their footsteps left in the frost like a good tracker. He wasn't going away. Dannek's boner however definitely was.

"Godsdammit!" It was no use now. He rolled off of Alixe, suddenly feeling the full bite of the cold. "I better go see what he wants," he said with a sigh.

"This is ridiculous," whined Alixe. "Just 'cause you're the best with a bow doesn't mean you have to do everything. Probably saw a squirrel he wants to roast."

"Mhmm."

"If this keeps up I'm just going to go with that Allard fella."

Dannek made a sour face. "He's damaged goods, you know. Missing a finger."

"Ain't a *finger* I'm interested in."

Dannek finished stumbling back into his wrinkled clothes. "Alixe, you're barely thirteen. You have plenty of good years left for screwing."

"Except no one thinks we'll survive the winter and I don't wanna die a virg—"

"*Dannek!*"

* * *

"What? What do you want already?" Dannek had doubled back on Corren's path and surprised him from behind, just to show that he could. Corren spun about.

"Ah, there you are. What's with the attitude? And what are you doing all the way out here anyway?" Alixe stepped out from behind a tree after rearranging the folds of her gown, a deep scowl on her face. "Oh. Sorry. Well, you can do that any time. Right now I need you."

Dannek sneered. "Oh? Didn't think you leaned that way."

"Funny. Here's a funnier one: Marchmen ambushing us, flaying our flesh, burning the rest of us alive as an offering to their ancestors, then wearing our skin to absorb our strength. There's a regular gut-buster, eh? That's how the north'rd tribes do it."

"You spot any?" asked Dannek.

"Not yet. But we're nearing the edge of where they wander, and I want to start regular outrider and foot patrols. You're captain of the first one. Congratulations."

"I am? You think the older folk'll take orders from me?"

"They'd better, or I'll flay 'em myself. Playtime's over. You head out in ten minutes."

Only when he was safely out of earshot did Dannek ask, "What's gotten into him? Playtime my ass."

Alixe shrugged. "Maybe he needs a girl too. *He* ain't missing any fingers, is he?" She laughed. Dannek didn't.

★   ★   ★

Dannek, Gant, Emony and another smuggler named Marella crept forward in a staggered side-by-side arrangement, ducking low branches and trying not to leave any tracks. Snow drifted gently down through the trees and would cover their footprints soon enough, but as Corren had told them, "Good practice is good practice." The constant peeking through the dead brush, then down to mind where they stepped, then up again over and over, left little time to imagine a Marchmen ambush. Maybe Corren had been exaggerating. Besides, would their fate be so different if they were caught by reds or greens? Better the Chthonii you knew he supp—

Crack!

The four of them froze, the echo seeming to take an age of the world to die away. Dannek snapped his gaze to the left. Marella stood with one foot suspended in mid-air above a broken twig, her face flushed pink. "Sorry," she said just above a whisper.

"All right," Dannek said with a sigh, "let's start back. Different path than the one we took out."

"What if we get lost?" asked Gant.

"Then hope we're not found by the wrong people. Plenty o' those about." They skirted the edge of a large clearing where wind stirred up the fallen snow before whistling through the trees around it. They were on a slope that marked the beginning of the land's long rise to the distant Edra Mountains.

Gant stepped, paused, then looked up toward the eastern horizon, then the west. As he did so, out of the corner of his eye – a flash. Weak and brief then gone, but it had definitely been there. In the sky. "What the – ah!" He slipped, tumbled off the rock and down the slope into the whiteness of the clearing.

"Gant! Great." Dannek hopped down and ran after him, careful not to trip and share Gant's fate. "The rest of you stay here!"

Gant kept rolling until the ground leveled out. Then he slammed into something solid. "Oof!"

Dannek only barely missed crashing into it himself, blinded by the drifting snow and the falling dark. He grabbed at a branch of the lone tree to stop his descent. No, not a branch, it was too soft for that. It was...Dannek looked up, squinted, then gasped.

Gant shuffled to his feet. "Oh, that was stu— Hey Dannek, what's the prob— *Gyargh!*"

Two bodies were strung up in the tree with arms spread wide. More than that, they'd been mutilated. Eyes gouged, bellies open with intestines forming bloody icicles, noses slit off, and their mouths.... "What, what is that?" Dannek stepped closer, revolted and curious at the same time. Then he looked down at the dead men's legs, and between them each on the ground, dark frozen pools. "Oh for the love of gods."

"They cut off their cocks and shoved 'em in their mouths," Gant concluded. "Hells of a way to die. Was it...do you think it was Marchmen?"

"Dunno. Maybe. There's no village or town around here, not with Firleaf gone. I don't know who else...wait a minute. Look at their tunics." Gant looked, squinted.

"Is that...are these bastards soldiers from opposite sides?"

Dannek nodded. "One red, one green. I wonder what they were doing out here." He eyed their belts still buckled about their ruined torsos. "The purses are cut away, see? Marchmen might take the belts for the leather, but they don't use money."

"Robbers, then. Maybe they interrupted some kinda undertable deal – frattin' with the enemy for fun and profit, like."

"Hmm. But this looks personal. Taking the time to do...this. There's gotta be more to it. But I'm not hanging around to find out."

Gant glanced up at the dead men, than back at Dannek. "That supposed to be a joke?"

"Uh, no. Let's leave this place."

They trudged back up the slope to where the women waited impatiently, and Marella asked Gant what made him fall in the first place. "That was clumsy, even for you."

Gant shook his head. "It's the damnedest thing, but I coulda sworn I saw it...."

*   *   *

Vinian could've sworn she saw it, and she felt a new surge of energy, certain that she'd picked up her quarry's scent. Well, sight anyway.

The jerks had been bad the night before, as she huddled next to her horse in the freezing wilderness. When sleep at last embraced her it kept its hold for longer than she'd intended and she awoke to full daylight, with no sign of the strange pair of insurgents. The spymistress cursed herself and her luck and started off up the road – it led northeast without crossroad or fork for miles yet but there were unmapped side paths leading to hamlets, hunter's rests and robber dens without number. After most of a day of fruitless pursuit she saw no choice but to admit defeat and return to the queen empty-handed.

Then she saw it – another fire arrow shot straight up into the sky. Just a wink then it went out, but there were no more so it'd apparently served its purpose. *And mine. It must be them. I'd thank the gods if they existed.*

Vinian turned back and rode hard to where she'd seen the signal. There was no one there, but a set of horse tracks drew a clear path into the forest and up the hill due east. Her elation was short-lived when the tracks petered out under the scant canopy of trees that denied the ground enough snow to lead her on. For another half-hour she pushed on in as straight a line as she could manage, only to be faced with a wide, open land that gently but inexorably rose toward the rolling hills of the east. She peered across the brown, tangly mess, the rise and fall of land marked out in mottled white and fading into the distance. *How will I ever find them in this?* she wondered. It would be impossible alone. With gritted teeth she turned around to begin the journey back to Lenocca.

*   *   *

The arrow sliced through the cold air and buried itself in the branch an inch in front of Ulnoth. He yelped, slipped on a patch of slush and fell face first into the icy mud. The horses nickered and jumped at the commotion, and Alessia whipped her knife out, determined not to be so easily disarmed again.

"Hold!" The command rang out, and the leader of the trio of swaddled interlopers stepped forward. "What did I tell you? You bloody identify your target before you loose! That's lesson number one!" He slapped the wayward shooter upside the head.

"I thought they was Marchmen!" protested the man.

"If they had been you wouldn't have lived long enough to see them. Surrender your bow for today, and enjoy a week of laundry duty."

"But—"

"*Now.*" The dejected figure handed off his weapon to the one next to him and moved to the rear of the pack. The leader pulled back his hood and offered a hand down to Ulnoth. "Sorry about that."

Ulnoth wiped slush from his beard with a scowl. "Nice welcome, Corren. Won't ask how you do for intruders."

"Much the same way it seems. Came across a bit of a gruesome sight yesterday. Everyone's on edge." He glanced at Alessia, who still held her knife out in front of her. "Looks like you've had a like experience."

"We'll tell you all about it," said Ulnoth, "but first I need a fire and some grub. You caught our little firefly I take it?"

"We saw. Bloody dangerous, that. Did you find out what you wanted to know?"

"Well, about that. Better gather everyone together, 'cause you probably won't believe it and I don't wanna tell it over and over."

★   ★   ★

"You're right, I don't believe it," said Corren when the tale was done. Ulnoth knew that the fact that he'd told most of it and not Alessia signaled that more had happened than he was telling, but he figured he'd told what needed to be known. "*Both* sides? At once? That's...that's monstrous."

"What, unlike everything else that's been going on the past few years?" Sally sat close to the fire next to Bedegar, who was nursing a cold. "Higher up you go the bigger the monsters are."

Corren shook his head. "It just seems too far-fetched. What are the odds of us coming across that Thazovi, out of this whole big country, bound for Sarpoor with something this important?"

Nan shrugged. "What are the odds of all of us coming together and doing what we've done?"

"Point taken, but what good could we even do with this?"

"We could tell Pharamund what Artabarzanes is doing," suggested Crander. "Expose the queen."

"Or we could tell Engwara," Emony answered. "But to what end? Even if one side knew, it's not like they'd refuse their own source of funding. And the other would just deny it and accuse us of making it up. So would the bank."

"We wouldn't even get close enough to do the telling either way." Someone from beyond the flicker of the fire said it, from the riveted council of all three dozen or so of them. That brought more argument, a cacophony of possible courses of action, raised voices.

"Quiet!" shouted Corren. "All of you. We don't have to decide now."

"Everyone's right though," said Marella in a soft voice. She rarely spoke, so when she did all voices piped down to listen. "It doesn't matter which side you give that letter to. They'll disbelieve and kill whoever tries to deliver it. There's really only one option."

"Well, don't hold us in suspense, love," said Allard.

"Give it to both sides. At once."

There was a moment of silence as everyone listened for Marella to give some further clarification. Finally a voice asked, "But how? That's just twice as suicidal."

"No idea, but there's an old gambler's saying – when the odds are split twixt the favorites, bet on the long shot. How? That's for our glorious leaders to decide." Eyes turned to Corren and Alessia, and a few even to Ulnoth. The gazes weighed heavy on each of them.

CHAPTER TWENTY-FOUR
Chthonii

"Come on, it ain't much farther," Banwick said when Ulnoth paused to catch his breath.

"Aren't you supposed to be on laundry duty? You know, for almost killing me?"

"Nope, my week's finished. I'm a free man. That's how I found it – I was out on my own looking for game."

"Found what?"

"Come on."

Banwick's glee unnerved Ulnoth more than even a column of soldiers would have – no one so recently suffering Corren's disapproval should have cause to be excited about anything. So when Banwick had gone into the hills morose as he'd been all week then come back positively giddy, Ulnoth figured something was either really wrong or really right. He trailed behind at a jog. "We're makin' a lot of noise, you know. We shouldn't be—"

"There! There it is. Bask in the glory."

All Ulnoth saw was a rock formation in front of him. Rock and bare trees and snow, just like everything else for miles around. A stream trickled, and somewhere nearby the rush of a waterfall. "I'm looking. What exactly is it I'm supposed to see?"

Banwick laughed. "Look closer. You see the pool between those boulders?"

"That puddle? I see it. So what? I – wait. It ain't frozen."

Banwick shook his head. "Nope! Look closer."

Ulnoth clambered up to the formation. A big section of the hill jutted from the ground like a stony bone ripped out of the earth in a great wound, and a cleft where three large fragments of rock came together held a small pond. Smaller than that even, no bigger around than a wagon wheel. And not only was the water trickling from it not frozen, it was *steaming*. Finally Banwick's attitude made sense as Ulnoth realized what he'd discovered. "A hot spring. You found a hot spring!"

"Yes!" Banwick danced and hopped from one foot to the other like a lunatic, ecstatic. "Hot, plentiful, and free."

"And that waterfall—"

"Regular stream. The spring drains into it a bit downhill, hot and cold together."

"You could do a lot of laundry in this."

"Forget laundry, my term's done. We can all have *baths*, my friend. Remember those? Merciful gods, I'd love to climb in there with that Sally tart...."

"Hey!"

"What?"

Ulnoth shook his head. "Nothing. Keep dreaming, I'm getting in there now." He began to rip off his clothes, suddenly conscious of how grimy and foul he must be.

Banwick took hold of Ulnoth's shoulder. "Whoa, hold up there. First we have to agree we tell no one about this just yet. Plenty of time for everyone, but there are finder's rights to be observed. I need you to keep Corren's precious patrols from stumblin' over our little find. Just one day, agreed?"

"Hmm. Well that's fair I guess, not that fair's exactly a thing anymore. All right, one day."

"Good." Banwick nodded. "Now if you'll step aside...."

"Wha— Why do you get to go first?"

"'Cause I found it. You go fetch some cloths."

★   ★   ★

"Well. I'm lost." Bestre *was* lost, and had been for a while. The realization didn't come all at once but spread like a mold on bread until it was too green to ignore. Saying it aloud crystallized his irritation – and more than a little bit of fear – into a thoroughly ugly frown as he plodded through the woods looking for his squad. They'd gotten separated in the dark, and he dared not call out for aid. *Not in this place, hells no.* He lifted a wineskin to his lips but tasted only the last dregs. *Great. Lost, cold and dry too.*

General Duelleigh had sent them to investigate reports of Engwara's partisans operating in the area. To seek, to find, but absolutely not to engage. What could the enemy be doing out here so far from any castle or town or port of worth, no battle or siege to join? But there were other reports too, and far more terrifying. The attacks, the disappearances, the bodies found all up and down the river valley with unspeakable things done to them...all officially attributed to outlaws, or Marchmen, or outlaw Marchmen. Word of mouth told different stories. Stories of invisible monsters, ghosts, of things even more sinister that men could not conceive of for fear of going mad. Like every Bergovan lad, Bestre had grown up on nighttime whispers of the Chthonii, the ancient gods-before-the-gods banished to the primal chaos yet doomed ever to seek out cracks in the bones of the world through which they might squeeze and wreak their havoc. He'd thought those tales themselves gone from memory long ago. Now....

Bestre shook his head to clear the cobwebs. "Stupid," he said out loud with more certainty than he felt. "Just drunken stories, that's all." *They must be.* He looked up at the bright full moon and tried to remember his thoroughly inadequate navigation training to get some bearings. "Let's see, downhill is that way, and the moon is to my left...wait. *That* way is down too, so...." *Should I risk a shout?* What was he truly afraid of? He lived in the real world after all, not some storytime dream. *Man's the worst monster I have to fear. Maybe I'll walk on just a little further....*

Bestre picked through a tangle of branches dragged down by the weight of snow, and some annoyed birds overhead made his heart jump when they flew off. Ahead he heard something – water gurgling over rock. *Maybe I can follow it back down.* He crept toward it, faster now that he had a direction to fix on. He stepped out of a thick patch of underbrush and was faced with the rising solid ground. Then he looked up. *No....*

A Chthonus towered over him. It shimmered silver at the edges and all blackest dark in the middle. It had the vague shape of a man but rippled with muscles and was enveloped in an ethereal vapor that twisted and writhed all around it like a skin made of live serpents. In one claw it held a sword the likes of which he'd never seen. And it was looking. Straight. At. Him.

It snorted a stream of smoke, and Bestre managed to force his trembling, piss-soaked legs to turn and flee back into the trees. He screamed in terror, and he kept screaming when he heard that the thing was chasing after him. He tripped, scrambled to his feet, ran some more. He came to a sharp drop of more than ten feet, and without a thought threw himself over the edge. *Just get away get away get away havetogetawaygogogo....*

He landed hard, knew something was broken but ignored it and shambled on. After some nameless amount of time he realized he was no longer being pursued, and only then did the pain hit him. Bestre lost consciousness.

In the morning Bestre's squad mates found him where he'd dropped, curled up into a ball with a fracted ankle and whimpering about Chthonii. "Coming for me," he said over and over. "It's coming for me...."

*   *   *

After some nameless amount of time Ulnoth realized he was no longer covered in a layer of hot water but of ice, and only then did the cold hit him. "Argh, that was stupid!" He gave up the chase after stubbing his toe on a rock, then limped back to the hot spring's warmth before hypothermia could set in. He tossed the antique sword he'd grabbed just before leaving camp onto the pile of his clothes and slithered into the pool. "Oh, that's better." Who had that fellow been? It was dark but it looked like it could've been a soldier. "Thanks, Banwick," he muttered, "great job guarding the place." *I guess we have to let the secret out*, he thought. Too bad – they could've been very comfortable living by the spring for a little while anyway, but if soldiers were moving in.... "Oh well. Least I got my bath." He luxuriated for a few more minutes before crawling out again steaming. He dried and dressed quickly then headed back to camp.

*   *   *

"Argh, it itches!"

"Of course it itches," Alessia replied. "Water from hot springs is full of minerals. When you let it dry without rinsing off, you get salts on you. Which is what you two deserve for trying to keep it to yourselves."

196 • ERIC LEWIS

She poured a jug of cold water from melted snow over Ulnoth's head, making him shiver and moan some more. Corren and Nan encircled the pair lest they try for a quick getaway.

"Well, we're sharing now," said Banwick. "Didn't think we'd have to move on so soon. What're them sloggers doing up here anyway? We're in the ass-end corner of nowhere."

"How many did you actually see?" Corren almost snarled the question through grinding teeth, furious at the two for pulling something so selfish and at himself for not covering their tracks well enough.

"I just saw the one," said Ulnoth. "Which is one more than *he* did."

Banwick held his hand in front of him defensively. "Hey, I was havin' a piss break. I swear I was vigilant—"

"Enough! They never travel alone," said Alessia. "There must be more nearby. Do we hunker down and hope they miss us or risk moving out?"

"We could just…." Ulnoth made a slicing motion across his neck.

Nan rolled her eyes. "That's original."

"That'd just bring more when they didn't return," said Corren, shaking his head. "Besides, we can't even be sure it's us they're looking for."

"If we are they have a funny way of showing it," said Ulnoth. "He took one look at me and tore off screaming bloody murder."

Banwick grinned and seemed about to make a cock joke, but Corren's smoldering gaze kept him silent – one week on the receiving end of it was enough.

*　　*　　*

Two days after the fires of the Lenocca military camp were put out, a watch captain was discovered in his tent, lying on a pallet soaked with blood and piss with a gaping hole in his throat. A day later a patrol went out looking for some lost new recruits and never came back.

In Eikenstead, a woman who'd gone missing and presumed dead along with her babe turned up with an unbelievable story of capture and rescue. One of those lost recruits overheard the telling of it, and between the two the village went wild with rumor and speculation. Soon after, a band of local brigands who robbed the villagers under pretense of 'foraging' for the queen's army was surrounded by an emboldened mob armed only with pitchforks. The day ended with the brigands tied to horses and torn into quarters, and the pieces piled at a nearby crossroad under an effigy of a woman labeled 'The Warrior Priestess Sends Her Regards'.

In Carsolan, a ragged caravan of smugglers arrived unusually tight-lipped regarding their journey through the war-ravaged country, but after a few days in the tavern district tongues loosened a bit, much to the interest of Vinian's many paid informants.

$$\star \quad \star \quad \star$$

Vinian herself was much surprised when Carthagne Fadhlan ven Xedrusia himself arrived in Lenocca with a letter of safe conduct and a company of mercenaries. He presented Vinian with another letter bound by Engwara's seal, and marked in all the secret ways Vinian had shown her that ensured that it hadn't been opened.

V,

I'm writing this with my own hand because I do not trust any other. I cannot believe what you've told me, though I must because it comes from you. A peasant uprising! It is beyond unimaginable!

I have commanded Taurix and Ludolphus to advance immediately, together, to stop this treasonous plague from spreading. That is my only command to them, and to you. By any means necessary, is that clear?

The banker has volunteered the use of his mercenaries. I do not know why, but he claims it is to secure the bank's investment in the form of our victory. Maybe. He seemed to become most distressed only when I mentioned the location of the disturbances.

Make what use of them you may but act in haste, for when Taurix arrives I fear his methods will be far less precise. And be careful.

Work your magic for me, Vinian. I need it now more than ever. Remember how I love you and I know you will remember your faith to me. It is my only comfort.

Engw Q

* * *

A flash of warm indignation seized Vinian. *Remember my faith?* Did Engwara mistrust her baseborn spymistress, whatever the letter claimed? Or was it just paranoia? And to sign it with her official signatory title....

Vinian shook the thoughts from her mind and looked up at the banker. "An intriguing offer, Mister...what was your name again?" She said it just to needle him.

Carthagne rolled his eyes dramatically. "As if you don't know. As if you haven't been spying on me from the moment I landed on this accursed continent. But I suppose 'banker' will do. My name seems to be a matter of some local difficulty."

"Fine, fine. But tell me the truth, why *are* you involved in this?"

He inclined his head just a bit, paused. "It's embarrassing but...I sent a messenger this way with some, er, important financial documents to an associate of mine. He's yet to return and I fear he may've fallen victim to this unpleasantness."

Vinian raised an eyebrow. "That was stupid. This way? Where?"

Carthagne sighed. "Very well. To Vin Gannoni. I said nothing because the city is still under Pharamund's control and I didn't wish to present the appearance of a conflict of interest. Completely unrelated bank business, I assure you. Profit flows everywhere, my dear. But I would know the truth of it."

"It would've been safer to take a ship and come down from the north. This county's a choke point going west to east – you sent your man right into the jaws of the beast."

Carthagne opened his mouth to say something, but paused. Then a weak smile. "Time was...of the essence, I'm afraid."

He was lying. She could've told that even without her agents' reports. Oh, he was a master of deception, no doubt. But only so far as his job required, and thus Vinian's job necessarily required her being better than that. *Best to keep him under close watch. I shouldn't be convinced too easily, though.*

"Well, I'm accustomed to using my own people. People I trust. Why should I be inclined to use your...personal security contractors, as you put it?"

"Oh, they're quite skilled in domestic pacification techniques. Good hunters and trackers too. Why, I recall a nascent rebellion against a Pelonan doge in Ayala that was put down with exquisite speed and precision by the company I employ. It was simply a matter of locating the leaders' children, appropriating them all at once then returning them a little bit at a time, if you take my meaning. The affair was over within a week. They're Cynuviks, primarily. Hardy and strong, inured to pain and toil. Gods help me but they consider this country soft. Most of all they're sworn to absolute obedience. Even without your trust they could prove useful."

"Hmm." Vinian shouldered past Carthagne, making a bit of a production of circumnavigating his bulk in the small tent. Outside, the mercenaries busied themselves tending to horses and erecting tents of their own. They were an ugly, muscled troupe of brutes sporting either long flaxen hair or none at all. Blue tattoos adorned their bare chests and shoulders that defied the cold. They grunted at each other in their own tongue, sounding to Vinian like a ward of consumption patients. "Any of 'em speak 'Vani?"

Carthagne smiled. "A few, though none be great conversationalists."

"Then I hope you paid them well. I plan to put your claims to the test."

"A plan already? I'm impressed."

"Oh, I've been stuck here brooding long enough to come up with dozens. I've got an idea of where these rebels are – I just need to pin them down. Thanks to some…recent events, I couldn't risk using any of these." She waved a hand contemptuously over the camp of edgy soldiers. "Let's waste no more time. I just need to grab a few props and we'll be off."

"Props?"

"Let's see…cart with horse, couple of sloggers, dogs—"

"Dogs? I don't comprehend, mistress."

"Hungry ones. And a few of those trash pickers out there. Yes, that'll do nicely…."

PART THREE

CHAPTER TWENTY-FIVE
Total War

"It's right here, m'lord. We left it just as we found it, so you could see for yourself."

Taurix glared up at what was left of the boy. *Looks like I'm in the right place.* The cold held the worst of the smell back, but Taurix wrinkled his nose anyway. The flesh had started to rot away yet still hung lashed to the crossbeam, arms wide as if to say, "Behold, the fortunes of war, my lord." And it was indeed a sight to behold. The wreckage of the manor house had not weathered the winter well, the foundation and frame all that remained of the place. That and the Qassorian oak door. The soldiers hadn't even bothered to bury their comrades. Taurix couldn't really blame them for that – bodies had become part of the landscape, no more remarkable than the snows that covered them or the scavengers that fed on them. But in this case....

"And you're telling me this is the work of *peasants?* Why exactly are we spending all this money on weapons and armor and training when some underfed dirtfuckers with sharpened sticks can do *this?*"

"W–well, Marshal, we think they at–attacked at night, like cowards they did—"

"Oh, well," Taurix said, tongue dripping acid sarcasm, "a *night* attack, was it? That's completely different, of course." Taurix stepped forward and the soldier stepped back, pinned against his horse. "Truly cowardly. Tell me, which do you think is more useful to my purposes – cowards that win or a pile of *burnt fucking corpses?*"

He grabbed the man and shoved him face-first into the festering hangings on the cross before them. "You think this does me any good, eh? Idiot!" Taurix threw him into the muddy slush. "You could take a lesson from those cowards. Get up! Did you question the villagers?"

The soldier wobbled to his feet, fighting to hold back tears. "Y-yes lord, of course! We put half of them to torture. They all said the same thing – the folk what done this robbed their food stores and left weeks ago."

"And where did they go?"

"They wouldn't tell them. But they claim the band hasn't been seen since."

Taurix sighed. "Then the village is of no use to my purposes either. I want you to round them up."

"Them? Who?"

"Everyone. Every single peasant, villein, laborer – anyone you can get your hands on. Everyone. Bring them here and hold them. You have one day."

"But, my lord, that would take—"

"Whatever it takes, do it! That's what an army's for. Now go!"

Taurix turned back to the dead boy, considering. *Mockery*, he thought. *They're mocking us, mocking me. Putting him up there like that for all the world to see. They'll live to regret this. But not for long.* He sent for his engineers – they had much to do and not much time.

★   ★   ★

It was a pathetic haul, all told – less than a hundred souls, all too old, too young, weak or sick to run away. But they'd had only one day. *There'll be more to come*, Taurix thought as he looked at them. Plisten was no walled town and the county boasted no castle of note, but it was difficult to herd sheep without a fold so the mass huddled and wept within an enclosure improvised by the engineers.

He mounted the tree stump set before the human cattlepen. Would these southerners even understand his words? No matter. He cleared his throat and blew a glob of phlegm onto the ground. "My name is Taurix. Baron of Ólo and of Vin Gannoni, Lord of Phenidra, Count of the Northeastern Marches, Defender of Bergovny, Chieftain of Ar'Vaddhfa Edrai, Admiral of the North'rd Fleet and High Marshal of the armies of K— er, of *Queen* Engwara of Greater Argovan. I am also the last spectacle most of you are ever going to see." He paused for effect. If they did understand they gave little sign.

"In the brief hours or days before you die, I wish you to tell any that pass by here the cause of your grievous sentence. And that cause is the most unspeakable, unthinkable, unforgivable act that a vassal can dare to commit — open, violent rebellion against a sworn lord. The gods themselves have ordained the order of this earth in which some must rule and others obey. Defiance of that order is not only a sin against mortal law, but against the very divine universe. And who, I ask you, *who* can be against the gods? *None!*" He almost laughed at the hypocrisy of his words, and he glanced briefly at the units under Ludolphus for any rolling eyes.

"Your queen," he continued, "in Her infinite mercy and love for Her loyal subjects, has decreed that this perfidious plague of insurrection must not be allowed to spread further. Therefore, take comfort in the knowledge that the example of your punishment will stanch the flow of this pestilence, and restore peace and prosperity to this most blessed of lands. May the gods light your path, because I certainly will not." He stepped down.

Beside him Ludolphus stood scowling. "Nice speech," he muttered.

"Thank you, I so rarely get to declaim these days." Taurix motioned to an engineer, who motioned to another farther off, who motioned to another. Finally from behind a stand of trees came a line of soldiers marching one by one. They each held a cross.

A cry went up among the penned villagers. If they did not understand the Marcher lord's words, they certainly took his meaning now. A few tried to jump over the two-yard-high planks of the fence, only to be beaten back by watchful sentries.

"Ah," said Taurix, "much like when a kitten realizes it's being drowned and there's nothing it can do about it. Sort of beautiful, isn't it — that moment of terrible inevitability."

"Positively captivating," Ludolphus said, wearing a bitter frown. "Let's just get on with it."

Taurix regarded the old general with deliciously false sympathy. "Oh that's right, I forgot – you come from humble roots yourself, don't you? It must feel like I'm crucifying your own people. Well, I'm sure your ancestors weren't so squeamish about doing the same for mine when you drove the Marchmen into the mountains. Just be thankful we're both on the right side of history this time round. And you haven't long to wait – see, here they come now!"

Taurix strode toward the enclosure escorted by a retinue of spearmen and ordered the gate opened. The wailing peasants shrank back before him, but he finally picked out his prize – a young, heavily pregnant woman, sprawled on the ground and nearly senseless with fright. *Perfect*, he thought.

"No," she whimpered when she knew she'd caught his gaze. "No, please—"

"Oh, yes. Yes, yes. Come here!"

He grabbed the woman and lifted her up. So near starved was she that she put up only a token resistance that evaporated after a single blow. Amused that not a one of her neighbors dared to defend her, he carried her out of the pen and tossed her on the ground next to the first cross-bearing soldier. "Witness," he yelled in his best divine retribution voice, "the wages of treason!" He took a dagger and speared the woman's wrist straight through to a crossbeam, and she howled in agony. Cries of "Butcher!" and "Chthonii take you!" rang out among mostly incoherent moans. The soldier tied her arms and legs to the beams and used a large construction staple to nail her other wrist down, then he and another carried the cross to the nearby stretch of road where a post hole had been dug, leaving a trail of blood behind them. They hoisted the whole ghastly assembly, and the center beam sank home to stand upright. The cross was thicker and twice as high as the one that'd held Lupold and then the boy, and bore its victim to the sky to be seen from far off, as Taurix had ordered. The woman jerked, then sank into merciful oblivion.

"Wake her," said Taurix, "we ain't done yet." He pulled out his sword. The woman writhed in half-awareness after someone tossed a bucket of cold water up at her. He stepped back, taking care to judge the distance just right, then raised the long gray blade. Most of the soldiers turned away with tight grimaces, knowing what was next.

Taurix swung the sword up, grazing the woman's belly just enough to open it. Blood sprayed everywhere, and then her skin exploded like a lanced boil and her unborn child tumbled out. The red little thing swung from its umbilical cord, quivered once, twice, then dropped to the ground with a string of ripped entrails flailing behind. It stilled, and the woman sank into shock and did not recover. Taurix turned back to the panicked villagers, face splattered with blood. "Now. Who's next?"

One by one they went up, man and woman and child. Some fought while being dragged to their assigned place, most didn't. Some fainted or even died from heart attack before their turn, but they went up anyway. Many of the soldiers had to leave to vomit after doing their bit. The crosses were spaced about fifty yards apart, all along the road like signposts pointing the way to hell. The screams flew over the treetops and flooded the valley, stretching on over hours and miles while each of the condemned succumbed to blood loss or exposure. Only one remained. When it was his turn at last, Taurix stood over the brewer Ludrig, smiling his bloody smile. "Now. *You* my friend are having a very lucky day. Very lucky. I've a task for you, so listen carefully." They gave him food, coin, warm clothes and even a horse and told him to ride far and wide and tell all what he'd seen.

The work was hard and took all day, and when it was done Taurix rode past each one, looked each in their eyes and smiled.

★ ★ ★

"You know, I think I might be getting used to this damnable cold at last."

"Indeed. Might I ask a…philosophical question, my lord?"

Taurix lay on the table in his tent while his secretary Tobius worked oil into his aching joints. "By all means, General Ludolphus. My intellect is feeling invigorated today."

"What exactly is the point of this butchery? And that speech? If you were going to execute them anyway, I don't understand—"

"It wasn't just for them," said Taurix.

Ludolphus frowned. "It wasn't?"

Taurix waved the secretary away. "Give us two minutes, Tobius, then come back. No, it wasn't. You read that spy's report – the things these rebels have done. My guess is they've at least one good soldier among them, leading or giving advice. Maybe even officers. Deserters. That display, well—"

"Was meant for my army," Ludolphus finished.

"*Our* army. We foul things up enough and we're just feeding these terrorists more recruits. They're still out there, you know, hiding in the forest like the cowards they are, just waiting to welcome the weak-minded with open arms and then turn their spears against me. But trust it, after today that'll be less likely. You smell the stench of puke in the air? It's sweet to me, general – the more afraid they are the more afraid they are to betray me."

"You mean, to betray *us*."

Taurix nodded. "Precisely. Now, if you'll excuse me – it's been a long day and we've as much to get done tomorrow. Tobius! Get back in here!"

★ ★ ★

When Taurix moved on he peeled off the least useful five hundred from his army and sent them to relieve Lenocca's garrison. Those so relieved in turn made their way back to Carsolan and carried with them the stories of events both lived and heard from their comrades, and the Crucifixion of Plisten was foremost among these. Like the smugglers before them their words spread through the lower city and grew with each retelling. Two nights later three city guards were found floating in the harbor with their bellies slit open, bloated and fish-eaten. In response, Engwara ordered six taverns and the fishmongers' and dockworkers' guildhalls burned to the ground.

CHAPTER TWENTY-SIX

Where There's Smoke

"You know, it's not so bad," said Alessia.

"Easy for you to say. It's not your face." Nandine kept her eyes forward and scanning while they talked, finding it easier by the day to pick out any movement that might signal danger or dinner.

"I've tended many, many wounds, and I can tell you in a year you'll barely notice the scar. Besides," she shrugged, trying to sound casual, "I kind of like it."

"You do?"

"Sure. Like in a…a fierce beauty sort of way."

Nan lowered her bow and stared at Alessia with a look of concern. "Are you feeling well?"

Alessia looked away, face flushed. "I-I'm fine. What do you mean?"

"Ever since we found that hot spring everyone's been acting funny. Maybe there's something in that water making people sick. Bathing," she said, shaking her head, "it's a dangerous business."

Clean bodies are a dangerous business, Alessia thought. *Clean, soft… stop it stop it! Focus!* "I don't know. We'll be gone from here soon anyway. Maybe—"

"*Aaargh!*" The scream was followed by a series of snarls echoing through the trees.

"Where did that—"

"There! Come on!"

They raced toward the sounds, all thought of scars and baths banished as arrows were notched. They leaped over a hillock and below them they saw it – two vicious hounds snapping at a huge, bearded man curled up on the ground in a ball and utterly failing to avoid the flurry of teeth descending on him. A limp chain dangled from a manacle around one of his wrists.

"Gods," hissed Nan, "shoot!" She raised her bow, and hesitated for fear of hitting the man. Alessia took a shot, which grazed one hound and sent it yelping off into the forest. Nan took hers and it speared the other clean through the heart, fixing it to the ground. They jumped down to the bloody site.

"Are you all right?" Alessia asked, kneeling.

"I...thought...they had me," he breathed. "Thank you." They gave him some water and sat him up while Alessia checked him for wounds. "I fear...the dogs get everyone else. Perhaps more still out there."

Nan eyed his mangled feet. "Can you stand?"

"I try." He winced when they lifted him up. "It hurts, but a short ways can I go. Is there somewhere...?"

Nan looked at Alessia, questioning. *Should we?*

Alessia looked back, nodded. "Yes, not far. Let's go – wait, what is that?" She followed the chain hanging from the man's wrist. It snaked along the ground behind him, and at the other end was another bloody manacle.

The man gathered the length of chain up in his arms. "As I said, dogs get everyone else. The other fellow beyond hope was, so...I freed myself." He spat a red clod of something onto the ground.

* * *

"They were hauling us north. For what purpose I know not. Only that they take folk such way before and none seen to return."

Alessia wrapped bandages around the man's feet while Corren stood over them, brows furrowed. "They? You mean the queen's soldiers?"

"Yes. I know not whose idea to overpower driver and guard. Only I heard shouting, shoving. Then the wagon was turned over and we were free. We went in all directions – I and my chain-mate up the hill with two or three others. Then we heard dogs. I manage to fight them off, but...." He turned away. "I am ashamed."

"It's not your fault," said Alessia while Crander pried the manacle off the man's wide wrist. "Sometimes getting away is all you can think of. And they chased you all the way up here?"

"Dogs were starving I think, like everyone in Lenocca. They don't return to their masters."

"You were in Lenocca?"

"I was trapped in the city when war came. The soldiers wanted me, but I will not fight for that evil woman. Nor do they let me leave. Picking over trash, no life for a man, so after some recruits revolt I try to break out." He spread his arms wide with a sour smile. "I injured four before I was taken. Maybe they decide I be most useful in the mines up north."

"And this revolt," Corren said slowly, "what exactly happened? What caused it?"

"I know not how it starts, only that many officers and men were surprised and murdered. Many fires set. Most of the rebels were caught and executed, but some escaped. Luckier than me."

Corren nodded. "Well you're welcome to remain with us until you're well enough to travel, so long as you heed our rules."

The man grinned broadly. "Thank you. I knew there is still kindness left in this dead land. You...you are in revolt also, yes?"

Corren and Alessia exchanged a glance, just for an instant. "We," said Corren finally, "are just trying to keep our heads low for now."

"Ah, a good plan," said the man. He offered up a large hand. "Kryte am I called."

When Alessia finished her bindings Corren took her aside. "What do you think?"

She shrugged. "I don't know. I never saw him in Lenocca, but it's a big city. Or was."

"And his story?"

"Sounds about right...it is a bit convenient though, isn't it?"

"Mmmm. Keep an eye on him, don't leave him alone or let him go off alone."

"*Me?* Why me?"

"You found him – he's your pet."

*   *   *

"Kryte! What are you doing?"

The man looked up at Alessia with a surprised and hurt expression.

"Only feeding fire, madam, to boil some broth. Was this wrong?" The little pile of tinder sent a dark column wafting up through the branches, stark against the solid white sky.

Alessia grabbed a pail and doused the flames. "It's too much smoke. It'll give away our position."

"Ah," said Kryte, looking down on the black mess of sludge. "I am sorry. I had not thought of that. This is very new to me."

Alessia sighed. "It's all right. We're all still learning. We need to—"

"Who built that fire? You tryin' to send up a godsdamn signal to the— oh." Ulnoth came running out of somewhere spitting daggers at their new guest. He did not trust the foreigner or his story any further than he could throw him. Which was not very far at all.

"It's fine," said Alessia. "It's out now. There's no harm done."

"You don't know that," Ulnoth countered. "Someone still coulda seen. And *you*," he pointed a half-mended arrow straight at Kryte, "use dry wood next time." He stalked away, muttering curses under his breath.

"Sorry about that," Alessia said. "Tempers are a bit frayed right now."

"You will move from this place soon, yes?"

"Can't stay in one spot too long. Crander's figured a way to take the wagon apart so it can move through thicker forest, but that just means more to carry. And we're weary."

Kryte nodded. "This can I see." That was an understatement – the encampment presently looked as though some giant had smashed a great fist through everything. Clothes, half-finished bowstaves, odds and ends pilfered from a dozen raids and more lay strewn about the tromped-out space among the trees. The only thing that didn't litter the enclosure was food. It dwindled once again even with the contribution from Plisten. True, the hot spring had lifted spirits at first. Just enough to remind them of the few comforts they'd once had but left behind. A mood of indolent despair hung over the place. "Is there some task I can do, to help? Perhaps not one with fire-building."

"Oh, there are a thousand things that need doing. But it might be better if you did join up to fight for the queen, then you could send some food and medicine our way."

Kryte rubbed his chin, a comically studious gesture from one so rugged. "Hmm. I cannot go back now, but perhaps what you say is still possible. Before they send us from the city I hear many discussions – they think a man chained like an animal somehow cannot still comprehend, for the fools spoke openly. The queen pushes ever closer to Thoriglyn, but this means her supply lines grow longer. More and more must pass through Lenocca. One such train was spoken of, to be sent five days after us prisoners, along the same road. From what I see here, you could go and get it with little difficulty."

Alessia kept her stare perfectly neutral. She said only, "I see." *Yes, very convenient indeed.*

"Well," said Kryte with more insistence, "will you not?"

"I'll speak to Corren about it."

"If you fear to risk many of your folk I will come to help."

Alessia looked at the man's feet, still wrapped in bandages. "Does that mean you're healed enough?"

"Oh," he replied, as though he'd forgotten the vicious dog attack and been suddenly reminded. "I.... If you think it so."

"Then I'll speak to Corren. Until then no more fires, agreed?"

Kryte smiled, and it sent chills down Alessia's spine. "Yes madam."

★   ★   ★

"Nah, too good to be true."

"You think so?"

"Come on, it's a trap. Even I can smell it a mile away."

"You're getting cynical in your old age. So sad to see."

"Funny."

"Well what if it's not a trap? We could really use that food."

"The dead don't eat none, do they?"

The five of them sat arguing in a circle inside a rough hide tent – Corren, Ulnoth, Alessia, and now Dannek and Nandine.

"I'm not saying I trust him," Dannek said now. "Just that it's worth checking out, ken'ee?"

"Much as it pains me to," said Nan, "I agree with him. We need that food, and we've taken risks for less before."

"We'll track 'em," said Dannek, "get a good look first. The right team, we could keep up without being seen, I guarantee it."

"You know who to use?"

"Aye, we been out enough times I know who can be counted on."

"Not Banwick I hope," said Ulnoth.

"No."

"All right," said Corren finally, "do it. If you say yes, we go in. I'll personally take Kryte along. Meanwhile keep him a bit away from everyone – no need to let him get too cozy just yet."

"And if it turns out he's lying?" Ulnoth asked.

"Then a pack of rabid dogs'll seem like a pleasant memory."

★　　★　　★

A day later twenty Heron Kings crouched with eyes and ears peeled for the approach of the prey they'd tracked for several miles. One ambush team waited on a slope above the road just south of the fork, another on the other side, with Alessia kept back just far enough to notice if any needed aid when the killing started. It was the last ambush point for miles, their last chance. They all wore the same drab brown as the tree trunks around them, bows strung and short swords loosened at their waists. They kept Kryte between and a bit in front of them, trusted only with a staff.

An hour passed in silence and grim determination. A second hour passed with impatient sighs. Every so often hand signals flashed to and from Ulnoth's team on the other side: *When? Wait. Now? No, wait.* When the third hour brought audible grumbling, Marella threw a little ball of packed snow at Corren's shoulder and waved. When she saw she had his attention she pointed south.

"There they are," Corren said quietly, though they were still well out of earshot. "Get ready." He spread his arms wide, palms facing downward, then knelt. As one, any still standing sank further into the brown, into nothingness. Across the road all movement disappeared.

"Oh, godsdammit," Nandine whispered.

Alessia gave her a quizzical look. *What is it?* she mouthed.

"I gotta take a piss."

The caravan rolled closer. They could make out individuals now, drovers and sloggers both. It seemed to be ten men altogether, and three wagons. *Foolish to leave it so poorly guarded.* She knew everyone would be picking out targets – *first that one, then that one, I wonder could I hit that one on the far side?* She wouldn't have bothered, knowing how fast plans crumbled when things started.

The caravan was almost right below them. The tension was given voice by the sound of twenty bows being drawn or half-drawn and Alessia felt the anticipation quivering around her.

Movement. Not from the caravan or their guards, but from across the road. Corren glanced furiously toward Ulnoth's team. Movement and noise, both frantic. To everyone's shock, Ulnoth appeared halfway out of the trees and flashed the signal for *No. No, no, no,* over and over again.

"What the...." Nan gnashed her teeth when she saw the gestures. Ulnoth made a new signal, one whose meaning she couldn't remember.

"*Abort,*" said Corren. "Dammit! Send it down the line."

"But—"

"Do it!"

One by one the word took each of them by surprise, and they relaxed their weapons with confused and disappointed expressions. Below them the caravan rolled on, oblivious to the halted attack. In stunned silence the Heron Kings watched it go by, wagons loaded high with whatever each person's imagination supplied, lost and gone forever, leaving empty bellies growling behind. "He'd better have a damn good reason for this," Corren said.

"I do not understand," said Kryte, only now seeming nervous. "Why did you not—?"

Dannek and Ulnoth sprinted across the hard-packed track and up the hill in a mad dash. "Stay down," hissed Dannek, dragging Nan to the ground when she tried to rise.

"What are you taking about, why did you—"

"Quiet!" Ulnoth took out his knife and held it to Kryte's throat while kicking away his staff. "Especially you, shitpot."

"Wha—"

"Quiet!"

They stayed quiet without knowing why. Then they heard it –

someone else, coming up the road. Many someones, with many horses. They moved in relative silence for mail-clad men bristling with weapons, and at a leisurely pace. Exactly the same pace, it seemed, as a supply caravan. *Disciplined group*, Alessia noted. *Don't look like sloggers, these. In fact they look a lot like....*

Her eyes turned to Kryte. Ulnoth pressed a knee into the man's back, holding him immobile. "One move," Ulnoth whispered, "one sound, and it'll be the last you ever make." Kryte only frowned back.

The men passed by just as the wagons had, eyes darting back and forth as though in expectation of something, then faded away as well. Wind whistled through the trees for a minute more as they all stared at Kryte. The truth of it plain, there seemed little to say.

"You were right," Nan said to Ulnoth at last. "A trap. Mercenaries! If we had attacked we would've been cut to pieces. How did you know?"

"I didn't," Ulnoth answered without relaxing his hold on Kryte. He cocked his head at Dannek.

"Just a feeling," the youth replied. "I was coming up to join you, then decided to make a quick double-back. That's when I saw them riding up behind. I ran here as fast as I could chance it, told Ulnoth to call it all off."

"Glad you did," said Corren. "Saved a lot of lives today, son. Exquisite work." Dannek looked away, embarrassed. "Now, as for *you*...." The rest of Ulnoth's team melted out of the brush to join them as a forest of blades pointed down at Kryte. "Here's the deal. You answer every question I put to you and I'll give you a somewhat quick death. Or we can drag this out. Your choice."

"I have nothing to say," Kryte replied.

"Ulnoth, take an ear."

"My pleasure." In a moment his knife was out and biting into the Cynuvik's earlobe. Alessia moved to stop him, but something had taken away her will to do so. She just watched with an attitude of...what? Enjoyment? Righteousness?

The man grimaced, ground his teeth, but did not cry out. Steam rose from the bloody wound. Ulnoth held the bottom half of the lobe in front of him. "Halfway there!" He tossed the raw slice of meat and cartilage onto the ground where a swooping cardinal quickly snatched it up then flew off.

"No hurry," said Corren. "Ain't no one going anywhere. Let's start with something simpler. That smoky little fire you set the other day. I'm guessing that was no accident, but a signal. Am I right?"

Kryte said nothing.

"Ulnoth, if you please…?"

Kryte began to struggle and was met with three or four sword blades poking into his backside. Before Ulnoth could finish his task Alessia at last stormed between them. "Stop!"

Ulnoth looked up. "Why?"

"Because, he won't talk, whatever you do to him." She looked down at him. "That's the way of it, isn't it? You serve whoever pays the most. Merc's code."

Kryte smiled through the pain of the wound. "Not so dumb as you look. No matter. You're already dead. Only a matter of time." He tried to laugh, but instead coughed on blood dripping into his nose.

"Let me make you a better deal then," she said, kneeling down to look into the Cynuvik's eyes. "We'll let you go, as whole as you yet remain."

Ulnoth and Corren and Nan all stared at her, brought for once to total agreement. "We *what?*"

"There's naught to be gained from simple revenge, we all know that."

"But he'll tell them where we—"

"We'll be gone soon enough. He doesn't know where we're headed, what kind of shape—"

"He knows we're short of food!" Nan protested.

"They knew that already," Alessia countered, pointing up the road the way the caravan had gone. "We, on the other hand, don't know anything. How about it, Kryte – is your life coin enough to turn your coat?"

"Why should I believe you?"

"I don't care if you believe *me.* You just need to believe that fellow above you just itching to slice you up like a saint's day pheasant."

"What," he snarled after a long silence punctuated by his ear dripping blood onto the snow, "must I do?"

"Who hired you?"

A pause. "The…the queen," said Kryte.

"Personally?"

Another pause.

"That's a no then. Who then, Taurix?"

Kryte furrowed his soaked red brows, but said nothing.

"He doesn't know that name, I can tell," said Gant, caressing the handle of the cleaver he'd taken from Plisten and itching to use it. "Don't lie to a liar."

Corren folded his arms, stepped forward. "Some other lord? Why not use soldiers to hunt us down?"

Kryte spat contemptuously. "Those idiots are useless. You have no idea what you stir up, do you? Well, you will."

Alessia felt a furious heat welling up from her gut. "Ulnoth, the other ear please. Don't stop this time."

Ulnoth knelt down, wrenched Kryte's head around and set the blade against his other temple. "I shoulda been a chef...."

Kryte growled more in anger than in fear. "Wait! Fine. One bitch or another, what do I care? But she's a far sight harder than you."

"*She?* Who, the queen?"

"No, the other one. At 'Nocca. Some burned bitch does the queen's shadow work."

Nan snorted. "What do you mean *burned*? Not some highborn lady from Engwara's court playing shieldmaid?"

Kryte sneered back. "If she's highborn then so am I. Face like seared lamb, uglier than yours even. No, you have a death-worshipper after you. I counsel you cut your own necks now and save some suffering."

Corren furrowed his bushy brows either deep in thought or troubled. "Where's this burned bitch now? Still in the city?"

Kryte shrugged as much as a man in such a position could. "Somewhere 'twixt here and there I ken."

"Emony," Corren barked, "keep him alive!" He grabbed Ulnoth and Alessia, dragged them further up the hill where they could talk without interruption. "You know what this means?"

"Umm," Ulnoth said, "kind of?"

"This is what we've been waiting for – someone with connections we can show your letter to. Someone the queen will believe."

"Someone currently hunting us to death," said Ulnoth. "Don't exactly inspire confidence. Who's this burned woman?"

"Probably an assassin," Corren said. "A touch smarter than your average slogger. Maybe even one of Engwara's personal agents."

"If so," said Alessia, "this could be our chance. If she has the queen's ear—"

"Heh, ears all over the place today."

"Shut up, Ulnoth! If we tell her about the bank's scheming, she'll tell the queen in turn."

"It's half the equation," Corren mused, "but what about Pharamund?"

"Burn that bridge when we come to it. You're right – we have an in now, let's not waste it."

"But how to be sure our friend there'll deliver our message?"

"You just let me and Dannek worry about that," Ulnoth said, wiping his blooded knife clean. "Satisfaction guaranteed."

*　　*　　*

That very night they released Kryte with a very odd proposal, along with the distinct impression that he'd be followed at close remove by more than one arrow ready to ventilate his lungs should he stray from his course, or the lantern he'd been given go out. Ulnoth in fact did so for the first hour, and when it was clear he was headed straight south Dannek led a team to observe him at regular intervals. Before dawn Kryte approached a small party of riders camped upon the wayside and Allard, ready to drop from fatigue, watched from his hidden post as they blurted out exclamations in some foreign tongue at the sight of him alive. Kryte spun around, scowling more darkly than ever, held up the lantern that was almost burned out, then laid it on the ground as if to say, *See? I've done as you said!*

"Gotcha," Allard whispered. He backed away and faded into the forest to find a place to take a nap.

*　　*　　*

To the Burned Bitch,

We apologize for the unseemly moniker but your emissary seems not to know your proper name. Alas the trap you set for us did not meet with much success, though we commend the effort. Do not despair! We believe we can offer a far greater prize than our heads to adorn Engwara's pikes. We've sent your man – and we use that term most loosely – back to you to request the courtesy of a parley. By pure chance we are in possession of a certain piece of information which could have a profound impact on the course of this campaign of terror that your supposed queen has loosed upon our country. To whet your appetite we say only that it concerns the activities of a certain wealthy entity native to the uttermost west, as well as another to the east. If you agree signal so with a fire arrow – trust we'll see it. And please do not attempt any further actions against us. Considering your numbers and position, rest assured that at this moment it is you who are at our mercy, and not contrariwise.

With warmest regards,

The Heron Kings

★　★　★

"Cheeky bastards," Vinian muttered when she finished the note. "Fire arrow, warm regards – no doubt these are the rebels that riled up Lenocca." She cast a glance at Kryte. "*Burned bitch*, is it?"

"They tortured me," said the Cynuvik, pointing to his subtended ear. "I had to say something!"

"I thought," spat Vinian as she turned to Carthagne, huddled and shivering in his furs, "you said they could endure any hardship."

"Indeed, madam," the banker replied through chattering teeth, "that has always been my observation. Until now."

"Endurance was nothing to do with it," Kryte said plaintively. "They offered to let me go if I spoke, or kill me if not. A simple business decision it was. Surely a man such as yourself can understand this?"

"Surely. What does that note say, anyway?" Although Carthagne spoke fluent Argovani, his reading was slower and peeking over Vinian's shoulder didn't reveal much.

Vinian summarized the message, saying only that they offered useful war information and left out the bit that obviously referenced the Marimines Isles. *What of value could these wretches possibly know?* she wondered. *And what is this eastern entity? Pharamund? Strange....*

"Heron Kings," Carthagne repeated with a snort. "What a silly name."

"My experience, when it comes to bandits the bigger the name the smaller the game."

"They certainly saw through your plan well enough. What now?"

"Why not agree to this meeting? Obviously they think they have the upper hand. As well they might."

Carthagne's entire face went as red as his runny nose. "You can't be serious. You don't know their numbers – they may be bluffing. Or worse, they may not be."

"Yes," said Vinian with more than a little relish, "and I was willing to spend the lives of all your men just to find out. I still am. Let's see what these bandits have to say. Then we can decide whether to 'attempt any further actions' against them."

"Erm...one moment. Let me confer with my man here, make sure he's suffered no injuries beyond the cosmetic." The banker wrapped an arm around Kryte and pulled him away from Vinian, whispering in a crude approximation of the Cynuvik language. She tried to listen while appearing not to, but could only pick up what sounded like the words for 'fast' and 'best trackers'.

★　　★　　★

"Send it up."

The arrow arced across the sky. It was a clear and blue day, and the signal stood out proud before it. But Vinian didn't watch. She stared instead at the message lately put into her hand. Not another insolent note from those terrorists; no, this was from the secretary in Lenocca pressed unwilling into her service. *So, Taurix is on a rampage, killing everything in his path. How predictable.* She had to give it to him, lining the road with crosses and pinning up peasants the whole way would certainly make an impact. *Though perhaps not the one he intends. Savage blood or not, he has the mentality of a highborn. Thinks they'll be shocked into submission. I almost pity old Ludolphus.* The whitened face of the courier that'd delivered the message attested to the truth of it, having ridden through Taurix's advance. "He'll be here soon," she said to herself. "Not much time then."

"Madam?"

"Nothing," she said to the courier. "You can go." The courier nodded glumly, not keen to ride back through that highway of horrors again.

"News?" Carthagne waddled up to her, appearing for the first time that day outside the warming tent to watch the signal arrow fly.

"You might say that," replied Vinian, handing him the note. "Our lord marshal's coming this way, along with his distinct flavor of wrath. If we want to catch these terrorists we'll have to do it before he arrives – I doubt they'll stick around for this...."

Carthagne read the message, taking his time to make sure he got it right. "Is...is this true? Is he—?"

"Whole villages, aye."

"By all the gods...."

"By none at all," Vinian snarled. "This is man's work, as ever."

"Foolish, and short-sighted. Well, the invitation is answered – what now?"

"We wait," said Vinian. "The next move is theirs."

Carthagne gave Kryte a quick look, and it was answered with an almost imperceptible nod.

CHAPTER TWENTY-SEVEN
Merry Meetings

Near Wengeddy, the lone survivor of Taurix's crucifixions happened upon a camped gathering of townsfolk hiding from the depredations of General Pertinax, Taurix's most trusted officer. As he told his gruesome story his eyes blazed with fury in the firelight. Before the next dawn, the ragged band set upon the bridge across the Carsa River with tools of their former lives – axes, mattocks and saws. Not to destroy it, no, but to make it as weak as a house of twigs. Pertinax's army streamed out of the recently reconquered town to march south and join Taurix. When the first soldier set foot at the midpoint the bridge crumbled, spilling a dozen men and beasts into the icy waters of the Carsa.

In Carsolan, the unrest caused by rumors continued, and when the entirety of Harlot's Row burned to the ground, a grain factor named Marek publicly accused Reynal's smugglers of causing the disturbances, and Reynal himself of treason. When palace guards came to arrest him, a young boy with a leg wound tried to interfere, and the affair ended with the blood of both of them spilled between the cobblestones, and the guards torn limb from limb by an angry mob. The factor Marek was found drowned, most curiously, in a pot of millet porridge with a silver coin shoved in his rectum.

Above it all Engwara sat in her palace with the gates locked tight, effectively under siege, and looked down on it all in utter disbelief. Vinian might well have explained it quite exactly, but she was far away.

★ ★ ★

"I'm *hungry*."

Alessia patted Lalaith on the head after strapping the baggage to her back. "I know, dear, I am too. And cold. But we have to go now. Just a little longer."

"Everyone always says that."

She took a last look at the clearing. They'd gotten good at picking up and moving – but for the mess in the snow you could barely tell that anyone had lived there at all. Tents, canopies and supplies were rolled up and hoisted onto weary shoulders, animals weighed down with packs and the wagon collapsed to fit between the trees. The Heron Kings had become true nomads. "Go on," Alessia said, "join the others. Stay in the middle of the pack."

She turned to see Dannek running toward the remains of the camp. "That's it," he said excitedly. "They say yes! I saw it."

"Good," said Corren, stepping into the saddle of their one unladen horse. The children had taken to calling the dappled gray Phaerie in mockery of King Pharamund, but Alessia couldn't bring herself to name an animal they might be forced to eat soon. "I'll go oblige them. You and Nan get to the head and keep the course to safety."

Alessia looked up at him. "Why you? Whole thing was my idea – I should go. These people need their leader."

"The *parley* was my idea. And I've taught everything I know. I'm not special anymore, you are."

Alessia's face darkened into a scowl. "Corren, the other day I ordered a man tortured for information and felt nothing. This goes on much longer the bastards'll do worse than kill me – they'll make me into one of 'em. I want this over. Besides, I've got the letter and I'm not giving it up. I'm going." She took hold of Phaerie's reins and lifted herself into the saddle – in front of Corren, forcing him to shimmy backward.

"You're mad, woman," he groaned. "At least let's take along some iron in case things turn sour."

"If that happens," interjected Nandine, shrugging a pack from her shoulders, "you'll need more than two. Let me come—"

"*No!*" Corren and Alessia both shouted at once.

Crander handed up a sword and bow with a full sheaf of arrows. "Here. One thing we ain't short of is weapons. If only we could eat metal.... Be careful, these ain't nice people."

"Neither are we," said Corren. "Keep east, take winding paths, and leave decoy tracks—"

"Aye, aye, we know that. We all do. Catch up quick, eh? I get nervous with Ulnoth in charge."

★   ★   ★

The Heron Kings meandered single file up the hill, a cold red sun bathing them through the branches as it sank. Few spoke, saving breath for the task of porting their worldly possessions on backs. With one free hand Ulnoth led a roan gelding – this one named Enga in honor of the queen – loaded with grain at the head of the great gray human train. He was so intent on negotiating the slippery incline he jumped with alarm when Dannek appeared next to him.

"Dammit, boy, don't do that! Like to take you for a Marchman and perforate you like Banwick nearly did me."

"Sorry. You seen Gant? He's got my sparker and he's sure to lose it on this death march."

"I think he's somewhere halfway back, pestering Sally."

"Is it just me or have they been spending a lot of time together lately?"

"Have they? Hadn't noticed."

"It's just, I thought they hated each other."

Ulnoth laughed. "Opposites attract I guess. 'Course that'd make Sally just about everyone's opposite."

Dannek moved to catch a sack before it fell from the horse's back. "That doesn't bother you? I mean you and she were...."

"Nah," grunted Ulnoth. "I got no claim on her. Besides, after I lost everything I don't seem to want much of anything."

"Oh...."

"Listen, don't pay me no mind. You got your own pretty little yellowhead to think over, ain't that right?"

Dannek blushed. "Alixe is great. I just wonder what we'll do, you know, later. If we survive all this whether she'll still want me. I mean we've all kinda just been thrust together without much say-so."

"Aye, we all heard some of that *thrusting* last night, thank you very much. Look, I'm no oracle for sage advice, but I say just keep your eye on makin' it through the day and worry about later, later."

"Well, what for you then? If not women, what comfort would the grim and terrible Ulnoth wring from what's left of the world?"

Ulnoth looked up, appeared to sink deep in thought for a moment, then said in a low rumble, "A thousand-year-long howling wind, to drown out all my thoughts forever. Yes, that would be nice...."

Dannek laughed nervously. "You're fracted in the head."

"Oh, you've no idea."

★   ★   ★

Sometime after dusk an arrow was found lodged in a post holding up Carthagne's tent. No one saw where it'd come from or who'd shot it. Unnerved that they could get so close – *as intended, of course,* she thought with grudging admiration – Vinian unwrapped the note around the shaft. *North along the highway one quarter mile then turn right at the deerpath. Alone and unarmed.*

"Ha! Fat chance of that," she said.

"What is it?" Carthagne peered over her shoulder.

"Our instructions. Your men ready?"

"As ever. And with some delightful new equipment – gifts from Lord Taurix." He held up one of the cross-bows they'd taken. Carthagne had been playing with one for most of the day, nearly impaling more than one of his mercenaries. "You know, I don't think he puts much faith in technology."

"Just keep that thing pointed away from me," said Vinian.

★   ★   ★

The tension in the air was so thick you could cut it with a...well, a knife was overkill. A spoon would do. Or a blunt stick really, proper utensils being a rarity in these parts. *And they haven't even shown yet,* Vinian thought. She knew they could be walking into their own deaths, but somehow doubted it. *Why bother with a meeting at all? They could've shot us down anytime.* Carthagne's six mercenaries with their cross-bows eased her apprehension somewhat, though the banker himself rather added to it.

"How much further do we have to go?" he wheezed, trying in vain to keep his fine leather shoes from sinking into the mud. "This is ludicrous."

"It's 'farther'. We go until our friends make themselves known. Quit complaining. You could use the exercise."

"A low blow, my dear, hardly worthy of your keen wit. I'll have you know that in my youth my belly covered hard sinews strong enough to wrestle an ox."

"A roast one maybe. Here, the path disappears just ahead – can't be very far now—"

"Correct. Stop." The voice stabbed like a falling icicle. The party jerked to a halt; the mercenaries raised their weapons and cast about for targets.

Vinian licked her lips, pushed down the pit of anxiety in her stomach. "We're here. Where are you?"

"You didn't come alone. Or unarmed," said another voice, barely recognizable as female.

"Let's not quibble over trivialities. My time's valuable so come forth and we can get to the fun part, shall we?"

"First tell your thugs to lower their…whatever those are."

Vinian waved to the mercenaries. They looked at the banker, and he whined, "Are you sure about this?"

"Not remotely," said Vinian. "If you want you can go back to your tent, let me deal with this." *I dare you. I dare you to leave me alone with them. What might they say about you?*

Carthagne glowered at her with a twisted lip before turning to the mercs and snarling something in Cynuvik. They slowly dropped the bows but kept tight grips on them. Kryte, who instead carried a torch, rested his hand on a long sword at his hip.

"There," called Vinian into the darkness, "we're at your mercy, just as you claimed."

At last in the flickering torchlight appeared two of the most pitiable excuses for human beings Vinian had ever laid eyes upon. The man might've been strong and strapping once, but like Carthagne seemed to have fallen from grace, dreadfully thin instead of fat. The woman Vinian remembered from Lenocca was worse off – starved and breastless, she might've been taken as a boy for the chausses and tunic she wore. Both held bows notched and taut, arrows aimed only slightly downward.

"That's better. So *these* are the Heron Kings. The ghostlords spreading terror and death across half of Bergovny. I must say, I'm underwhelmed."

"That's yourselves you're describing," the man spat, his words dripping with hatred. "You're the ones burning everything in sight, murdering as you go all so you can rule over the corpses."

Vinian thought, *You've no idea – wait 'til Taurix gets here.* "Yes yes, save your breath. I don't make policy, only enforce it." She nodded at the bows. "Not exactly a parallel gesture on your part."

The woman sneered. "Don't make the mistake of thinking this is some kind of negotiation. We brought you here to make an offer. I suggest you quit quibbling over *trivialities* and listen."

Corren took a cautious step forward. "You must be the 'burned bitch' that bastard behind you spoke of."

"Vinian, Her Majesty the Queen's royal spymistress." She made a sarcastic bow.

"Impressive. Who's the landwalking manatee?" He motioned to Carthagne with his still-drawn arrow.

"Ah," the banker said with more confidence than he felt, "you know of sea beasts. Are you a sailor?"

"Have been. Answer the question."

"These gentlemen are mine," he said, spreading his arms to encompass the mercenaries. "You should be proud – they've been engaged specifically to track you and your friends down. Expensive."

"Could've saved some money," said Vinian. "Seems all I had to do was let you come to me."

"It's of money that we wish to speak," said Alessia. "Do you know where your queen gets the funds to continue the war? You must if you're truly who you claim."

Vinian turned just enough to put Carthagne in the corner of her eye and watched him fidget. "What if I do? That can hardly have anything to do with your little band of traitors, now can it?"

"How about Pharamund? How is it possible Engwara hasn't spent him into the ground yet?"

That took Vinian aback. "I...we've been wondering that. What of it? Quit dancing about and tell what you know."

"I'll do better than that." Alessia slowly lowered her bow, opened her belt pouch and pulled out a roll of tanned red hide. She unfurled it and displayed the document it held in front of her, stepping just close enough to let Vinian see the writing. "Can you read Bhasan?"

Carthagne tensed then took half a step toward Alessia. "Ah! Uh, um...I can. If you would...?" He extended a hand.

"Stay right where you are," said Vinian, stabbing a finger at him. "The parley was addressed to me. I can read Bhasan too."

As Vinian read, so many pieces fell into place. She lost track of how many times she thought *Of course!* and *How could I have not seen it?* Only when she reached the end and saw the ridiculous golden signature – C. F. v X. – did her mind begin to race. Should she reveal the banker to the strange pair? What would happen? What would his men do? *Careful, careful.*

"It's...a fake," she said at last, knowing full well it was not. "A fabrication. How could such as you get your filthy hands on this thing?"

"A messenger cutting through dangerous country," said Alessia, "*our* country. Tripped over us, took our presence as something it was not and...well, he's long dead."

"And you'd give me this supposed evidence why? Out of the goodness of your hearts? You've already shown you have none. In exchange for gold? You've stolen more than enough. To spite a far-away emperor?"

Corren felt his temper flare, heedless of the danger they were in. "To make you royal idiots stop slaughtering the world long enough to look up and see you're both being deceived! Don't you get it? We want it to stop!"

"You say you're a spymistress," said Alessia. "Tell me this is really the kind of spycraft you prefer, I dare you. Starving conscripts bashing each other into oblivion and taking the rest of us with 'em? Is that truly the height of your skills?"

"How dare you. I've worked without rest to end the war as efficiently—"

"Then do it! You want a chance to make policy, *here it is!* Take this to your queen, and to Pharamund also, get them to agree—"

"I tire of this farce," Vinian said with a swipe of her hand. "I'm here to find you and wipe you out and I intend exactly that. How many of your fellows surround us?"

"More than you could find before being cut down," said Corren, desperate to hide how tired his arm grew. Sweat glistened on his brow.

"Oh, I think not. If it were so they'd have their weapons trained on us and you could lower yours. You're afraid. And I think you *are* alone. And, I think these men shall seize you now."

At once the cross-bows were hefted upward, pointed at Corren's chest before he could react. "Don't," snapped Vinian, "unless you desire a very painful death. I'll take that." She reached for the letter, still held in Alessia's right hand, while the left hovered frozen above the hilt of her short sword. "A fine forgery, I admit—"

"Actually *I'll* take that."

Vinian turned to see three of the cross-bows now pointed at *her*. Carthagne strode forward, fear now replaced with a smug grin. He snatched the letter for himself, gazed at his own handwriting with almost sexual longing. "Apologies, but your act could not quite fool one who sails seas of lies as often as those of water. I appreciate you doing the hard work for me though."

"You treacherous sack of cack," Vinian hissed. *Never trust a traitor.*

"From you, I count that a compliment." He nodded at Corren and Alessia. "As for you two, I don't know what you thought you were doing, but your stupidity this day has given me great comfort. Now I can rid myself of several irksome insects all at once. I will graciously allow you to die knowing you have the sincere thanks of both Bank Isle-Euderico and Emperor Artabarzanes. Boys, put these animals down."

★   ★   ★

The mercenaries braced their cross-bows against shoulders and raised to aim, and a strange calm washed over Alessia as she tensed to at least try and dodge the bolts she already imagined ripping through her organs. But when the action began, something went very wrong.

No, that's not right, she thought. It seemed that it was one of the Cynuviks that was struck, not her. The man screamed more out of alarm than in pain as an arrow lanced out of the darkness.

"*Gyaaargh!*"

The others pulled the triggers of their weapons, and iron went flying. Alessia dove, felt Corren tumble into her. Screaming, then more screaming. Knives and swords, flashing in the light of Kryte's dropped torch. Their spooked horse bolted into the night.

"Get them!" someone yelled. Corren drew his blade as a mercenary fell onto him. He buried the point in the huge man's belly, straining to push it deeper through hard muscle until the weight atop him went limp.

Alessia grappled with Vinian, neither woman sure where the other stood in this sudden violence other than in front of her, and they both went to the ground. A hot flare of pain shot through Alessia's thigh, and she looked down to see a cross-bow bolt protruding from it.

While two of the mercenaries scrambled to reload, the others drew swords and attacked. Then, out of the forest a raging cry came on the heels of another arrow shot.

Thank all the gods for ever and ever, Alessia thought. *Nan!* Another merc went down wounded, and she swung her sword wildly to fend the others off. Meanwhile Vinian had produced a blade of her own and slashed at Carthagne while he made clumsy attempts to pummel her into the ground. The blade opened a stretch of his face, and as he jumped back Vinian snatched the precious, crumpled and bloodstained letter from him. "Come," she said to Alessia, "we'll kill each other later!"

Kryte pushed Carthagne out of the way and raised his sword for a blow that would take off three heads at once. But before it could fall Corren jumped out from under his kill and buried his blade in the Cynuvik's back. Kryte let out a sharp puff of air and his eyes went wide. Corren ducked the backward swing of Kryte's sword, then used his body to shield himself from another volley of bolts. Rather than press the attack, the remaining mercenaries clustered around their employer as Carthagne scuttled backward along the pathway, bleeding profusely and whimpering.

"Let's go," said Nan, panting and sporting a dozen cuts and bruises.

"I can't," Alessia hissed through clenched teeth and tears, "I can't walk—"

"You can," Vinian replied. "You damn well will!"

Carthagne's voice echoed through the trees. "You fools, don't let them get away now! Kill them!"

"Lessi, you must," Corren insisted. "However much it hurts, you *must*."

They hoisted her to her feet, and she wailed as blood spurted from the wound. Vinian took an arm around her shoulders and carried Alessia deeper into the brush.

"We'll cover you," said Nan as Corren handed her an arrow. They turned back, drew and loosed just as the mercenaries came one more time. Two were hit and their bolts went wide. A third sailed through Nan's tunic in a one-in-a-million shot, straight up her sleeve and out the shoulder without tasting flesh.

"Now, while they reload!" They turned and ran, and within two seconds the night forest had swallowed them up again. Cheated of both his prey and his incriminating letter, the banker howled in fury.

CHAPTER TWENTY-EIGHT
Sacrifices

"Wait, stop."

Ulnoth almost barreled into Dannek. "What is it?"

"Something's wrong."

"What do you mean—"

Attack! Ulnoth thought it even before the first bodies hit the ground. A harsh cry rang out, a voice he couldn't immediately place, then another. Another. He dropped the sacks and whipped his bow up around his shoulder. "Down, get down! Cover!"

"*Where?*" someone screamed. Bolts sailed through the darkness, invisible comets of death. All along the line people panicked, or huddled together or writhed on the ground. Children wailed. Ulnoth and Dannek frantically sought shelter behind a pile of sacks.

"There," grunted Ulnoth, pointing somewhere into the black, seemingly at nothing. Then...the tiniest movement.

Without thought or conscious aim Dannek loosed a shot and then heard a low moan. "Alixe," he whined, "where's Alixe?"

All around them shapes moved in random directions, collided, fought, fell. Others who'd had the good luck to be armed took shots of their own, not knowing whether it was friend or foe they targeted. Then the attackers advanced in force. Ulnoth pulled a sword. "Scatter!" he yelled. "Everyone scatter! Give no target!" Ignoring his order, Dannek charged the nearest shadow, swinging wildly. The big figure ducked, and Dannek barely avoided having his shoulder cleaved away. He scrambled on hands and knees, and as the attacker moved to impale him through the back an arrow appeared at the base of his skull. The man said something angry in a foreign tongue then fell back, twitching.

"Come on," said Ulnoth, wrenching Dannek to his feet. "More of 'em out there – we gotta get out of here!"

"But Alixe—"

"Come on, we're alone. Nothin' you can do now!"

Dannek groaned with impotent hate while following Ulnoth into a grove of trees. They picked up two others wounded, then pressed themselves as hard as they could near the ground, not feeling the cold for once. Screams erupted on occasion, and once Dannek rose to take a shot at a menacing shade that strayed near.

When all fell silent they forced their burning, frozen limbs out of a crouch and Ulnoth crawled from his hiding spot. "Dannek. Gimme your sparker." He tore a strip of worn wool from the nearest body he found. The little red flare of light confirmed his suspicions. "Cynuviks," he spat, then stomped his heel into the upturned face.

Others came out, slow and terrified. Ulnoth took up the dead man's long sword and wrapped more wool around it to make a crude torch. He held it up before them.

Dannek gasped. "All the gods and all the Chthonii...."

It was Wengeddy all over again. Figures both dead and nearly dead littered the slope. Their baggage and supplies, once so precious, were strewn all about like garbage. Overhead the moon appeared from behind clouds and its silvery light revealed dark swaths in the snow. Moans, cries of anguish. Not many though. Not very many at all.

"I don't know, Bed," came a terrified voice from somewhere ahead of him. "Maybe got 'em all, maybe chased off, or still out there. Stop asking!" It was Gant, his tunic steaming with blood not his own. Noticing Ulnoth, he said, "There you are. Quick, help me. Emony's doing what she can but we can't see shit. What happened?"

"Mercs, looks like. Good ones. Prob'ly tracked us and used that meeting as a distraction. They hit us all at once."

They pulled a barely moving form from under some crates. It was Crander, skewered by two cross-bow bolts. He wheezed and coughed blood. "Hold still, old man," said Ulnoth. "You'll be fine—"

"Nah," Crander whispered. "S'all right. Always knew. Done...."

"Hush," Dannek pleaded as he tried to stop the obscene flow of blood from Crander's belly. "Save your strength."

"I'm done...bein' afraid. Done. S'all right...thank you." Crander's eyes closed, his head went limp in Ulnoth's shaking hands.

"Damn it all," said Ulnoth. He stood. "Come on, plenty more around still in need."

They rescued two or three more from the worst of the carnage, unsure of how many might yet be waiting just out of sight. The sameness brought by the stillness of death made some of the less fortunate hard to identify in the darkness, but Ulnoth thought he recognized Marella. A fellow from Wengeddy. A smuggler whose name he couldn't remember. Then Ulnoth froze and Dannek followed his gaze downward.

"Oh, no. No, please no...." It was Lalaith, the little girl. A blade had cut her nearly in two. Ulnoth sank to his knees, huddled into a quivering ball. Dannek reached out to touch the man's shoulder. He flinched away and buried his head in his hands. "No. Just...give me a...."

Dannek left Ulnoth alone. He came across a Cynuvik, barely alive. Dannek stood over him while the dying mercenary eyed him with contempt, an arrow buried in his chest and a series of sword blows on one side. He uttered something nasty, and Dannek raised a knife to dispatch him, then halted.

"No. No, you don't deserve it. You can bleed out." He kicked the merc in the gut and turned away, only to find Banwick before him.

"You...better come," he said, not meeting Dannek's eyes.

"Why? What is it?"

"Emony says...better come. It's Alixe."

*   *   *

The girl was in bad shape, and there was nothing Emony could do with the training she had. Nothing anyone could do, really. A bolt was through Alixe's lung and her ribs had been crushed by a falling horse. Her eyes were glassy and drowning in tears but still focused on Dannek when he raced to her side, though she could not speak. Ulnoth stood watching, feeling more dead inside than the bodies strewn around them.

"Oh gods," Dannek whimpered, "save her!"

"I cannot," said Emony. "Not even Alessia could, not out here—"

"Godsdammit, do *something!*"

"Dannek," said Ulnoth in the gentlest voice he could manage, "she's drowning in her own blood. All that can be done...is to end her suffering."

"*What?* No! How could you say—"

Alixe shuddered, gurgled something. Dannek held her tighter. "It's all right, I'm here. I'm right here. Listen...remember, remember the other day? We were talking about...about what we were going to do, later? In the spring, maybe. We'd leave everyone behind, slip away in the night, go far away where no one would bother us. Just you and me. Maybe build a cottage somewhere. You remember that? You need...to pull through, so we can do all that. I'll travel the towns and become the best carver around, and you'll smuggle in the best fabrics and spices and everyone will envy you...but we'll always be alone, together...." As Dannek mumbled all this Ulnoth forced himself not to notice Emony take something small and pull it gently across Alixe's wrist. The girl didn't even flinch. Dannek held her and talked to her until her eyes closed and she stopped breathing, and then until her heartbeat faded away. He held her still, mumbling nothings to himself. Everyone else stood silent.

Eventually Gant knelt next to Emony. "Did...did you happen to see Sally?"

"No. Allard?"

"No. Maybe they got away."

"Maybe." Emony looked around her at others who still needed care. "I don't think we can go looking. If there are more of those bastards out there—"

"There are." Ulnoth walked in between them, his eyes puffy and red, his voice even more leaden than usual. "I spotted some on the horizon, just past the trees. Think they're hoping we'll lead 'em to the rest. Don't think they know we're only three dozen. Or we were."

"What do we do?" asked Gant.

"Give them what they want. Get everyone able together – we'll lead 'em away. Don't ask me where, just away from here. Emony, stay and care for the wounded." He looked down at Dannek, still cradling his lost love. "All of them."

*   *   *

Ulnoth and Gant took four of the least wounded in a close pack formation and crept out of the cover of the forest. They were high into the foothills now, miles from road or river. Wind whipped through the icy gorges where trees grew scarce. Not far ahead was the crest of the ridge.

Ulnoth pulled his cloak tighter. "They still behind us?"

Someone crawled up next to them. "Aye. Ten at least. Keeping up well enough. They think we don't see 'em."

"Good. We're going over the top."

The man blinked. "Over...over the top? But that's—"

"Yup. Marchman country proper."

"Don't seem much of an improvement to me."

Ulnoth looked at the fellow. "What's your name again?"

"Verrell."

"Verrell, when the odds are against you, you can give up, fight to a glorious defeat, or change the rules. Over the top things can't get much worse for us than they are. For our friends back there, they absolutely can."

*   *   *

"What by all the nameless saints is *that?*"

Ulnoth eyed the object of the fellow's gape-mouthed question with a mix of terror, disgust and elation. "That, Kuther, is a Marchman Tel."

They'd hoofed it for an hour, stopping only to make sure the mercenaries were still behind them. Gant had taken Dannek's sparker back and used it to build a tiny fire to keep them from freezing. Then it was over the crest of the ridge where the land flattened a bit. Just beyond it loomed a village-sized hill, but not any made by nature: perfectly round at the base and a straight slope up to the pointed top like a perky tit towering from a maiden earth. The only trees clustered at the very summit, obscuring who knew what horrors.

"A Tel?"

"They build them, in high places like this. For their rituals."

Gant swallowed hard, their pursuers – mortal men at least – momentarily forgotten. "To worship the Chthonii, you mean?"

"Nah," replied Ulnoth, "that's just tall tales. Marchmen don't *worship* anything. But they honor their ancestors, make offerings for favors and such. At least that's what Bed says."

"We best steer clear then."

Ulnoth shook his head. "No. It's just what we need. Make for it." Not waiting for argument, he ran. The others reluctantly followed, snow crunching loud underfoot. Closer and closer it grew above them – so simple a structure, yet terrifying. Finally they came close enough in the gray early light to make out a stream of smoke wafting from the high treetops.

"Holy hells," hissed Verrell, "that thing's occupied!"

"Just as I hoped," said Ulnoth with an evil grin. "Half moon, right on time. Run hard right to the base, then break left for them bushes yonder. Whatever you do, do *not* set foot on that slope."

"What is he doing?" breathed Kuther as he sprinted away what little reserve of energy he had left.

"Don't...ask...me," said Gant. "Too tired...cold...pissed off to figure it."

"Quiet down!"

When they hit the base of the Tel Ulnoth made a breakneck leftward twist midstride then somehow managed to run even faster. The others followed as best they could. Half a heartbeat before they dropped from fatigue they crashed into a wall of frozen brambles. Ulnoth clawed a path before them using only fingernails and spite, and when the last of them was firmly enwombed in branches they collapsed, scratched and lathered but alive, breathing heavy.

"Hush," spat Ulnoth. "If you fear death and worse, hush!" He maneuvered himself through the growth to turn around and watch the Tel. "Now we wait."

They waited. Before long – frighteningly soon, really – the Cynuvik mercenaries came running into view, hot on their trail or so it seemed. But where Ulnoth's crew broke for the thorns the mercenaries followed the signal of smoke, climbing right up the Tel's slope.

"So that's what you planned," someone whispered.

"I hoped. Cynuviks might be tough customers but they don't know the local riffraff. Now if we're real lucky...."

No one spoke, even long after Ulnoth failed to finish his thought. They waited, eyes fixed on the summit of the Tel waiting for... what? When the first scream rang out high and mad like nothing you'd expect from big tough sellswords, all except Ulnoth jumped half out of their skin. Then there was another, then another, then ten others, screaming the screams of tortured lunatics. Even after all they'd suffered it was hard to listen to, and Gant covered his ears. After what seemed like an age they faded away, and the fires began. They flickered through the trees at the summit, then flared high and higher.

"Give my regards to the Chthonii, you babykilling pricks." Ulnoth began working his way out of the thicket. "Let's go, no one after us now. Stay close along the bushes and we'll keep it that way."

They crept back toward the ridge, seeing it now as some magical boundary between the violent but familiar world they knew and... this. A sickening smell like charred pork drifted through the air. But before they could reach their destination something reared up in front of them, something out of a drunken madman's nightmares. Everyone froze.

It bore the rough shape of a human but surely could not be. Large, muscled and hairy, mostly naked with broad splashes of unnatural colors across its torso and sporting the antlers of a stag, it towered almost as tall as the Tel itself, or so it seemed. Its face was obscured by the gloom but the fires from atop the hill danced in its eyes. It smelled sickly sweet like rotting flesh and wildflowers. Before it the Heron Kings – how ridiculous that name sounded now! – cowered small and pathetic.

The thing glared at each one of them in turn. At their knives and bows and desiccated faces and tattered clothes and cloaks. Its gaze at last rested on Ulnoth. Somehow leaders always knew each other, even ones as unlike as these. The creature reached for something swinging from its waist. Something big and roughly round. What was it?

The growing light revealed the creature's prize when it held it aloft – a head. A human head still dripping blood. The creature let out a hard, repeating sound. A cough? Or....

Is it laughing? It tossed the head, and it rolled to a stop at Ulnoth's feet. The man – or was it truly some creature? – waited. Expecting? Slowly, cautious as a newborn fawn, Ulnoth knelt, picked up the head. He held it aloft, mimicking the creature's gesture, and bowed, all without breaking eye contact. Still laughing, the thing made a waving motion and all around them as though from thin air a dozen like shades materialized, though none of these wore an antler crown. They rose from the tall dead grass with barely a sound from spots that a sane man would swear had held nothing a moment before. And just like that they left. They broke into a run back toward the Tel, a long loping run more like deer than men, swift and silent.

Ulnoth and the others stayed fixed in place for seconds that seemed like hours. Long after all sight and sound of the fearsome beings was gone they stayed while the wind whispered softly through the grass. The Cynuvik head swung by its hair in Ulnoth's grasp. At last Ulnoth forced himself to turn around and face his crew, knowing there would be more than one pair of wet braies in the bunch.

It was Verrell who spoke first. "Was that...?"

"That was a Marchman," said Ulnoth after clearing his throat. "A chieftain. And yes, we're still alive. They must've been watching the whole time."

"But why did they—?"

"I don't know. Maybe since we supplied their offering they decided not to make another out of us. Doubt we'll enjoy that courtesy a second time." Suddenly remembering what he held, Ulnoth threw the head away with a revolted grunt. "Come on, I want nothing more to do with this place."

CHAPTER TWENTY-NINE

World Movers

"Hush," Vinian insisted. "Keep quiet or they'll find us!"

"...what...you wanted," Alessia moaned.

From behind Corren Nan materialized, and together they scooped Alessia up with a practiced gentleness that took Vinian by surprise.

"Fast," Nan said just above a whisper. "They're not far behind."

"Where?"

"Doesn't matter, just go."

The slope was too steep to carry Alessia uphill, so they made their way north, weaving through the brush and boulders and trying not to go too long in any one direction. Alessia faded in and out of consciousness. After a time Vinian dared to comment, "We can't keep going this way much longer."

Corren didn't bother to look at her. "Why not?"

"Because, this is enemy territory. Pharamund's got patrols – um... oh." She nearly tripped over the torn and bloody riding gown she wore. "Never mind."

"No, that's good," Corren said. "If you wouldn't come this way, neither would they. Means we can go back toward the road to move faster."

"Doesn't matter how fast we move," Nan said, "without a kitted physic...."

"I'm...sorry," Alessia mumbled. "I should've...."

"Ssh, you just relax," said Nan, pausing to wipe sweat from Alessia's brow. "You've taken care of us long enough. It's our turn."

Corren looked up the mountain. "But we'll never find the others in time. All right, back to the road. Maybe...maybe someone will happen by."

The highway to Thoriglyn narrowed after it split from the river road, and was not much used those days except for the aforementioned patrols. There were no waysides carved out for travelers, or if there were they were long overgrown. "Lay her down here, easy," Corren said, choosing the least uncomfortable spot he saw. "I need some light. Nan, do you have any— good." They tore up a top layer of grass to get at the relatively dry stuff underneath that was sheltered from the snow. After a tedious harvest they had a few handfuls of kindling and set it alight.

The bolt was buried through inches of thigh meat but not quite protruding out the other side. The look on their faces made Alessia come more fully to her senses. "Set me up...lemme see."

"Are you sure—"

"Now!" They raised Alessia's head and shoulders while hoping to avoid putting stress on her lower half, but she bit her lip trying not to cry out. "Chausse...off." They cut her legging away from around the wound, leaving a skinny bloody leg sticking out. She felt the flesh around the bolt and winced. "Deep."

"Tell us what to do, Lessi," Nan pleaded. "Tell us how to help you."

"Need my kit...."

"We don't have it. I'm sorry."

Alessia closed her eyes again. "Knife?"

Corren nodded. "Aye, girl, you know we've plenty o' those."

"Put two in the fire. Make 'em hot."

"I'll do that," said Vinian.

Corren packed some snow atop the wound to numb it as much as possible.

"I don't understand," said Nan. "We can't cut through you to get this out. We can't pull it out – it's barbed, it would—"

"You know," said Corren, "what we have to do." He looked at Alessia. "You do."

Alessia nodded with gritted teeth. "Do it."

Nan and Vinian held her down, and Corren put a twig wrapped in cloth between her teeth. Then he knelt over her, directly above the bolt. Not giving her the chance to lose heart, he held the bolt steady in one hand and with the other pounded the shaft further into Alessia's thigh. It popped out the other side with a sickening squish, the broad head dripping. Alessia howled as much as her packed mouth would allow, which was still quite a bit. Nan squeezed her eyes shut and looked away while Vinian sat stony-faced.

Corren snapped the head off the bolt, then yanked the remains of the shaft back out of Alessia's thigh. While Alessia continued to shriek he plucked the knives – not red-hot but they'd have to do – from the fire and pressed them onto both entry and exit wounds. The smell of burned flesh filled the air and Alessia's cries went up an octave. Grinding his teeth almost to the bone, Corren forced himself to hold them there until the searing sound faded.

Alessia's last thought before sinking into senselessness was of Lannie, the boy whose own arrow she'd removed. *We need more practice....*

★   ★   ★

"Let me guess," said Vinian. "If she dies I die, right?"

"Don't feel special over it," Corren answered. "If she dies we *all* die. You see how well we practice physic. I should kill you now just to be safe, but you're too good a castra piece."

"That banker won't put any value on me, that's certain. He'd only want me back to make sure I—" Vinian suddenly realized Corren's meaning. "Oh."

"We'd just need her head," Nan said, putting a hand to her sword. "No mistaking it for another...."

"No," said Corren, "more than that. He wants that letter back. He's the one, isn't he? The one who wrote it."

Vinian dug through the folds of her gown. She'd shoved the document down her front while they were fighting to get away, and though it was torn on one corner the hide it was rolled in still protected the essentials. She held it by the waning firelight. "I'm not surprised he'd pull something like this. It's what banks do, after all. I am surprised he'd be so reckless to put it in writing and cast it into the world. Taurix switching sides must've really spooked him."

"Why *did* Taurix betray Pharamund in the first place?"

"Well...I might've had something to do with that."

Nan blinked. "You?"

"The right pressure, applied to the right place at the right time can move entire worlds. One ill-tempered Marcher lord is child's play. Hard to believe you've survived out here this long without knowing that."

Corren looked down at Alessia. Her breathing was shallow, her pulse weak. Her eyelids fluttered through what he hoped was a dreamless sleep. "We might not much longer. Can you get back to your queen and tell her what you know?"

Nan stood up, angry. "You're not letting her go!"

"It's half of what we aimed at anyway. We still have the letter. Well?"

Vinian shrugged. "Taurix is coming, should be here in less than a day. He won't easily be convinced, not after that banker pours poison into his ears. But I still have my resources."

★   ★   ★

Alessia awoke to a gray light and pain, and a certain face hovering above her that she'd hoped was only.... "Oh gods," she rasped, "... wasn't a dream. Water...." Vinian fed her some fresh snow, and Alessia nearly choked on it so dry was her mouth. Slowly but still too fast it came back to her – the meeting and the letter, the double-cross, the mad getaway.... "Aargh!" The pain burned anew even though her wound had been bound and packed in more snow, now red. "Where...are we?"

"North and east from where we started," said Vinian, her voice all fatigue. For the first time in a long time she hadn't needed a bottle to fend off the nighttime jerks – sheer exhaustion had done the job. "Somewhere between certain death and unending misery. Disputed country all around. Your friends keep watch southward. Lie still – you don't want to reopen those pokes now."

"What...what's it to you? You tried to kill me last night."

Vinian shook her head. "Capture, ideally. Your little insurgency intrigues me. The killing would've come later at someone else's order."

"Your tenderness warms my heart."

"Well, things seem to've changed around a bit – we're in the same boat now. A funeral barge to be precise. But I might be in a position to help, should you survive. Her Majesty does not take kindly to being duped. We—"

"You're awake! How are you feeling?" Nan and Corren had once again managed to sneak up on Vinian without notice.

"Like I been eaten by bears," Alessia said weakly, "then cacked out and eaten again. But I'm still here."

"We can't stay out in the open," Nan said. "Smoke on the horizon, lots of it. An hour off yet but definitely coming our way."

Vinian nodded. "That'll be Taurix. Slow and steady beats the race to a bloody pulp. Master ven Xedrusia won't be far behind so I suggest you use that famous magic of yours to weave a concealing mist."

"The only magic we have," Corren said angrily, "is rumor and superstition."

"You don't think that counts? What about your friends uphill? Can we get to them?"

"With any luck they're far from here. We're on our own—"

"Oy!" The shout came from the road, from northward. "Oy, you there! What do you think you're doing? Stand to!" The man wore a ragged tunic with a faded red badge hanging by about four stitches. His companion wore no badge but looked every bit as mean. *Pharamund's men*, they all thought. The twists in the narrow track had concealed them until they were too close to avoid.

The pair came upon the motley crew with looks of half consternation, half suspicion and another half spite just for bad measure. "Who're you sorry lot? Look like you done ten rounds with a frost giant then clawed outta yer graves. Declare y'selves!" He put a hand near the hilt of a ragged sword.

Nan and Corren exchanged a glance that said much. Corren took the initiative. "Who do you think we are, you dolt? We *were* contracted to supply the forward post, but you can forget that now!"

The soldier frowned. "Supply? But there ain't no post for'rd of the fort!"

"No shite! Someone shoulda told that arsehole cap'n what hired us that. You see the result." Corren waved a hand at Alessia laid out as what he hoped was a convincing prop.

"Wait," said the unbadged soldier. "What cap'n? What happened here?"

"I don't recall his name," said Corren, "but he was outta Duelleigh's fort."

"Ah, that explains it. That place is full o' fools don't know their arses from a hole in the ground. So you get hit by that green bitch's partisans, or…somethin' else?"

"Bandits," said Nan. "Same trash been all over the valley for a season. Took everything and nearly did us in. We just got away."

"Bandits? Uh, so you don't mean, well, you know."

"What?"

"Come on, you musta heard. *Them.* Chthonii! They's crawling all over the mountains, woke up by the ruckus of the war. They been seen even!"

Vinian raised an eyebrow. "Have they?"

"Say," said the badged soldier, "you're a touch well-armed for a company of carters…."

"In this place you better believe it," said Nan a bit too quickly.

"And overly feminine too. What lord granted your license exactly?"

"Erm…Lady Nostrado?"

The soldier sneered. "Well now, that is a bit of a problem. Y'see, Lady Nostrado's dead."

"What?"

"Aye, half a season dead. Bloody flux they say. Before the contracts was renewed." He took a tighter grip on his sword. "Who are you *really?*"

"Uh…."

"You best come wi' us," the soldier said. Or began to say, as he was then inexplicably hit with a hail of arrows. Corren jumped back.

Actually only a few arrows hit their mark out of the flurry that leaped from the opposite end of the road. The other soldier let out a wordless yelp and turned to run, and a wiry figure appeared from the cover of the trees brandishing an axe. They both disappeared around the first bend before a horrible shriek rang out, then cut off suddenly.

It was a messy action, certainly. When it was over several skittish folk drifted from cover, indecisive and doubtful and looking with fear on the four they'd rescued. One man a bit more confident than the rest approached them. "Good bait yinz're, no doubt. Sorry abaht dat, waitin' so long but we's unused to comin' aht for strangers. Thought yinz might be some o' us, but y'ain't, huh?"

"I was just thinking the same about you," said Corren, though he strained to understand the man's accent. "But thanks all the same, mister, uh...."

"Oh, my name ain't important. Names just makes us easier to track dahn...." The man stopped and looked down wide-eyed at Alessia. "Wha—? You. Don't I know you from somewheres?"

She smiled. "You should, Wrenth. You helped build my hospital, for all the good it did."

"Alessia? It...it is you! Damn girl, you look terrible."

★　★　★

"Been a rough winter," Wrenth said later, "but when ain't it? Guess I don't need to tell you that. Woulda been a worse but for the rumors goin' round. Marchmen, monsters or whatever rainin' hell down on the soldiers. I guess we have you folks to thank for it?"

Alessia hobbled through the trees with a branch for a crutch, the others trailing behind. "Don't thank us. A big joke's what it is. Where've you been all this time? What happened after Firleaf? And... Quen?"

"See for yourself." They broke through a wall of whitened brush into a clearing set low in the ground, and a campsite far less than the Heron Kings had managed but no less welcome opened to them. They moved Alessia into a grove of oaks that'd somehow held on to a few leaves through the winter, and as the strangers tended inexpertly to Alessia's wounds Wrenth spread his arms and a familiar eight – no, now *nine*-year-old jumped into them.

"Quen!"

The girl, grown more desiccated and angular and dirty yet undoubtedly Quennet, turned and laughed. "Lessi! You look terrible."

Despite pain and fatigue, Alessia smiled back. "So I've been told."

"I was so afraid when you didn't come back." Quen's smile faded a bit. "Momma died. I was sad for a long time. I still am sometimes. But we revenged her a hundredfold."

"Now," said Wrenth, "no more talk like that. Did you catch anything today?"

Quen held up something brown and furry and limp. A groundhog. "It came out early. Big mistake."

"Good girl. Take it to the spit—"

"I know, I know." Quen moved toward a fiery pit with a spit slung empty above it, then turned. "I'm glad you're back, Lessi."

"So am I, dear."

Wrenth bade them sit by the fire while the animal roasted. "Welcome to New Firleaf. Not much to look at but does the job. I heard about certain goings-on, didn't quite believe 'em. Sure didn't figure you for one to join up, Lessi, but whatever. Some of us even felt like adding to the soup, and any slogger we come across better watch out."

"Adding to the soup," said Corren, "wouldn't happen to include a couple pinned up in a field on a hill a few days from here, would it?"

Wrenth grunted. "Saw that, did you? Weren't my idea, but there you have it. That's bad enough. Some o' the other stories though, well I don't right know what to believe."

"Believe what you like. Thanks for your help, but we really must find our own people. Things are heating up beyond what even we can deal with."

Wrenth frowned. "Meaning what? What exactly are you folks about?"

Corren and Nan looked at Vinian, who'd held back and kept silent as a precaution. Now she took a step forward. "That, erm, might take some explaining."

*　　*　　*

"Delayed! A week delayed!" Taurix hurled the message against the wind, and when it blew right back in his face it only made him madder.

"What? What's delayed?" Ludolphus had come to accept his role as observer in the bloody affair Taurix had wrought on the Carsa valley. The Marcher lord's idea of pacification surpassed even his own jaded experience, and the miles of crosses had worn him thin.

Confident in the county's depopulation, they rode now in the shadow of the wild Marchman-infested hills that separated them from Thoriglyn. He'd stopped vomiting at the stench of rotting peasant, but his sleep remained restless even for one of his years. So he asked the question disinterestedly, as a bit player in an unpaid role.

Taurix did not respond in like manner. "Pertinax! He let himself get boxed in at Wengeddy. Someone sabotaged the bridge before he could cross – whether he rebuilds or cuts south and over, it's a week either way. I wanted to finish this hock-chopping and take the war to Pharamund's doorstep at last. No chance now."

"If we push hard we can take some ground at least, and hold until the spring thaw."

"Aye, I'll have to be content with—"

"M'lord!" Tobius sidled up alongside Taurix, shoving Ludolphus out of the way without ceremony or apology. "Outriders are returned – they report smoke from the highlands. Likely Marchmen."

"Your own people," mused Ludolphus. "Think you might like to go up and say hello?"

Taurix laughed contemptuously. "Hardly. The tribes hate each other even more than they hate the Argovani. No, we'll give them bastards a wide berth. One problem at a time – wait, what's that?"

"What?"

"Up ahead!"

Ludolphus squinted. "A clutch of riders, too few to be any harm – it's that fatass banker! What could he want?"

When the company drew near enough they saw the banker sported a nasty face wound, attended by far fewer mercenaries than previous, and those in sorry shape.

"Ah," said Ludolphus, "Master Carthana. Seems some ill has befallen you."

The banker drew rein five yards from the pair of generals. "Carthagne," he said, pronouncing each syllable as one would instruct a toddler – "*Carr-thahn-yaa fadh-lahn*...oh, never mind. It matters not now. Who'd ever trust one so marred by violence?" He barely brushed a finger across the poorly treated scab that meandered across his cheek like a red river and inhaled sharply.

"Oh we ain't trusted you before, never fear," said Taurix, brightened just a bit by the man's misery. "What happened?"

"It was that witch what happened! That...that *woman*, Vinian!"

Ludolphus frowned. "What about her?"

"She turned on me! On us! On...on the *queen!* She was in league with those rebels all along. We were about to apprehend the ringleaders when she ordered them to attack us. I myself barely got away, lost my best man to a knife in the back—"

"What is this cack?" Ludolphus almost fell from his saddle, shaking with incredulity. "You lie, that cannot be!"

Carthagne's jowls bobbed up and down rapidly. "Oh it be! How else do you imagine I suffered *this?*" He motioned to the wound, careful not to touch it this time.

"Banker, there is no one – *no one* – in this world more loyal to Her Majesty than Vinian. Not even I. What have you really done?"

"Why, it's all true, I swear it!"

"Oh good, you swear it," said Ludolphus with a snort.

"What cause could I have to dissemble?"

"You've no cause out here at all. What game—"

"Enough, both of you." Taurix sliced the air with a mailed hand. "I'll give orders to capture or kill the bitch on sight, but one more damned rebel or less I care not. I care about getting my arse and the arses behind me up this road and in Pharamund's ugly face, so step aside, banker, and *stop delaying things!*"

The army pressed on, wending its way unknowing past scores of eyes that watched with both fear and hatred, but more of the latter.

★   ★   ★

"Must be over a thousand men," whispered Corren from his hiding place. "Pharamund holds all the country beyond – are they actually marching toward battle?"

"His orders," replied Vinian beside him, "were to put you lot down, but if he sees an opportunity he'll take it."

Corren turned to the woman with suspicion. "So you aren't at all of a mind to go join him?"

Vinian shook her head. "He's got no love for me. You see that pig riding next to him?"

"Hard to miss."

"Taurix won't believe anything I say now. Besides, thanks to you folk, things aren't so clear-cut, are they?'

"You're welcome."

"A winter battle," Nan mused, buried in the grass nearby. "Will he risk it?"

"Maybe not," Vinian answered, "but that's good. Gives us time to work your magic. With a little help from a spymistress."

★　★　★

"Will she live?" Nan asked.

Wrenth shrugged. "How do I know? She's the physic. We done what we can, followed her 'structions close as our supplies allow. Depends on luck now. If it gets affected...."

Wrenth, Quen and their companions took turns watching over Alessia like mother hens fawning over a single precious egg. Vinian sat by as well, pondering her strange status somewhere between hostage and ally. When night fell she wondered whether she'd be spared the jerks for a second time. *Almost makes being a prisoner worth it.* There were other annoyances though.

Nan glanced at Vinian's marred face over and over again, and the spymistress could no longer credibly pretend not to notice. "Don't worry, girl, you're still prettier than I if that's what you're wondering."

Nan instinctively put a hand to her own scar. "What? N-no, it's not that. Just...what happened to you anyway?"

"What do you care?"

"Maybe I like to know my enemies."

"Good policy. Nothing entertaining, if that's what you're hoping for. When I was a kid some baron's son took a passing liking to me. Not knowing the finer points of feudal etiquette, I... constested his advance. So he threw me into a kitchen fire. I got burned. That's all."

"Oh. I'm sorry...."

"Why? Best damn thing that ever happened to me. With this

beauty mark my dear parents, gods rot their souls, could never hope to marry me off, so they treated me like one of the cattle. Even made me sleep in the barn. Everyone was like that. People didn't want to see me, and eventually they didn't. And when people don't see you, they can let slip the most interesting things. Valuable things. I learned to use that."

"That's how you became a spy?"

Vinian nodded. "Got pretty good at it. One day I aimed a bit too high, tried to blackmail that very same noble whoreson. I was lucky. Rather than getting skinned alive on the manor green I was taken before the countess, to be made an example of at court. Instead the countess was intrigued by my story, so she offered me a choice – a job in her household or burning at the stake. And as you might expect, fire held few secrets left for me."

"Countess...Engwara?"

"Just the same. Gave me education, training, position, and in time agents of my own. And a certain baron came very much to regret his decision not to flay me."

"Yet you're still her creature. The choice is still service or the stake."

"That's true for everyone. At least I know it."

"It's not true for us."

Vinian's temper flared. "No? Making a good go of it, are you? Fighting the good fight for freedom from tyranny? You fools have no idea what Taurix has done because of you."

"Then why don't you tell me?"

Vinian rummaged through her purse, the slivers of paper and whatever was writ on them now worthless except as kindling. When she found the one she sought, she hesitated. "I want you to know I had nothing to do with this. I never would, if only because of the sheer stupidity as a long-term governing strategy—"

"Gods' sakes, what is it?"

Vinian handed Nan the note from the secretary in Lenocca and tensed for violence. Nan scanned the message, fire dancing across her eyes. Her lip began to tremble. The paper fell from her shaking hands, and for the first time since the debacle at Duelleigh's fort, Nan curled up in a ball on the ground and wept.

★　　★　　★

The hillside was still littered with five or six corpses, shown in all their gruesome glory by the noonday sun. But it was a welcome sight for all of that, since it was now only dead mercenaries, the others mercifully having been moved somewhere else. But whoever had done it was gone now.

"No sign," said Gant after making a cursory circuit of the area. "Maybe it means we're getting good, but I can't make out where everybody went."

"Maybe they're all dead," said Verrell. "Maybe more of them Cynuviks came and finished 'em off. W-what if we're all that's left? What do we—"

Ulnoth slapped Verrell just hard enough to shut him up. "Cut that! If we're it then no use panicking, is there? Calm down and light a fire. Figure out what to do after I thaw my feet out."

Ulnoth barely had time to get one ragged boot off when Gant nudged him. "Hey. Don't look now but there's someone coming up the left side, real sneak-like."

"You sure?" Ulnoth slowly put his boot back on and took hold of a blade while keeping his gaze straight ahead.

"I'm sure."

"All right, tell the others. Sneak-like as well, eh?"

The figure darted between trees, stepping lightly to avoid any sound but not doing a good enough job of it, and when it was nearly upon them Ulnoth nodded to everyone. "Now!"

They leaped to their feet armed and ready for a fight, but the intruder jumped back flailing. "Wha— Hold, I surrender!"

"Godsdammit, Banwick," breathed Ulnoth, unable to hide his relief under a layer of annoyance, "what were you thinking, pulling a stunt like that?"

"I wasn't sure who you were. I thought maybe they got you and came back for the rest of us."

"Huh. Turnabout serves you right, almost gutted you. Where is everyone?"

"You won't believe it," said Banwick, "but we found us a place. A good place – a cave. It—"

"A cave. Figures...."

"It's not as bad as it sounds, really."

"Don't see how that could be. Our dear leaders come back yet?"

"Not yet," said Banwick. "We lost a lot of folks and Emony's got her hands full. How'd you get rid of those pricks anyway?"

"You wouldn't believe us if we told you," said Gant.

When they came to the site of the cave, Ulnoth recognized the land and the sound of the waterfall above. "What, here again? Our hot spring. I never saw no cave under it."

"Couldn't. Too much snow."

"Almost too good to be true. Ain't no bears in there, are there?"

"Uh, I don't think so."

Ulnoth eyed the mouth of the cave – a smallish opening under an overhanging wall of rock, easily missed. Up above the water trickled and the spring steamed. Outside a dozen people sat nursing wounds, and just beyond an ominous cairn of stones. "What—?"

"We buried them as best we could. Every walking body carried one that wasn't. Listen, be light with Emony – Allard didn't make it."

"Shit," spat Ulnoth.

"It was him what found this place. Me and him and Sal, we got separated in the attack, an' this was the only place we could figure to find before we froze. Allard was hurt too bad, but he found it. Last thing he ever did, probably saved us all."

"Sally," Gant asked nervously, "is she...?"

"She's fine. Helping out inside."

Ulnoth went into the cave. Crawled in more like, and while his eyes adjusted he smelled sweat and warm death all around him. Weak red rushlights were set along the length of the short tunnel, and past that a wide chamber with water pooling in one corner. In the midst of it Emony labored over a small form that barely breathed. "More light," she said in a hoarse, angry voice. "I need more damned light!" Someone brought a torch closer, and Ulnoth saw her hands flying furiously over a jagged cut and he decided not to interrupt. Finally she collapsed back onto the stone floor. "That's it," she breathed, "either he'll live or he won't. Who's next?"

"No one," came Sally's voice as the patient was carried away to await his fate. "That's it for now."

"Thank the gods," said Emony.

"Nah, fuck the gods," Ulnoth called out, "thank yourselves."

"Ulnoth!" Sally found him in the gloom and wrapped him in her arms. "You did it!"

"I did nothing but run. I'm good at that. Go see Gant, he's havin' kittens out there." She shuffled past, and Ulnoth fixed on the petite shape before him. "Em...I'm sorry about your brother. He was a good lad. A good man."

"A lot of good people are under those rocks out there," Emony replied, too tired even to cry.

"Dannek?"

Emony nodded toward a small hollow worn in the side of the cavern. Ulnoth laid a hand on Dannek's shoulder, afraid of finding it cold. Then it quivered, and the boy looked up at him in the dark. "Are...are you all right?"

Dannek shook his head. "No. Not...not right now."

Ulnoth was searching for something to say when he heard his name being called from outside the cave. He scrambled out expecting some new terror, and found Kuther leading a very familiar horse. "Phaerie! Where'd you find her?"

Kuther jerked a thumb downhill. "She was just wandering around, following the stream I think."

"Corren? Lessi?"

"No. What do we do?"

Ulnoth turned around to face the wall of ice and rock towering over them. "For now? Make ourselves at home, I guess."

CHAPTER THIRTY

These Dark Days

Taurix's progress ground to a halt in the face of a new-built fortification filled with a hodgepodge of Pharamund's generals, vassals, retainers and associated riffraff. A ridge with two manned watchtowers bisected the path through the hills, and on the other side of it red flags fluttered like a thousand flames in the wind. Each side dug in to stare down the other just out of bowshot.

"It's perfect for us," Vinian mused from a hidden spot overlooking the camps. "We'll eat from both tables." Next to her Corren nodded agreement.

"You're seriously overestimatin' my folks' burglary skills," said Wrenth. He fidgeted and looked about in every direction, expecting to be ambushed by scouts any minute.

"Don't worry," said Corren, "we'll teach you. It's easier than you think – armies are big, strong, dumb things. We'll be away and belly-full before they know aught's afoot – hello, what's this?"

Wrenth started, like a kid just caught peeping through the bordello wall. "What?"

"Those flags," said Corren, squinting and pointing to one cluster among many. "I know those."

"You do?"

"I should. I marched and sweated under the fist and mace for near a year – that's Nostrado's banner. They said the Lady was dead...."

"What, you mean to say you was one o' them babykillers?"

Corren nodded. "Another life, my friend, though the only killing I did was my own mates. I was saved from it just in time."

"And that's your old outfit down there?"

"I think...if only I could get closer, have a look."

At New Firleaf Alessia had grown healthier by the day, to the surprise of no one who had to endure her mouth when the bouts of pain hit her. And her vocabulary had grown admirably filthy over the winter such that even infection fled from it. This day Corren and Vinian both found themselves facing one of her least accommodating moods.

"When were you going to tell me?" She glared at them with a fevered intensity and curled lip that spelled out exactly what she meant. Taurix's reprisals.

Corren sighed. "When you were stronger."

"I'm stronger. How could you keep this—"

"What was I supposed to say? That our raids led to the crucifixion of...hundreds? Thousands? Tell me, physic, exactly what condition do you need to be in to hear that kind of news?"

"*We* didn't cause shit," Alessia snarled, no less fearsome for coming from a bedridden waif without a bed. "I had the pleasure of meeting Lord Taurix once. His kind look for excuses to cause misery and always find 'em. The Polytheon teaches revenge is for the weak-minded, but that one...I'd pay gold to slip a knife between his ribs."

"No chance of that." Vinian marched to the heat of the firepit with a half-dozen river carp strung from her waist. "I paid him a visit once myself. He probably sleeps with ten guards and twenty swords now. You're lucky you survived him."

"For that," said Alessia, "you can thank the Polytheon. There were others there deserved as much and didn't get it."

"Best not trouble yourself too hard on who deserves what," Vinian replied as she gutted a carp. "No one gets what they deserve in life, except by accident."

With that somber pronouncement Corren went away somewhere to sulk and a silence fell over New Firleaf. Its fifteen or twenty souls busied themselves with whatever tasks were at hand. Spending so long clawing at the jagged end of survival had that effect, Alessia supposed. All the nonessentials stripped away left only...what? A sword? Or a scalpel. "Vinian."

The spymistress looked up from the half-grilled fish she held over the embers.

"Let's talk plain. I still mean to try and end the war any way possible – you know we don't care who wins it, but you're our best chance."

"Best? In these dark days, I'm your *only* chance."

"Fine. I need to know now – are you in or out?"

"I'm loyal to the queen, no secret that. But this scheme – the bank, Artabarzanes – it's a bigger threat than that wet noodle Pharamund. I'm in. If we can get the two of 'em talking, much as it turns my stomach…that could do it."

"But how?"

"I need to get inside that fort, see the situation over there. If the letter's genuine they'll be in dire straits about now. Make no mistake," Vinian added hastily, "I'm no ally to you – your crimes against Her Majesty and the feudal order, imperfect as it is, have led to chaos and needless death. But I have bigger fish to fry." Looking down, Vinian yelped, yanking her charred and inedible carp from the fire. "Godsdammit!"

"Calm down, it's only a fish."

"No matter. I can't afford to be careless, not now. Not ever."

★   ★   ★

With Taurix's advance his supply lines necessarily stretched, so Alessia and Corren decided to use the opportunity to take Wrenth and a couple likely candidates – they purposely avoided learning their names – on their first raid. The target was a slow convoy caught flat-footed by the push, but also made careless and overconfident by it. "Ten men," said Nan from her oak tree perch above the track. "Figure no more 'n half properly trained by the look. Two wagons loaded lighter than they woulda been not long ago. Six of us against ten of them." Her mouth filled with bile. "I suppose I should feel sorry for 'em."

"Somehow I don't think you do," remarked Alessia from her own hidden spot far to the rear. Though she was in no shape to fight, she could still manage to crawl to any wounded if the need arose.

"All right, remember your drills," said Corren in the high dead grass. "Quiet count, draw, aim, loose, repeat, repeat again. Don't get scared – trust we're covering you. Then rush 'em and attack with *intent*. Intent beats a skilled but unwilling foe every time."

"What if we miss?" Wrenth asked.

"Don't worry, we won't. *We* won't. We're a team, never forget. That's our strength. Get ready now."

The convoy came. A tree trunk lay across the way, blocking it as though a winter storm had blown it over, snow and brush concealing the marks of the axe that'd truly done the deed. Corren gave the hand signal to start the countdown, and they readied their bows.

One of the convoy guards jumped down from the lead wagon and began shouting orders to the others to draw weapons, take cover. At once they scrambled off mounts and huddled up in lines close to the ground.

"That one..." Alessia whispered. "Been through this before. He knows what's coming."

But the quiet count was already started. And remembering their drills, like clockwork the New Firleaf crew performed. *Draw*. The bows creaked as one. *Aim*. Silence pregnant with held breaths and thumping heartbeats. *Loose*. Iron and gray goose wings flew.

Not a one hit a target. The soldiers hugged the earth, hid under wagons or between horses. "Again!" Corren hissed, trying not to show his alarm. But they barely had time.

The leader called out, "To the left side, advance! Quick!" As one, as a team, the soldiers rushed the growth that concealed the new-made insurgents.

The new recruits managed a few hasty shots, then panic took over. One man rose and ran, only to be brought down by a cross-bow bolt. Alessia hobbled to him, ready with her instruments. Corren forced himself up and thrust his short sword into the shooter's belly.

"Huaargh!" The body fell atop him. Corren scrambled out from under it and no sooner did he find his feet than another raised a sharp halberd to cleave him with all the intent one would have for a venomous snake dropped suddenly into a ladies' parlor. The spearpoint glittered in the sun, then fell.

A shriek echoed out of the trees. The shriek changed to an animal roar and suddenly Nan was stabbing the soldier over and over, howling something incomprehensible. Blood gushed upward and bathed her in sticky warmth. When the meat beneath Nan shuddered no more she leaped toward a fellow grappling with Wrenth. She plunged her knife into the exposed neck of the man and ripped out his trachea. Alessia spared a moment from her ministration to look on in a mixture of awe and terror.

True to Corren's order, the last archer picked off two more of the guards, then pulled a hatchet after another. Robbed of their leader, the surviving soldiers broke and ran back south screaming bloody murder.

"Hold," Corren yelled when he saw Nan move to chase the men down. "Godsdammit Nandine, I said *hold!*"

For a moment it seemed she would ignore him and go off on her own anyway. Then she halted, chest heaving, and turned back. Her entire face, neck and shoulders were red. "Why?"

"Because," Corren said, "the raid is over. We won. That means you hold."

"No," she replied, her voice all poison, "it ain't. It's never over. Never."

★   ★   ★

"What the hells was that? Tell me," Wrenth asked while he dabbed at a wound, "is that what we gots to look forward to? Will I get crazy like that? Will Quen?"

"I can't say," Alessia replied. The raid had brought much-needed food, warm clothing and horses. It also brought casualties. She twisted in place to keep her leg immobile and also extract the bolt from the back of the man who'd run – not barbed this one. He'd live, but it wouldn't be an easy life. "Nan's always felt things more closely, but she's tough. But after what happened to Plisten...."

"What?" The small voice came out of nowhere, making both of them jump. "What happened?"

"Nothing, dear," Alessia said. "Nothing, just boring grown-up talk. I think Vinian's back – why don't you go help her with the fish—"

"I know that's not true," Quen said with deadly seriousness. "I know people talk about things they don't want me to know."

For a moment neither Wrenth nor Alessia could think of a response to that. Finally Alessia said, "Quen, do you trust me?"

"I...I guess so? Yes."

"Then trust me now. I won't lie to you – bad things are happening. But just as I wouldn't give you a pail too heavy for you to carry, neither will I nor your father weigh you down with matters too burdensome even for us old folk. Now please, go help Vinian."

Quen stared at Alessia for a second, then said, "All right." She tottered off, unconvinced but trusting nonetheless.

Wrenth exhaled, relieved. "Thank you."

"I didn't do it for you. I won't have her follow Nan's path...or Ulnoth's or...."

"Who?"

The bolt came out at last, and the man whimpered softly. "Never mind."

Some time later she tried some light walking with her crutch. It hurt but it felt better than being an invalid. She hobbled up next to Vinian and her latest attempt at cooking, which smelled better than the first one. A rough grill had been made from a stretch of mail strung above the flames.

"Thanks for the 'helper'," Vinian said. "You know, most of my job is getting people to *start* talking."

"I had to send her somewhere. Did you learn anything?"

Vinian turned a partly grilled fish. "You know, I think I'm getting better at this. I went to the reds' fort. Embarrassing how easy it was to get in. I played the part of a poor washer boy. Not a hard sell for me you understand. By the way—" she pointed to a smelly pile of red-badged tunics and surcoats, "—make what use of those you can. The soldiers are all lagered up and without enough officers to keep order they're scared shitless of Taurix. A bunch of companies from the north are making it a crowd thanks to Pertinax but the ranks are worn thin of men with any sense."

"So nothing useful."

"Oh no, I've saved the best for last. He's coming. Personally."

"He? Who?"

Vinian smiled. "Him. *Pharamund*. King Milksop himself. Seems the golden-haired fop is most unsatisfied with his fortunes in this war and has seen fit to take the field personal-like. As if that would improve things."

Alessia gaped. "This…this could be—"

"Victory, my lame temple wench. Or at least survival for another season, which is much the same thing these days."

"But will Pharamund listen to you?"

Vinian looked away. "No. Not to me, but…well, there's someone else."

"I don't understand."

"I don't make a habit of talking about it but, despite my appearance I have had…acquaintances. In the past."

"You mean men," Alessia inferred.

"I mean *a* man. My counterpart at Pharamund's court. One of the finest minds in Porontus, and Pharamund snatched him up just before the country fell to the emperor. Before the war we worked together, and then…."

"Other things."

"Trozas was attracted to my skill, and I guess my razor wit. I don't know, I didn't ask. It was a casual thing. Obviously it ended when Pharamund chose to usurp the royal right but…he might listen to me on this. I think he will."

Alessia smiled in spite of herself, in spite of the pain shooting through her thigh. "I've heard of the enemy of my enemy is my friend, but nothing about my enemy's lover."

"He'll arrive beforehand to make sure all is safe and secure for the idiot's appearance. I'll be there to meet him. But Trozas is good – I'll need help just to get into his presence alive."

"Then you're in luck. What better help than one of Pharamund's own soldiers?"

CHAPTER THIRTY-ONE

Filtration

"This isn't gonna work. Let's go back."

Vinian elbowed Corren in the shin in a manner most unseemly for a page boy. "Too late – they've already spotted us. Calm down and press on. We'll be fine." Her hair was tied behind a linen coif and her breasts bound tight, but her less-than-deferential attitude undid some of the illusion.

Vinian could see that Corren strained under the weight of the armor – it was bits and pieces cobbled together from a dozen sources and not at all befitting a noble retainer, and he'd clearly lost a lot of weight over the season. He rode a nag donated by someone from the New Firleaf crew that no one with working eyes would mistake for a destrier. A helm of foreign design and a faded surcoat with some random lord's crest completed the outfit. Every ragged thread threatened to give him away. But it would have to do.

"You better be right," he growled, more to relieve frustration than anything else.

"Or what? You'll kill me?"

"No. I'll turn you in to the first red general I find. Imagine they'll have a *lot* of fun with you before they're through." Vinian shut up.

The wooden stronghold had no definite shape, having been built from whatever space could be wrested from the hilly forest. It was big, though – timber walls five yards high were topped with pointed stakes, sentry platforms and men with bows, cross-bows or other devices. Corren and Vinian rode toward the stockade from the north side making every effort to be seen, and the last hundred yards found eyes as well as ballistae fixed on them, axles creaking as the tips of the great iron spears tracked their path.

"Remind me whose get-up I'm wearing again."

Vinian glanced at the surcoat even though she'd already committed it to memory. "Lord Munrath of Hardscrabble. Far enough away that no one'll ask questions."

"Hardscrabble. Sounds pleasant. What about the original owner of this fine garment?"

"Dead when they took it off 'im. Gave it to me to wash for some reason."

"Did you wash it?"

"No."

They halted their mounts twenty yards from the gate and Corren drew a breath. "Ho there! Hail His Grace the King!"

"Who goes?" The voice was all nerves and fatigue.

Corren raised a hand. "C— Er, Qworthem, sworn man to Munrath of Hardscrabble, on business! Beg entry!" He straightened up in the saddle to display the device on his chest.

They waited to see if they would be nailed to the ground on ballista shafts. After ten or ninety heart-pumping seconds a hard snap rang out – a shot? No, a bolt sliding back. Then another, and another.

The wall of fresh-cut logs opened and a warm stormfront of stink wafted out. Vinian wrinkled her nose. Whatever impression the fort gave from the outside, inside was even more of a disgrace. Companies clumped together where they wished in no semblance of discipline while trash piled against walls and in ditches. Dogs snarled at each other over bits of bone and men diced, fought and in some cases humped in the open with no one to say a thing against it.

"Incredible," said Corren. "It's like Vindis all over again, minus the plague. If Taurix knew what he was up against…well, no matter now. There's Nostrado's flag – let's go see who's in charge of this fine mess."

They walked quickly past a pole where a sheep had been tied up, and one enterprising soldier collected coppers from men waiting in line for their turn at it. "The glory of the royal struggle," Corren remarked.

Vinian looked away with a hand clamped over her mouth. "Disgusting…."

"Yes, I'm sure *nothing* similar takes place in Her Majesty's stouthearted legions."

In the farthest corner a cluster of tents surrounded a company that Corren pointed out. "This is it," he muttered behind his helm as Vinian walked the horse beside him, "my old unit. I hope this beard and the helm adds up to enough disguise. New faces but the stink's still the same. If they suspected...well, we'd join that lot up there right quick." He nodded toward the corpses of unlucky deserters decorating the palisade.

"Where's the general's tent?"

"There," he pointed, "in the middle. No idea who commands now – Lady No was, to put it mildly, capricious in her bestowing of favors. But if she's kicked it...let's take a peek."

They didn't need to peek. The flap whipped open and out marched the most ornery, cantankerous excuse for a commanding officer ever to shamble across the earth. "*Gadanga!*" Corren whispered, then froze. The old man wore a general's medallion, leaving no doubt of his rank. He stomped past, and paused only to give Corren the most cursory of frowning nods before going on his way. Only when the man's shuffling gait faded from hearing did Corren exhale.

"That was close. Last time the cap'n and I met there were some unpleasant words exchanged. Also some unpleasant blades. Thank the gods I've become like a beggar's corpse since then."

"A riveting tale I'm sure," said Vinian. "Can we use him?"

"Maybe. The old man's a mean bastard but give 'im credit – he cares for his men. We need...we need to find Sergeants Jaxa, or Vastain. Assuming they're still alive."

"Who are they?"

Corren curled a lip. "Pressure points. Been with the unit long enough they're like sons to the cap'n."

"My specialty. Point 'em out to me. I'll make sure to take good care of them."

Corren scanned the flow of men throughout the camp, and eventually focused on one strain of loud, drunken laughter he seemed to find familiar. Following it, he indicated a pair dicing before a pitiful fire. "That's them," he said. "No mistaking those two."

Corren loitered a few hours, bumming what food he could without raising suspicion while Vinian followed the two soldiers. Neither was a fellow she'd care to get to know better. Putting them briefly out of commission was an easy task, and Vinian found Corren again just after nightfall. "Packages are secure. Let's find that old goat of yours and make sure he knows the situation."

"What *is* the situation?"

Vinian held up something – no, two small somethings, and offered them to Corren. He half laughed, half gasped. "Jaxa's crooked dice! Won't ask how you got him to part with those. I'm glad you're on our side."

"I'm not. I'm on *my* side. Now go do your part."

⋆   ⋆   ⋆

"Someone to see you, General," said the sentry, asleep on his feet.

A groggy, irritated voice spat from the interior of the tent. "At this hour? Tell 'em to come back tomorrow. Or even better, don't come back at all. Chthonii, can't *anyone* do a thing without me signing for it?"

The sentry frowned. "He seemed most insistent, sir."

"Well, so am I, ain't I?"

"Yes sir." The sentry ducked back out of the tent where he exchanged low words with Corren. When it seemed words were going nowhere, Vinian stepped out of a shadow behind the sentry and seized just the right blood vessels. He struggled but grew weaker as Vinian dragged him back into the darkness while Corren covered his mouth.

The tent flap flew back, and the old man looked up from his wine bottle in shock. "Who – who are you? What do you want? Guard!"

"Guard's taking a break," said Corren. "It's just you and me, Cap'n. I mean *General*."

"Who *are* you?" Gadanga demanded again. Vinian moved to the entrance of the tent so she could see and hear both within and without. "And you, mangled boy? What is this?" Corren wrenched off the helm.

"Oh, no," said Gadanga, "not again. Corren, you, you traitor. I hoped you dead by now. You come back to finish me off? Well, I ain't goin' down so easy as Tancred!" He went for his sword, but

Corren reached out and twisted Gadanga's arthritic wrist ever so slightly, a subtle move Vinian regarded with approval. Gadanga cried out and dropped to his knees. "Cheater...make it quick at least."

"Rest easy," said Corren, "I'm not here for your blood. I'm here to offer you lives."

Gadanga looked up at Corren with utter loathing. "What's that mean?"

Corren produced Jaxa's dice. "Recognize these?"

The old man squinted to see. "What have you done with him?"

"Nothing, yet. Jaxa and Vastain are safe, in better condition than they deserve. If you want them to stay that way I'll be needing a small favor of you."

"I still can't believe it," Gadanga said almost wistfully. "You was one of the good ones, one of the best. Bound for great things...."

"Great things! What great things? Sacking towns? Raping children to death? Harvesting heads by the thousand?"

"*That's what it means to serve!* To do what needs to be done as your lord and king command. How could you not know that?"

"I know better now. But I'm not here to debate with you."

"What then, damn you? What do you want?"

"Pharamund is coming here," said Vinian. "Soon."

Gadanga gave her – a boy as he still assumed – a nasty sneer. "What of it?"

"Another will arrive beforehand, tomorrow. A man named Trozas to make all secure against...well, against folk like us. I need to see him alone, and you're our key."

Gadanga spat on the hard-packed dirt floor. "To kill him too? You take me for a craven. Maybe I am, but not your kind."

Corren nodded. "Aye, you're a general now I see, right high and mighty. You answer for many lives now. I'm trying to save 'em. And yours into the mix, though you'll never believe it."

"What are you babbling on about? I don't know what type of cack you've got yourself into—"

"You don't serve who you think. Sit down and pour us some wine – I've got a bloody tale to tell."

★   ★   ★

After a night spent in recrimination and argument and just enough wine to make it endurable, Corren marched Gadanga out of his own tent, almost no space between them except that taken up by a compact, razor-sharp dagger. "Just as we discussed now," said Vinian, "no tricks."

The dawn wrapped them in its mist, and the fort looked to be even worse off than the previous night if that was possible. Hordes of men sprawled hungover or still drunk on casks of imported Bhasan cherry wine, some face down in their own vomit. The unfortunate sheep lay bloody and lifeless, victim of someone's overenthusiasm. Only a handful of guards manned the towers.

"No tricks," Gadanga spat back as he stepped over the senseless bulk of his sentry. "You'll both hang for this though."

Corren tried and failed to stifle a bitter laugh. "Undoubtedly."

"Even if I did believe a word of what you say, it don't change nothing. Far's I see you're a turncoat coward and a murderer."

"Seems the fashion these days. Keep walking." Corren poked Gadanga in the back with the tip of his knife.

"Ow! Stop it. Cap'n Nera – *Lord* Nera now, the snake – is the one handlin' the king's visit in the absence of anyone of real station. This bloke you want'll be with him."

"Then we wait." Corren pointed up to a vacant watchtower with his free hand. "Up there."

For one hour then another they gazed eastward, Corren's knife hard against Gadanga's back the whole time, even as the old man relieved himself over the edge. In the better light he glanced over at Vinian and gave a sour smile. "Say, you're a woman in truth."

Vinian raised an eyebrow. "In truth."

"Maybe I should keep this old cock out to – *aargh!* Gods, sorry! Just old soldier's talk."

When the sun had almost reached its zenith a faint movement appeared on the horizon – a party of horses and men, and a coach in the midst of it. "That'll be them," said Gadanga. "Bunch of cock-arsed lords along to scream at us to clean the place up I guess."

"That's the least of your worries," said Vinian. "You just get me in front of Trozas."

Over the next half-hour the train grew nearer and larger. The gates opened to welcome the party, many of the sloggers no doubt cursing their luck that playtime was over, and their few officers grateful for someone of authority at last. Seeing the sorry state of the fort a bevy of generals and barons began shouting orders even before they'd dismounted. The doors of the coach opened, and into the middle of this storm a man emerged – slender, dark and rather out of place in such a rough setting, yet the calm eye of it all. Encircled by attendants, he moved with practiced ease toward one of the few solid buildings in the fort – the headquarters. None of his men wore badges of allegiance of any kind.

"That's Trozas," said Vinian. "Keeping fit I see."

Gadanga grunted. "That scrawny whelp? Don't look like much."

"That scrawny whelp," Vinian countered, "could disembowel you and half your precious captains before you finished any thought that it was happening, then blackmail the rest into cleaning up the mess all for a morning exercise. We'll let them settle in a bit, then go down."

★   ★   ★

After scanning a brief, stilted introduction written in Gadanga's hand, the sergeant poked a head into the inner office. "You have a visitor, sir."

"Complaints already? That was fast."

"A page boy, with a message from a General Gadanga."

"Fine, fine, show him in."

Vinian shut the door to the office behind her, the freshly cut pine planks still fragrant. Trozas looked up once from a pile of paper on a small desk, then again. He jumped out of his chair. "Y-you! You're here!"

"Perceptive as ever," Vinian said. Trozas's right hand flashed toward his left sleeve just as Vinian's did the same. "Don't! You know I'm faster than you on that score. It, um, it's good to see you again."

Trozas gave a sarcastic snort. "Miss me, did you? I never forced you to leave."

"Don't be obtuse. We both chose our loyalties."

"I won't insult you by asking how you got in here," said Trozas, eyes scanning intently for any sudden movement. "You can't be here to kill me or you wouldn't have shown your, well...."

"Face," Vinian finished, "you can say it."

"Do I dare hope then that you're here for that drunken lech Nera? I've got him out digging fresh latrines to take some of the stench away from this place."

"No, assassination isn't my mission. I'll be long gone by the time your precious Pharamund arrives."

"And these, whatever they are – partisans, rangers you have sowing terror all along our lines? It reeks of your training. Half the army thinks they're evil spirits out for vengeance. Couldn't have done better myself."

If only that were so, she thought but didn't say. "I've always said, the right pressure—"

"Yes yes, can move worlds, I remember. So you want to turn me like you did that mountain of rusty nails Taurix? I'm assuming that was your doing too."

"It was, thanks." Vinian peeked over his shoulder at the reports on his desk, and he moved to block her view. "Sorry, habit. No, much as it'd stroke my ego to flip you I'm here about a different man. A fat one."

"Ah, I've heard of this kind of fetish, tales from back east—"

"Be serious."

"I'm always serious. All right, tell me about this fat man you fawn over."

"Carthagne Fadhlan ven Xedrusia of Bank Isle-Euderico, Marimine Sardicchio Esquaralle." The fountain of foreign words rolling off Vinian's tongue caught Trozas off guard for just a moment; anyone else might've missed the reaction. "I see you know the name. Funny thing, so does the queen. Just so happens she owes his bank a great sum of gold, at a painful rate of return. Sound familiar?"

"You—" Trozas faltered, then covered with a grin. "You've got little snakes at Pharamund's court, despite my best efforts. Impressive. But you must know this is a poor use of them."

"You give me too much credit. Trozas, he's using us against each other."

"To what possible end?"

"Artabarzanes."

Trozas went silent again, but only for the couple of seconds it took for him to piece everything together. "I see. Of course you know my prejudices on that subject...."

"I know Artabarzanes swallowed up Porontus whole like a python does cattle, and would do the same here. But not for what it'd cost him to do so openly."

"—and you've had plenty of time to invent all this. Give me a moment to catch up."

"Take all the time you need," said Vinian, "just remember Taurix is at your doorstep."

"And now knows the king is coming, thanks to you. Well played – my options are limited while yours are wide open. Assuming you leave this room alive, of course."

"Don't be a fool. I have proof—"

"Oh, *of course* you do," Trozas sneered, "you're very good. You've always been my greatest weakness. I'm sure your queen was counting on that."

"No, I—" Vinian broke off.

"What?"

"I'm not here at Engwara's order. She doesn't know anything about this, thanks to that banker. I've been betrayed—"

"That's poetic."

"Fine, don't take my word for it. Don't believe anything, just consider. We're at a stalemate – no one's taking any more ground this winter and we both know you'll keep Pharamund safe from capture. What harm in just getting them talking?"

"Last time that happened it was almost a royal bloodbath."

"I remember. We barely stopped it. How many more bloodbaths since? You must know what Taurix is doing to the commons on our side. Yours can't be faring much better. Is...is that really the kind of spycraft you prefer? Mention it to Pharamund, will you, for old time's sake?"

Trozas sighed. "I'll consider it. In the meantime...." His brow furrowed, almost as though holding back tears.

Vinian frowned. *Oh, no....*

"Like you said we both chose our loyalties. It never felt right, you and me on opposite sides." He drew a hard breath. "Sergeant! Intruder!"

Could've at least given me a running start. "Trozas," she said quickly, "the banker's here, now. When next you see him, look for a cut to his face." Vinian whipped past him and onto the desk, sending papers flying. In the half-second before the delicate thing collapsed she jumped again to the rafters of the building. Soldiers and attendants both burst into the room, and Trozas pointed out the interloper by hurling a slender stiletto concealed in his sleeve at Vinian. She ducked and the blade stuck in a beam an inch from her ear.

The frame of the building was made to support a loft, which hadn't been built yet. Vinian danced along the planks, avoiding more thrown knives until she came to a ceiling hatch. Shoving it open, she shouted, "Think about it, Trozas!" She leaped out into the sun.

* * *

"What the—?" Corren started as Vinian jumped down to meet him.

"Run!"

Corren had stripped off most of his heavy armor, and now tossed away the helm to run after Vinian while Gadanga reluctantly trailed them both.

"Wait!" Gadanga breathed heavily, not having exerted himself since Wengeddy. "What...about my men...."

"Already free," said Vinian as she ran, "soon as they wake up anyway."

Perversely enough, as they ran through the fort chased by four of Trozas's men they attracted little or no attention, such disorderly squabbles not being anything out of the ordinary. "Get rid of him," Vinian breathed at Corren.

He slowed a bit and let Gadanga catch up just long enough to say, "Sorry about this, Cap'n," before throwing out a foot and tripping the old man into the trodden mud.

"Huah!" Gadanga went down easily enough, and two attendants in turn tripped over him, leaving several still on their trail.

"What now?" asked Corren.

"How...about...there?" Vinian pointed.

"What? No!"

"It's that or nothing. Come on."

A man sickened by a night of drinking can produce some truly revolting waste. A thousand men after an entire week of pugilistic debauchery...well, it was a thing best not thought long upon. Vinian tried hard not to think on it as they dove toward the filth of the newly dug latrine pit's drain gate. *If pain is nothing, stench is less than nothing. Control. I am in ...* "Yeach!"

Trozas's training was thorough but wasn't tough enough to motivate his operatives to swim through cack and puke to catch their quarry. Tumbling in a state of utter disgust down the slope into the encroaching forest, Corren chanced to open his mouth to breathe and was rewarded with a mix of air and piss. Next to him Vinian took hold of a protruding root and jerked her descent to a halt while Corren in turn clung to her shoe to stop his. A tiny brook intersected their path, and Corren frantically buried himself in its icy flow while Vinian peered back uphill. They were alone.

Corren spit mouthful after mouthful of water and bile in a desperate attempt to clear himself of the sewage. "Oh my gods...."

"All told," said Vinian, her nostrils still burning with the acrid sting, "I'd say that went ...rather well."

CHAPTER THIRTY-TWO

Just End It

"Hello? Anyone there?" The voice echoed back through the cavern. They still didn't know how far back it went but Ulnoth figured this was far enough to store one of the precious few sacks of grain they'd managed to salvage. He set it down and took up one of the last remaining candles to light his way back out.

"Step light," he answered. "Ground gets rough around here. It's...wait. Who's there? Nan, that you?"

"In the flesh." Her tall form emerged into the candlegloom, looking years older than she had the last time they'd been together.

"Shit girl, where you been? The others, are they...?"

"Whole, more or less. Fine setup you've got. Too bad they put you in charge of it. Where is everyone? Seems a bit sparse out there."

"Oh, you ain't heard then. Let's get outta this hole awhile – it's a hard story I got."

"We'll trade them then," Nan said.

They walked toward the daylight together. "How did you find us?" Ulnoth asked.

"I went out for a walk...to clear my head, I guess. I must've got turned around when I came upon a couple sloggers."

"Hope you hid the bodies."

"I...let one go," Nan said.

"What? Why?"

Nan shook her head. "I don't know. It was just a kid. Started cryin', begging for his mummy, if you can believe it. All seemed... so pointless all of a sudden."

"Huh," grunted Ulnoth, "might be more than a few points pointed at us soon."

Nan shrugged. "I made him take off his shoes, threw 'em down the hill. It'll take him hours to find 'em or get back to where he came from. That's when I saw the smoke, figured it was either you or an end to this godsfucked nightmare."

"The former, I'm afraid...."

It was a sad palaver, no doubt of that. Truth be told, Ulnoth had the worse of it. Wengeddy had been bad, but at least there they could entertain the fantasy that some had got away. Taurix's slow, methodical slaughter in Plisten and beyond was more like a sawmill with every bit cut, measured and accounted for. "All of 'em? Really? ...all?" Ulnoth whimpered with his head resting in two filthy hands.

"I'm so sorry," Nan said. "You must want the bastards dead, so badly."

"This...this is my doing. *I* brought this. I.... Just end it, please," he begged, broken out by a fresh weariness. He'd taken all the revenge a man could take, hated all the hate there was and by it accomplished exactly nothing. Now, emptied even of these things, the price of it all weighed heavy. "Don't care how, just end it. Please."

★   ★   ★

Winter wore itself out as it always did, and the brown death of an early spring gripped the forest. Here and there a few splotches of green poked up among the leaves and twigs, but mostly it held its chilly breath in anticipation of the new growth that had not yet begun in earnest. Several weeks passed with welome rest and uneventfulness, and when Alessia could walk they made the trek up to the cave. Corren nodded approvingly at the excellent shelter and Alessia wept at the stone cairns before it. The surviving Heron Kings and the folk of New Firleaf worked together to bleed Taurix and Pharamund both of what they needed to survive without raising too much ire. Emony and Alessia tried to guide Dannek back to his senses, knowing he'd never be the same.

"None of us will," said Emony as the two stood over Allard's cairn. "We'll never live in the civilized world again, will we?"

"Not for me to say," Alessia asserted, "but probably not. The person I was before is, well, gone. I could never go back to the temple." She forced a smile. "Mother Tanusia would never allow it, with the habits I picked up from you lot. Nor would Livielle, gods bless her."

Corren came out of the cave entrance. "Have to make a proper door to this place, then hide it well. It's good," he said. "Secret, secure. We can build on it. Yes, I think just maybe we're home."

★   ★   ★

They kept Vinian well away from the cave though she suspected with all their coming and going that they'd made a base somewhere close. She also watched Pharamund's visit from afar, and had to admit it was impressive – even from a distance the fort looked cleaner by the time the great red banners plodded past the gates and newly dug latrines. She wondered time and again if Trozas had let her escape, and decided it best to assume not. But would he keep his promise? What then? If only she could get to the queen. But without her writ of safe conduct, no doubt now firmly in Carthagne's grasp, what chance of making it did she have?

"Not terrible actually," said Alessia while she packed her things. "But not certain either. It's tough country, and as much your fault for that as anyone's."

"Not good enough," said Vinian as she gutted what she hoped would be her last carp in the dwindling camp of New Firleaf. "Her Majesty needs to know everything; I can't risk failure."

"Well, who does have safe conduct? Surely Taurix?"

Vinian laughed bitterly. "He hates me. Hells, he'd put me in irons on any pretext no matter the consequence. If only there was someone...Ludolphus!"

"Who? Oh, the fellow Taurix was chasing when he invaded my temple. He'll help you?"

"He might."

That night Vinian donned her page boy clothes, which still smelled vaguely of sewage despite repeated washings, and crept into Taurix's camp. It was a rectangular plot ringed by an earthwork palisade with sentries spaced along the edges. Inside it officers' tents were surrounded by the legion of sloggers set under meaner shelters or none at all. *Still plain and predictable as childsong I see.* Taurix's sentry placement was unchanged from the last time she'd infiltrated his camp. *Some lessons must be learned many times....* She easily evaded the cold and tired guards, ducking and rolling overtop the frozen earthwork, down the inner slope and picking up the first object she saw – a pail of something. *Look busy and you'll avoid scrutiny*, she taught her operatives.

Taurix's tent was the biggest, and very well-guarded. He'd learned something at least. Not far from that the banker had erected his lodging – a white pavilion adorned with the golden scales emblem of the Marimines Isles. She avoided that one.

At last Vinian spotted Ludolphus's tent, recognized from experience – the old general owed her many favors over many lost rounds of sneak-and-spy games to train his men. But tonight was no game.

Backside of the tent. Moonlight. Cloud...cloud...cloud in front of the moon. *Drop the pail.* Dark. *Down. Squeeze through. Quiet. In.* Easiest thing in the world.

She knew Ludolphus by the sound of his snoring. She knelt and crept close. "General."

"Hmmhmm...."

"General Ludolphus."

"Wha...what the—?"

She pressed a hand over his mouth. "Ssh!" He struggled. "It's me!"

He shook off her hand. "Vinian," he said, "where've you been? That banker, he said—"

"I'm sure he did. Listen carefully, if you serve Her Majesty...."

★   ★   ★

Before sunup Vinian left the camp by the same route she'd entered, and soon afterward Ludolphus announced his intention to return to Carsolan for 'critical consultations with the queen'. Taurix was furious but dared not interfere for many of the men were yet loyal only to Ludolphus. He grudgingly let the man go with only a small entourage to accompany him. Half a day later Carthagne also decided to pack up and return to the capital, ostensibly to sail home. Nobody objected to that.

"Did you know?" asked Alessia while they watched the banker and his mercenaries depart. "Did you know he'd go too?"

Vinian grinned. "I didn't know, but I suspected. He's afraid Ludolphus knows something, which is true. What he doesn't know is that if the good general follows my instructions exactly, he'll have a little surprise waiting in store."

"So why didn't you go back with Ludolphus?"

"Because," said Vinian, "whatever the next move is, one thing's sure – I'm gonna need your help."

Pharamund led an attack on Taurix's camp. Taurix beat it back. Then Taurix launched an assault on the fort. The walls held. Men died on both sides and no ground changed hands. Taurix ordered catapults and ballistae and waited impatiently for them to arrive in pieces, and Pharamund pressed his barons for every last handful of grain to feed his troops.

New Firleaf died a slow unlamented death as people moved up to the cave, their 'winter lodge'. Finally it was only Vinian, Alessia, Wrenth and Quen, lingering only to erase all traces of their presence. It was on the first day above freezing that Trozas strode with obscene ease into the nearly abandoned clearing.

"Not the most enviable of accommodations," he observed, "but I've seen worse."

Wrenth jumped up and trained a bow on him. "Stop right there!"

"It's all right," said Vinian stepping between Trozas and the bodkin tip. "I imagine he's had this place in his sights for a while now."

Trozas nodded. "Long enough to notice your petty thievery. You've fallen on hard times."

"We all have at that."

"Hmm. Can't believe those green idiots haven't winkled you out yet, but whatever. I'm here alone in case you're wondering. This isn't exactly the type of visit you announce in a place like Fort Pharamund."

Vinian raised an eyebrow. "Fort Pharamund? Bit egotistical, innit?"

"Not my choice, believe me."

After convincing Wrenth to put up his weapons, Vinian sat Trozas by the dwindling fire. "Did you talk to him about—"

"Yes. He doesn't believe you."

Alessia felt the energy drain out of her, replaced with a new despondence. "Oh for...." She sat down hard as a bolt of pain shot through her thigh wound.

"...but he doesn't entirely *dis*believe you either," Trozas continued. "I did as you suggested, paid a visit to the edge of Taurix's camp. Surprised how easy it was to get close.

"I saw the banker himself – you were right about his face. Which proves nothing, only that he's here and got hurt somehow. I can't take that to the king and seriously expect—"

"Show him," said Vinian to Alessia. Alessia took out the letter. The thing was grown now so precious and legendary in her mind that she never parted with it, even for a moment. Vinian unrolled the leather and held it out to Trozas. Like any educated Porontan he scanned the Bhasan text with ease.

"Hmmm...."

"I know, I know," said Vinian, "it could be a forgery, I'm a very good liar, blah blah blah. We could go back and forth like that until the sun burns out. But what do you *believe?*"

"It's exactly the kind of thing Artabarzanes would do. I'd like to take this back, verify—"

"No," snapped Alessia, "that's our leverage – I'm not giving it up only to you. Try and take it and you won't leave this place alive."

"All right, all right. I'll talk to the king again. I'll try to convince him to hold some kind of conference with Engwara, for all the good it'll do."

"Trozas, we both know Pharamund does only and exactly as you tell him. You must tell me where it's to be held. I can produce—"

"By the gods, woman, it's not even agreed to yet. War's put Pharamund on edge and he doesn't listen to me as he used to. The stalemate helps, but...we'll see. Meanwhile, I'll have to work on my knife-throwing."

"You do that."

Trozas turned to go, then paused. "One question. I didn't dare to ask it before, but...."

"What?"

He looked square at her. "Did you kill the old king's son?"

Vinian's mouth hung open in genuine surprise. "No."

"Did Engwara?"

She frowned at him angrily. "Did Pharamund?" They parted in silence, neither question answered.

*   ★   ★

Over the next few days a series of strange mishaps kept the two forces precariously balanced. Taurix prepared a new assault on the fort, only to awake on the chosen morning to find his siege engines sabotaged beyond repair. Pharamund sent secret parties to raid Taurix's camp but found them ready and waiting, warned by some unknown method. In this way the enemies were reduced to glaring at each other in helplessness. Artabarzanes himself couldn't have achieved a better balance.

★   ★   ★

"That's it, it's just us now," said Corren. "Wrenth and Quen moved out this morning."

"I don't suppose you'd like to tell me exactly where you've all got to?"

Corren gave Vinian a bemused look. "What do you think?"

"Had to try." Vinian shrugged. "If by some miracle we end up surviving this…well, maybe I could convince the queen to look the other way just so long as you behave yourselves."

"Us? None of us started this. All we wanted—"

"All right. Bad choice of words. All I'm saying is—" Vinian was interrupted by a hard thwack from somewhere behind her. She spun around. "What the hells was that?"

"There," Corren pointed. An arrow protruded from a tree, its bark made soft by the thaw. "That wasn't there before." He walked over to the arrow and tugged at the sheaf of paper wrapped around the shaft.

"Another message from your people?"

"Don't see why there'd be need for it. It's not one of our arrows either…." He unrolled the paper, frowned, and held it out to Vinian. "It's for you."

"Me? Who could possibly know— Trozas." She took it and read aloud.

V,

    First,
    let me apologize for the unusual way in which I've
    elected to deliver this note. I hope the archer's
    shot was true and caused no injury.
    However, the news is not good. His Grace has
    ordered that there will be no meeting with his enemy the
    Lady Engwara – no queen is she. Alas the war must continue.
Furthermore he
    desires that I have no more contact with you, as it is treasonous.
    —T.

★   ★   ★

"Dammit," spat Corren, "all our effort for nothing. Your man's not so impressive as you—"

"Hush," said Vinian, "it's not as you think. We have what we need."

"What do you mean?"

"This was meant for me, but he couldn't know who would read it. Look at the spacing of the words, look at the letters on the left edge."

Corren looked, squinted at the tiny script. "I don't—"

"Go find Alessia, and whoever else you need for hatching plans. We might not have much time."

CHAPTER THIRTY-THREE

Someone to Stand for 'Em

"Fleshold," said Ulnoth. "What's that?"

"An island," replied Alessia, "in the Lacaryc Sea. And it makes our job a lot harder."

Ulnoth stole a mistrustful glance at Vinian, not having met her in person before. "Never heard of it."

"No reason you should," said Vinian. "It's a useless, jagged pile of rock half a mile off the coast. Scholars say Marchmen used to make sacrifices there before they were driven into the hills. Impossible to assault or approach in secret, and there's only one place to land. Which makes it the perfect choice for a secret parley – no chance for a double-cross by either side, everything in the open once you're there but hidden from outside eyes. Before the war got so bloody there were plans to meet there, but it never came to anything."

Corren fidgeted on his log by the fire. "Then how are we supposed to get in front of these two and make our case?"

"I have an idea, but it's risky."

"Risky," snorted Ulnoth. "Maybe you ain't been payin' attention, but out here every hour of every day's been—"

"I mean it," Vinian said. "We'll only get one shot at this and it's likely not everyone'll come back from it."

"We've lost so many already," said Alessia. "Are you sure about this?"

"No. We need to find out some things, like when this is going to happen. Stay here and keep an eye on Pharamund and Taurix – if they leave here at the same time we'll know for sure the parley's happening. Do you have people that can help me run messages quickly and safely?"

Ulnoth nodded. "We're good at hiding and running, if that's what you mean."

"It is, exactly. We'll need transportation, and I think I might know someone who can help us...."

★   ★   ★

"Who's going?"

Corren's words echoed down the walls of the cave then faded away to nothing. They worked to make the place suitable as a permanent hideout, but it was slow-going. A crude gathering hall had been hacked out near the mouth, and the faces looking back at him in the torchlit gloom were stretched gaunt and threadbare, desiccated mockeries of the people they'd been. "It's closer to certain death than anything we've done before, so we'll only take volunteers. Lessi and I'll go alone if need be, but I hope we won't have to." He described Vinian's plan as best they could understand it, trusting to hope that certain details would prove less insane in execution than they sounded. Corren was about to speak again when Ulnoth rose.

"I, uh, don't need to tell you what we been through – you all lived it. Only half of us made it through to now, and I can't say for sure which half is the luckier. I don't see us weatherin' a second winter. If this plan – using the term loosely, mind you – has even a chance of putting this shitshow of a war down, I owe it to Athewen and Lisette, to Plisten, and all those we've buried, to try. Won't speak for any other, but that's what I say."

"Thanks, Ulnoth," said Alessia.

He shrugged as he sat back down. "Not like there was any doubt, o' course."

"All right," said Corren, "who else?"

Silence. Haggard eyes looked left, right to see who else would volunteer. From the back came a bitter voice that'd been heard all too seldom these days. "I'll go." Heads turned, bodies parted, leaving the speaker standing out for all to see.

"Dannek," said Alessia, her heart searing for a moment. "Are you sure?"

He nodded. "I'm sure. Like Ulnoth said, I owe it. To Alixe."

"If he's going so am I," said Nan. "For Crander, and all of Wengeddy."

"And me," said Gant, "for Staphenil."

Emony stood also. "For Allard."

Alessia shook her head. "No, Emony. This is my burden – I have to see it through. But if I fall the others will need you to help keep them alive. I'm sorry."

"But—"

"I'll go." Banwick laid a hand on Emony's shoulder. "I'll go for Allard."

Unable to make a counterargument, Emony nodded and sat down. "Anyone else?"

When it seemed no others would, Kuther and Verrell came forward together. "I guess us," said Verrell, "for anyone else ain't got someone to stand for 'em. I guess."

"Good," Corren said with a nod. "Then I'd say we got a fighting chance. Rest of you, especially the new folks from Firleaf – stay out of sight. Practice your drills. Raid only when you absolutely have to, and above all stay alive. Better days have to be ahead – they can't get much darker."

CHAPTER THIRTY-FOUR

Fleshold

Cold. Cold and wet and dark and pain was their universe as they held on for dear life while the ship plowed toward Fleshold. It would've been rough enough atop the pitching deck, but unwelcome guests such as they clawed at the outer hull instead, frozen knuckles clamped like barnacles with only a few stretches of rope to secure them.

"Lying pirate," Ulnoth spat into the roaring ocean, over and over though no one would hear it. "Said it'd be a short trip. He said it." Next to him Nan – or was it Alessia? His brain had gone numb – seemed to shout similar epithets that were largely swallowed up by the wind and the waves. Maybe on a calm summer day it was a short jaunt across the water, but tonight it seemed like the gods themselves ached to keep Arnaud's little cargo vessel from reaching port.

Another wave crashed into the ship, thrashing Ulnoth in a furious attempt to drive him into the deep. *Let it try*, he thought, *I've stood worse.* Maybe that was true, maybe it— *Aaargh! Cold!*

When it seemed he could take no more and the urge to let go and hurl himself into watery oblivion was its most seductive, everything stopped. It was shocking how suddenly it stopped, as though those ornery gods now shrank in fear at the great black lump of island before them. The wind ceased, the roar of the waves grew silent. Harbor.

It was anticlimactic really, when Arnaud's ship drifted almost softly casual toward the single pier built only the week before. Ropes flew out, were caught by men no more concerned than if they were threshing wheat in autumn, tied off then forgotten. A plank was thrown over starboard and more men unloaded barrels and crates.

One crate in particular proved especially hefty, needing six strong men to move. Throughout this Ulnoth and the others clung to the taut foot- and hand-hold cables portside – despite all they'd endured, this was the most critical test. *Still. Still and silent. Hold. Still.*

Only when the sounds of activity ceased and the lamps and torches were carried far away did Ulnoth try to relax his grip. After using his teeth to force his fingers open, he reached up toward the bow of the ship, the only dry thing on him the oilskin-wrapped bow on his back. Arnaud pulled him aboard and didn't spare a moment to listen to his shivering insults before moving to the next figure strung along the hull, and the next. Dark forms crawled up then collapsed, coughing up water and breathing hard to warm fingers.

"Is everyone here? Did everyone make it?" Alessia flitted among the gathered to match faces to names, limping on her not-quite-healed leg. When the count came to only nine, she grew frantic. "Who's missing?"

"Kuther," said Corren without hesitation. He didn't know how he knew, but live with people so close for so long and you can feel their presence. Or absence. "Kuther's not here. Damn!" He slammed his fists onto the planks. Barely begun and already they were reduced to nine.

Verrell looked once into the dark sea before them, the Bergovan coast and Kuther lost somewhere in that expanse. "What do we do?"

"Keep going," Corren answered. "We've a job to do, and if nine can't get it done I doubt ten could."

Finally Arnaud pulled Vinian onto the deck. "Ah," he said with a smile, "be you yet alive and spitting, my dear?"

"J-just barely." Vinian shivered. "Tell me it was worth it."

"Indeed," replied Arnaud, "it was as I suspected – so suspicious they searched us stem to stern. You'd have been found, no doubt of it."

"And my special cargo?"

Arnaud nodded gravely. "Safe on its way, compliments of the friends of Reynal. "

"Thanks, captain – there's one more I owe you."

"My dear." The smuggler put a finger to his head. "Arnaud keeps the tally all up in here. Accomplish what I think you seek tonight, and it pays for all."

★　　★　　★

The ship shoved off again and was enveloped by the night. Ahead loomed the audience hall built just for its current purpose atop the steep slope, glowing watchfires from the walls to guide them. The squalls they'd cursed only minutes before muffled their steps, now joined by rain and thunder. Tired as they were, they climbed, far from the well-guarded footpath over flesh-shearing stones toward the dark structure. It was mostly wood but a wall of stone blocks protected it, like a tiny castle. Every few seconds each pair of eyes flicked up at the ramparts. *Surely they'll see us! They must by now.* But no alarm went up, and they pressed on.

Far above, two soldiers discussed everything except the weather, for what was there to say about that except that it was nastier than a witch's tit? One of them broke off a stream of bored insults when his young comrade went suddenly silent, staring out to sea unmoving. "Uh, boy, you all right— Aargh!" The slightest nudge sent the lad clattering to the deck of the wooden parapet, and in the fleeting lamplight the older soldier glimpsed the straight line of an arrow shaft bisecting his throat.

"What the fu—" An arm enveloped his own neck and he had the briefest sensation of breathing through a hole in his trachea before blood loss sent him to his knees, then to nothingness.

"Nicely done," said Corren as the others clambered up the hooked rope and over the battlement.

"Lessi might be the physic," answered Ulnoth, "but in this work I'm the chirurgeon."

"You flatter yourself," said Nan, her face still wet and corpse-white from the journey. She yanked her shaft from the body and returned it still bloody to her quiver. "I did the hard work."

Quick and quiet and dark, the Heron Kings spread across the battlement. The last member of their party crept over the wall. "Is all secure?"

Ulnoth sneered at Vinian's question. "Secure? Never heard the word. We ain't dead yet though, and that's miracle enough."

Vinian eyed the bodies at her feet. Green-badged bodies. "Is this slaughter necessary? If we succeed, by tomorrow these men won't be your enemies—"

"Tomorrow!" Ulnoth raged right in her face. "Tomorrow don't exist. 'Til then anyone 'tween us and them's the enemy, and too bad for them. I'm sorry for that, but not really. Now, where's this meetin' at?"

"Down there." She pointed at the hall in the middle of the courtyard, separated on all sides from the wall. Guards ringed it and patrolled the courtyard. "They'll be in the center part with smaller rooms around it. Looks like the same layout as the council hall at Murento where this whole thing got started. Poetical."

The wind died down a bit, and from the hall a shrill shout of "*Liar!*" rang up to pierce it.

"That's my queen," said Vinian with pride. "Yelling means Pharamund's not dead yet. He must be doing well."

"Let's just hope that pirate of yours delivered his package as instructed," said Alessia.

"Don't worry, Arnaud marked it as Cynuvik apple brandy, the queen's favorite. It'll get through."

They snaked their way along the parapet, snuffing watchfires as they went. In each corner a tower house was built with windows looking outward, but the doors were shut against the storm. Corren leaned against one to listen. Through the wind, a voice. Then another. He waited nearly five minutes while the others held back with strung bows. *Two, no – more,* he said in their improvised hand-language. He nodded and rapped hard on the door.

After a few seconds it creaked open, and a soldier wearing Engwara's livery poked his head out. "Wha— Who's there? I just come up, so sure it ain't time for relief...." When the man was fully out of the tower house, Nandine pounced. An arrow hit the soldier's chest but impacted in the rings of a mail shirt and he staggered back. Before the man could cry out Banwick rushed forward with a rope and whipped it around his neck while Dannek shoved him clear over the outer wall. The rope tightened and the soldier's neck snapped without him ever uttering a sound of alarm.

Corren charged into the tower house. The place was three yards on a side and the only occupant was bent bare-assed toward the small stone hearth built into the wall. He barely had time to stand upright and shout his surprise when Corren barreled into him. This soldier – red-badged for Pharamund, one of each to a pair it seemed – went into the fire and howled. Gant burst into the room and cut the man's cry short with a swift cleaver blow to the face. They pressed on through the opposite door, Gant taking the lead and Vinian the rear.

Halfway along the next stretch of the wall they came to a stairwell, twisting dark and downward. They were forced to descend single file and blind. Just as they emerged into the courtyard a guard of one faction or the other turned to face them. Doubtless figuring them for intruders straight away, he drew a sword and yelled an alarm. Only the most extreme good fortune saved them when a crash of thunder directly overhead drowned out his shout. The guard swung a clumsy blow and the flat of a blade bounced off Gant's shoulder to lodge the edge in his neck. He fell against the steps.

"Bastard!" Banwick chased after the fleeing guard into the open courtyard, jumped on his back and twisted his head at an obscene angle. The guard fell, twitched once or twice then was silent. Banwick and Verrell dragged the body back to the cover of the stairwell, hoping to the gods no one had noticed. Gant bled.

"We're in," muttered Alessia. "You go ahead – I'll stay with Gant."

"Don't bother," said Banwick bitterly, "he's dead." He felt for a pulse once, then laid Gant's limp head back as his blood gushed all around them and down the stairs. Banwick kicked the stone with a snarl. "Can't stop for 'im though, or it's for nothing." They left him there. The remaining eight huddled against a shadow-draped corner of the wall, their goal within sight.

The conference hall was ringed with guards standing shivering in the rain, their oilskin ponchos obscuring each's loyalties. "What now?" asked Nan, raising and lowering her bow uncertainly. "I can't shoot fast enough to take 'em all, none of us could."

"Verrell," said Ulnoth, "that trick we pulled on the crew outta Fort Dunsmere? Let's do it."

"You think?" Verrell fidgeted nervously. "I dunno, it barely worked last time."

"Perfect record then. Let's go."

The pair staggered out into the courtyard and the tiny perimeter illuminated by what watchfires hadn't been extinguished by the storm, babbling and swaying back and forth. The guards came instantly to alert.

"Hail," slurred Ulnoth, "hail the king 'n the queen 'n all th' others! Is they the best or what? Hail! All us…we's the best."

"Nah," said Verrell, clapping Ulnoth on the back, "you, my friend… are the best. Ain't he, boys? This guy, *this* is the guy—"

The guard nearest the door stepped forward, face screwed up in fury. "What the— Are you kidding me?" He turned to the one next to him. "One of yours I take it?"

"Ain't none o' mine," the other protested. "See, who's your captain, you drunk son's of – you'll be crucified for this, whoever y'are!"

"Ahhh," moaned Verrell, "done lots of cruci…crucia…crosscification in my time. Ever'one of 'em gone up high! Hail 'em!" He raised a fist to the sky.

"Sure sounds like one o' yours," said the first guard.

"Shit." He waved to several others stationed along the wall. "All right, reel 'em in." Three or four peeled off from their posts and stomped toward the pair, their anger and embarrassment evident even amid the storm. But before they could be apprehended Ulnoth and Verrell darted off toward a far corner of the compound.

"You'll ne'er take me aliiive!" Verrell called in a singsong voice. Two more guards broke off from their stations in pursuit, and just like that the number blocking the hall was halved.

"Not bad," said Vinian from her place of cover, "even if they do get themselves killed for it."

"What about the rest?" wondered Nan, her bow still half-drawn. "Can we take them?"

"We better," answered Corren. He gave the signal, and in perfect unison five arrows were loosed at the remaining guards. Five seconds later another volley took the remainder. Dannek ran forward and began dispatching those still living. Vinian shook her head in wonder at how she ever thought she could wipe out folk such as these. If they knew what kind of power they truly possessed…. But she would not be the one to tell them, not tonight.

A second later Ulnoth came jogging out of the darkness, blood coating his face and chest. He came alone.

Alessia frowned. "Verrell?" Ulnoth shook his head.

Corren glared at the undefended hall. "This is it then – we don't stop until Vinian stands before the idiot royals themselves."

Banwick held a fist before the large door. "Shall we knock? Worked last time."

"No!" Vinian yanked his arm away. "Don't, not while they're inside. If it opens and they see you and these bodies it won't open again until an army surrounds us. We'll have to find another way." She stood back, took in the whole of the building. "Just like the hall in Murento...." *No windows, no other doors. But the roof....* "Up there. The roof'll be all planks. The original was thatched, but I'm betting they didn't quite get around to...there!" She pointed to a series of beams that protruded horizontally from near the rooftop. "If we can get up there...you still have that grappler?"

Banwick had it. After a few misses it looped around one of the crossbeams, and Vinian tied the other end around her waist. "Hoist me up."

In this manner they ascended one by one to the roof. They pulled the rope up after them with Banwick left behind on the ground to watch for more guards. They spread across the angled planks, searching for a loose one to gain entry. They began to despair when Nan called out.

"Here, help me with this!"

Corren put his sword under the mislaid board to use as a prybar. He heaved. The board creaked and groaned. "Almost...got it." When it snapped so did the one under his feet from the reverse pressure. There was a loud crack, a crash, and he disappeared through the bright hole.

"Corren!" Ulnoth stood too fast, and lost his footing on the wet roof. He slipped, reaching out for Nan. They both fell and slid through the breach after Corren.

"No!" Alessia knelt over the opening, her face bathed in yellow light from within.

Corren and Ulnoth hung from rafters, clawing at the beams with bloody fingernails. Nandine writhed on a feast-strewn table below them, clutching at her leg, and all around her stood the royal party of Engwara, Pharamund, and about a dozen shocked guards of both camps. Against the far wall a fire roared, and on either side luxurious tapestries of green and red, banners of serpent and fox, whose adherents now looked poised to kill each other.

"Ambush!" Engwara shrieked. "All that love me, kill them!"

Pharamund threw up his hands. "You bitch, I'm betrayed!"

Vinian shoved Alessia aside and poked her head through the hole. "Wait!" She quickly hooked the rope on a secured plank, threw the end into the hall and slid down. She dropped the last two yards, landing on the remains of a roast boar next to Nan. As she did one of Pharamund's guards plucked a lit torch from a wall sconce and hurled it at her. *Hello, old friend.* Vinian caught the brand in one hand by the flaming side and tossed it away, unfazed. "Majesty, I beg you wait! It's no ambush."

"V-Vinian...? Is it you?"

"Hold!" The voice boomed above the confused shouting. A slender figure fought through the crush of raised spears. "Heed me, Your Grace." Pharamund had retreated under the table, and Trozas shielded the spot with his body. "King's men, hold!" He turned to Vinian. "Welcome to the party."

"Sorry I'm late," she replied. She knelt next to Nan. "Alessia, get down here!"

"Stay here," Alessia told Dannek above, then shimmied down the rope somewhat more carefully than Vinian had.

"Vinian," said Engwara, "I can't believe...how did you get in here?"

"By skills I learned at your command. And with the help of these rebels."

"Rebels! So it's true—"

"Many things are true, Majesty." Alessia landed next to Vinian and paused a moment to pass her the red leather packet before tending to Nan.

"Is that what I think it is?" asked Trozas.

A meek voice came from under the table. "Is...is it safe? Trozas?"

"It's safe," said Trozas, as though comforting a child frightened of the storm outside. "Come out, Your Grace." A frightened man of middle age, middle height and middle build crawled out from underneath. A man with a pleasant but plain face that you might greet kindly in the street but would not long remember afterward. Engwara's was the polar opposite, yet both vied for the same kingdom, both had been duped by the Bhasan emperor. Vinian wasted no time, taking the momentary uncertainty of the two warring monarchs for her best ally. She unrolled the letter and began reading.

"...Profit flows everywhere, Your Radiance. Your ever-kneeling and humble agent...." She handed the letter to Engwara and finished the rest from memory. "Carthagne Fadhlan ven Xedrusia. Bank Isle-Euderico, Marimine Sardicchio Esquaralle."

Not a word, not a breath, not a heartbeat could be heard in the hall. Corren and Ulnoth had shambled down from the rafters while she read and now crouched in a corner, watching and glad to be ignored.

Vinian waited, then waited some more for someone to speak. "Is it not clear to both of you? Your true enemies are Artabarzanes and the bank. While you claw at each other they spur you on and wait to pick over the bones of what's left."

Engwara cleared her throat first. "I...I thought it was a trick. It seemed so impossible...."

"And I," said Pharamund, glancing red-faced at Trozas as the letter was passed their way.

"Who says it's not?" The voice that still brought Alessia nightmares made her cringe as its author tossed aside a guard to gain a spot near the table.

"Taurix," spat Vinian, "how disgusting to see you again." He was no less imposing without his battle armor, and no less ugly.

"Likewise. And...you." He laid eyes on Alessia. "I know you – that mouthy bitch from the temple! I might've known you'd be part of this." He reached for Alessia, who scrambled away from his grasp.

Ulnoth dashed in between them. "Get away from her!"

Taurix shoved him aside with casual contempt. "Queen, *we* have the initiative. You're a season from victory, no more. I don't believe this wild story and neither should you. I told you what the banker said about these peasant scum and your precious spymistress—"

"And I told you different!" answered Ludolphus, firm at Engwara's side.

Pharamund sneered at the Marcher lord. "Who'd listen to the word of a traitor like you?"

Taurix sneered right back. "As opposed to a mewling incompetent?"

"Quiet, all of you!" Vinian trembled at how she spoke to the highborns, but the hardships of the winter had worn her patience thin. "Forgive me, Majesty, but I had to come before you both like this. It had to be a true surprise to be believed. I think now might be a good time for a drink. Some brandy, perhaps. Why not send for some?"

Engwara frowned. "Brandy? How can you think of—"

"Trust me, Majesty, if you've ever trusted me before." She risked a glance at Taurix, wondering what he suspected. "Send for your crate of apple brandy, special cargo delivered just tonight."

"What – very well. I know you have your schemes, but this one better be good." She nodded to a guard. "Do it."

The crate, again needing six men to move, was brought from the hall's cellar. But when pried open it yielded not brandy but a very fat banker, unconscious.

Engwara gasped. "Carthagne! Drugged?"

"Ah," said Trozas, "so you *do* know him. Take heed, Your Grace."

"I take heed, my friend. I take heed very well. Wake that mountain of lies."

A few hard slaps and the banker slowly came to wakefulness. "Eh? *Dovastra ela tenessi lo…?*" He was dragged dizzy to his feet and realized where he was, and among whom. "Oh dear…."

"My agents found him trying to buy passage to Bhasa, to his true creditor," said Vinian. "With Ludolphus's help I got to him first. Mercenaries and smugglers – simply a matter of who pays them more, isn't that right, banker?"

"Your Majesty," Carthagne stammered, "I-I can explain—"

"*Majesty!*" Trozas fumed, furious at having been taken for a fool. "What happened to Pharamund having the greater right and title, as you claimed when you delivered us a fortune in gold and silver?"

"It's true," snarled Engwara. "It's all true, godsdammit! I've heard enough. Put that pig in chains, if you can find any of sufficient length."

"No, wait— *Aiee!*"

She turned to Pharamund. "Well, so-called king, it may be that we have more to discuss than first I supposed."

"Um…." Pharamund glanced at Trozas, who simply nodded. "It seems. I won't be tricked into giving my kingdom to Artabarzanes any more than to you. But before I entertain any proposal I've one condition." He pointed up at Taurix. "*This* turncoat's head. Preferably in a box. That before anything else."

Trozas squirmed. "Your Grace, is that really necess—"

"I have spoken!" Trozas flinched at Pharamund's newfound resolve.

"What…." Engwara bit her lip. "What would you give for such an extreme gesture?"

Taurix almost choked on his own breath. "You cannot be serious. I'm the only advantage you have, you stupid old cow—"

Ludolphus lashed out with admirable speed for an old man and smashed his fist across Taurix's jaw, and the Marcher lord stumbled back into the waiting arms of Pharamund's guards. "Humph," Ludolphus grunted with a smile. "Been waiting for that. Be rid of him, my queen, he's a wolf beyond taming. And if he's the coin that buys peace, what value is he afterward?"

Taurix spat blood at Ludolphus's feet. "One betrayal paid for with another, eh? Best get on with it then. But I can tell you this much... you'll have no peace so long as I draw breath." He exploded, wrenching himself from the guards' grasp and took hold of a sheathed sword. He drew it upward and in so doing slashed its owner's chin. The man fell back, clawing at his bloody jaw and dropping a cross-bow.

Carthagne used the distraction to bolt from his own captors. He took up the bow, and in a last-ditch bid to escape leveled the weapon at Pharamund's chest and pulled the trigger just as Taurix lunged at Engwara, slowed only a fraction by his bad hip.

"The queen!" Vinian yelled. "Protect the queen!"

"Save His Grace, all to me!"

What happened next, and in what order, would be the subject of debate in universities and taphouses for decades to come, but half a second later the scene stood still and bloody. A bolt was burrowed deep in Pharamund's groin, and the author of the errant shot himself transfixed with a shaft sprouting from the top of his head. And Taurix....

Taurix's blade was halted an inch from its target, stopped by – to his own surprise more than anyone else's – Ulnoth. Somehow he'd flown into the path of the steel without any conscious choice to do so, and the length of it passed clear through his midsection. "Huh..." he said, looking down, as though mildly fascinated.

Pharamund howled, Carthagne came crashing down, and Alessia gave a shrill yelp. Ulnoth's eyes fixed with Taurix's and he staggered forward, still impaled on the blade. He took a final step and slid his knife into the Marcher lord's chest. Taurix gasped in surprise as his blackened heart stopped. "Wait, that ain't how it's supposed to...."

Ulnoth used his last ounce of strength to twist the knife, then fell to the floor.

Dannek scrambled down the rope to join Alessia at Ulnoth's side, his last arrow buried in the banker's skull. Corren descended on Taurix to make sure of his end. "Oh gods," whispered Alessia, "hold still. Just hold...." But she knew it was no use. She'd seen too many grievous wounds to think there was anything to be done. She cradled Ulnoth in her arms. "Just...please—"

"Ssh," Ulnoth wheezed. "Doesn't hurt...finally...doesn't hurt anymore. Gods lit my path...after all. Didn't...we almost win?"

Alessia smiled through tears. "We did. Almost won it all."

"Just end it...please. End...." He breathed out once more and then stilled, finding his peace at last.

Engwara fought through her protectors to stand over the rebel who'd died saving her life. "I...don't understand. Why?"

"Why?" Nan looked red-eyed up at the queen. "Didn't you hear? He just told you."

"We've been telling you all this time," said Corren, his sword dripping with Taurix's blood, "if only you'd listen. *End it.*" He looked toward Pharamund's party. "Just end it!"

"Save him," Trozas pleaded. "Save my king and I swear, I'll do what I can." Alessia nodded, still weeping for Ulnoth, and went to work.

Vinian stood before Engwara, surprised to feel the heat of tears on her own cheeks for the first time she could remember, and the pain of fire was indeed nothing compared to their burn. "Consider it, Majesty. I'm your very best, and I cannot defeat these people."

CHAPTER THIRTY-FIVE
The Quiet at the End

Alessia lingered in the yellow sunset that washed over the hidden entrance to the lodge, watching Corren and Wrenth lead the last patrol of the day back inside. Sally brought up the rear and paused as the others passed by.

"They're finally cleared out – no reds, no greens anywhere in the valley. Never thought I'd be thankful to have only Marchmen to worry about."

Alessia nodded. "That's good to hear."

"I heard from smugglers coming through that lots of places are being settled again...Lenocca, Wengeddy, Plisten even. More of us managed to survive than anyone thought. Ludrig's reopening his bar, if you can believe it."

"You're going back, aren't you? Into the world." Alessia tried not to make it sound like an accusation, but it came out that way.

Sally looked away. "I thought about staying. But I'm not really one of you. There's land aplenty now, even for the likes of me. Bed needs looking after, and with Gant gone...did Corren tell you?"

"He didn't have to. I knew. It's all right."

"You're staying out here for good then," said Sally. "Why? It's all over now...isn't it?"

Alessia shrugged. "I get the feeling it won't ever be, not really. Something ends, something begins. Besides, in the world I never really knew who I was or what I wanted or what I was doing. Here I know."

"Those highborn lords'll never stop hunting you after what we've done, no matter what Vinian says."

Alessia grinned. "Then we'll never stop hunting them right back. And we're better."

⋆ ⋆ ⋆

The peace negotiations had plodded on for some while, and ended just about as well as they could have. When the bank's money ran out, Pharamund and Engwara were forced to an agreement. Effectively castrated by Carthagne's wayward shot, Pharamund's chance for a dynasty was snuffed out before it began. He'd remain king of Bergovny for the remainder of his days, and thereafter Engwara's successor would rule both kingdoms united – her 'Greater Argovan'. Which is probably how it would've worked out before all the bloodshed started. But nobody really cared about these details, only that the War of the Bergovan Succession was over. Whether the events here described shortened it by a season, or a year, or ten years no one could ever know. There were more important things to worry about: towns to be rebuilt, crops to be resown and children to be born without the ghost of despair in their eyes. Life went on as it always did – lords still schemed, bankers still stole, and though discredited and despised by a dozen other kingdoms for his conspiracy, the specter of Emperor Artabarzanes ever loomed in the formless east. But in the shadow of every soul from the lowliest swineherd up to kings and queens themselves, a memory of the few who stood for the many still crouched with blade and bow at hand, and a wicked smile.

It's best left that way, Alessia decided. *It's as true as it needs to be, and I am tired.* The westering sun dipped below the cleft horizon, and under the old mountains the Heron King slept.

FLAME TREE PRESS
FICTION WITHOUT FRONTIERS
Award-Winning Authors & Original Voices

Flame Tree Press is the trade fiction imprint of Flame Tree Publishing, focusing on excellent writing in horror and the supernatural, crime and mystery, science fiction and fantasy. Our aim is to explore beyond the boundaries of the everyday, with tales from both award-winning authors and original voices.

∙

∙

Join our mailing list for free short stories, new release details, news about our authors and special promotions:

flametreepress.com